JAIME MUNT

# WHITE CHILD IN THE WOOD

# WHITE CHILD IN THE WOOD

Published by Jaime Munt

Cover Design and Illustrations by Jaime Munt

Background photo of trees available by royalty and license free site: www.pixabay.com

Art copyright © 2015 Jaime Munt

ISBN-13: 978-0692522578
ISBN-10: 0692522573

Printed in the United States of America

To my sister, Donna, who, for all we have in common, too many we share are fears:

Thank you for all the brilliant edits and suggestions. Thanks also for the encouragement, inspiration and making a lot of really normal and perfectly explicable events utterly terrifying just for sake of a story about a bunch of evil little "children".

# CHAPTERS

## CHASING A BETTER KIND OF DEATH

◆

Maniacal laughter resounded through the fog drowned northern wilderness. Only cackling registered on the terror anesthetized mind of the hunted young man. The woods were a dreamy blur. The only sense still functioning was touch and feel. Trickling blood felt eerily like the touch of fingertips on Quinn's body. Falls and collisions with jagged branches left large bloody mouths among other rips and snags in his soiled and sweated flannel shirt and jeans. He didn't know how hurt he was—there wasn't time to.

*They* were coming.

Behind him, the dense boreal woods groaned as the trees appeared to lean away—away from *them*. The horrid wooden moans preceding the pack soon surrounded him. The gnarled wrist of a broken limb clawed the side of Quinn's face as he fled past. Oblivious to the alternative, he could not be grateful that the crowded timber kept so much snow from reaching the ground.

There were merely two or three inches of wet snow on the forest floor, compared to two or three feet everywhere else.

"Where are you?" a voice with neither age nor gender cooed, so impossibly close he could almost feel its hot breath inside his mouth. He tasted it.

Fear can drive a person to do things they normally could not. Quinn was lean and healthy, but he rarely worked out. Normally, after running only a mile or so, Quinn would have lost his breath, lost his footing, lost his will to continue—nothing about this was normal.

With little sense of time or distance anymore, every step seemed to go nowhere. The night was everlasting. It was impossible to keep up this pace. His lungs rejected the shards of cold air shredding their soft tissue—each refusal somewhere between coughing and retching.

Quinn was running out of time.

It was painfully clear his life was at stake.

*Have you ever run for your life?*

More than once, the pursued made tracks across earlier ones. The darkness saved him from demoralization, but was helpless to do much more.

The tree ribbed stomach of the forest was a labyrinth of suffering and helplessness intent to swallow Quinn alive or dead.

Suddenly silence engulfed the fleeing man. After all the heckling and movement, the quiet pressed in on him like devastating news. The trees turned black like a cloud of volcanic ash wrapped its arms in a ring around him. There was a sound like a generator losing power. The toes of Quinn's shoes dug deep into the snowy slush mingling with the mossy forest floor.

His gut was right when it said the pursuers were now ahead of him. The only thing to do was run another direction… again.

Quinn felt them smiling through the dark, surely he saw their little bodies glowing softly beyond the formidable trunks of towering evergreens. Small eyes glittered in the shadows. He felt them perched in the rungs of branches waiting for the perfect moment to slash and bleed him. The wilderness had done all the damage so far.

In the dark, Quinn barely had time to raise his arms before finding the solid body of an enormous pine with his face. Staggered, he gasped and heaved to collect himself.

A small weepy laugh came from the other side of the trunk, only one yard from his fear whitened face. Beyond the obstruction, an ageless voice told him:

"You can die now."

Quinn opened his mouth and his lips formed the words he meant to say, "Please don't!", but terror held them fast within his throat. His body was more afraid than his soul, but then his *soul* would not be hurt. His *soul* wouldn't feel them ripping him apart. His soul would flitter away, leaving the agony and the body behind. The soul thought Quinn might plead with the beasts, the *things*... the giggling and gleaming things that screamed like delighted banshees playing tag with prey—the body did *not* want to take chances.

His breath staggered loudly out of his chest in one rusty breath as he pushed off the rough bark into the chase one last time.

Quinn felt like he was slapping the trees aside. His heart jumped wildly in his chest, like it wanted to abandon the body and try to escape on its own. Slivers of glass struck his ribs, leaving painful little cracks above his heaving lungs.

They were running too—no, they were *chasing* and without guile. Without games.

They looked something like emaciated child-sized white rabbits, with small and long faces. God, they moved so fast. A flicker here. A flicker there. Was that a patch of mist or one of them? A heap of snow dropped from a tree—or one of them? Some laughed hysterically but most of them were bestial, howling and yipping hungrily. Their bedeviled noises resonated eerily around him with an almost physical presence. He didn't know where to run. No place was better than the next. He didn't want to die, *that* he knew. This couldn't be his time. He didn't ever want it to be his time.

All at once Quinn felt like *he* was chasing, chasing a better kind of death, like a frantic shopper on a time restricted spree.

Then the forest spit him out.

Quinn stumbled and fell into the wide ditch before him. A foot of freezing water opened beneath the snow as his foot passed through the ice, biting him savagely. He felt like he'd been shot.

A car hissed past, spraying a salty sludge blanket across the desperate man struggling to find safe footing. Quinn found a fistful of long grasses peeking through the snow's surface for a secure handhold. He pulled and moved, trudging through the heavy snow, stopping once. Slowly, Quinn turned his head, daring only to rotate it enough to see the woods out of the corner of his eye. The threatening presence subsided, slunk back into the cavernous dark of the forest.

In both fear and hope, Quinn turned fully, searching the tangled darkness for a flicker of white, a trace of what chased him and found none. Disbelief quivered sourly in his stomach. They couldn't really be gone. Frantically looking, eyes straining, ears aching until a dizzying migraine erupted.

Not a simper in the dark, not a whisper in the branches. Now, maybe, he was out of reach of the twisting trails, the unforgettable things and the white child in the wood.

There was time to breathe, time to think, time to feel. He didn't want either—thinking or feeling could only provoke more pain—he'd settle for breathing normally, but feeling and thinking were faster.

He could still hear the sound of them on top of the camper. *She just opened the door to throw out the cold coffee*—the screams would resonate forever in his tortured mind.

From somewhere deeper than flesh, were tremors of his soul and body feeling safe to inhabit the same space. His body was shaking so badly, Quinn had to squat to keep standing. His hands pressed into his face and an abysmal cry rose up his throat and out, not as sound, but as tears.

Out of the stillness, out of the forest, a horrible, desolate, graven voice came from everywhere and nowhere:

"Suffer me…"

He could not scream.

A sigh escaped Quinn's lungs that sounded like an aluminum door grinding shut across a floor of standing nails. Strength spent and weak he stumbled along the side of the road.

A second car sped past. Quinn watched it numbly. Alone for most of this horrific night, it felt strange to have been, for a moment, so close to life. Something that could save him, spare him, understand him. Nothing those *things* would do. He shivered, somewhere between feeling cold and sick, and staggered up the road.

To his horror, the snow began to churn in the ditch parallel to each step he managed. Quinn stared dumbly as the snow raised like rabbit tunnels through cartoon gardens.

Reality tripped him—the stumble brought the man so near to falling that his fingertips touched the earth.

No, they weren't below it, not anymore.

His soggy shoes made wet sounds as they struck the gravel shoulder, quicker and quicker.

The horrible things themselves were like snow or fog— almost perfectly lost against the winter. They ran on top, on all fours, but faster than any animal. Their legs blurred. They hung in pace with Quinn—legs working at one hundred times the speed of their actual progression. Playing.

They were waiting for him to tire. Waiting for complete exhaustion. If they took him now he could still struggle. He would fight them and they were just children. They would wait for him to collapse, wheezing, and take him at the pace they chose, kill him as they wanted—he'd whimper and make all the pretty dying sounds they love.

Tires squealed behind Quinn.

He spun on his heels, discovering an otherwise unannounced broken ankle as it folded over on the pavement. Inconceivably bright light stunned him.

*Like a deer in the headlights.*

He giggled a little.

Behind the light a motor purred. The car pulled up beside him and the power window was eaten by the door.

*No...*

Quinn shook his head urgently. The man behind the wheel talked loudly, but all Quinn heard was the clicking of claws across the pavement.

"Goddammit! I could have killed you! What the hell're you thinking?"

Words scuttled up Quinn's throat as he desperately sought the strength to speak.

"Help…me!" Quinn croaked, slapping shredded, skinless, bleeding and frozen palms against the open window. He tore at the locked door.

The driver's hands creaked as they constricted on the vinyl wheel, finally taking in the poor semblance of a man that stood tattered at the passenger side window, sea-blue eyes blazing against skin black and red with blood like he'd been mauled by a grizzly or three.

Something like anger swelled in Quinn's chest, his brow pinched, veins throbbed on his temples, and fire surged through the tendons in his neck. He had no time to be surprised by what happened next, when the desperate, raging, bestial howl ripped free from where words start out as feelings:

"*HELP!*"

"What?"

Rather than the man's own reflection against the opposite window, a little girl looked back at Quinn.

"No!" he wailed.

The driver's door burst open and six of these children were waiting, greedy hands open and grabbing. Blood sprayed from the man's throat and across the face of the creature biting into it. In seconds, the driver was torn from the seat, leaving bits of flesh and lots and lots of blood. Blood everywhere. Quinn heard the clitter-clatter of nails beneath the vehicle and painfully scrambled through the open window. He pulled the driver's door shut and locked it as he slid inside. He threw the car into overdrive, raised the window and floored it. Something ran across the road. Part of Quinn wished it would cross again. He wanted to see if they could bleed too.

Quinn's tearful eyes found the band of cheap gold hugging his finger, but quickly moved that hand to turn on the interior lights. His right hand took control of the blood slicked wheel. He felt the dangerous emotions he'd swallowed flood his throat like bile, an eruption of grief, anger, and confusion shuddered him until he could hardly hold the car steady.

*This is not the time, Quinn. This is no time to lose it,* he told himself.

*You're not safe yet.*

Tears pooled into the splotches of blood sullying his face. He dared not wipe them, not with hands so soiled with blood; not when he could hardly see as it was. Exhaustion crept in, promising blindness and sleep… and death.

Quinn turned on the high beams and every light available. He even opened the glove compartment. He turned the radio up and swayed out of rhythm with the music. He didn't really hear it. He couldn't even tell if it was a song he knew. It didn't matter.

Something pale hurtled across the highway.

Suddenly the car filled with light, blackness then a dull red glow. Everything stopped. Pain. Dizziness.


"God," Quinn groaned, raising his head from the wheel. Hot white pain danced between his eyes and filled his vision with sparks. He shook his head to clear it, unable to believe he hit something. He didn't remember anything on the road. He hardly even remembered the road. All he thought was to escape. The realm of awareness shrunk to almost nothing.

There were little noises outside.

The door was ajar but Quinn still had to throw himself against it to persuade it to open. It groaned loudly, giving into his efforts, spilling coolness into the chamber of heat where he sat.

The seat creaked as Quinn swung his legs from the vehicle. Clutching the door and roof he found footing and stood. Crosshatched light blazed against the hood like Hollywood spotlights. Only then did he realize what had happened.

He saw the other car, a wrinkle of metal like a crumbled piece of foil tucked into the grill of the vehicle he'd commandeered.

Sounds came from the other car. Soft sounds, almost like purring. His shoes scuffed against the tar through thousands of tiny squares of bluish glass.

Blood trickled from the seam of the rear passenger side door. Scarcely a thing remained of the front seat or its passengers, but these Quinn ignored, feeling beckoned by the sound. He moved steadily to reach for the handle, peering into the shadows beyond the cracked glass. To open it took less exertion than expected.

Quinn heard the click and easy complaint of the door as it swung open slowly, lighting the interior bulb. The cooing continued as Quinn backed away from the square of light that smiled at him knowingly. The white wolf child licked at the blood weeping from the open eyes of a little girl. The wolf child had bit away the lids and now lapped at the bleeding as it gained access to the smooth orb below. The course tongue's pull made the iris bob in its socket. After a few last flecks, the beast leaned back on its bottom and turned around slowly, sloppily wiping blood coated hands on its ragged white sundress.

"Scream…"

# CHAPTER 1

◆

# DAVID

"Take this out to the car, David," Noah Asheborne said to his six-year-old son. He handed the boy a cooler, smiling lovingly as the child wrapped his small arms around it, balancing it against his chest and underneath his small chin. Small as he was, his father couldn't believe how fast he was growing.

The boy's dark brown eyes shone proudly as he gripped the cooler tight and hurried out to his daddy's cobalt blue '96 Grand Prix; the one his mommy hated *so* bad.

He'd finally consoled David that the belongings the movers already took would arrive safely at the new home. Noah himself was not comfortable with knowing most of their worldly possessions—as well as the new house—were entrusted to strangers. There was no way to know who was aware that no one would be at the house for days. He told himself those fears were a result of living in the city—in truth, he was a distrustful person and wasn't exactly ready for his second international move.

His life improved so much the *first time* that he told himself the same quality of change could happen again. Only *this time*, he told himself, he wasn't running away.

But that was a lie.

"Are we there yet?" David sang. The faintest echo of Noah's English accent, played softly in the boy's voice.

Noah was born in Liverpool. He felt he did pretty well disguising himself among the other college students when he first came to the U.S., but not until about four years ago did he feel completely emancipated from that British inflection. He was American now and didn't want to stand out.

He hadn't any real kind of life in England anyway and left as soon as he could make the arrangements—wanting to start over completely.

Somehow the six-year-old picked up a little, so subtle, almost unnoticeable. Noah surprised himself that he thought it was cute, when the accent could give him away. He didn't want to explain himself. It was easier to just be perceived as American. Even though the whole of England wasn't responsible for why he felt the way he did—anything English was enough to remind him of what *was* responsible. As a result, the young father told himself he would never again underestimate what David noticed.

In a lot of ways the six-year-old was like Noah when he was young, small for his age, stubborn infant qualities of the wide eyes, nose, and baby fat. The biggest difference, the most important difference, was that David was happy and safe.

Seeing David enjoying life gave Noah back a little of his own childhood.

Everything about David raised conflict in the man who never wanted to be a father. His wife, *ex-wife*—Terri—said "*it*" happened because Noah worked too much. If she was pregnant maybe he'd pay more attention to her.

The following years were filled with growing numbers of similar complaints—not because they involved him being inattentive, but similar in that he couldn't figure out what he was doing to make her feel the things she said she was feeling. When Terri said he wasn't paying attention to her, for him, they were still on their honeymoon. He often left work early just because he missed her. He'd take extended lunches to meet her for rendezvous at hotels or motels or anywhere else where they could get an hour of privacy.

It took a few years before Noah started to suspect she was conditioning him to accept blame for things falling apart if the marriage failed, because everything he did was wrong. It was his fault that she wanted to leave. And, even though she made the decision on her own to tamper with their condoms and get pregnant, it was *his* fault that she'd been so desperate that she turned to pregnancy. It was his fault that she had stretch marks and all that weight to lose. His fault she was "no longer attractive", when, despite himself, he felt drawn to her more than ever when she was roundly pregnant and flushed and lovely. Only then did he really start to believe he could do it—be a father.

Now, Noah was having doubts about fatherhood again, well aware this would not be the last time he heard 'Are we there yet?'

He didn't answer, but bent to pick up the last of the boxes and luggage. The gravel crunched beneath his shoes and the cool air revitalized him. The roaring, flashing, grinding city could have been a million miles away. If he looked up he could have seen skyscrapers stabbing through the sky. He let himself see only the house. It was the object of his dreams, goals, and his success in both—the product of putting in the overtime as a bachelor, but during the pregnancy his priorities changed. Traditional work supported them, several books on the press paid for the house, and inside was the sum of all he'd ever wanted. Someone to share love with. Nice things. A happy home.

David called Gilder, a mutt of black lab and shepherd, and squealed in retreat when she whipped, half crazed around the corner of the empty house.

"No!" David howled, twisting away when she tried to seize his blankie from the backseat, even though he purposely allowed Gilder to catch a corner. They yanked each other back and forth on the driveway behind a young father caught deep in reflection.

"It's all fun and games until someone gets hurt," the six-year-old recited in a condescending way that would have made Noah smile if he'd been paying attention. David liked to say that when he'd jamb his thumb or stub his toe. Horrifically, at the age of four, David offered this bit of wisdom to a shopper who crashed their cart into a kiosk at their local mega-mart. Noah doubted the shopper appreciated the words of wisdom and apologized. It wasn't the first or last time that David shared his point of view with strangers. Unnatural cuteness, by father's bias, might have spared them from unfriendly responses. Who snaps at a toddler? Who knows? There's always someone willing to volunteer to be that asshole to ruin your day.

The small house looked unfamiliar, dark and empty—only the shadows of morning deceptively filled it. David did not feel the emotional sickness of leaving home because he had his dog, his father, and his blanket.

The "For Sale" sign caught Noah's eye. He turned to it, but would not look right at it. The red "Sold" sign swung idly on two tiny silver chains. The realtor, knowing what the house meant to give up, assured him it would be cared for. An aunt bought the house to keep it a secret from her nephew's fiancé, at the time. The newlyweds said it was their dream house. Noah once felt the same way.

*Don't think about it.*

He needed to busy himself—leave no time for regrets. Just get away, as soon as possible. Tell himself there's no other way. When you don't have a choice, there's no room for regret either.

Even so, vitality drained out of the handsome immigrant like a gluttonous succubi was attached to his spirit. Twenty-nine, feeling ninety-nine. He was afraid of change. Afraid of making mistakes.

*What happened?*

"Why does Gilder get the front seat?" David grunted, tearing the blanket loose, and diving on top of it. Gilder caught a hold of David's bibs, shook him hard twice and then urgently licked the mounds of curly brown hair. Noah shoved the last suitcase behind the driver's seat atop a mass already half filling the space.

"I don't want the seat belt across your neck," Noah answered tiredly. David knew this tone. Dad was thinking about mom again. The child shoved himself off the ground and brushed the dirt and grass off his red and blue locomotive bibs. Noah was awestruck at his son's smallness as the child reached up to open the front door and let Gilder in, then at the effort to close it afterwards.

"It's okay dad," David assured him, climbing into the backseat, and buckling in. He immediately yanked his stuffed bear backpack from between the front seats and rifled through it for the chubby fruit-scented markers. Gilder pushed her head between the seat and door, bug-eyed, whites showing, staring and sniffing at the red marker that smelled like cherries, but not real ones.

"No, Gilder."

Noah slid into the driver's seat. He reached back glancing to check that David was securely buckled in before pulling a seatbelt across himself.

"Give Gilder a break, David," Noah urged, rumpling the dog's thick black hair affectionately. The boy smiled mischievously, but nodded with exaggerated speed and force to emphasize a sincere effort to obey.

"Okay dad."

It was a weird feeling to pull out on the familiar street and know they wouldn't be coming back in an hour or two—that it wasn't an errand, a night out, or otherwise—they were leaving their home.

At the first stoplight Noah plugged in his M.U.S.E., Media Ultra Storage Engine, MP3 player and handed it back to the color splotched paws of the grubby six-year-old.

"Find your songs, David," Noah referred to David's personal playlist. It would be a challenge to see how long the father could stand it. His personal best was an hour and a half.

Noah looked over at Gilder, wriggling in the "navigator's" seat. The young mutt loved to watch the city. She probably had a little ADHD. He wondered what she would make of the woods they were moving smack dab into the middle of. After New York City she might be bored. This was all she knew.

The English immigrant fondly remembered the very first moment he saw her, one of the last two puppies, in a cardboard box with a sign that read "PUPPIES FOR SALE – FIFTY BUCKS". Even though Noah wanted one, he hadn't planned on pets, but when the sweet black face with large teary eyes fixed on him and then the roly-poly puppy followed him to the other side of her box, he melted. He paid with three tens and a twenty. Noah recalled one of the tens being pretty beaten up.

When he held the little black puppy in his arms he felt lost and in love all at once, not unlike the first time he held his son.

"What am I going to do with you?" he had asked her and the reality of all the other immediate expenses crashed down on him. Food, bowls, shots, neutering, toys, pet bed, leashes, tags, registration? After all that he still had to explain all this to his wife.

Would the truth work?

"She looked at me. What could I do?"

By the time Noah got home there was nothing else he could think to say. How do you explain love? He loved the little mongrel, helplessly, and completely in just the time it took to see her, buy her, purchase what things he could immediately afford, and walk home. The whole of about an hour and a half.

Terri was actually pretty good about the puppy. She told her husband she would feel a lot better about him running in the park if he wasn't alone. He'd never thought about it, but suddenly felt better about it too.

Noah felt better about a lot of things with Gilder around. When he wasn't home the dog was with his wife. When both of them were at work, the dog would mind the apartment, where they lived at the time.

Whenever he ran errands by himself Gilder sat shotgun. Briefly, he pictured the little fat puppy in the seat. Noah felt blessed then and blessed to have happened to look down in that pee soaked cardboard box.

Speaking of blessings in disguise, five months after that day they were pregnant with David.

◆          ◆          ◆

Noah's best friend, Derrick, told him about a place far north, in Canada, where his great uncle ran a small printing and publishing operation. He'd been working short-handed and under skilled for a long time and could really use the help. It wouldn't be nearly as sophisticated as the business he'd worked at for the past four years. Derrick's uncle could only pay a fraction of what Noah was making in New York, but the cost of living would be a fraction as much. None of that really mattered, since he wasn't going to work full-time, at least at first, and Derrick's uncle was happy with whatever time Noah had to give.

Noah knew he *probably* didn't need to work. Enough royalties came in from his books that they would *probably* be okay. It's fine to play those odds when you're only responsible for yourself. He wouldn't work full-time so he could devote more time than before to writing… and to David. There was the money from the house—half of which was reinvested in their new home.

Derrick joked they'd be living like kings. The idea kind of scared Noah. He started to imagine tarpaper shacks and toothless drunks shooting beer bottles off their porches, but his old college friend was pretty persuasive, and Noah was finally convinced this was just what he needed to get his mind off things—keeping busy and getting the hell away from New York. Or rather, leaving the hell *in* New York. Okay, so Canada might have been farther than most would feel necessary, but Derrick sometimes went fishing up there and insisted it couldn't be more different so there'd be no chance for old ghosts to haunt them.

Derrick thought it would be easier if Noah applied for Canadian citizenship, but he got a work visa instead, as a precaution. Just until he got a sense of what things were like up there—Derrick shrugged and was a little put off that his advice wasn't heeded. He might have felt differently, had he known Noah had been through all this before and was nervous about doing it again, especially with a little kid.

The trip was roughly 1,025 miles north near James Bay. The father and son would pass hundreds of beautiful places before they'd even reach the new home—all places that *could* have been home. He and David took turns claiming houses as they passed through town after town after town. Noah couldn't make time to see the actual new place for himself—so it would be fun for both of them to imagine other homes might be like theirs.

He *was* worried that he might not have taken the time to get everything ready for moving in—worrying constantly that he forgot something. Noah had to arrange for the movers in New York. The realtor arranged for the place to be tidied up a little. The utilities were turned on and gas delivered. He closed accounts that needed closing for the house he sold. He left other accounts, like banking and insurance, as they were, just in case.

Setting a pace of about 340 miles of driving a day, Noah thought both he and his son would survive the trip better. They hadn't done a lot of travelling. His ex-wife was estranged from her parents too, so the furthest they ever went was to Jersey to see friends, though most lived in New York. Many within walking distance.

He didn't really know how David would cope with the trip. Luckily, he thought, his son was adventurous and curious. Even when he was shy about new things, Noah recognized how his son's eyes would gleam with interest, or his fingers would squirm with a desire to touch or pet the strange item or animal. If he introduced David to new food, all he had to do was say it was foreign or exotic and the child would immediately become interested, at least in trying it—that was the most, for such a little kid, Noah could ask for.

He might not have wanted the responsibility of being a father, and sometimes he didn't know how to handle different issues, but he knew he never wanted to mess the kid up. He didn't always know how to express his love, as if the lack of desire to be a parent inhibited that integral part of human behavior. Of course, he'd known a lot of parents who said they wanted to have kids who should have been locked up for even thinking about conceiving. One thing Noah knew was discipline and hurting didn't have to be the same thing. His own parents didn't know that.

So, not everybody likes every kind of food. He didn't think it was worth putting a little kid through tension and intimidation because of something like brussel sprouts.

Noah had printed out a list of all the pet friendly lodgings along the way. Their first night would be spent in what was deemed "Fun for the WHOLE Family." After bathroom breaks, lunch, and stops for gas it was about three o'clock when they arrived at the hotel. Enough time for David to swim in the pool if he wanted, check email, order pizza, and watch a few movies on TV or on the computer before bed.

*Thank God for credit cards*, Noah thought for about the tenth time since they left New York. He wasn't ready for Canadian currency. He couldn't imagine anything but greenbacks in his wallet. At least Visa didn't care where it was.

"Can I go swimming?" David wanted to know. He wanted to know everything. If there was room service. If there was a gym. If there was a sauna. Did their room have a hot tub—Noah told him he watched too much TV. David was completely amazed they were staying in a hotel, something he'd never done. They were "checking in" which was apparently the second most exciting thing compared to there being a swimming pool.

"Yep."

In the heat of August, who could say "no"?

"Can Gilder go swimming?"

Noah and the desk clerk looked at each other. The clerk was smiling.

"I don't think anyone would want Gilder swimming in the pool. With the way she sheds, people would think the water was a carpet and fall in when they tried to walk across or she'd plug up the filters and we'd get kicked out," Noah teased. He palmed and shook David's head affectionately.

"Gilder likes to swim," David remembered from one of their trips to Jersey. The only time he ever saw Gilder in water that wasn't a kiddie pool or a bathtub.

"I know, son."

The clerk turned his smile on the little boy he could barely see below the opposite edge of the counter. Their eyes were able to meet.

"Are you on vacation?" the clerk tried to help by changing the subject.

"No," David said like it was obvious they weren't.

"How are the camera's in the parking lot?" Noah asked, "Do we have to worry about stuff we had to leave in the car?"

"Nah," the clerk waved his hand. "We've never had anything like that here. That was reported anyway."

"Thanks," Noah said. He looked at the clerk's name tag and added, "Ian."

"No problem. Gimme a call if you need anything, aye."

Father took son's small hand and the sweet faced black dog, with large loving eyes, led them down the hall.

The room was typical. Noah didn't expect dramatic differences, but you never know. There would be a lot of little things—mostly culturally, he suspected—they would have to adapt to, but as he learned from his first international move, you take it in doses and you can digest it pretty easily.

"One bed?" David pointed. "So we don't have to fight over who gets Gilder?"

"If you ever want that fart-knocker in your bed, you can have her. This was the only pet room with a view of the parking lot," he explained.

"I don't mind," David told him. Actually, since his mommy left, they had been sleeping together a lot. His daddy often slept on the couch and David would end up falling asleep there because they were watching TV. Or sometimes David was feeling bad and needed to sleep by his daddy. Sometimes they both were feeling bad and lonely and missing the way things were. When they all slept in his daddy's bed, they talked a lot about stuff, but not about mommy. David was afraid to. Something inside him said that it would break his daddy, like the last move in Jenga. It wasn't that they didn't both think about her. His daddy often talked about her passively, like when he assured David they would be okay. They would get through "this". Maybe just thinking about it was so hard they couldn't talk about it, even if they wanted to. Even though his daddy often said David could talk to him about anything.

"Can I interrupt the swimming plans, kiddo?"

"Wwwwwhy?" David tossed his bag on the side of the bed that would have been his mommy's side.

"I think we owe Gilder a little exercise and fresh air."

"And a chance to take a dump," David added. He ran for Gilder's pack and took out a small plastic bag. "I'm ready for poop patrol!"

Gilder's tail wagged enthusiastically.

Noah looked bewildered at the two creatures he'd be bunking with. David was always quick to volunteer for the job of picking up after Gilder—calling it "poop patrol" since he was four. Shortly after Gilder learned that this meant she was going to get to relieve herself. He wondered if the boy would still be interested once they were living up in the woods in the middle of nowhere. Then they could let Gilder out and train her to come back to the door, much like she already knew to go to the door to let them know when she needed out.

*It could be like a treasure hunt*, Noah mused.

He knew he better enjoy it, instead of be perplexed by it, because in not too many years, David would probably become less interested in doing any chores. He probably was only interested now because he had to beg to be allowed to do them.

That night they passed on pizza after David convinced his dad they should only eat food from vending machines.

*Visa can't save you now*, Noah thought.

They stayed up past David's bedtime watching the same shows they would have watched at home, but were somehow more special, according to David, that they were watching them at a hotel.

After sleeping restless, all three woke up feeling sick from the meal.

Noah really hated to stop unless they had to—his mind constantly calculating the miles, miles per hour, and how long that would mean before they got home. But his body, one he *thought* was young, couldn't handle too many hours in the seat and—God knew, both Gilder and David were half nuts to get out and run by the time he gave in and stopped at wayside rests or city parks for a break and another drive-thru meal before hitting the road again.

Through fast food litter and cheap plastic kids' meal toys, Noah watched David in the rearview. The boy's head rocked against the seat as he watched the trip become less and less fun with every passing mile. The boy glanced up at the mirror and found his father's coffee brown eyes seeing him. David offered a weak smile to say he was still enjoying himself, but that was no longer true. The pleasure of drive-thru dinners lost their appeal the slowest, but after 560 miles David was craving raw veggies.

They spent the second night at a motel with hard beds, funny smells, and noisy neighbors. Noah was just too tired to look for another place.

◆         ◆         ◆

Highway 11 felt like the longest road in the world. A mile and a half to Kapuskasing. Kapuskasing, Ontario. The sun had only just set and still lit the horizon under the weight of falling night when they rolled up beside the Number 4 of four gas tanks at, hopefully, the final gas station before reaching their new home. The odor of petrol thinned by breeze mingled with that of crushed out cigarettes whose charcoal flesh was ground from their crumpled bodies. The amber lights of the service station glared over Noah, drowning his shadow in royal blue darkness. His shoulders ached like someone had beaten them with a mallet. He tried to stretch his spine, but felt permanently hunched. The cold night air of late summer had a particular smell tonight, a sick and earthy smell, something like that of rotting grass under old melting snow. Between that and the gasoline fumes Noah's stomach turned. Gilder sniffed the peculiar scent when Noah opened the driver side door to slip the map back above the sun visor. The rush of gasoline ceased with a click in the pump when the tank filled. There was a brief gurgle like a toilet flushing and the air was almost perfectly quiet. A wave of guilt and pity washed over the young father as he leaned in to talk to his weary traveling companion.

"Do you want anything when I go in?" Noah asked the half-buried child. David's head rolled in his father's direction. The clearly contrasted orange and blue of light and shade made the boy look painted. David could not help but scowl at the question, he heard it at every stop between there and New York City. He wanted to snap, snarl, and throw a fit, but he told himself how much dad needed him to be good. He had enough on his mind and David did not want to be a part of that drained look Noah tried not to let him notice—that pained inflection father did not want son to hear—loneliness he didn't want David to feel. He pressed his small lips and grunted an, "uh-uh." David was so worn out he almost looked ill. Noah felt like a piece of shit to put his child through all this. He couldn't make sense of it himself; much less explain it to anyone else. *To confine a six-year-old to a car for three days must be something like abuse*, he thought regretfully. There were no words, no hugs, no games that could appease an under slept, bored and grumpy child.

"I'll be right back."

Noah closed the car door and hurried past the gas pumps to the service station door. The bright yellow-orange lights were speckled with dead bugs and dangling webs. His eyes fixed on this as he pushed the touch-blackened bar in to open the tall glass door.

"New York, aye?" the clerk noticed, leaning away from the wide window behind the counter.

"Yeah," Noah sighed.

The man behind the counter smiled friendly enough, though from the grime of working in the attached garage, he looked burly and intimidating at first.

"Where you headed?" the voice was booming and warm to match the broad smile.

"Nibebiitam, or pretty near it."

"Kapuskasing's the largest city to it or from Thunder Bay to Temiskaming Shores for that matter. If you need anything and can't find it in Nibebiitam you're sure to find it in Kapuskasing."

Noah inwardly winced at the thought of having to drive thirty miles every time they needed something.

"Doesn't Nibebiitam have stores?" Noah worried. That was only fifteen miles or so from their new home. That was where he worked. Derrick got him the job so he'd never seen the town. He'd never seen his boss, only spoke to him on the phone. He was more than a little alarmed at the idea of working in a town without a single store. Was it even possible?

"Sure, but just the essentials."

Noah paid for the gas and thanked the clerk as he yanked the door open. The cool air swung around him like walking through a curtain, but then that unusual odor struck him with its pungent, musty breath.

"That's the pulp and paper mill," the clerk said knowingly.

"People aren't bothered by that?" Noah wondered aloud. Visions of frivolous lawsuits danced in his head. From the stink most city people live in on a daily basis, natural stink like mills and farms were just too wretched to exist. He snorted with disgust. A call to a lawyer would be the first thing his ex would have done without considering a company going under because of a lawsuit could mean hundreds of people out of work. He shook his head and tried to imagine the day when he wouldn't even notice the smell anymore.

"Hell no, no one's bothered. No one's jumping to make its fragrance an air freshener, but most people who work around here work there or the hospital. Used to be a nice hotel, but that's burnt down. Quite a few people worked there before that, but it's always been the mill at the heart of things," the clerk laughed. "You'll get used to it—*if you'll be around here a while.*"

"We plan to."

Noah started out the door again.

"You going to stay in town tonight?" the clerk asked, a hint of anxiousness played beneath his words. It made Noah's skin crawl. The clerk was looking out the window, piercing the shadows inside the car for whatever or whoever might be there. To Noah, the man might as well have been looking for a car to jack, a stereo to rip off. He felt violated by how the clerk studied the vehicle. There was more to his discomfort than just of material things. Was he trying to be seductive? He cast a fresh eye on the under washed, overly haired stranger. A hard working middle-aged man who wasn't afraid to get his hands dirty was gone. A panty wearing, candy-man, with prick tickling whiskers replaced him. He didn't want to tell this guy anything more about them. The clerk watched the car so intently, Noah got paranoid that he spotted David.

Was that it?

When the clerk noticed Noah noticing what he was doing, he appeared embarrassed. A little color rose first to what little neck he had and then what cheek showed above the ratty facial hair. A grin shoved through the clerk's unkempt, frizzed gray beard. A shiver went up the back of Noah's neck and arms.

"You planning to stay in town tonight?" the clerk repeated.

"No."

"Got a good sixty miles ahead of you," the clerk pressed.

"I've got a shortcut, a friend of mine told me about."

The clerk frowned and edged toward the side door of the counter, "You *don't* want to go exploring those backwoods at this time of night. Do you know how late it will be by the time you get there? Why don't you just—"

"Thanks!" Noah hurried and fairly jumped out of the building. The clerk came from behind the counter and stood in the open doorway when the car from New York hurried away with its three passengers.

# CHAPTER 2

◆

## The ENDS of the EARTH

"Kapuskasing, population 8,196," Noah read aloud as they crossed the city limits. He looked at Gilder as if to ask, what do you think of that? Gilder seemed impressed, but she was only glad for the attention. Night had fallen fast once it started dropping and by the time they actually entered town the stars were brilliant, the streetlamps were already warm, and the population was, for the most part, fast asleep. The lone car murmured through the empty streets. It was so very quiet and open.

Where was the graffiti? The gangs? No hookers running out in front of traffic hustling dates. The sirens—God! The constant sirens! The whine of ambulance sirens. The piercing, stop your heart, make you run to the window to check if it's yours, car alarm. The blipping, crying siren of squad cars. The endless growling traffic and horns, shouting, fighting, crashing, thumping—thumping against the paper thin apartment wall behind your head when your neighbors screw, thumping over your head, even cracking the plaster in the only shit-hole you can afford to live in straight out of college.

Noah's smooth brow furrowed remembering. This was a complete 180 of the Big Apple, not that he hadn't felt fine about raising David there. He'd have had certain advantages the children here could only dream of. The advantages for a child growing up here... he breathed deeply as his eyes devoured the passing town. He felt himself smiling and it surprised him. He hadn't smiled and meant it in so long. He took in the trees, the starry sky—what a sky!—the ambiance of small town homes and their broad yards. It wouldn't be a fantasy anymore.

With the paper mill at the epicenter of the community, he imagined a lot of blue collar laborers lived in the homes he passed. He'd probably be considered a light weight or something to these northern men. He was an artist, writer, something of a computer geek. It'd been years since Noah was a "skinny little dork." Access to the fitness center in college and hitting the gym for lunch breaks once he started working put an end to the "nosebleed" he'd been in grammar school. So he was fit, but not in the way he pictured guys here to be. That thick natural muscle, toned and heavy from labor—the kind you can never achieve in a gym. Not sculpted muscle, no BowFlex bodies—the kind of muscle that is for show, for sex and for guys in movies.

So what would the women be like here, he began to consider, but Noah could only think of *her*. The Pilates Princess. He felt himself cringe instead of that looming feeling of misery just waiting for him to let down his guard. He was proud of himself for that, but decided he wasn't ready to think of anyone else... even in speculation.

Reaching the edge of town, Noah was relieved to see an airport. That would save a lot of time if a trip to New York were ever necessary.

Beyond the airport, a graveyard stretched out across acres of mostly grass. A quiver started in the lining of his stomach and lurched up his throat. The hairs of his arms and neck prickled. The car floated by, his eyes a witness with no body, flying inside it; he felt weightless except for that guttural tremble. He felt like he'd been slapped in the face. It seemed an unlikely place to find a graveyard, but there was more to the chill crawling through his flesh and he didn't know what.

Thoughts clearing, Noah realized he'd let the car slow—he actually must have braked, the car barely crept along.

He pressed gently on the accelerator. David was fast asleep when Noah glanced at him as they reached 50MPH. With all the critters running around at night, he didn't want to take the chance of hitting anything because he was driving too fast. He imagined what hitting a bear or moose would do to a car at any speed.

Having just looked at the map back at the service station, the image of this area was pretty clear in his memory. It kind of bothered him that, other than for a few towns farther west in Ontario, they were really driving to the end of the world in a sense. Beyond Nibebiitam there were no roads. No roads. There were other towns, but ones only accessible by plane, train, or boat. He'd heard there were some condemned roadways, because you never knew if hitting that pothole in the road would just jolt the car or send you crashing through to a mine and ultimately, he guessed, your death.

It would be three in the morning before they'd arrive at the new house. David slept fast in the backseat, head rattling against the window. Gilder looked at him, eyes asking, *Are we there yet?*

Noah wanted to turn up the radio. He could get in six radio stations. MooseFM played softly through the speakers. He looked uncertainly at the volume dial. David could sleep through almost anything, but he didn't want to take the chance and deal with a grumpy six-year-old when he was barely awake enough to stay in his lane. He *hadn't* planned on taking the shortcut, but it would trim the last miles of road by half. If he stayed on the tar road going north, it was about forty miles to Nibebiitam, from there he'd have to head south again on a better maintained portion of Mitigomin Road, for fifteen or twenty miles, to get to the house.

The shortcut was a right hand turn off of the tar road onto the other end of Mitigomin Road. His friend, Derrick, said it was narrow on this end with a lot of growth near the road, but not to worry, that it was wide and maintained by the house.

Apprehension filled Noah when he turned down what turned out to also be a *winding* dirt road. The muskeg exhausted a dense fog, illuminated by the nearly full moon. Passing through the patches of unyielding whiteness proved difficult and unnerving. His eyes strained to see beyond it and relaxed when the car started uphill and out of the bottoms. It seemed to last forever, but what the road became was no better. Here the trees leaned out over the road, scraping the roof while low bushes slapped the car doors when he swerved to miss sinkholes and corduroy.

He glanced at the mirror to see if David was restless or waking. When he looked back at the road, the top of the hill passed and the car started slowly down a steep slope. Through the glow of moonlight Noah saw broken trunks of rotted trees half drowned in swamp water and the broad white lake of fog across it.

"Shit," he breathed and reached the level ground of the bottoms, sinking into the blinding white. The instant they entered the fog a shiver ran up his back. He turned to steal a look at David. His eyes never made it past the passenger seat.

Gilder sat upright, like a human, but hairless and body distorted so it was ape-like. Her front legs were so long that, even sitting on her "bottom", her elbows rested on the seat and her paws were lost somewhere in the dark below. The skin of Gilder's head drew so tight the flesh rippled and pinched along her lips. They pulled back over broken human teeth.

The car fish-tailed, Noah cried out, slammed his foot on the brake, white-knuckled, clenching the wheel to regain control. Something thudded against the front bumper. He heard it scamper across the dirt road. The reeds crackled and parted. His eyes shot back to the dog. Noah threw himself against the door.

Gilder looked normal again, but she was almost on top of him, baring her teeth, and growling fiercely. Her warm breath puffed against his cold and sweaty collar and throat. Her eyes fixed over Noah's shoulder at something else. He was afraid to look, but had to.

The light from the dashboard lit his face and cast a reflection on the glass of the driver's side window, but *not* his own. He blinked hard and then saw only his own strained face staring back. He was so terrified he hardly recognized himself. Heart pounding, Noah leaned back into the seat. He cast a listless glance upon the window; a patch of steam whitened the outside of the glass and ten crescent moons of white slowly dissolved on its smooth surface.

Then he heard David whimper and turned quickly to see if his son was alright. Awakened, the boy's small mouth pressed tight, a face flushed from trying not to cry. At the boy's first sound, Gilder shoved her head in between the seat and door to lick David's hand.

"What is it, dad?" David wondered, staring and confused.

"I—" Noah stammered, scanning the fog uneasily. "I'm sorry, daddy's just tired."

"Did you have a nightmare?" David pressed, the red in his face drained to blotches of pink.

"Um," Noah hesitated.

Before he could answer:

"Can you have nightmares when you're awake?"

His father's eyes flicked up to him and he suppressed all signs of fear to answer, "Yeah, you can. But nightmares aren't real, right?"

"Right," David answered promptly.

Noah wasn't so sure. Perhaps he had fallen asleep.

As the car crawled down the long dirt road he couldn't shake the pretense of warning he tried desperately to ignore the nearer they got to the new home. Alert with fear, a terrible trembling danced above the heavy clay-like weight in his stomach. He'd fallen asleep at the wheel, the father decided, no matter how real it felt. They could have went off the road or worse. That scared him more than anything.

A skeleton of an old cabin rose out of the headlight beams and Noah slowed when he neared the grown over driveway, marked by a rust shelled mailbox. The name scrawled on it was eaten away so what remained looked like Braille only in scattered dashes and curves instead of bumps. There might not be a better place to pull over and rest instead of taking the chance of falling asleep again.

As Noah braked, a crawling sensation spread through his skin like millions of lice. His heart pounded. Deafening silence pressed on them. What remained of the cabin stared at them with a patient, predatory hunger.

The night had presence and scrambled nearer the slower the car went. Noah's pulse beat in his throat. Gilder looked at him expectantly—a yearning look in her large brown eyes said, "I trust you know what you're doing."

Dread cooled his blood. He tried to tell himself his imagination got away from him. The tall reeds and unkempt grass slowly bent toward the car without even slightly swaying, despite a steady moaning wind seeping out of the deep thick forest like breath.

His foot pressed hard on the accelerator. With a little roar and spitting gravel they hurried down the road. He had a terrible feeling like he'd been running and had only just escaped. There was no risk at all, he realized, of falling asleep.

All at once Noah felt alone, or at the very least, vulnerable because his senses said a million malevolent eyes were watching. Always, he thought, it was the man who made a family feel safe and whole. The first time he had to do anything without Terri was when he woke up that morning to her note and her absence. Waking David by himself, calling in to work—he would not be there—that was what he felt she had done to their life. As when he called work, as with her note—no real explanation. But Terri did say it was over. Now he wished more than ever she was there. He felt safer making his family feel safe.

Does that make sense?

Yeah. Then you have to forget your own fears.

As they crept deeper and deeper into the wilderness, his thoughts drifted further from his fear and into dreams of what he remembered as life. There were no significant problems. He tried, but couldn't wring anything from their past to explain her leaving. Which raised one suspicion and he prayed earnestly his heart would not break wondering if she'd been unfaithful.

Abruptly they reached their driveway. The number on the mailbox flashed brightly in the headlights. He passed it by a few feet and had to drive back.

They were finally home.

The huge log house towered over the semi-open yard. Derrick had arranged with his uncle to get someone out there to clean up the yard, mow the grass, and haul out fallen trees and branches. There was very little else to see in the middle of the night. The great black silhouette blotted out a huge section of wilderness and the lot seemed to spread before it like open arms. As ominous as it might have appeared under any other circumstances, on this night, after the long drive, it was the most beautiful thing he'd ever seen. He imagined the warm glow of a fireplace casting light on the porch. That would truly look welcoming. Everything would be okay.

David was asleep again and draped like a towel across Noah's arms as he was carried to the front door with keys ready. The screen door whined and the keys seemed to clink together too loudly. Every sound was amplified in the tangible silence. Gilder pushed against his legs and forced herself into the house as soon as the door was open enough to squeeze past. With his back and his right foot, Noah carefully and quietly forced the door closed behind them and fumbled for a light switch. When he found one, he turned David's face against his chest and flipped the light on. With plenty of time to look around in the morning, all he wanted was to collapse anywhere and sleep.

His shins met the weight of their large mutt.

"C'mon girl," Noah whispered nudging the furry wall further into the house. Gilder didn't move.

"Gild—"

Hunched and bristled from tail to neck, she stared hard at the front door. Noah was tempted to let her alone. He'd feel safer with her right there.

"There," he turned the small notch in the center of the knob and locked the door. "Is that what you wanted?" It was weird not having to lock a deadbolt and a chain. He looked down at Gilder. A knot formed in his throat at the yellow puddle between her feet. She never had accidents anymore. The hairs stayed up and the large black mongrel trembled like she was freezing. Her eyes strained till the whites turned red, sparing every blink until she could not bear to stare any longer and stared again. She was beyond growling, she was threatening.

Perhaps moving to the middle of nowhere wasn't such a good idea for a city dog. He slid down the wall beside Gilder and let David sleep on his stomach. Noah was suddenly so tired he thought he was losing consciousness. Clean Gilder's mess in the morning. They could look around later. They would unpack whenever. He'd have the whole weekend before he started work. *I should have locked the car,* Noah thought as he drifted off to sleep. Everything could wait until after.

◆          ◆          ◆

"Eee!"

The squeal jolted Noah awake like a slap.

Daylight streamed through dirty windows. The warm yellow light filled Noah's skin and relaxed his nerves. Immediately past the entryway where they slept, a large kitchen, dining room and living room spanned from left to right. Last night he slept against a closet door. The front hall, which was basically only a closet on one side and room divider on the other, lasted only eight feet. Another hallway cut thirty-some feet into the other side of the house, dividing the living room, on the right, and kitchen and dining room, on the left. Both rooms were occupied by all their moving boxes and clusters of furniture. Noah hoped somethings he'd marked ended up where they belonged.

A back door stood exactly parallel to the front and on either side of it were two doors and a space, Noah guessed, would lead to stairs to the second level or basement, if they had a basement. He wasn't sure. The place was huge.

The man stretched and stood, taking in everything with a slightly clearer mind.

Gilder and David were nowhere to be seen.

The squeal happened again.

Noah stepped out of the small entry way into all that radiant light. Fully awake, he knew the sound was David and it was nothing to worry about even before finding him. The boy stood in the middle of the wide living area, in an ocean of hot golden light from a massive picture window flanked by two tall windows that could be opened with cranks. The high ceiling in the living room accommodated five large windows centered above those.

Behind them, in the kitchen, sliding glass doors divided counter space and let in abundant light on one side. Another window, over the sink, gave a perfect view of the front yard.

"Dad!" the boy screamed, charged his father, and tackled one leg. "It's huger than the old house! There's still only a bedroom and a bedroom! There's two potties, one with a shower! One with a bathtub. The kitchen is there and there's a basement and an attic and the porch goes all around the house!"

This wasn't entirely true. The front and a portion of the sides were covered. The rest was more like a large deck. Stairs led off it at the front and back doors.

Noah's eyes dropped to David's feet, the fabric dark with moisture. Strewn out on the living room floor were several of David's toys, markers, crayons, and a couple coloring books.

"So you like it?" Noah snatched the boy up in a bear hug.

David nodded furiously, "But Gilder piddled by the door."

Noah remembered and sighed, "I know. I'll get it while you pick out your cereal from the food we packed. The milk's in the cooler."

He felt childish for last night's panic. The events lingered like a bad dream and nothing more. There was no reason to be that way, except for being half asleep. That was all—unless fumes from a pulp mill cause hallucinations—which clearly isn't the same as half sleeping, but an equally acceptable excuse for the moment—to excuse everything.

When the phone rang his heart jumped and shattered any self-assurance he was calm and happy—that last night no longer bothered him. Then he had to find the phone.

"Hello?"

"Hey Noah, Jesus, how was the trip?"

His friend, Derrick.

"Long," Noah answered. That about summed it up.

"How's the new house?" Derrick asked excitedly. Noah heard him devouring his morning cigarette and blowing it around his coffee cup before slurping it because it was still too hot to drink. He'd seen the ritual play out hundreds of times—through college and coffee breaks at work.

Derrick was raised in Canada and, while he didn't know Noah wasn't American either, Noah felt an immediate kinship to the confident Canuck who was his first dorm roommate.

"Haven't really seen it yet. Got in late. Just woke up in fact." *Where's David?*

"I'd been trying your cell. I'm thinking no service up there."

"Great," Noah groaned earnestly. He took his cell phone out with his free hand and shrugged at the couple bars that showed up. He was just glad to see any.

"You'll have to tell me if you find hotties up there. I don't meet a lot of people when I get up there, but Uncle Jacob's friends. All of them are… well, I guess we never talked about if you get desperate. I bet there are some really sexy country bumpkins up there."

Noah grunted, both in answer and leaning down to pick up David's colors.

"I'm not shitting you, buddy. I want to know. You probably wouldn't tell me anyway," Derrick laughed then—to Noah it sounded forced, "You'll be staking out your own territory, moving on."

Noah didn't want to talk about that.

"So this Nibebiitam? It has a grocery store, at least, right?" he did want to know.

"Sure. Groceries. I think a couple restaurants and bars. You know it has a little school." Noah did, and it annoyed him a little that King Bachelor should point it out. Wouldn't any parent find out about that before moving? "It's just a cute little town, but with just about anything you want. I stress the 'you' part."

*Why am I irritated?* Noah frowned at and to himself as he went to the front door, prayed when it opened it wouldn't drag through Gilder's piss—it didn't—and stepped outside.

A heavy mist hung on the clearing. The trees loomed around them like walls. The silence—not entirely silent—birds, a pissed squirrel. There wasn't a trace of the mill smell in the sweet, clean air. Derrick was talking about jerks at his job, advertising, when Noah reached the car. It looked like Gilder'd been investigating the vehicle, circling it, circling it, probably peeing all around it. He took paper towels and a plastic bag out of one of the few grocery bags and started back to the house without realizing that the tracks were not Gilders. If he had looked closer, the tracks would have looked to him more like David had been running around the car on tip-toes.

"So you're sure this job is right for me?" Noah asked when it was a good time.

"You're the writer, buddy. 'Sides, my uncle's got at least three other people working for him, that's pretty big business in his business. You're not going to be alone or anything. You know how to do what you do and you'll sell that place like you sold your work here. Probably help business, in fact. Bring that New York edge. Fuck, when the word gets out he's got a big shot from New York, real author working for him, he'll rack in the dough right there. When they find out that you're good too—"

"So we'll be rolling in the dough anytime," Noah didn't bother to hide his sarcasm.

"You'll live as comfortably there as here, I promise."

"I'm not worried about that."

"Well then what?"

*Is Derrick irritated?*

"No one asked you to leave, remember? You were sitting pretty here."

"I know," it was Noah's turn again to be annoyed, but he discarded it from his voice. He got a feeling Derrick was going to blame him for the divorce, for being "stuck" with "the kid."

Noah looked at his watch.

"Sorry to cut you off here Derrick, but it's almost nine and I haven't got David breakfast."

"Yeah, s'pose. And *I* shouldn't even be up yet," Derrick agreed.

"I'll call you later today," Noah promised.

"Sounds good."

"Bye then," Noah pressed the talk button and his arm dropped limply to his side.

He took the handfuls of pee soaked paper towels and threw them away in the bag.

He was looking out the kitchen window, washing his hands (wondering where the nearest soap was packed) when he spotted David squatted at the end of the driveway.

David studied a small limp body from across the gravel road. He rubbed his mouth like a struggling alcoholic; then wrung his hands, indecisive if he should touch it or if he even wanted to. Its body lay in two masses of black and white fur, pear shaped self and two liter tail. Very fluffy—the morning breeze displayed its softness, flowing through it and pushing it this way and that.

His dad would never let him touch it.

Daddy'd stop him from even *watching* it, if he knew, but Noah didn't know and was left to smile quizzically from the window at the boy posed like a frog beside the road.

David reached a decision and started to stand.

A heavy 60's Ford pickup roared past and over his treasure. The little body jumped under the wheels and was tossed aside and ripped. Its pouch popped and the boy's stomach, already rolling with horror, now churned with sickness and rose and rose until its bulge filled the back of his throat—if he'd opened his mouth to a mirror he bet he could see it.

David retreated.

He ran until he reached the house and, breathing exaggeratedly, clutched one of the posts supporting the porch. The small boy realized there was a lot of space under it to explore and started looking for treasures.

The something that claimed the darkness down there as home woke up. It watched David enter the shadows. Though looking for nothing particular it felt that it alone was sought and would surely be found. That was fine, it thought, with no intention of abandoning its territory.

*Let him come.*

Flexing its claws and crouching in the concealing dark, it needed only to wait a moment before the boy came tramping over. That was when David screamed:

"Dad!"

Seconds later Noah ran around the corner of the veranda and to David's aid. He ran down like a wind-up toy when he saw David's back. The boy was bent and half lost beneath the porch and perfectly soundless.

"David?" Noah ventured uneasily after David remained motionless and quiet. There was nothing around but a few gaily chirping songbirds. Dread crept in through the earth, through his toes with a petrifying cold and weight. Later he would laugh at himself for being so afraid, but at the moment there was only fear, the kind of fear born only out of the deepest love and concern. The boy meant everything in his rapidly shrinking world. Suddenly—

"Dad!" David yelled impatiently. The child jerked backwards and stood, dragging out a tabby cat in a full Nelson, that would actually be thin were it not very, *very* pregnant. The child was filthy from the apparent power struggle that had just taken place. He grinned up at his daddy, proud of his big catch.

"Can I keep him?"

*Her,* Noah thought. He barely considered David's request before agreeing. It would be nice to have a cat around where the filthy things were actually useful. Hopefully it wouldn't bother Gilder too much.

"You better get her—it, him, some milk so sh—he'll want to stick around," Noah said.

"I *can*?" David shoved the cat out for his daddy to take and went for the milk. Human food was ordinarily off limits for animals, so this was a real treat, especially since it felt a little naughty even though he had permission.

"Poor girl," Noah cooed, petting her tense frame gently. He looked her over to get a vague idea of her health and immediately hoped there was a vet nearby. She had several sores and looked malnourished. He'd heard of mange, but had never seen an animal with it, so he worried about the sores. He would readily admit ignorance about this and tried not to think about it, but what concerned him most, for the kitty's sake, were unmistakable bite marks.

"Je-*sus*!" he breathed in two hard breaths. "Poor kitty."

He looked over his shoulder at the woods. Nature was a cruel master, Noah reflected, holding the cat protectively. What hell the poor thing went through just to be manhandled by a six-year-old. Caring for her came as easily as the grimace when he found the first bite. He promised her a good home with them.

He would eventually explain to David that she was a she and wasn't fat, she was going to have babies. After referring to her as a mommy cat a couple times, David would name her Mama Cat.

Noah was about to open the screen door when he thought about mange again. It was pretty contagious, he thought. They would have to leave her outside until they found a vet.

Add to the list: Find a vet. Under: Unpack. Buy Groceries. Check utilities. Call Work. Register David for school. And a half a dozen other "to do's."

It would be a long day.


After sorting where the boxes went, Noah worked hastily to unpack while David made his room his own. He had to leave his own work to move the bed and dresser to where David wanted them. Noah hoped that would be the only time.

The living room and bathroom were done by the time David tracked his daddy to where he was unpacking in his own bedroom, looking for something to do.

"Well, we're gonna need to pick a place for Gilder's bed."

"She always sleeps in our beds," David pointed out, while poking through one of the boxes.

"Not when we're in the kitchen," was about the only time when she wasn't on people furniture, at least where they used to live.

"Okay. Maybe she can pick a place."

"Good idea," Noah agreed. After, boy and dog wandered all over looking for where the bed should go. David was certain to stay with her after the bed was put in the spot and watch as Gilder scratched and straddled it to a place that felt right for the moment, or minute.

"After you finish that, why don't you draw a picture of the house to send Derrick? Then, when he comes up here to visit he'll know what it looks like and won't drive past."

David hollered "okay" or "yay" or something as he ran off.

After a half hour Noah went to check on his son, who was still wandering between the kitchen and living room with a dog looking very interestedly at what was happening with "her thing".

"I'm gonna move some of this stuff upstairs," he told the cute little face that was looking so serious about its work.

"The attic?" David exclaimed, dropping the bed like it weighed a hundred pounds.

"No way, mister. No Way Zone. You stay out of the attic—" he raised his pointed finger at the protest that was about to happen "—No. Take care of Gilder."

Noah lifted one of the boxes that had a few lamps packed away. They wouldn't fit anywhere he could think of, so he was glad there was a place for storage.

Standing at the bottom of the attic stairs, he was filled with the apprehension and curiosity guaranteed to most people at the precipice of such places. Beyond the door to the attic, almost against the door, began the stairs. Down them and softly illuminating the dust on their unpainted wood surfaces spilled the afternoon light.

He liked the way the dust and wood smelled and didn't feel threatened by the unseen space about ten steps above him, give or take a few. Noah didn't lie to himself about being able to feel the same way about it at night.

He'd look for a light switch on the way out.

The L-shaped attic floor and stairs from it were divided by railing. It only made sense, for safety, that it should be there, but you never know. Noah was glad to see it. It was easy for him to imagine David forgetting there was a large rectangular hole in the floor and dropping down it like Alice.

The spacious attic was mostly empty, beyond support beams and where the fireplace chimney passed through the levels. An old bedframe leaned against a wall. A box marked "Christmas" that had a rusty spring mousetrap inside it and a sock. He found two pennies, a nail, and some broken glass beside two boxes. One containing old glass pop bottles and the other was full of the glass caps or insulators, or whatever they are, from electric poles. A couple pieces of art that, beyond being filthy, didn't peak Noah's interest, hung here and there. Everything was a lot older than the house. Evidence, Noah reasoned, that the former owner was either old or into antiques.

He sat down the box and left the attic with a head full of ideas for the space.

Noah doubted he'd enter or leave the basement feeling the same way. Basements too reek of intrigue, but that which is largely composed of fear. He wasn't looking forward to it.

"There's no time like the present," he muttered to himself.

After a quick peek at what the kid was into—still wandering with the dog bed—he was ready to take on the basement, or at least, just see it. There was still a lot to do upstairs.

Noah was looking for the light switch while simultaneously trying to figure out the grayish-brown light that filtered through windows made almost useless by the addition or expansion of the porch and deck space. He would have put money on the lights not working, but they bloomed so triumphantly against the feel of "basement" that they almost seemed to give him a thumb's up.

Only the first few steps had backs on them to block the threat of being grabbed through them. He hated steps like that and decided he'd have them finished as soon as he could get hold of a contractor. He wasn't going to reawaken that childhood fear in himself or conceive it in his child.

The basement was cold and dismal feeling, even as the lights were warm and bright. The ceiling beams were exposed and draped with cobwebs. The cover for the coaster sized floor drain was sitting aside the hole it was supposed to fill.

He didn't like it down there. Didn't like the two foreboding doors set in the brick walls. He didn't like the bare brick walls. Didn't like the gunmetal toned paint that seemed to eat the light.

Noah didn't want to get off the last step. He didn't want to go out into that—and there was no self-bullying or teasing or motivational advice that could convince him to do it. Shivers raced up his body and ran visibly through his back and arms. He rubbed at the sensation as he leaned over the rail to look at the space under the stairs. He imagined the triangle of darkness filled with a colossal, demonic, monstrous spider folded tightly into the space—it would slowly unfurl like a contortionist climbing out of a box.

The washer and dryer stared back at him like they were caught making out in a basement they'd broke into.

"Yippee skippy," he turned to leave.

The monster was under the stairs again, reaching for his legs.

He ran up the stairs, shut off the light and closed the door. David was standing in the hallway, holding the dog bed. Gilder was standing underneath, her flattened out ears looked like they were trying to hold it up. They both bugged out at the grown up—at the wild look on his face.

Noah smiled hugely, hugely embarrassed.

"What'd'ya two think about us scrounging up some lunch? I'm so hungry, I just realized."

David blinked.

Gilder wagged her tail.

One fine little eyebrow raised on the boy's face as he shared his two cents:

"You looked like you had to pee."


After lunch Noah asked David to play in his room for a little while and then they would go through the house together to decide if everything was really where they wanted it to be. And, "No, that does not include the attic or basement." In the kitchen, the child of six would be challenged to guess what was behind the cabinet doors. Until then, Noah challenged himself to try and make his own room feel like "his room" since it was where he did most of his writing. The "feel" of the room turned out to be really important.

Gilder was interested in what was keeping her big person so busy—was it a bug? A treat? A sock? A missing piece of crinkly paper—when her master gave off this energy, it was usually for missing paper. She tried to help until she was driven out of the room.

It hadn't taken more than half an hour before David's room felt like David's Room. His stuffed animals were sitting where they were supposed to. His favorites, on the bed on the side by the wall to keep monsters from reaching up. His ultimate favorite, at the top of his bed, to hug onto and protect him all night. It didn't blink all the while David was sleeping so, just like his daddy told him it would, obviously the floppy grey dog would keep watch all night.

Even Gilders have to sleep. Sometimes light, sometimes so heavy that she hasn't waked when David has tripped over her, or that time when a spoon fell off the counter and landed on her rump.

Toys and books being considered for entertainment already littered the round rug partially hidden under the bed.

It felt a lot more comfortable, to Gilder, in the boy's room.

Noah stood up from where he'd braced himself against the weight of the bed and was about to change where it sat, again. He heard his son jabbering excitedly and paused to listen. He couldn't make out a single word from down the hall and the opposite side of the house. He was less interested in words than the tone of the child's voice. Excited and happy.

He looked at the room and wanted to care about making it right, but felt such a strong compulsion to be with his family that he suddenly didn't care about it at all.

The hall felt a little familiar now as he entered it—and in not too long he hoped it would feel like home.

The laughter that erupted in the back bedroom gave Noah comfort that it might be sooner than later. He had a lot of doubts about the move. A lot of doubts if the change would be good for David and for him and for Gilder, for that matter. In his heart, he secretly dreamed of reconciling with David's mom—that whatever had gone wrong would mend itself as secretly as it had torn apart.

Noah's neck crackled painfully as he whipped his head around to chase the movement he caught out of the corner of one eye.

When he didn't see or hear anything he shrugged it off and went on his way.


Later, while Noah looked over the improvements recommended by the appraiser, and added a list of his own,

David was sentenced to amuse himself without exceeding the parameters of the "Okay" zones into "No Way Buddy" zones—which anyone could guess were far more interesting than anyplace "Okay".

Some "No Ways" included playing in the attic, basement, and woods. This trio was guilty of "Don't know what's in there". It may as well read in neon and promise cupcakes by what that means for a child. Noah didn't say "there might be monsters"—that was never inferred—what *was* implied, as far as David was concerned, was that there were things in these places his daddy had to explore first, in case there were things to throw away—one person's trash is another person's treasure—or possibly of value or interest Noah didn't want his own little monster to vandalize or break.

The "Okay" zones: David's bedroom, the living room, the front yard, the kitchen table (if he played quietly) or his dad's bedroom ("though I'd prefer if you didn't and if you have to, don't get into anything").

Noah wasn't anxious to poke through whatever was stored in the couple outbuildings, after the basement and attic. Probably none of them would see much use. It wouldn't be worth the effort. Understandably, however, David was obsessed with their secrets. When the fear is taken out of the unknown, for children at least, there is only reward or disappointment.

David drew pictures and said they were of stuff stored in the shed, buried in the basement or stuffed in a chest in the attic.

How could anyone discourage their child from being so hopeful? Noah couldn't blame anyone, given the state of the world, for feeling only hopelessness.

"Where's Gilder?" David barked and threw himself backward with a thump, like a just split log, against the living room carpet. His fingers raked the dense fibers like he was scratching an itch. Noah didn't hear, or didn't register that it might be directed toward him.

With another adult in the house—if anything was called out it probably had purpose. With a six-year-old, they could be talking to themselves, a teddy bear, or a houseplant.

David knew another thing that made places "No Way" places was if they could be dangerous—that was intriguing too—not to experience, but just to see what it could be. There might be broken glass or nails or something in the attic or basement. In the woods, there was the risk of getting lost or poison ivy.

Some dangers in the woods would come to them.

David rolled on his side and listened to the heavy silence of an occupied parent. This was a good time to explore, but there were things in the back of David's mind. Things he was afraid of that he would not say aloud, because in the heart of a child lies the fear that this might make those things real... to speak of the Devil, as it were. Things like getting hurt, getting killed. Bears and rattlesnakes and other things that attack people in the wilderness. He'd heard his daddy say "bears" when he was on the phone. They were real. They might eat his head off—or worse, only half his head. They might eat his daddy.

What if he got snake bit and couldn't get back to help. How bad does a snake bite hurt? How long before it kills you? Could the hospitals here fix it?

*Town is a long ways away.*

At the same time, there was something else thinking this too.

# COMMON MISCONCEPTIONS

◆

Cannonballs flew through the air. They rose slightly and fell short, landing inside a skirt of splashing water, amidst a wave of laughter. The cannonballs unfolded and became children again. The four friends were trying to enjoy the last of their summer before entering fourth grade. So far, they were doing a good job.

The three boys and one girl, a cousin to one of the boys, had spent most of the day throwing a ball around on the shore, but they got so hot that they convinced themselves the water would feel good. It probably wouldn't have felt that great if they weren't having such a good time.

The water was dark and partially lined by large dead trees that lent their winding roots to the depths—with them the illusion of a thousand horrors.

Jonas McKenna was keeping some distance after the other two boys started to tease him for being too protective of the rogue female of the group, Mandy. So that must mean he liked her. So he punched his friends, yelled a lot, and stayed away—

like any boy would do when there was some truth to the teasing. He was a little embarrassed to have this crush, it being his first.

"Hey Baker," yelled Timothy Whipple, "Time me!"

The head of dark red hair disappeared below the surface. Numbers in sequence, separated by "Mississippi" were counted out by the breathless friends.

Under the water, surrounded by a color they'd always likened to Root Beer, he stared down into the deep black shadows shrouding the pond bottom. A chill ran through his gut. He still had a few Mississippi's in his lungs and was confident he would beat his personal best. He couldn't make out where the counting was at through the distorting layers of water, but he was keeping track himself.

Timothy was reaching the point where he would start to let the air out slow and then scavenge a few more seconds from his emptied lungs. A bad feeling preceded a physical one, and the air he meant to ration came out in a burst so big he felt like he'd vomited it up and almost puked because of the feeling. The warped sunlight seemed a long way away, but in a matter of two seconds he breeched the surface, gasping, and did throw up.

"Oh gross!" Mandy groaned and moved away. The boys laughed at him and told him his puke looked like the bread that's thrown to ducks in the city pond. He temporarily forgot that something had brushed against his foot down there. He thought something actually put its mouth over the end of his foot. Once, he'd put his foot into the mouth of a large mouth bass and that was the first thing he could think of.

"Hey guys!" he demanded attention. "There's something down there."

"Sure there is," Jonas agreed. "There are fish, and roots, and weeds, and don't forget, the body of Camper Quinn!"

The children squealed and laughed at the mention of the missing camper from last winter. There was so much gossip that the story was beginning to be treated like an urban legend. The popular joke around the elementary school was his missing body. The mystery meat in the cafeteria was, naturally, different parts of Camper Quinn, depending on how creative the jester was. They could always tease each other that Camper Quinn's body was hidden under their beds or that he was sleeping with this person, or that person's mom. Some people said that Camper Quinn killed some motorists that the local police had said died in a traffic accident. So that rumor led to warning that Camper Quinn was at the door or calling homes to find out if anyone was home.

"Shut up!" John Baker hollered. He didn't like to think about where Camper Quinn was, or what he might be doing if he was still alive.

The other three laughed at him.

"He's lying on his belly, scrambling up the pond bottom like a salamander—he's in a hurry to catch you! Run! Run!" Timothy cried urgently as all four splashed toward the shore. Real or not, no one even wanted to be in the pond with the idea of Camper Quinn.

Suddenly Timothy screamed. He was waist deep in the water and was losing his footing. It looked apparent to the other children that something was pulling him back into the water.

Timothy screamed for "mom", it wasn't missed by his friends, but they were in no mood to tease anymore. There was nothing funny about fear so tangible they could almost swim in *it*.

Then Timothy went under.

There wasn't a chance to dive after him before the boy was up again, gasping for air.

Jonas rose up behind him, but not enough to even fully expose his chin.

"Hey! Hey!" he cut through the screams and crying. "It's just some weeds, moron."

His hands worked under the water and shortly emerged with fists full of aquatic plants.

"Better call your mama!" Mandy was the first, but not even close to the last to joke about that.

The handful of children marched out of the water, a little more hurriedly than any of them wanted it to appear.

"Let's go home. This is stupid. We could be watching TV," John complained.

"Yeah, let's go," agreed Jonas.

Timothy agreed, but couldn't get a word out. He was afraid to turn his back on the pond, even with his friends between him and it—even if Spiderman was between them.

It didn't feel like weeds.

# CHAPTER 3

◆

# NIBEBIITAM

Noah didn't want to take David to work with him, but until he found a babysitter this was how it would have to be until school started. He hoped his boss would be understanding, since there really wasn't any other choice.

Already restless and grumpy about having to spend the day quiet and well behaved, David fussed in his car seat and scowled at the rearview mirror. It was weird how the frown reminded Noah so much of David's face when he was a baby—it was the "I'm shitting" face.

They had to get up extra early to drop Mama Cat off at the vet in Kapuskasing. It would be an awful lot of driving for one day.

"Dad, why can't I just go to school?"

"It will be school time soon," Noah assured himself as much as his son.

"How long do you work in the day?"

"As long as a school day."

"What will you do there?"

"The same kind of work I did back home," Noah lied, but he didn't feel like trying to explain the difference.

"Then why did we leave if you just do the same thing?" David whined even though he knew why. They were leaving bad times behind and were looking for better times. He didn't feel as grumpy then and tried not to be mad about having to spend the day with dad at work—that was part of dad's effort for better times. He would have to try too.

The trip to Nibebiitam was about twenty miles, add to it the run to and from Kapuskasing. They saw ravens, ducks, all kinds of songbirds, a raccoon, deer, and the rear end of a black bear retreating from someone's bird feeder.

Whoever built the Asheborne's house must have had money. Compared to the few other homes they passed within the first fifteen miles, their cabin looked like a mansion. Noah started to feel guilty.

The nearest home was a green trailer house patched with pieces of sheet metal. A chicken-wire fence was tacked to posts around the yard, separating the woods and underbrush from the uneven cut grass within. A reel lawn mower was propped against the three steps and black iron railing extending to a wind stripped white door with fiberboard showing through.

The next two homes were no better. The one small weathered home looked like it had cardboard for siding and only two windows, one facing the road and the other on the door. The third was a cabin, aged gray by seasons and sun. It too had a porch, but it stuck out farther into the yard than their own and only spanned the front of the house. It looked like something out of a western movie where a hermit miner might live. On the deck, a silvery haired Native man wearing a red plaid shirt, rocked slowly in a willow rocker, cupping an oversized dark-blue mug. Noah almost smiled.

"That's just perfect," Noah muttered and raised two fingers to wave. The man waved back.

*I could almost have guessed you'd be there. Or maybe Red Green,* he thought sarcastically.

Ironically, they passed a few better looking homes, but these looked abandoned and had obviously been so for many years. Several windows were broken on every home. One suffered significant fire damage. The shells of these homes were as big as their own.

Within three miles of town the houses were closer together and more typical looking. Nibebiitam, population 654, was only a small cluster of buildings itself, surrounded by patches of scalped forest. Two groceries, a hardware store, an auto shop, several small businesses he probably would never enter, a church and at least three bars passed by the time he arrived at work.

The car door sounded loud as it slammed closed. He looked disgustedly at the dirt and dust quickly turning his blue car brown. The town was quiet, nothing like stepping out onto the street in New York. He told himself not to compare the two anymore. He would never find anything alike about the two. Looking up and down the street, he could kind of see that now.

When he passed by the front of the car Noah noticed chips of yellow paint running away from the sidewalk about three feet from the passenger side of the car. Once, the parking spaces had been painted. He let out a "huh" under his breath.

No parking tickets, no meters, no ramps, no tolls. No smog, he breathed deeply, no shouting. He paused long, long, long— digesting. The bumper, the sidewalk, the only distance between himself and his job. Amazing. Twenty miles was a remarkably short distance now. Remarkably easy. For the first time in what felt like his whole life, something loosened in his body, somewhere between his ribs and shoulders. He had the sense, one he knew could only last so long, that this was a vacation.

Before he reached the back door, a truck rumbled slowly past. Three people were crammed into the cab, two middle-aged men and a woman, a few years younger, in between. They all looked like they got dressed out of the same wardrobe. Noah tried not to think about the driver's mullet—not only the longest he'd ever seen, but the longest he ever imagined. It was flapping through the rear center cab window. All three passengers stared at the New York license plate and then at the man standing near the rear, dressed like he stepped right off the cover of *GQ*. Not that any of them had ever heard of *GQ*. Noah waved with the hand that reached for the passenger side handle and only then yanked the door open after they passed by. David craned to watch the truck go and undid his seatbelt.

"Who were those people?" the boy wondered.

"I dunno," Noah admitted, reaching over his son for the bag David had packed with things to entertain himself.

"Then why did you wave?"

Noah wasn't sure, it just seemed right.

"Just being friendly."

"Don't talk to strangers," David reminded, smiling saucily as he climbed out.

Noah barely nodded in answer. He was about to face his somewhat vague new job. From what he could tell it was some kind of newspaper, print shop, photo mat. It was his job to do graphic design and layouts, maybe some writing. The entryway was lined with ads and examples of work they could do. He stared at the neon green paper advertising that they would now "Print Photos from Digital Cameras! New! New! New!" Several happy customers' photos of weddings and portraits were displayed. He held his breath and opened the next door into the main building. He let David move in under his arm before letting the door close slowly.

There was a tiny waiting room, on either side were four folding chairs with dark green cushions tied on the seats. Between the chairs were end tables with neat stacks of magazines and a single ashtray. Dozens of ads and pictures similar to those in the entryway were displayed beneath a glass panel on top of the pine reception desk. A tall office chair sat behind the counter where a lower desktop stored a phone and lots of papers. Filing cabinets and a single desk were just behind that. A balding older man sat there absorbed in typing, eyes bulging at the computer screen. He was so close to it, Noah bet there were nose marks on it.

"Excuse me," Noah knocked on the counter top.

The man started at his voice, but laughed easily through it as he got up.

"Mr. Asheborne!"

David looked surprised at his dad. He barely ever heard him called that.

"Hi, Mr. Cle—"

"Jacob to *everyone* around here," the man interrupted, waving a hand across the air like he was making a rainbow. Noah looked up from the history of coffee stains on the chest of the old man's jumbo thick beige sweater. The French and Italian ancestry was as vivid in Jacob as in Derrick. Though all the swarthy tones were just washed out in the elder. It made him wonder when he'd see Derrick again and realized how much he already missed him.

"Then call me Noah. This is my son David. I hope you don't mind. Because school hasn't started and I don't have a sitter yet—"

"Don't mind at all. Not too many children around. No daycares except people's own family and friends unless you head to the city—" which Noah assumed meant Kapuskasing "— you'll find someone certainly."

"That's good to hear," Noah said relieved. He got the sense that by the end of the week the whole town would know he needed a sitter.

"You've quite a drive out from your place, ain't you?" asked Jacob. His tone shifted in a way that sounded nosey.

"Farther than I used to have to drive to work, but took *way* less time. I think I'll get used to it," answered Noah, smiling easily.

"You'll want a four wheel drive come winter. I promise."

"I hadn't thought of that."

Noah looked at the doors behind him and tried to imagine his faithful old car plowing through several feet of snow. The idea of being stranded somewhere out in the boonies made him sorry he hadn't considered something like this and bought a truck where he had good choices. He might even be willing to take the horrible trip back down that road just to get to a bigger town and a more reliable vehicle sooner.

*It probably wouldn't be that bad in the day time, when you're not tired*, he told himself.

"Where do you want me?" Noah wanted to get started. He felt pressed for time like there was too much to learn. He'd so many questions and he didn't want to annoy his boss by asking them all in one day. He followed Jacob into the back room to a desk overflowing with files needing attention.

At least it looked like business was booming.

"Sweet steaming shit, what time is it?" Jacob exclaimed. Noah's eyes shot to David who, completely bugging out, had looked at his daddy immediately too.

"Uhh…" Noah looked at his watch, "Its eight o'four."

Moving with surprising speed, Jacob flew past them and threw the deadbolt on the inner door.

"Sorry to cuss, but I left it unlocked because I knew you were coming, but after today, so you know, we don't unlock until eight-fifteen, got it?"

"Umm…okay."

"Oh lord, come on back here quick," he glanced out the large front windows. "Quick!"

And ushered father and son into the back.

"Stand over there," Jacob directed, pointing to a little nook between a bookshelf and a file cabinet.

They went obediently while Jacob ducked out of sight, peering occasionally over the next five minutes until finally he went really low behind the counter.

Shadows gave away someone walking by, but rather than pass, they heard the outer door open and the inner door tried via several firm tugs. Then the shadow moved on.

"What is this, *Night of the Living Dead*?" Noah laughed as the old man groaned himself into a standing position.

"Oh, it's those damn Sneider's," the old man answered as if they should know the implications. Shortly after, when he realized they wouldn't, he explained. "The damn nosey creeps. They prowl around looking for people to talk to. Well, they knew we opened officially at eight, but unofficially at seven-thirty and damned if they didn't want to come in here and chew my ears off with their stories and questions. Enough people know that I hired the new guy in town, enough that they got wind of it too. Not unlike a dog to a ripe fart, they come looking to sniff out some information."

"So…" Noah began, "You 'avoid' them."

"*Yes*," said his boss exasperated.

Noah snickered as he led David back to where he could color and work on whatever else he packed. He couldn't meet Jacob's eyes as he passed by. No one should laugh at their boss, especially the laugh that would have erupted if he'd an ounce less self control.

◆          ◆          ◆

The day went quickly. For some reason the dull town made Noah think his work would be dull too. Not that there was anything exciting about the work. He enjoyed it because it was creative, but it wasn't the least bit interesting. Though he had a feeling that working around Jacob would make it easy to show up.

David surprised Noah by quietly entertaining himself all day. The worst thing he did was hum a song with no tune he made up while coloring, but he stopped that when asked.

At lunch they went to a diner attached to a gas station a few minutes' walk away. It had red vinyl cushions fixed to rounded wooden booths, like lavish park benches. The tables had red tops and chairs that matched the seats in the booths. It smelled of comfort food, grease, and sweets cooking somewhere behind swinging doors with portholes and the open counter where completed meals, ordered, and finished dishes went back and forth like slow juggling.

They had homemade burgers and fries. The burgers were huge. If Noah had known, they would have bought one meal and split it between the two of them. Each basket of fries was like four large fast-food fry orders.

*Well, it's a special day*, he excused. David could stuff himself if he wanted to. After Noah bought groceries he would make lunches, but when David was in school he would probably skip lunch and just have coffee like he used to.

After work they drove to Kapuskasing to pick up Mama Cat. The vet said she was healthy and didn't have much to say about the bites. Probably because she was outside and uncared for. No doubt something would try to make a snack of her. She was now up to date with all her shots, dewormed, nails clipped and, after a brief stop for some pet supplies, she was fully a member of the Asheborne family.

The drive home on the shortcut felt shorter than the first time. Aside from being in town, he saw three other vehicles on the whole drive. *A hell of a lot different than New York.*

"You weren't going to compare them," he reminded as they pulled up to their property among several other vehicles—three on the road and two more parked kitty-corner at the end of the driveway and yard. The occupants of the vehicles, nine men were milling around on the road. If they had been coming from Nibebiitam, the men would have had to move aside to let them reach their driveway. It looked like they were waiting for them. One of the men was the old Indian with the red plaid shirt. They were all Native, in fact, as were many of the people in town, according to Jacob.

The young father pulled in and stopped in almost the same place he had the night they first arrived—really close to the house. Before opening the car door he could already hear Gilder's frantic barks from inside the house. David's eyes were round with fear and excitement.

"Stay in the car," Noah ordered and got out.

A second later the rear passenger door clicked shut and gravel moved beneath the small feet that landed on it.

Noah went up the driveway to meet the men. He tried not to look as anxious as he felt. David followed, gently pinching at his father's loose pant leg even though this gave away his disobedience.

Most the men looked gut-flippingly serious—the kind of serious where you know you aren't going to like what you're going to hear—or what was going to happen to you.

His daddy said, "Hi. Is everything okay?"

Noah's hand reassuringly held the side of David's head as the men formed a half circle around them. If he was scared, his son couldn't see it, but thought he had every right to feel it if he was. And David thought his daddy was scared.

The tall dark men towered around the boy, talking over him to his father. They barely noticed him, in fact. They looked very serious. They sounded serious too.

David looked up at them, curiosity gleaming in his deep brown eyes. He wanted to touch them, touch the soft flannel shirt of the old man beside him whose silver hair was neatly pleated into a long thick braid. He yearned to stroke the fur-lined boots this man wore and the tawny leather of its deerskin. The other men wore work boots or regular tennis shoes. Most of them were younger than the silver-haired man. To David, his father's wide brown eyes were like a dog's and, although these men's eyes were dark too, they were dense and depthless like polished stone. He had, of course, heard of Native Americans, but had never met any as far as he knew. He wasn't even confident that was who he was meeting now.

The boy barely heard a word they said, so engrossed in seeing that everything else was just atmosphere. Some of what these strangers said were in words he didn't understand anyway and when these words were spoken another man would speak immediately after and his father would nod and reply. There was so much going on, so much to absorb, that the only thing the little boy was able to take in was his father's reaction—and it was mixed.

Occasionally, the old silver-haired man looked down at David while the others were talking. He didn't look as grave and serious as the others, in fact, he looked somber and tired. This man seemed helpless—like his father the morning his mother was gone and he'd sat at the table and stared and stared till it numbed the air and all David felt was his father's silence. The old man's eyes were filled with that same quiet, a restless and wounded quiet. David frowned up at the stranger, eyes scrunching to see deeper into those eyes—he thought were trying to speak to him.

At last, the sky nearly dark, his daddy and the men walked back to the trucks. David stayed where he was and watched them, still talking, even as some got back into their vehicles. His father leaned on the open window of the cab of one of the pickups and gestured a lot when he spoke to that man, as he did when he was frustrated. Like when he tried to explain things to David and didn't know just what to say or how to say it.

David felt vulnerable, alone in the middle of the driveway. The unfamiliar house stared at his back. The darkness of the surrounding porch lending deep shadows to the siding and the windows. The woods felt tight around the yard as if desperately trying to overcome it, pressing into the air like great black tidal waves. The child wrung his hands nervously into his shirt and turned a slow circle, suddenly aware someone stood near him.

He screamed.

Looking into the worn jeans of the silver-haired old man, David's mouth popped open like it was hinged with springs. He didn't even notice the tall old man hadn't went with the others. Then the man bent to one knee to look David in the eyes and said, "Tomorrow you and your pa will come see me."

David wasn't sure if it was a question or statement.

"Tomorrow you come over and meet my family," he continued, cracking a warm smile that drove fans of wrinkles out of his eyes, bows on his brow and wings around his mouth. David's smile only inflated the fat of his baby-like cheeks.

"I have a dog," the six-year-old announced, looking around to point out Gilder.

"Don't worry, I'll meet 'im," the elderly man assured him. "Make sure you bring him with you when you come to town—a dog from the city, with all the new sounds and smells, might run off into the woods after something without someone keeping an eye on him."

"Do you think she's run off *now*?" David squeaked. He was worried about his kitty too.

The old man chuckled, "Where was she last?"

David thought, pressing his forefinger into his cheek, just beside his chin as he looked for her.

"She's still in the house."

A smile bloomed on the man's face at the child's own smile of realization and the small abashed laugh.

"Solomon, time to head back," called the guy his father had been talking to at the truck window. He seemed anxious. Thunder rumbled in the distance. Ten men and one child raised their head at the sound.

Solomon straightened and smiled softly at this silly little white child, "Remember what I said, David. Take that dog with you tomorrow and everywhere after."

"I do," the child assured him and grinned secretively because he learned the stranger's name without being told it. Tomorrow he'd call the man by his name and see the same surprise David felt when his own name was spoke by someone he didn't think should know it. It occurred to the little boy, in the silence following the old man's departure, that it would be impossible to keep Gilder with him when school started. Unless schools here were different than in the states… *hmm*, he smiled to himself. *Wouldn't that be nice? Dogs at school…*

Noah lingered by the roadside until the taillights were out of sight down the tree shadowed road. Hands crammed into his front pockets, clamped in by each thumb, he slowly started back. Casting a look over his shoulder after them, the father mumbled something under his breath and shook his head. His son waited anxiously for all of this to be explained, but when they looked at each other the boy knew none of the words shared between the adults would be shared with him. Noah actually looked a little worried. He didn't know David was too preoccupied to hear the things being said over him and so the child was also completely unaware of the pressure his dad felt under to think up viable answers to the billion questions that would never be posed.

"Did you get your bag out of the car?" Noah asked monotonously as he took the cat and a fistful of bags full of pet supplies out of the back seat.

"No."

"Come get it, bud."

While David scrambled to retrieve his things, Noah's mind sorted through what the men came to tell him. The older man with long silver hair, Solomon, asked normal things. How was the move? Were they settled in okay? Said he stopped in to see Jacob while Noah and David were at lunch and found out he was stuck for a babysitter. His granddaughter, who lived with him, would be glad to watch David days during the summer, which was almost over.

After school started, she could ride the bus home with David and watch him until Noah returned from work. They were neighbors after all. All that sounded fine.

The rest, he didn't really understand, but disliked it nonetheless. He didn't want to understand it and he had no intention of trying. The men sounded urgent to discuss the matter with him, but hesitant too, as if they didn't want to tell everything. It was delinquent or wild children? Sounded like a bunch of punks, as far as Noah could tell. Pulling pranks, being destructive. He didn't know why the men should have felt the need to come in a herd just to tell him that. Didn't they think that might be a little intimidating… threatening?

The car door slammed shut and David hurried to catch up. Inside his pocket Noah pressed the "lock" button on the key ring and, with a honk, the car was locked up.

David slammed on his brakes, spinning on his heel to face the car again.

"Why'd you do that?" he wondered loudly.

Noah held David's hand and led him to the house.

"Just because we live in the sticks, doesn't mean we shouldn't be careful, right?"

"You should always be careful," David agreed matter-of-factly. But he thought people in the country *didn't* lock their doors. Derrick said so.

Noah wished they didn't have to be careful. He wished there were places like that on earth, but there apparently weren't. That a few punks should have to ruin things for everyone else, because they're bored or something, pissed him off. Same shit as, not just New York, but every damn place on earth. Lose the assholes—perfect world. Make people care about each other's feelings—perfect future.

After a brief struggle with the cat, the bags hanging heavily on his wrist, and getting out his keys, Noah got the front door open. He didn't take off his shoes, but went to dump the bags off on the kitchen table. Hands free, he tried to calm the car ride out of the frazzled kitty. He waited until David took off his shoes and was heading past, to put away his pack, to tell his son something he hoped he would only have to say once, at least as severe as he was going to say it now:

"David, when I tell you to do something—*you do it*."

"Yes daddy," the little boy said soberly and went to put away his things.

Only when Noah was setting the cat down did he realize how badly he was shaking. It hadn't escaped him that those men could have meant to do anything. *Anything*.

David was pretty tired by the time he had supper, brushed his teeth and had a bath. But he was afraid to be sleepy because it started to rain and it had thundered again, once or twice. Derrick said they get a lot of rain and a lot of winter up here. To a six-year-old, this translated into lots of hot chocolate and lots of sledding.

His daddy tucked him in, read him a short bedtime story, and kissed his head through the tangle of damp curls. Then they said goodnight.

After sleeping restlessly for what seemed like forever, though he'd actually slept a couple hours in between waking, the child decided it was hopeless and started amusing himself in bed. He talked to himself. Told a story to God about the burgers they had for lunch and marveled at the mass of Mama Cat's belly when he found her sleeping among his stuffed animals. David crawled to the foot of his bed, battling with his conscience. He wanted to get up and play, but knew he shouldn't.

Fat raindrops beat on the deck like thousands of small hooves.

Thunder crashed.

Windows rattled.

A squeal mewed in his tight throat, but he was too afraid to make a sound. David's footie-pajamas strained as one foot reached for the floor, stretching a cartoon dog's face across his chest and stomach.

Lighting flashed.

A small black form filled one corner of the doorway. A shape too small to be his father. Dizzying, strobe-like flashes illuminated the room. He saw dark eyes twinkle against the lightning. Patter. Patter. Patter. Was that laughter? David spun on his bottom, snatching his foot away from the floor and staring horrified out of the rain blurred glass. His hot breath steamed it.

CRACK!

Thunder like a cannon blast rattled the house. Beneath it, the sound of nails clinking rapidly on the floor. The boy threw himself into the corner of his bed and it was on top of him. Wet and shivering, whimpering, the mutt pressed hard against the trembling child.

"Oh Gilder!" David turned his mooing cow flashlight on the large black dog. The exclamation resounded in a sob. Something had bitten her ear.

When Noah came to the door, in just a matter of seconds, he apologized to the little body being trampled.

"I'm so sorry," he declared, once he realized David was wide awake. "I was so distracted that I didn't remember to let Gilder out. About five minutes ago she was making that sound, like when we came home from Simone's around Christmas? Do you remember?"

David smiled at the memory. "She sounded like a fog horn."

"Yup. Well I woke up to her making that sound and I let her out. When I opened the door she went tearing off. Didn't have a chance to dry her and—" Noah noticed the bite David was already comforting Gilder for. He dropped down on the bed beside her and examined the wound. He thought the bites looked like the bites on Mama Cat.

"I can patch this up, but I think she's gonna need booster shots."

"Making the vet a *lot* of money," David remarked smartly.

# NIGHT CREATURES

◆

Gina Graham assisted in almost one-fourth of every birth in Nibebiitam since she was twenty-four years old. After six years of schooling in nursing, she married a Nibebiitam man and took her master's degree back to the isolated town. That was fifty-three years ago, she reflected as she closed the stubborn, creaky door of her antique truck. How many more years could she keep doing this, she assumed was up to the truck and not her. She was not about to buy a new vehicle, at her age, and have to mess around with learning all their fancy new doodads and devices modern vehicles were filled with.

This was as typical a call as any, middle of the night, as always, "Baby's coming so *please* hurry." Of course.

The woman she'd assist that night already birthed three children and could probably do the job herself, but this was not the kind of country where one takes chances like that, not when the nearest hospital was an hour away. She resolved herself that there would be no problems tonight; she was too old for that crap and wanted to be back home by sunrise for her cup of coffee and a little snuggling with the hubby before church.

Gina smiled to herself as the thought of this crossed her mind, she pressed a little harder on the accelerator just when a deer bolted out in front of her with something clinging to its neck.

She braked hard and the tires slid on the loose gravel. She cringed at the thump she prayed she wouldn't hear.

For the moment, she wasn't thinking about what she saw—or didn't see—on the deer's back; she was just thinking about the creature that might be broken and suffering in front of her bumper.

Gina opened the door, grabbed her .22 on its rack in the back window, and stepped out into the starless night.

For a second she wished her truck had headlights like newer trucks. The ones that, even on dim, blind you to everything but their whitish blue light. The first time she met a vehicle with those lights, she thought it must be something like that legendary "white light" so many wonder about. After all, it often felt like a near death experience.

Then again, she didn't need good light to put the poor creature out of its misery.

Sure enough, it wasn't dead.

Gina uttered apologies under her breath and made quick to put an end to its suffering. The safety was off, the gun raised only high enough so the butt was just under her ribs. She didn't even use two hands. Her finger filled the space beside the trigger. She felt the cold metal against a fingertip that wasn't nearly as sensitive as it used to be.

The headlights went out.

There was a flurry of movement, like setting off fireworks in a chicken coop or gutting yourself among a school of man-eating sharks.

Her screams filled a night so lonely that not even nocturnal creatures were present to witness the toothy dissection of her small round frame.

And when the feasting was done, she lay conscious and suffering until—while she might have lived even longer—it seemed that even God could stand it no more and put the poor creature out of its misery.

# CHAPTER 4

◆

# The ORIGIN of PLAY

"Aren't we leaving early?" David wondered the next morning. He stabbed his Peanut Butter Crunch with a spoon. He'd fought getting dressed and fought getting his teeth brushed so much so that hot tears ran around his foam covered mouth. Noah didn't want to battle over combing the unruly mass of curly hair. David was in a mood.

"If you make a mess you're in trouble, little man," Noah warned, passing the table to put the milk away. David's face got red and he stabbed less forcefully—even though he felt like throwing the bowl across the room.

"I don't want to spend the whole day working," David protested, tears rimming his large dark eyes.

"That makes two of us, buddy. But *you* might get out of it," Noah encouraged. David leaned back from his bowl after biting down on a satisfactorily crushed spoonful of cereal. He looked around for a reason why he might not have to go.

"Can I stay at home with Gilder?" David asked. At her name, the large black mutt raised her head and one ear, where she lay on her side in a square of warm morning sunlight.

"That reminds me," Noah went back to the fridge and wrote "dog door" on the grocery list, right under deadbolts, bathroom ventilation fan, litter box, pet taxi, and "Videos for David." They only got three TV stations, he had a feeling it would be damn near impossible to get satellite out there. At least there was internet.

They may end up owing their sanity to NetFlix.

He gazed over the list thoughtfully, then scrawled two big black marks over "dog door". With wild animals all over, a child in the house, and possibly demented children running all over the place—no way in hell. The kitchen got a once over for obvious needs.

"Oh, shi—"

David's eyes widened and flicked up at the swear radar he knew as dad.

"We're gonna be late. Don't worry about finishing your cereal," Noah hurried, draining his cup of the last few swallows of coffee.

"But I'll go hungry!"

"Then you'll learn to eat when you can, won't you?"


David sat quietly in his car seat. His face was red again and he was mad. He was living in the world of self-empathy, where no one loves him but Gilder, nothing is fair, and "Why does everything happen to me?"

Noah smiled as he watched David in the rearview. He said a line he knew David hated:

"Keep it up, your face will freeze that way."

"You don't know—" David's voice trembled.

"Know what, buddy?"

"What it's like to be six. I got no friends."

The tears returned, bigger than ever.

By the time they reached the dark green mailbox with S. CRANE written in faded white paint, Noah was getting a headache from the grumbling coming from the back seat. They'd been in the vehicle a whole of maybe seven minutes.

"I was supposed to keep Gilder with me all the time!" David protested.

"She will be happier at home."

"You make me a liar."

Noah didn't know what *that* whine was about.

When the car slowed, David perked up to see what was happening. They bounced gently in the ruts of the short driveway. Where dirt ended, tire tracks continued through the grass into the back yard. Solomon was on the porch, sitting in his rocker with the same blue coffee cup.

"Morning, Solomon," Noah called, getting out.

David shot his father a wounded look. Now he couldn't even surprise Solomon by knowing his name. Everything was ruined today.

"You're sure this won't be an inconvenience?" asked Noah. He went around to let out David, who hadn't even unbuckled himself yet.

"Well if they don't get on then I can bring him into town to you. I'm sure it will be fine," Solomon comforted.

"I'm really stuck for someone to watch him. It hardly matters how they get on, to me."

Now David was really scowling.

Noah couldn't remember the last time he had to lift David out of the car when he wasn't sleeping.

"David, you didn't grab your bag," Noah noticed once he got him out.

The little monster he was really trying to love said something like "I don't care" but there might have been an "I wanna eat soap" word in there too.

"Good morning, David," Solomon called from the rocker.

"So where's—" Noah stopped when he noticed the young girl watching them through the screen. He couldn't see her expression, barely her face, through the tight silver mesh. The door opened just enough for her narrow finger tips to slip through and then pushed it open the rest of the way.

A pretty girl came out. Her long black hair disappeared past the slight inward curve of her waist. She dressed comfortably in boot cut jeans over sandals, and a long sleeved red t-shirt. More confidently than when she left the house, the girl tromped down the steps to meet Noah and David. Her hair flapped like an obsidian silk cape behind her. She smiled at them. Her closed lips making a lemon shape with gentle impressions on either point—that was her smile. Noah guessed she was about fourteen. He figured that was old enough to confuse David about treating her as a playmate or respecting her as an adult—which worked for the dad.

"Hi, I'm Noah Asheborne. This is David."

She stooped over with her hands on her knees. Then her hair really looked like a cape.

"Hey David," she said. "I'm Fawn."

David looked shyly at the older girl. She reminded him of a gerbil, with her small round ears, nose, and quick black eyes.

"I don't play with girls," David notified his father.

When no comfort came the only thing to do was retreat. His cords made sounds, "Vip-Vip", like a zipper pulled up and down when he ran back to the car.

"I don't play with girls either," Fawn said.

David froze, looking over his shoulder suspiciously.

"Then who do you play with?"

She smiled secretively.

David would later find her playthings and playmates in nature and learn there were few children her age in the area. He also learned she was not at all like girls he'd known in New York and would likely be the best friend he would ever have. She was not afraid to touch bugs or snakes and her patched knees and dirty nails proved she would not wimp out when the going got tough.

And it would.

Here there were plenty of places to be tough—the wilderness, the muskeg, the backyard… But for now she invited them inside for coffee. David wondered if she would have some. He couldn't tell how old she was.

The long gray planks of aged wood creaked beneath the four of them as they started up the steps and across the broad porch of Solomon's log home. Solomon went first, smelling of coffee and faint cologne, as if he might have worn it the day before. Fawn followed and held the thin aluminum screen door aside with a teeth jarring whine of rusted springs. The heavy wood interior door was wedged open with a sliver of pine shoved between it and a worn tawny carpet that was about 45 years old. That color of orange was at least that old when people actually wanted it in their homes.

A nearly empty suet feeder hung on the right corner of the porch, the slamming sheet of metal and mesh scattered half a dozen birds while dozens more only fluttered or ignored the sound altogether. Inside, only the warm morning light illuminated the home, gently tracing mementos of people who'd lived there and who loved there. A heavy knitted afghan weighed across the back of a blue-gray sofa, badly needing reupholstering. On the coffee table, among round stains where perspiring glasses sat without coasters, was a long knitted doily. Woven hand towels draped over the oven handle in a kitchen that was separated from the living room by only a cluttered island and different wallpaper. A chicken trim ran around the walls of the goldenrod-yellow kitchen, crashing against the washed out forest green of the living room. An older TV sat atop a second coffee table and upon it, like on almost every other surface, was a knitted something or feminine trinket. A single mounted Northern ornamented the living room wall, centered over the couch. The dust furred pike, with cobwebs strung between rows of thumbtack teeth, swam among a green ocean of carefully dusted photographs in homemade frames.

Though probably forty-years-incurrent, Noah spotted Solomon among the faces and, in another, a baby he was sure to be Fawn. The infant was held between the same man and woman in several of the photographs. He felt instant pangs of concern and sympathy for the little girl and Solomon too in the noted absence of the woman in more current photos.

"You have a nice place," Noah commented. From the upper middle class life he knew, it might seem likely he was being insincere, as Solomon suspected, but Noah liked the feel of a place with history and warmth, a place lived in, with the essence of family, holidays and hardships—a place with a memory. It was welcoming and comforting. These were good people.

"Fawn, why don't you introduce David to Naana so his papa and I can talk?"

David would go along with this, as always. He knew this meant adults were talking about stuff they didn't want him to hear. He resented that for many reasons, the foremost being that it was just because he was young. He looked back as Fawn led him down the short hall to the screen door on the other end of the house. He hoped Solomon knew that his dad still needed to get to work.

A couple of supporting beams cut across the frame of the screen door. Not like the ugly metal screen door at the front of the house. This doorway also had a heavy inside door, and it too was held open with a door stop. The faded rug running the length of the hall stopped a few feet short of the back door. By the time his small Velcro strapped sneakers reached the end of the rug he could see Naana, back to them, enjoying the morning. David saw the top of a head turn to one side over the rounded back of the wicker rocker.

Then Fawn was opening the door and they were entering the enclosed porch. His breath caught and he was overcome by clinking, chiming, and swinging columns of silver. He'd never seen so many wind chimes, not even in a store. They ran the length of the house like Christmas lights. Outside the few windows, long hooks were driven into the frame so at least three could hang at each of them as well.

*Holy shit*, David thought. He felt only a little wicked because there wasn't a more honest way to react. The sound was hypnotic. He wanted a long stick to run with along the back side of the house and ring every chime. "Why have—"

"David," Fawn interrupted, "this is Naana. Naana this is David. They're new neighbors of ours." Without realizing it,

Fawn had led him around the chair. He didn't know how long he'd been standing there.

The old woman made Solomon look young.

*She must be Fawn's great-grammy*, David thought correctly.

Her beautiful red-brown skin was faded, almost a gray version of Solomon's skin. The deep wrinkles carved a scar of every expression ever made. A crown of brilliant white hair was weighed down by a heavy bun of these snowy tresses. He was fascinated by her in the same way as a toy with lots of dials and buttons would immediately interest him.

A mechanical smile twitched on her thin lips.

He couldn't tell if the smile was forced. So David thought she didn't like him. He thought he knew "the look". He saw people give "the look" to other people. A couple times, David got it when he went home with friends from school. Sometimes his friends lived where almost everyone was the same color. He'd been called things he didn't understand. He'd been looked at like he didn't belong.

So sometimes his eagerness to meet people was tempered by uncertainty. He hated "the look". The look he sometimes got, the feelings he sometimes felt among a lot of people whose skin was a different color than his. Sensing a tentative rage and distrust, as though expecting David disliked them first. That he might do something.

At first he wondered what people could fear from a little boy, but he knew that it didn't matter how old you are, you can still hurt people. Kids know lots of mean things to say.

David smiled at Naana and hoped he had not been staring too hard or too long. That wouldn't help. He couldn't speak for other people, but he thought differences were great. Her face, its deep wrinkles, the puffs over each eye—below each eye—she looked like she was made of bark. He wanted to touch that face, then flatten his hands and push the skin toward her ears—glimpsing the past. Then he noticed she was smiling for real and he shot his most dazzling back.

She was amused by the staring boy. The mound of soft curls atop his head were tempting to pet. The baby cheeks, tempting to pinch. Fawn's left hand sank deep into the waves of hair and rested there, waiting for the two to exchange "hellos."

"Why do you have so many chimes?" David went to the screen windows and looked up and down the rows of dancing metal.

"It's for the children," Naana answered, voice slow as though remembering.

"What children?"

Fawn shot Naana a look of mixed emotion and warning.

"David," the girl intervened. "Do you like stories?"

Fawn sat down on the sprawling rag carpet and patted the ground beside her. David used her shoulder for leverage, threw his legs out from under him and dropped to his butt with a thud.

"What kind of a story?"

"It's...," she considered carefully, "folklore. Do you know what that is?"

David wasn't sure so he shook his head.

"It is things passed down through people. Art, customs… stories. Okay?"

"Does it have to do with wind chimes?"

"Ours," Fawn answered. "Some people say—"

A picture clattered onto the hallway floor.

Fawn's hand jumped.

"Mr. Nobody!" David declared smartly.

Fawn muttered something under her breath and hurried to put it back. She looked nervous.

"Playful, aren't they?" Naana whispered.

"He gets *me* in trouble," David countered, squinting to see through the screen, which proved harder from the side hit by sunlight. The door pushed open as Fawn returned. David saw his father standing at the other end of the hall. He looked tense. He was having coffee, every knuckle of the hand holding the cup was white.

"They're *very* playful," Naana repeated. She had a glazed, absence in her eyes.

"They won't play with you if you don't understand what's happening to you…" then absently the ancient woman added, "or if they don't scare you…"

"What?" David wasn't sure if he heard right.

Naana didn't appear to have heard him ask—she didn't even appear to remember they'd been talking.

Fawn tried to answer.

"David, they're—"

Thunder rumbled in the distance. The wind was beginning to pick up and drive the buzzing mosquitoes away from the outer screen. The wind chimes jingled enthusiastically.

"I have to go," Noah apologized. "Are you sure this is fine?"

"It'll be nice to have him around," Solomon assured him.

Noah sat the coffee cup on the island and started down the hall. David heard what they'd said and realized they must have been whispering the whole time or he could have heard their conversation. He met his dad in the hall where a hug and a kiss goodbye were waiting. David's little body was lost in folded arms—Noah felt a surge of love fill that hug—completely forgetting that he felt like he'd spent the morning with Regan MacNeil.

"You be good for them," Noah ordered on his way out the front door. The car purred to life and he was gone.

David felt like crying, even though he felt fine being there. The Fears snuck up on him. The Fear he usually controlled or could sometimes forget. But he felt abandoned. Would he go away like mom and never come back?

Solomon watched the car hurry away and sighed as he picked up the coffee cup. He hadn't expected the New Yorker to accept what he was telling him hook, line and sinker, but it was important to put the thoughts there. A little caution, a little fear, could make all the difference. Until the family got used to the way things were, he and Fawn would look after them. When they learned the rules… it would be nice if the Asheborne's could stay there. The American took it, or *didn't* take it, worse than most. *Most* at least found it a little exciting.

Something in Noah's past made him resistant. Not just because it might seem far-fetched, but that the young father was so determined to have a good, normal life. Even more so than any other good, normal person…

"David," Fawn called him from the porch. "Don't you want to come back and hear a story?"

He nodded agreeably and returned to the carpet, folding his legs underneath him.

"Naana, can you tell David the story of the wind-chimes?"

"Folklore?" David pressed smartly.

"Mm-hmm," Fawn touched his shoulder reassuringly.

"A long, long time ago, when the earth was cold and even the smallest beasts we know today were so great they shook the earth when they stepped. Spirits wandered the earth. They were quiet and solemn things who were very tired and very bored. One day this little spirit, when meaning only to sit in a tree heavy with snow, shook the branch and it dumped on one of these great beasts.

"Something happened inside that little spirit and two things happened for the first time in all time," Naana leaned in close to David. "Do you know what?"

David shook his head.

"The spirit *smiled*. And then… the little spirit laughed.

"Other spirits came from all across the world to hear the sound. And when the little spirit told what it had done, the other spirits did it too and went back to their homes. But some places did not have so much snow or even trees, so the spirits had to think of other things to do. Like rolling a rock into a stream beside the large toothed cat that was only trying to drink when— SPLASH!—it was soaked and ran away to pout as the little spirits laughed and laughed and rolled and rolled on the ground.

"After many, many, many years, there were some spirits who fell in love with mischief and did it all the time. Some animals even liked the games and would play them with each other, especially the tall, almost hairless animals who walked on two feet. At first this animal was no good to play with, but after time he learned to walk better and faster. He learned to think as good as the other animals. And his body changed as he became more clever, until he was man as we know him today, who is just as good at playing as the spirits and the tricksters—raccoon, raven, coyotes, fox, crows—all the animals who love playing and laughing.

"Tricksters are important. They make us laugh. They open our spirit and purge out the bad. But sometimes people don't feel like playing. Do you always feel like playing?"

David shook his head.

"No," he answered.

"Tricksters like to surprise you. It is a lot easier to catch a naughty raven or raccoon before he plays a joke on you, but to catch a spirit you have to be more clever."

Naana pointed at the wind-chimes, "When spirits come to play they make the bells sing. Then they pout and throw their hands up in frustration—they cannot surprise you! And must go play somewhere else."

"You have the chimes because you don't want to play?" asked David wondrously.

"I am too old to play their games," Naana laughed. "So they must go on to find fun."

David and the old woman snickered at her cleverness.

"I *like* that story!" he declared loudly.

"I do too," Fawn said earnestly.

"And as I am too old for them, I am way too old for playing with a rascal like you!" Naana rumpled David's hair. She was more than happy to touch all those soft lamby curls.

"Come on, we can go to my room," Fawn offered. She took David's hand and led him off the porch.

"Bye Naana! Nice to meet ya!"

"Bye David," she called with only a whisper of the little boy's energy.

"Do you have any toys?" David asked as she opened the door into her room. She didn't have a lot of stuff, David noticed, unless she was just good at keeping her room clean. There was an almost filled bookcase at the foot of her twin sized bed. A single shelf ran the length of the wall above her bed, on it were the only visible toys and they were for someone a lot younger than Fawn.

"No, but we can play outside or we can play games on paper."

"Do you have board games?"

"Yeah," Fawn said like it was obvious that they should. "We can't play videogames because I already played today and *mishomis*, my grandfather, won't let me play for more than two hours at a time."

"I could still play," David pointed.

Fawn laughed, "You're slick, but I don't think he'd want me to sit there watching either."

"I like any games," the little boy said amiably. "I want to know what your favorite is."

"We can do this. It's not my favorite, but it's fun and easy," Fawn took out a sheet of paper from a stack of last year's homework and turned it over to the blank side. "We cover the paper with rows of dots. They have to be even. Then we take turns making lines between the dots. Whoever makes a box first, by connecting dots, we put our initial in it and whoever has their initial in the most boxes at the end, wins."

"Initial?"

"That's the first letter of your name. So when you make a box, you put a 'D' in it. D for David. Duh-duh-Dee. David. See?"

The six-year-old smiled and hugged her boldly.

"Yup," he said.

He watched as she starting laying dots over the paper.

"Why don't you have toys, Fawn?"

"I ask for books."

"Aren't those your toys?" David looked at the shelf over her bed.

Fawn looked too and looked away just as quickly.

"They're my baby toys," she replied flatly.

◆          ◆          ◆

There is a sense, in the country, of being watched—ironically more prevalent than even in large cities—perhaps because amongst so many people you are obviously being seen, but in the wild there are fewer people, but no less life and you just don't know what is watching you there.

The young man hovered over the kitchen sink, holding a cup of coffee he hadn't sipped in several minutes. He smiled occasionally at the little boy out in the yard. There is no end and no beginning to a child's patience and his son had been standing still for almost half an hour.

David was distant and seemed even more so when he didn't respond at all when his father finally called his name—though this was only because his son was ignoring him.

Noah shut the kitchen window, watched David a second longer to check if he'd heard and was just dawdling, but the child still didn't show any sign of coming in or even having heard his name. Something told him not to leave the window, that if he let David out of his sight he would never see him again—a horrible sense of doom brought the sting of tears to his eyes. But that was nonsense and at last he made himself walk away.

David had a similar feeling. He was sure whenever he blinked that something of interest would appear if only for that split second—so he tried not to. When his daddy started calling, David was sure when he, at last, was forced to go in that he would miss a brief second to catch *it* out of the corner of his eye. He had to be sure—look in just the right spot—that chance to catch *it* was always there, but were lost to less advantageous positions.

"I said 'bedtime', rascal," Noah called from behind the screen door.

David resigned and ran for the steps.

"What were you doing?" his daddy looked amused as he watched his son pass under the arm that held the door open.

"Trying to see something."

"Something?" Noah pressed.

David shrugged. With completely sincerity he answered "yes".

After having a bath, brushing his teeth, and having two stories after being unsated by one, David finally started to get sleepy.

Gilder curled up at the foot of David's bed. She had been tense and jumpy most of the day, but she almost seemed like herself tonight.

She would be restless for a long time getting used to the sounds and smells of nature, his daddy said. New York was a lot louder than here and she was never afraid. Gilder was relaxed, even when they went for walks on busy streets or in the park. What would they do if she never got used to it? What if she never stopped rolling in deer and rabbit crap? What if she didn't stop trying to eat it? What would they do if she ran into the woods after something and was too dumb to know her way back?

Just a city dog and city kid.

He was beginning to feel that his father, Gilder, Mama Cat, and he were the only people in the world. The drive took at least fourteen eternities and the only people he'd seen were the tall, kinda dark people from Thanksgiving. But they didn't bring any food and they drove cars and pick-ups. Pick-ups mostly, like the white-haired man, called Solomon or *mishomis* to Fawn, who warned him about city dogs in the country. The best thing about city dogs in the country was no more sandwich bag snatching Gilder's warm messes. Now maybe David could actually eat a sandwich from a zip-lock bag and not examine it first.

# *PIECES OF GLITTER*

Corina Orville, unmarried and unbothered about it, had worked at the library in Hearst for almost twenty-five years. Very little about her had changed in all that time, endearing her to the libraries patrons by her consistency, in more than just service. Her dishwater blonde bob was now mostly gray and white. She always wore some kind of sweater, over some color or pattern of blouse, over slacks or skirts that looked like they were made from similar patterns.

Since her second year, Corina—sometimes called "Cori"— was first to arrive and last to leave. She never had anything to do after work and secretly really liked to have the place to herself sometimes.

After having the library all to herself for several hours that evening, the librarian swatted "off" the five sets of switches and watched the fluorescent lights wink out.

Corina couldn't be sure, but she thought something moved beyond the rows of books directly across from her.

She blamed her mind for playing tricks—after cataloging new books all day, filing the new issues of magazines and stamping, stamping, stamping under these damn fluorescent lights—she was bound to "see things". Corina would see things on the way out to her car. When she got home. When she entered her dark home. When she lay awake trying to sleep—

*I'm overtired and under-caffeinated*, she thought. She took the quiet tranquility in the library so seriously she became a chronic listener in and out of work.

Now the listener's ears twitched at something she was sure she didn't really hear.

She *couldn't* have.

So overworked, after such a long day, she was bound to hear things.

She always did.

It sounded like little shoes, like little dress shoes, the kind she loved to just clip-clop around in when she was a child.

Whoever it was liked the sound just as much as she had.

Then she didn't hear anything, not a thing in the unbearable minutes she stood their straining, eyes almost popping as if it helped her listen, to hear *something else*. Just when the feeling something was creeping up in that silence became unbearable she practically dove out the doors, locking them behind her.

Corina trembled so hard she dropped her keys. When she stopped to claw them up she heard the sound of shoes again. She heard the familiar "thump" that heavy books make when they fall on carpet. Someone always drops a book. But maybe it sounded like it was thrown against the carpet. Then the lights came on.

"Ohh" was what came out, but it squeaked and moaned from a mouth gaped in horror.

She backed clumsily down a short flight of cement stairs, on legs that felt no stronger than string cheese. Corina was almost crawling by the time she got behind the wheel of her car.

She heard a click by her temple, barely registering the flash of steel as the blade jumped up under her chin.

"Your purse," demanded a gravelly male voice.

"I forgot it," she comprehended just as she said it. She also realized she was crying over tears already drying on her fear stricken face. She felt dumb dwelling on it, even as the angry man cut her just to spite her. A sheet of blood surged out of her neck like her throat was the world's fastest printer.

*How does somebody not realize when they've started to cry?*

*It must have been when I dropped my keys. I was so scared,* she decided as her mind tried to take her away from the moment, only for her to come to a merciless realization:

*I guess there must have been something in my house after all.*

And as the car shook when the man jumped out and ran off into the night, even as she was one gurgling breath from death, she wondered what book it was that fell and it bothered her that it wouldn't be put away.

Small black eyes sparkled like pieces of glitter in the suddenly darkened library. They were bothered too.

They didn't like it when their fun was ruined. They didn't like cheaters. And no one invited *him* to play.

But if he wanted to participate so badly, he would.

He most certainly would.

# CHAPTER 5

―――――◆―――――

# COMPANY

David's brow furrowed with concentration as he pressed the paintbrush to the last of twelve hard multicolored noodles. The oblong black blob represented the last of the passenger car windows.

"When you're feeling quite insane and you wanna ride a train, macaroni! Oh, oh, macaroni!"

Noah cringed and looked away from cooking.

"David!" For the third time.

Careful short fingers pushed each painstakingly painted noodle on a piece of bright red yarn.

"If you think it's really nummy and you wanna fill my tummy, macaroni!"

The stirring spoon rattled freely inside the kettle as Noah shoved it out of his hand.

"David! Don't make me tell you again."

The ends of the yarn lowered to the tabletop and he slowly focused on his dad as if coming out of a dream.

"Can I use toothpicks for the track?" he asked.

"I don't know if we have any," Noah turned back to the stove, glancing at the stacks of neglected packing boxes.

"Look-it!"

Noah jumped. He hadn't even heard David get up. The noodle train shoved up at his chest between hands streaked with primary colors. His whole torso recoiled from the brightly colored hands and glistening noodles. He'd only an undershirt at stake, but it was supposed to go underneath his suit. His suit pants were partially shielded by a dishcloth tied around his waist.

"David!" he thought he sounded old and tired. "You're covered in paint."

"It's Crayola."

*As if I'd let you get your hands on anything else,* Noah thought.

"The babysitter will be here in a few minutes and I still have to get ready."

"I don't need a babysitter; I have Gilder," David pointed to the shepherd lab mix urgently cleaning herself with wet black nose bobbing between splayed legs. She always snorted when she craned her neck down like that.

"To protect you, yes. To protect the house from you... no."

An image flashed before Noah's eyes of what havoc the six-year-old and paint would create if left to their own devices. For a second he doubted if Fawn would be able to handle things if David got crabby or restless. Not that it mattered. There was no one else to ask and he didn't have a choice to stay. The photographer from work was supposed to pick him up shortly to attend a wedding on the other side of Kapuskasing. Hearst, he thought. Jacob convinced Noah to go along for the ride. Kapuskasing would have a selection of trucks and, if the shop was open, he could do some low pressure wheeling and dealing with a local for support. If the dealership was closed, then Noah could do some looking around and have an idea of his choices. But it meant attending a wedding where the photographer was hired to work. It meant hours of boredom. An essentially quick trip turned into a wasted afternoon and evening and however long the reception lasted... late night babysitters were one thing he thought would be over now.

"You remember Fawn. You'll have a good—David go wash up. I'll set out some PJs—you'll have a good time. You and Fawn can have your mac n' cheese and camp out in the living room. She can help you pick out a video," Noah hurried the pot to the colander in the sink and poured the pale steamy noodles into it. He was thinking about a million things at once. At the moment thinking about the hundred and fifty dollars in kid's shows Amazon just shipped and what a Godsend they would be. It was always good for finding a lot of used children's videos that someone's kids or grandkids had outgrown.

David yanked his t-shirt off and stomp-shuffled down the hall.

His daddy hollered something about paint on the cat. David didn't remember that, but he did remember having to move her out of his way. She wanted to rub her face all over everything.

Outside an engine rumbled to a stop. Then a door slammed with a heavy metallic thud. Something was called out and lost through the walls, but it was Fawn's voice. Probably saying goodnight or goodbye or whatever. It might not have even been English. Noah wasn't even sure yet what kind of Indians they were.

"Come on in!" he called when her footsteps passed the steps and started across the porch. Her small fist hovered before the door. She was glad to enter quickly. Outside it rained and rumbled. Solomon backed out and started back for home. The beams of yellow light pushed the darkness they hit into the shadows—where they did not, ever deepened the blackness therein. This was a bad place.

In the entryway, Fawn removed her light jacket and almost new looking tennis shoes. They were a couple of years old, but sandals, bare feet and boots can get a pair of shoes through more than a year in Nibebiitam—where there only seemed to be two seasons.

"Hi, Mr. Asheborne," she surprised herself with how timid she felt and sounded. She was more nervous than she realized. She'd intended to explain some things to David that night, but she was afraid. Ignorance is bliss.

"Hey there, Fawn. You're doing me a huge favor," he said earnestly. "David has some movies and supper's on the stove. There're a couple sleeping bags in the back closet. I thought you two might just camp in front of the TV. You know I probably won't get back til' late tonight. You sure you're okay to stay?"

She nodded.

"Is it okay if my grandfather just picks me up when he heads to town tomorrow. It might not be until around noon, is that alright?"

"You bet," the boy's father agreed with a smile that struck her as dazzling.


"You-put-both-hands-in," David's hands thrust into the sink of cold water. "You take both hands out. You-put-your-face-in and you shake it all about. BRRR-ah," David shivered as he doused his paint streaked face with water and rubbed it. The colors mixed and ran through the lines in his palms and made small thin clouds like smoke when he shoved them back into the water. He grabbed the bar of hand soap with both hands and was careful not to squeeze too hard. When you squeeze a frog too hard its stomach comes out its mouth. When you squeeze a bar of soap it goes flying. When you're six, your best intentions always get you into trouble.

He carefully rubbed the bar around his face, nowhere near his eyes or mouth. He learned a long time ago about avoiding soap in the eyes and he got soap in the mouth for saying the "F-er."

When his face was clean he clawed up his comb and stared helplessly at the mess of thick brown curls atop his head. The comb had very few teeth left. It didn't seem to matter how short David's hair was it seemed to tangle, knot, and weave in unnatural ways. The mess on the back of his head looked like matted dog fur or fuzz more than hair.

Suddenly a hand clamped on the back of his head. David started at the touch and a crash of thunder. He squealed like a stuck pig.

"Daydreaming, buddy?" Noah shook the mess of curls as he moved around the child to reach his own comb and do last minute adjustments to his own hair.

When he leaned around David, the boy caught the fragrance of cologne and the still damp scent of grown-up body wash from the shower he'd taken just before starting supper. David hated baths and stuff, but he envied the routine of men "cleaning-up". He often played it out, aftershave and all. What he didn't understand was why it's okay for adults to use kid stuff, but not the other way around. He loved the way his dad smelled when he was dressed up. The shirt and suit jacket were laid out on the queen sized bed in his daddy's room, still steamed and pressed from the New York cleaners. Everything with adults seemed so much more important than children get. He glanced resentfully at his bottle of strawberry toothpaste and sighed. It didn't even come in a box.

"You look nice dad," David kissed the inside of Noah's upper arm, because it was nearest his face.

"Thanks, kiddo," he carefully kissed the top of David's head and scooted out of the room. He could hear his daddy move to the bedroom. Probably picking up the suit and coat and holding them together in front of the mirror, second guessing himself. David shook his head and finished cleaning himself up. His daddy was the most handsomest, strongest, smartest in the world. His mommy left them, like so many moms or dads of other kids from his class. Why was his daddy like half that person now? When Noah might never look in a mirror before—here came a second and third glance. Sometimes staring long into the dark brown eyes staring back, as though it was not quite the face that should be there. Sometimes gazing into himself like he was trying to read his own mind.

The boy dried his face among the folds of the pale green towel hanging by the sink, drying his hands on the opposite side. He knew his dad would be lost without him.

David stepped off his stool and returned it to its space beneath the sink. He padded down the hall to peek in on his dad. The door was mostly shut, so David knew the babysitter was already here.

They never closed the doors when it was just "us guys".

With utmost care he tiptoed down the hall and peeked around the corner to spy on the girl. Her back was to him, sitting stiffly at the breakfast table. She looked like she'd done something bad, in David's opinion. Like she knew that she was going to get in trouble and was just waiting for it. Her hands clasped tightly before her. Corners of the table pressed the edge into her elbows. Back stiff like a scarecrow. He lowered to his hands and knees and crawled along the floor until the chair was within arm's reach. Carefully rising, his arms spread and fingers wriggled eagerly.

Fawn's scream pierced the nearly silent house.

"David!" Noah hollered, a nearly forgotten accent drenching the name. He'd been startled too.

The boy's small hands slipped back through the dowels on the back of the chair. Fawn could still feel where his tiny fingers had pinched her muffin top. He caught the outermost post of the chair back and swung on it with his left arm so he could face the girl.

"Hi Fawn," he said in his sweetest voice.

A car horn called weakly from outside.

Fawn leapt out of the chair, knocking David off his feet. She went to the window to look outside. Maybe Solomon changed his mind, that it was too dangerous to be there, but it was not her grandfather's truck out there in the dark and rain.

"That's my ride, David. Do you want to grab my shoes?" his father called.

"Why do you need a ride?" David wondered.

"Because they're going to take me to a store that sells trucks and help me make a deal," Noah emerged from the bedroom, adjusting his tie, "Hopefully I'll be driving a new vehicle back. How would you like that?"

David made a face.

"She's coming up to the house," Fawn announced.

"Oh," Noah groaned.

He sat at the two-part sectional coffee brown couch to put on his shoes. He was still thinking about bringing a pair of street clothes. He didn't want to go to any dealership in a suit.

"Why?" David wailed and ran to the door. He yanked it open just as the woman reached it.

"Patience is a virtue!" David recited.

"*David*!" Noah cried in alarm.

The child scowled up at her in disapproval. She was Indian too, but David thought, he didn't like *her*.

She backed up a step and looked uncertainly to the man getting up from the couch, stamping his left foot into his second shoe.

"Jesus, I'm sorry," Noah apologized as he reached the woman and his son.

"It's fine," she stammered, pushing an errant length of damp black hair behind her ear. She looked back at the growing storm with nervous black eyes. "Are you ready to go?"

"Yeah," Noah confirmed, but patted himself down to make sure. "Just a sec."

He turned on his heel and returned to his bedroom.

David studied the woman studying his daddy.

She met him briefly, at work, when Jacob arranged this, but felt like she was seeing him for the first time. Maybe he just cleaned up that good, or maybe she was just too busy or tired before. She dropped her head shyly and gave herself a once over. Patting her tight thigh-length braid and checking her long brown sundress and tan sweater. She seemed to be regretting her choice. Noah returned, dressed to the nines; hair, skin, suit—all perfect. David was proud. He thought his daddy was handsome. He knew other people did too. His mommy's girlfriends often said so. He didn't understand a lot of what was said in those conversations, but he followed this much. And his mommy and all her friends, David thought, were beautiful. They always dressed like magazine people and smelled pretty too.

This woman looked so plain.

When Noah apologized and snuck out past them, she followed his dad all the while with her tadpole shaped eyes. Though slender, her face was amply soft; between that and her cheekbones they pinched a tail from her almond shaped eyes so they looked like tadpoles. She had the same lemon shaped mouth as Fawn. But he didn't like it on her; in fact, he didn't like anything about her.

"Be good David," he shot his son a look that said, 'we're gonna talk about this later.'

David didn't care.

Noah hardly looked at the lady, even as they descended the stairs and crossed the driveway together. He heard his father apologize, but that was that. David felt a little better. His dad would never pay her any attention. His heart was still with mom. This lady could smile and drive him around all she wanted, but she was nothing like mommy. He closed the door with a victorious thud and almost walked into Fawn's legs.

"You better watch yourself little man," she warned. "That's the daughter of the top dog in municipal police here."

David raised his eyebrows, not fearfully, but with an opportunistic energy.

"Tell me everything you know," he demanded.


Noah slid comfortably into the seat beside the woman who, in passing briefly at work, had introduced herself as Rising Moon. By the time the door closed he would not think of David and Fawn until later that evening, while standing idly on the sidelines of a wedding reception, making notes on another book while Rising Moon got the shots she needed.

He automatically fastened his seatbelt and Rising Moon watched this with interest, as though people in small towns didn't do that. In fact most people there didn't, but after he did she felt obligated. Perhaps he'd heard her father was a constable.

"Do you know the family?" Noah asked.

She pressed her lips together thoughtfully and tucked invisible hair behind her ear. She wasn't used to wearing it any other way than out. "I know who they are," she offered with a shy smile.

He studied her a moment after an internal alarm went off—he sensed she was attracted to him. Was it physical? His hair, eyes, ethnicity, where he was from, had she caught his faint accent?

She was attractive, but The Alarm made him feel uncomfortable with it. The Alarm went off when he was married and might be talking to a woman and sense she was trying to do more than just socialize. Why it went off when all Rising Moon did was answer a question, he didn't know.

His conscience thought it was protecting someone who still belonged to someone else.


"Nothing to tell," Fawn shrugged. "She works at that print place. Quiet. Just takes pictures all the time. You only see her taking pictures or getting lunch at the diner. Egg salad sandwich and a shake, every time."

"Why do you know that?" David wanted to know.

Fawn shrugged, "I don't. If this dumb town wasn't so boring, someone getting the same meal all the time wouldn't be newsworthy, but people talk about everything. Remember that.

"The only other thing is that she and her dad, Phil, came up from Thunder Bay about five years ago. That's pretty much all there is to her. If her dad didn't run the police no one would even know she exists.

"Why are you so worried?" Fawn added.

"I'm not," he contradicted.

"I understand," Fawn pressed gently. "My mom's gone too."

"Divorced?" David said the word reluctantly.

"No, my parents and sister died in a car accident," Fawn explained. "But I felt like my grandparents were trying to take their place when I went to live with them. I resented them and everything they tried to give me for a long time because of that."

David looked at his feet.

A distant rumble vibrated through the house. Nearer. Nearer. Lightning brightened the yard, bleaching the windows and the world outside while it turned the rain black. Thunder cracked like a gun shot and David screamed again. Fawn put one hand on his shoulder.

"You don't have to worry about her, David, your dad's a city guy and I'm sure she's too plain. Did you see? He looked right through her. But you're going to have to get over worrying someday, because he has a right to care about someone who makes him happy, right?"

"I dunno," he felt really bad. He wanted to chase after the car so he could hold his dad, apologize, and kiss his face all over. He never ever, ever wanted to hurt him.

◆          ◆          ◆

Settled before the glowing TV, *Aladdin* in the player, Fawn couldn't concentrate. She kept looking at David and waiting for a sign that the time was right.

Now?

*No.*

Maybe now?

"There's folklore about this very place, you know," she was careful to use the same term she used before.

David shook his head and scooted instinctively closer to Fawn.

There is a certain tone people use to say things they want people to *really* feel and believe. This tone was so thick in Fawn's voice one could almost chisel it. When people talk this way, a child likes to snuggle close and listen because it is too important to not be a little nervous and excited about.

"What kind of folklore?" David asked.

"There is an old belief," Fawn said in a low, secretive voice, "that these forests are busy with spirits. They are old woods and expansive—"

"Wow!" David exclaimed, "How expensive?"

"*Expansive,*" her voice snapped into normality. "It means that it spreads far and wide." Then her voice lowered, "It means that these woods are deep and long and many a man, child, and even beast has been lost in them."

The little boy thought of Mama Cat.

"The legend goes that there are lots of spirits in these woods. There is a great spirit who looks after all of us and is the creator of and is nature itself. There are the spirits of the animals. There is the Silver Fox Man whose domain is the muskeg. He eats the spring and summer. When he is full and cares to eat no more than the season dies. While he is content the leaves are hot reds and yellows. The air smells sweet and the animals fatten themselves on his leftovers. As autumn ends, he is getting hungry again and, because there is no more to eat, Silver Fox Man becomes bitter and resentful. In the old days, more people harvested from the earth and the animals. They say he was angry that people took his food and ate well the whole year. And while he didn't care in the spring, summer and autumn... He cared when there was no more to eat and he was hungry. So Silver Fox Man grows cold and the earth is bitten with frost. When his anger shows, all the birds escape the north and the little animals hide in their dens. They are so afraid that they can't sleep, until they *have to* sleep, and by then they are so tired that they sleep for almost half the year. Only the fox man's dearest friends do not go into hiding and suffer the winter beside him. These are deer, some rodents, and other beasts you see in winter, but especially the fox whom are his brothers and sisters."

"Does he look like a fox?" David interrupted.

"No, he is a man. Even though sometimes they say he takes the form of Old Man Owl. A pale and *huge* great grey owl. Some call him the Old Man of the Woods or the Muskeg Miner, because of the way he dresses. He looks like an old miner or trader, they say, with bundles and tanned fur over white man suspender pants and flannel shirt. They say he wears a wide brimmed hat atop a head of long hair tangled with branches and cobwebs from living in the wood. In the spring and summer all his things are brown and black. His hair is long and black. He is youthful, swift and strong, like a young man. In the autumn his hair burns the warm red of his fox brother and all his leather is the warm golden hide of deer. But in the winter, they say he becomes all gray and old like an ancient statue collecting dust for years and years—that his eyes frost over like cataracts and by midwinter he is so bent and withered he walks with both his hands and feet. His head swings to and fro like a blind man's walking stick—listening his way through the hinterland. He is so thin he looks like a skeleton horse built of branches—his clothes like dead skin clinging to its bones. Since a horse's head and neck are long and a man's is not; the Fox Man looks like a decapitated horse with a withered human face on the end of his throat."

"Decapitated?" David echoed in a tiny fearful voice.

Fawn drug her finger across her neck while the genie with the peanut shaped head made a prince out of a thief.

With a gulp and a shiver David pressed closer to her.

"Is the Silver Fox Man bad or good?"

"He is neither," Fawn supposed. "He is the spirit memory of days and seasons. But they say if he is near you—that nothing can harm you."

"He's scary," David simpered.

Fawn quickly shook her head and hugged his small shoulders.

"Are there any animals you're scared of?"

"Some spiders."

"He's like a spider," she pointed and squeezed his shoulder with her left hand. "They only look different, but *looks* can never hurt you. That ugly spider may make your skin crawl, but it doesn't know you, want to hurt you, or want anything to do with you. A spider will not plot against you. Like the Silver Fox Man, they would *never* hurt you unless they felt threatened. Spiders are so delicate—God made them spooky to keep things away that can hurt them."

"I bet people want to hurt them more *because* they're spooky than if God made them cute."

Thunder boomed—the lights flickered but stayed on as the wind picked up, moaning through the woods, groaning against the house.

Fawn perked up like David saw deer do, eyes round and blazing, ears and body alert and tense.

"Did you hear that?" her voice was almost shrill.

It'd begun to rain hard, each heavy droplet pounding on the porch roof.

*Sure*, David thought, he heard lots of things, only which "that" did she mean?

"There are children outside—don't you hear their footsteps on the porch?"

David listened hard and the harder he listened he did indeed hear something like small footsteps.

"Children?" the idea filled him with curiosity.

"Listen to them," Fawn breathed fearfully, knowing well the signs of escalating danger—as clearly as when rain turns to hail and howling winds begin to scream. "They may be loping around like dogs or scampering like hunch-backed hyenas on fingers and toes… grins on their lips."

"What do you mean?" David demanded.

Fawn looked surprised. "The white wolf children."

"White wolf children," David echoed.

"You mean you *don't know*?"

He shook his head.

"When the first white people came here, my people told them, you will not make it here and they thought we were warning about the terrible winters and wild land. Soon bumps in the night and tricks of the mind revealed a life of their own and really started to scare the settlers. Children were dragged out into the lakes 'by hands', they said—*the children that survived.*

Mostly they did. Men working in the mines, trapping, and logging were tricked by the cries of lost and frightened children. Trappers were led over traps themselves and to bear. They were led into the muskeg and came stumbling back to town trembling and sweating like they were sick—the *children* had 'played' with them—out there… where no one could hear the men scream. They are naughty, selfish little things because they are children at heart—they take what they want and are thrilled and curious about others' discomfort and terror. You can see by the abandoned homes on the way to town that many have tried to live here that could not. Grown men never go into the woods alone. Solomon fills his boots with sage before taking a step beyond the yard. It helps some, but only as much as the belief you have in it," Fawn dropped her eyes to the hangnail she'd been nervously picking while she spoke. "He still feels them everywhere.

"David, I guess you don't know any better, but you must pay attention to what people tell you about them—attention to what's around you, because no one is completely safe in the woods. Only the Silver Fox Man, who has strong magic," she considered the statement again and added thoughtfully. "He is magic."

Fear and curiosity wrestled David's tongue until at last, he could not resist the "need-to-know" and asked, "What *are* the white wolf children?"

Fawn considered this and looked earnestly into David's eyes.

"They are spirits. They are the things that go missing, are misplaced or broken. The sound of feet or voices in the rain," she reflected. "When you hear creaking in the house for no reason or catch that movement in the corner of your eye. That sensation of not being alone when you think you are—when you know you are. Sometimes you think someone is talking to you when no one has. They are the reflection that seems to have a life of its own. When you feel that hand in the shadows beneath your bed or between the stairs waiting to catch your leg—they are the something that looks back at you from the dark."

Fawn started to look sick and made a sound in her throat that made David want to run for a bucket. When she continued she looked at David with color blotched on her cheeks, "When you get the feeling that something's about to happen… they are there. Or when you see something in the dark corner of your room—there has *always* been something there. For some reason, in other places, they don't hurt people very often. It's different here. Up until now, when someone told you there was nothing to be afraid of—they were telling the truth."

The thunder crash sounded like all the furniture in the house was lifted and dropped on the roof. David almost jumped out of his skin and, in all truth, peed a little in his pajamas. He hated to leave Fawn when he suddenly had to go to the bathroom. It had nothing to do with peace of mind, safety, or security. He was shit scared to go all the way down the hall by himself, in the dark, and close himself into the small bathroom—by himself. The light for the living room was so far away. The light for the hall was farther away than the bathroom. Glowing softly on the walls was the flickering blue aura of the humming television, but that only emphasized the creepiness of the dark. Gilder was under the kitchen table where she drug her bedding and would come out for nothing. Not five hundred pounds of steak.

He patted his thigh.

Gilder looked at him, as if to say, "*Yeah* right."

David didn't want Fawn to see because then she would know that he wanted Gilder with him. If she knew that he wanted his dog, then she would wonder why. With the pounding rain, crashing and flashing of the storm it might take her a millisecond to figure out that he was terrified. Then she might offer to come with him to the kitchen or wherever he might want to go. When he said no to all the places she would guess, then she would eventually guess that he needed to use the bathroom and there was no way in hell he was going to let some girl escort him to pee. No way!

"I'm kinda cold, ain't you?" David wondered.

"A little," Fawn admitted. "Is there a window open?"

David shrugged. That wasn't the point.

"Could you go get me a blanket from my room?" he asked.

She nodded and pushed off the ground. A small shower of crumbs and popcorn rained off her as she stood. Mostly from the side David had been curled up beside.

With utmost satisfaction the boy smiled as she turned on the lights on her way down the hall.

He went to the bathroom and returned in record time, while it seemed like Fawn was gone forever.

As he sat before the TV in a kind of daze, his subconscious tried to swallow what he was told. He couldn't feel the change, but it was there just the same. Forever after, he distrusted his senses, watching the world suspiciously and listening like a parent with a disobedient teen. Every deceitful shadow and touch of wind left his flesh trembling. Every fiber of the world had a million curious eyes and a secretive grin.

Fawn came back empty-handed.

"We should probably be thinking about getting some sleep," she reasoned. "Where are those sleeping bags?"

"Cuh-clos—" but he couldn't find the word. Instead he pointed.

When she spread out the bags in front of the TV he felt a sense of relief that he would at least sleep close to another person since Gilder was being a wimp.

Another feeling ate at David, one he couldn't understand— the resentment of his child-spirit and his soul discussing what Fawn's story had done to both of them.

Before she returned with the sleeping bags he'd settled on some conditions for not declaring her a liar then and there.

"What do they look like?" David challenged.

"Some say you only *really* see them when they know they can kill you."

The six-year-old thought on this a minute. He was scared at first but talked himself into thinking that she only said that part to scare him.

"*Naana* said they were playful spirits."

Fawn looked him straight in the eyes and warned, "You won't like their games."

The sincerity of this warning wasn't lost on David. He knew, Fawn believed what she was saying. That was enough to tie a knot in his guts. But there had to be a happy ending. A light at the end of the tunnel. Something to make him wipe his brow and think, "Whew! That was close." And thereby making all of this scary stuff fun. So more than a little casually he asked, "How do we stop them?"

"*Stop them*?" Fawn shook her head. "You can't, any more than you can stop nature," she explained. "They just are. You have to learn to live safely with them."

David nodded, even though he didn't entirely understand. People stop nature all the time.

"So why is this place so bad?"

Pushing a section of thick black hair behind her ear, at the same time making a "hmmm" sound, Fawn took a moment to prepare her answer, "My great-grandfather said some miners dug a tunnel to a part of hell too near the surface. Only no one has ever found it, if it is. A lot of people looked for it too and they had all the mines for this area on maps so they're pretty sure that it's not a mine. I think that it's Black Martin."

David's wide eyes asked for her to continue.

"Black Martin is the spirit of an angry boy who was taken from his people a long time ago. The richest man in town, a dentist who retired and tried his hand at mining, and his young assistant, bought Black Martin for a couple bucks off a logger who owed him for some dental work. Black Martin was brutalized—tortured—for fun and, while he was a slave, had a lot of mean jokes played on him by the people that lived in the town where his kidnappers lived. They would make Black Martin drop and break things he was sent to fetch from the mercantile, because they knew he would get in horrible trouble. They would lie to him and get him punished.

"And all the people knew he was stolen, and all the people knew he was mistreated. Some people helped abuse him in the house. Some people borrowed him and abused him in their own houses. Most of them were men, but there were a few women. For a little pocket change, when the dentist didn't need him for himself.

"Some people say, when Black Martin's family found out where he was, the warriors of his people came together to get him back by force, if they had to. And when his kidnappers got wind of it they had to get rid of the evidence. They say that one of his captors strangled Black Martin with the chain of a pocket watch and when it was over, the chain was dug so deep he couldn't remove it.

"Other people say Black Martin died very young and sick and so angry that all that was left of him was hate and so that was all that made up his spirit. Because Black Martin was a child, the white wolf children don't know he's not one of them and so he can use them to get vengeance.

"Either way, Black Martin was never seen again. At least, alive."

"Prove it," David demanded, no matter how much he already believed. Believing in what's frightening is one of many things children do with no effort in their marathon to discover the world. Fawn already knew her answer.

"Wait until the first snow fall. Other places in the world this might not be true, but *here*, you will find their tracks. You could find tracks in frost."

"Tracks…" he echoed.

They looked at each other. His small round face transformed from sickly pale to blotchy pink and white. Was he getting mad? Going to cry? By the time he turned away the red blossoms had spread across his whole face and the tingle of it started down his little neck and shoulders.

"David?" she asked, suddenly, inexplicably afraid that while she was gone he'd been replaced by one of *them*. It made her want to shake David and hurt him. She wanted tears, some kind of reaction she would never get from a wolf child. But the idea that he could be or might be one kept her frozen in place. She didn't even know if she could get his name out again. So you can imagine how relieved she was when he turned grumpily to her and protested, "It's not even fall!"

Fawn burst out in a crazy, half hysterical laugh that scared her, but seemed to entertain David.

"Jesus, David. Do you have a bad temper or what?"

"Do your people believe in Jesus?" he asked wondrously.

She laughed easily and shoulder hugged the boy still too small for his age.

"Why not," her voice still laughed. "Jesus, Buddha, The Great Spirit, whatever. They all have the right idea, the right plan."

"Plan? What's that?"

"Be good people."

"That's daddy's idea too," he added smartly.

"You're pretty close to your daddy, aren't you?" her voice no longer laughed, but sounded breathless like she'd been braying for some time.

"I'm his best buddy," David repeated the endearing answer as he had for anyone who asked. And if someone said, 'yeah?' He'd say, 'My daddy says so.'

Fawn wondered if that would last if Noah went to bed with Rising Moon or any other woman. She could already hear the rejected, 'I hate yous' and 'I'm running away' in resistance of a presence she already knew was unwelcome to the child. She felt bad for David then. Noah was still young. How broken does a heart have to be to resist another love? Or the prospect of sex? David felt he was taking care of his father through whatever they were going through. Anyone else loving Noah would mean trying to replace the role David found crucial in his father's survival and, unknowingly, using that position to shelter himself.

"Where's your mom?" she blurted regretfully, but David did not react with the tears she was afraid waited behind the "m" word.

"I don't have a mom," he said firmly, resentfully.

"She died?"

*What are you doing*, Fawn thought in alarm and disgust. She thought of herself at his age, how she would have reacted to such a question. When words like suicide just meant, going away, and threatening to kill yourself embodied the powerful newness of child emotions and sparked equally strong emotional reactions in adults.

David shook his head and moved his face so he was not quite looking at her, "Nah. She went away."

A terrible restricted misery slithered in the boy's dark eyes. It had always been there, Fawn realized, but hadn't recognized it until that moment. She had known a similar pain as a child and relived it with any long look in the mirror. Eye scars. Her grandfather had them too. In David's eyes were deep lakes of hurt, sadness, and confusion. They were slowly icing over with the struggle to understand the purest versions of these feelings. The flat tone in David's voice cooled the water a little more. She thought of how the little boy said the word 'divorced.' She knew there was a reason he said it that way. Noah apparently had custody, otherwise he'd jumped the border to keep David. But Fawn got the sense that the mother didn't care where they were as long as David wasn't with her. Most bitches, no matter how little they love their children, hold out for child support.

She started to like David pretty darn quick and Noah seemed nice enough too.

*Cute enough*, she acknowledged fleetingly.

Fawn already told herself she wasn't going to think of him that way. She couldn't keep her shit together around boys cute enough to think of as cute. To all *other* boys she was a tomboy who could hold her own in any scrap, but with cute boys—

giggles, blushing, stumbling through simple sentences, and easily blurting out any stupid thing that comes to mind *and* Noah was older.

Through her few friends and from listening to their mothers, Fawn learned what she should look for in a good man. What was quality in shoulders, stomachs, thighs, and buns, and…

She felt her face burning and a stupid giggle inside her. Then she couldn't remember what she and David were talking about.

"Do you get much snow here?" David asked scooting down into his sleeping bag. He hadn't noticed that she wasn't paying attention.

Fawn laughed. "*Oh* yeah."

"When it frosts…," his voice was sounding heavy and bored.

Fawn didn't really want to talk about that anymore. She would have enough trouble sleeping as it was. At least it was done. Soon things would happen. Then David would already be wary and learn the rules. Rules that adults often dismissed because they interfered with normal life. Then they die. For children it has always been easier. The danger is clear, automatic, for the beasts *themselves* are children, in a sense—or at least they *want* to be, and the understanding between children who torment and children victims is almost telepathic.


David woke drained.

Inside the sleeping bag his PJ's stuck to his skin from sweating in the night. Now he was cold, stiff and aching. He wanted to know what time it was. The easiest way was for him to look out a window. The big picture window was just above and behind where he ended up sleeping. Laying on his back, he arched his head back to try and see, and found himself staring up into large shining black eyes staring down with interest into his own.

David screamed, "Daddy!" and shot up in the sleeping bag.

The scream in her face sent Gilder bolting down the hall and under Noah's bed. Fawn screamed herself awake and threw back the top of her partially zipped bag.

Too many mornings she woke just like this—with *someone else* screaming—deathly shrill screams. For her it was the old woman on the other side of a wall that almost seemed to amplify sound.

Would it be David screaming in this house?

Fawn had never gotten used to it—would probably never be desensitized enough to just grumble, pound on the wall, demand silence, and roll over with a pillow pinned over her ears.

Before Fawn could react, David was on his feet, to his father's room and back. He was at the front door before she got herself out of the bag. Morning light streamed around the boy's silhouette as he stared, panting at the empty driveway where his dad's car should be. The garage?

David disappeared from sight. She heard him run across the porch and heard his feet on the rain dampened gravel. Then Gilder was at the door, whining to be let out, and scratching at the screen that just slammed in her mug. Before David reached the garage, he remembered the car would be there because his daddy rode with that woman.

So where was he now? And where were the *children*…

His eyes locked terrified on the dark forest across the road—a darkness that could hide a million eyes, a hundred-million sharp teeth. The garage could too. The shadows beneath the porch and all the forest on the other three sides of the house. The cellar. The attic. Where were all the birds and their happy morning chirping?

Mama Cat waddled over to him and stared where he stared. David noticed her only when her long tail twitched at a fly. The screen door slammed shut and he heard running behind him and the creak of a few steps taken too.

He was startled at this *and* the threatening hiss of Mama Cat.

Then Gilder was licking and sniffing her. Fawn was leaning on the heavy post right of the steps to the porch. Somewhere deep in the throat of the forest or the back of his mind, David heard a low growl like distant thunder and a giggle so faint it almost sounded like bells.

"Come back inside, David," Fawn said and suddenly held the boy's tiny shoulder like it was a handle and led him back in.

"Where's my daddy?" the six-year-old demanded.

"I dun—"

With little warning a pickup pulled into the driveway, driving both of the kids up the stairs and against the front door.

The driver waved at them and turned off the engine.

"What'd'ya think?" Noah asked as he climbed out of the cab. Before either could answer, he added, "David, you're gonna need your stepstool to get in here."

"Cool!" David exclaimed, knowing nothing really about trucks, and ran down the steps to his dad's open arms. The hug lasted even while the child was lifted onto his father's hip so he could see the truck from higher up.

While David was absorbing this, Noah turned his attention to Fawn.

"I'm sorry. I thought I'd be back before you two woke up. I hoped I might be back early, if I found the right vehicle, because I would have just come back, but the dealership was closed when we got to Kapuskasing. You guys were sleeping so cute, I didn't want to wake you up. I decided to take the car in to see if I could trade it. Did you see my note?"

Fawn shook her head and said matter-of-factly, "I've been up for about three minutes. I can't believe you didn't wake me when you came in. I guess I stayed up too late."

*Or didn't sleep very well...*she thought.

"I'm glad. I didn't want to stick you with taking care of him all morning."

"It would have been okay," Fawn assured him. "Until *mishomis*, grandfather, comes, it doesn't really matter."

"Well, let's get you guys in, get you breakfast."


Noah started coffee before getting to the bacon, eggs and toast he offered first—Fawn agreed hungrily, but David wanted cereal.

Fawn folded the eggs and bacon into a single slice of toast and ate ravenously. She had no idea she was so hungry.

"You ready to talk shop? We never talked about your rate," Noah smiled at the stricken look on the very tired looking girl's face. Pop Quiz!

"Ummm," she had no idea what was fair. She wasn't even sure, after he smiled, if he even expected her to answer.

He passed an envelope across the table. It was wrinkled enough that Fawn could tell it was had been ready for a while. She squeezed the thickness and looked at Mr. Asheborne questionably.

"I hope eight dollars an hour before bedtime and ten after, for the inconvenience, is fair," Noah sincerely wondered. "I don't know what the going rate is here."

"Neither do I, but it seems like a lot," Fawn tried not to obviously squeeze the envelope. "We didn't exactly go to bed at bedtime," she confessed.

"That's okay," he assured her.

"What time's Solomon coming?" David asked with only half interest because he was also studying the cereal in his spoon.

Fawn shrugged, "Sometimes Naana is a handful; that can change plans pretty fast."

"David thinks she's pretty neat. He says all those wind-chimes are hers?"

Fawn nodded in a somewhat exhausted way.

"Do they keep pests away?" the young father wondered.

Fawn and David exchanged looks.

"Maybe they let her know when pests are there," David offered a little too obviously.

Fawn rolled her eyes and dropped her face into her arms. The envelope was against her chin. Was this a good time to peek inside?

"Fawn-along-a-ding-dong," David sing-songed and stuffed an oversized spoonful of cereal into his mouth.

"Hmm?" she picked at the edge of the envelope.

"Your hair is in your bacon juice."

Noah turned away from the counter to see, just as she started collecting the portions of her hair that pooled in her plate.

He grabbed up a dishtowel and opened it to catch the couple drips and gather her tresses.

"I'll assume this means you were okay with your breakfast. I really wouldn't have been offended if you had left the grease."

She threw back, "If you're competing with David for 'cute', you're losing."

"Okay, missy. Let's take care of this," Noah held her hair in the towel and led her to the bathtub to let her clean up. When he left the bathroom, Noah unceremoniously tossed a bath towel across her back and called over his shoulder, "I'm gonna have to spend some time with Solomon to come to some understanding about these Native customs."

"Oh my God," Fawn said in a breath. She thought about what had happened and was smiling by the time she rinsed her hair. *He's so hot.*

# MISERY LOVES COMPANY

◆

At fifteen, Angela Cleary thought she was too old for babysitting. There is a hiatus in people's lives, she thought, when people just aren't supposed to do it anymore. To her, that period began at sixteen and ended at sixty—that is when you babysit because your kids are all grown up, maybe your grandkids live far away, maybe they live close and you don't see them as much as you'd like or you can't have kids yourself. That's when parents take advantage of free babysitting. No matter what, Angela told herself, she would never babysit for free.

Woe be her parents, Angela never really wanted to do anything for free.

"How much will you give me?" was the traditional response for extra and even ordinary chores.

The reason why she said "yes" to babysitting for the Coventry's was because their daughter, Sable, was such a sweetheart and never a problem. Ironic, Angela's parents thought, that their daughter should so admire the sweet and obedient disposition of this little girl and be repulsed by being asked to even consider trying to conjure any of those qualities in herself.

Sable's parents were shy and kind-hearted people, who quietly participated in a lot of community and church events.

They made supper and the plates, one for the sitter too, were left to warm in the oven. Their daughter would have to be in bed in two hours, they'd be home three hours later. The evening would be a breeze.

But a breeze hardly covered the weather, it was blustery and prematurely dark via the ominous bluish-black clouds hanging heavily among smaller and finer clouds visibly moving over the tree line. The air was thick and charged with malevolent weather, among other malevolent things sensed in the air.

Never before had the Coventry's been hesitant when they left. When they finally told themselves they *had* to get going, the father mentioned their little girl being a little jumpy because of the weather. Both parents appeared spooked themselves.

"Poor little thing," Angela said whole-heartedly.

As soon as the door was closed and locked she went to look for the little cutie, starting in the living room.

She swallowed down the lump in her throat that kept her from screaming.

"Oh my God!" Angela gasped after almost plowing over the knee high darling with chubby cheeks, exactly three freckles, on only one side of her face, untidy hair, and a limp wrinkly nightshirt that was probably her mom's when she was that age—can you even buy stuff with classic My Little Pony that isn't used?

Two hands that seemed the size of Oreos reached up for the babysitter to pick up and cuddle.

"Are you getting a little hung—"

"BAHH!" Angela screamed loudly when the phone rang. The toddler thumped against the ground when the hands supporting her flew to cover the mouth sounding alarm.

It took two more rings before she was composed enough to answer. Sable was crying and had crawled to the arm of her daddy's chair and pulled herself up so she could throw her face and arms into the seat and let it all out.

"Hello?"

"If you want to babysit, I'll give you a baby," said the pseudo-manly teenage voice on the other end.

"Who is this?" she was sure she knew the voice.

"The one who can git it done."

"Oh yeah," Angela snorted. "If you're that eager you'd probably come off before you got your pants unzipped."

"Yeah, baby? Tell you what, then you make sure you're ready and I'll wear sweats."

"I'm vomiting."

"Yeah?" the voice almost groaned.

"What?! Are you choking it? You sick bastard! Don't call here again or I'll give your number to Phil."

"My num—oh shit!"

The line went dead.

"Dumbass," she looked at the caller ID: G & R TOULLET. "Charlie, you ball-muncher."

She looked at the small stricken face peering at her over the crook of an almost shapeless elbow.

"Sorry honey, but you know not to say bad words right?"

The ratty head nodded awkwardly in the nest of arms.

"Ready to eat?"

PHWAM! PHWAM! PHWAM!

The teenager threw herself away from the door. The

pounding was right beside her head.

In an instant Angela was more terrified than she had ever been in her whole life and she had no idea why. In her gut, it was almost like she expected to open the door and find Satan himself standing there. She wasn't about to peek. Every ounce of her nerve prickled flesh begged her to hide.

BOOM! BOOM! BOOM! on the floor above her head, like the heaviest person on earth, with the biggest feet too, still managed to run down the hall upstairs.

The babysitter threw herself on the little girl just in time to catch the scream in the palm of her hand. The tiny angel turned so she could clutch the neck of the temporary parent.

"Shh," Angela whispered against the side of the little head that, this close, she realized smelled sweet of being newly washed—her mind took the time to understand this was why she was looking kind of ratted.

They both listened for the sound, more sounds.

A single "thump" and the cops were going to get a call.

They sat still for a painful hour where neither of them really breathed and rationed their too-loud heartbeats to not give themselves away.

"There *has* to be an explanation?"

"What?" Sable worried.

"I'm gonna find out."

The tiny arms constricted on her neck.

"Okay, you can come too."

The hall at the top of the stairs was blocked by a wall of shadows where the light from the kitchen and living room couldn't chase it away. After turning on the lamp atop a small table beside the right side of the stairs, Angela decided the second floor was officially fucking terrifying. The railing threw a row of dark shapeless figures on the wall behind it. More than a few seconds passed before she realized it wasn't actually people standing there.

"I think I might have to wear one of your pull-ups tonight," the babysitter said as she climbed the dark blue oriental runner over oak steps. Her eyes fixed on the panel of switches on the wall to the left at the top. The hall light was the second from the left. She wanted it like that unattainable god at a party that you feel a one-sided magnetic attraction too—one, in fact, you are pretty sure you share with half a dozen other single girls. Hell, maybe even not-so-single girls.

Angela reached out for the switch long before she could reach it. She imagined her arm stretching to close the distance, and in her fear impaired mind, she actually thought her arm was longer than it should be.

Seconds later, the smooth plastic shape of the hall switch met the tip of her middle finger. She flicked it, like a fly. There was a moment of warm light, the pop of a weak firecracker, and the flight of stairs and hall were reunited with the darkness that apparently had no intentions of surrendering them.

"We'll just go check if something fell over," the babysitter tried to sound nonchalant.

*Yeah, something just tipped over. It happens all the time.*
*Yes it does.*

Mr. Nobody was the busiest citizen of Nibebiitam. He was blamed for almost everything—the accusations were almost always followed by uneasy chuckles. Yup, things fall over a lot. And buildings settle. There must be a draft. Must have sat it too close to the edge. Boy, I'm just so scatter-brained, I keep misplacing things!

Who did it?

*Mr. Nobody.*

"Mr. Nobody must have knocked over some of your mommy and daddy's books!"

Sable got an "uh-oh" look on her face and put one small hand to her oval-shaped mouth.

They were halfway down the hall when lightning obliterated the ink-like blackness. It hurt the girls' eyes.

BOOM!

The thunder was so close it sounded like it came from the middle of the house. It sounded like it was in the hall with them.

"It was thunder, you dummy," the sitter said lovingly to the light, but heavier and heavier, child in her arms.

"It was?"

"Yeah. Oh my God, I've had us in complete house arrest over a stupid ass storm. Let's go down and eat some supper."

Angela Cleary was so distracted she didn't notice the long-faced, chimp-like creature perched on the dresser as she passed the guest bedroom.

Supper was good, as always at the Coventry's. They knew how to use spices and weren't afraid to try new things. Sable wasn't fussy, maybe that was why there was never any trouble getting her to eat. Because she already had a bath, after supper a bed time story and a hug and a kiss were just about all that was left to do.

The nightlight fed a warm glow into the cloud of resin that surrounded it. Outside the house was likewise surrounded by clouds and, while windy, the storm didn't seem to have any interest in moving away. Every thunder clap made the house rattle and hearts race. So when she went back to check on Sable the teenager couldn't believe how heavily she was sleeping.

Angela smiled adoringly when she whispered to the little

tyke that she hated her and went back to sit on the couch and channel surf.

"Are you fucking serious?" she groaned.

A small red line, like marker, was on the cushion she had just been lounging on. Laying her hands flat on the waist of her jeans, Angela arched out her hips and hunched over to see a red stain growing on the crotch.

"Men suck," she muttered as she roughly searched her handbag and tore a tampon from the contents. The tirade continued inaudibly as she entered the bathroom, punching the lock button after closing the door. It didn't catch.

She pressed it more firmly and it always sprung back.

Angela had used this bathroom a million times. It wasn't the kind of lock where you have to turn and depress it, or depress it and turn it. The door didn't have to be closed for the button to lock.

"Whatever, fuck it," she dropped her bottoms and plopped down on the toilet.

The lights flickered and for a split second she thought she saw something, *someone*, hiding behind the shower curtain.

A second look proved it was a large brown, bunched up towel.

BAM!

The lights went on and off, on and off, on and off, on and off in rhythm, not flickering. *Pulsing*.

In between a pulse she saw the door open.

Then it was closed.

Then it was open.

Then it was closed and something was standing there.

Something with gray-green putrid flesh.

Something with long arms and skin so thin it almost looked

like there was none at all.

Something with a long thick maw like a wart-hog, but with chimp-like features on it and its emaciated body.

Something that's body didn't move when its head moved, or when its neck stretched out impossibly far—that struck with its mouth thrown back like a snake and found the girl's throat like it was the only place it could ever bite.

In the meantime, Sable was finding out there really were monsters under the bed.

# CHAPTER 6

◆

## The ART of BEING NEIGHBORLY

When Noah left England, and for most of the time he could remember growing up, he was nervous around people. Eggshells were a lot sturdier than what that child and then youth had to walk on to not only feel safe, but stay safe. Maybe if Noah had gotten mad instead of withdrawn, the fear of what could or would be done to him might not have lasted as long. He might have become belligerent and jaded. Instead he walked around with a stiffness in him like someone cursed to play Red-light/Green-light every waking moment. He was no good with people.

Becoming roommates with Derrick was the best thing that could have happened to him. Derrick was courageous and fun— he knew how to live and dragged Noah along with him until he could walk on his own.

If not for that Noah wouldn't have been as excited about entertaining company. It was something he grew to love, attending as well as hosting get-togethers mixed with friends, co-workers, and acquaintances. He was thrilled to get to meet interesting people he might have never known because they were dating a guest, along for the ride, or as a guest at a party he and his wife went to. He remembered crying in the shower, after they got home one night, when he first realized it was possible to feel so good and welcomed around so many people—people he didn't know. It made Noah feel like he had a pulse for the first time in twenty years. Proof positive he was passing as a human being, a normal one.

Even so, Noah was nervous, cutting potatoes and rechecking recipes. In a way, he felt he was starting from scratch. At least there weren't a lot of people coming over.

It was time they had company in the house to warm it—resuscitate whatever that feeling is when a house switches hands that makes a home a home.

He was distracted by a few things he noticed were missing or found rearranged while he was getting things together to cook. Things he was sure where they should be and how much should be left of them, if the items were to be found at all. When Noah found only two slices of bologna left in its plastic container, he suspected David. But he couldn't explain away why he found the lemon pepper in the fridge, or a loaf of bread hidden behind the good glasses. So he just shrugged—that was the easiest thing to do, being short on time.

"Which plates?" David asked. He was standing on a chair holding cupboard doors open, staring in like a teenager into a refrigerator.

"Uh..." Noah left the potatoes to pick his son off the chair and move it back where it belonged at the table. "Not plates, but you can do silverware if you want to help."

"We're not going to eat on plates?" the six-year-old was surprised.

"Yeah, we will."

"Then why..." the boy trailed off, his left pointer finger hovering toward the open cupboard doors like a drunk playing darts.

"They're pretty heavy. I don't want them to fall and break or worse, to fall and hurt you or one of the pets following you around."

"Plates aren't heavy," David contradicted with an impatient frown that Noah returned. David was feeling a little cranky and Noah felt it. "*My* plate I can hold in two fingers."

"My plate" referred to a cheap plastic character plate he'd bought at a supercenter when David was four. It was $1.50. His baby loved it and wanted to eat everything off of it. After a hundred million washings the character wasn't quite what it used to be, but it was still *his*. And yes, it was light. But David knew—

"We're going to use the good dishes."

"The white ones?"

Noah nodded and said, "Mm-hmm."

David stared at him dumbly. His IQ was visibly melting away. Mannequins have more going on in their heads than was registering in that boy's eyes.

The father waited as long as he could bear before beginning to talk again, but no sooner did he open his mouth when David asked, "Gilder and Mama Cat too?"

"When have you ever seen Gilder get to use people dishes—," he quickly corrected, "—special dishes."

David shrugged and ran to the drawer where placemats and tablecloths were kept.

"Can we use these too?"

"Do you want to?" his daddy asked.

The child's tiny neck delivered a ferocious set of nods.

"Ok."

"Then silverware?"

"Yep."

"Daddy?"

Noah looked past the towel slung over his shoulder and saw most of the face of the small person squatted at the drawer.

"Yeah, kiddo?"

"I think there's potato juice in my pits."

Noah looked down at his work. He was, at that moment, cupping the last handful of cubed potatoes. Neither father or son really cared about it. Noah didn't like a mess of any kind anywhere, but it wasn't going to stain or stink. David was disheveled and sticky and splotchy with God knows what. Potato juice in the armpits sounds like accessorizing.

"Do you like it?" his daddy decided to try.

David sniffed them loudly. He tried his left armpit three times, his right only twice.

"They're just wet."

"Wait 'til you're a teenager," Noah forewarned with ominous large eyes and a secretive smile.

David chuckled as he roughly drug out a deep crimson cloth.

"This one okay?"

"It's your choice," the father answered, but deep inside considered it and approved. If he hadn't, Noah would have still honored what he said, but he was sure the Christmas tablecloth was going to come out. He would have put money on it.

Timing meals so everything was done on time was something neither Noah nor Terri was great at. It would have helped a lot, in the beginning, if they had more reliable appliances. You can't plan for something to be done if you can't count on the temperature being what it's supposed to be or the burner heating through the whole coil. There was something romantic and fun about incidentals like these. They were doing it on their own, but they were doing it together. They didn't have family to turn to for help, but they found out they had a lot of friends who loved them. While some of their friends climbed the financial ladder a lot faster than they did, they got well-meaning hand-me-downs and gifts that sometimes, laying together in the early hours of night, the young couple agreed that they felt bad about how nice this or that was. They couldn't wait to be able to return the favors.

Now all the appliances were right, but miscalculations, like not accounting for prep time and preheating times, had thrown them off schedule. To conceal the inadequacies in the planning, as useful historically as in the present, there were enough appetizers strewn about to keep rumbling stomachs from wondering where the food was.

"How many seatings?" David interrupted his, apparently grunt-worthy, efforts to spread the tablecloth out evenly to ask.

"Me, you, the Cranes, Jacob, Rising Moon is working—"

"Aww.." the child tut-tutted.

The man cleared his throat and mouthed the earlier listed attendants, "—Jacob may be bringing someone. Toullet's, the couple who does the actual printing for Jacob is coming and they are bringing their son."

"How old is he?"

"He's a big boy. I think he's almost done with school."

Noah sensed David's disappointment.

"You're going to have lots of friends again, just like you did in New York."

"What if Canadian kids don't like the way American kids are? What if I'm weird?"

"Kids are weird. You are definitely weird, so you'll fit in just fine."

"Are you sure?"

"I promise-promise."

David looked across his work and started pointing at each chair in turn.

"How many people?"

"Ummm. Nine or ten."

"How did we get room for ten chairs?" exclaimed David.

"Hey, hey. Watch the volume. What's the crisis?"

"How did ten chairs fit?"

"I put the extra parts of the table in."

His son looked under the table to confirm it. Not one, but both of them were added.

"So is this ten chairs?" he wondered.

"Yep."

David went for the silverware, he knew what to take out and where to put them. They had "special utensils", but he'd never saw them used, even at Christmas, so he wasn't sure what they were for, but he had a pretty good feeling this dinner wasn't the time. The only time David saw them was when his dad would take them out, now and then, to polish them. They came in their own small suitcase with special places for all the kinds of forks and spoons—and there were a lot of them. David liked the tiny forks the best. They were funny.

Gilder made a sound like "moww moww" and raised her bat-like ears as she faced the front door.

Noah looked up at the window over the sink, the sheer

curtain was stroked with light as a vehicle turned into their driveway.

"Good girl," Noah praised his furry baby. The towel came off his shoulder and he dried his hands with it.

"Who is it?" his son asked.

"Dunno yet," Noah answered as he passed the partition between the kitchen and the small hall that was basically coat hooks on one side and coat closet on the other. It wasn't long enough for much more than that.

Noah had felt a sarcastic answer, as he had for a lot of the questions David asked that night. *Maybe*, he wondered, *I'm a little cranky too.*

He was smiling to himself as he peeked through the curtains on the front door. The people coming up were black and shapeless.

"Oops," his smile broadened as he flipped on the porch light before opening the door, without bothering to look out the window again.

"Jacob, hi!" Noah offered his hand to the older man and shook it robustly. The woman with him was probably five or so years younger than her escort. When she smiled, the dimples that pierced her cheeks were so deep he was sure you could see them if she opened her mouth.

"Noah, this is Polly. She owns that print shop over in Kapuskasing, *IN*-PRINTS."

"Oh sure," Noah shook her hand and impossibly her dimples deepened as she added teeth to her smile. "Jacob's looking for ways to deal with the competition."

"I'm flattered if he thinks I am," she demurred with a bird-like laugh. Jacob laughed too, but in a nervous 'you caught me' way.

"Sorry, if we're a little early," Jacob apologized, following Noah inside and shimmying out of his light coat. "I like to start drinking before other people so I can get a little drunk and people will just think I'm naturally fun."

Polly laughed loudly, clearly thinking he was joking. She laughed harder when Jacob didn't laugh and Noah only managed a weak chuckle. To him, Jacob could have been joking, but he didn't know what he was going to do if his boss intended to get shit-faced.

"I think you will know everyone here, so.."

"Oh, you're kidding? None of your friends from New York came up?"

"I think that would have been a lot to ask," was what Noah answered, but he hadn't even considered it. The dinner was a housewarming by merit of the presence of people who he thought would be in his life now and would be good to get to know. Immediately he worried that he might have misconstrued what the premise of this get-together was and didn't want to have to deal with refusing gifts or anything like that.

"Jacob said you were from New York," Polly was looking around the spacious joined rooms, she went to run her hand over the cushions and back of the sectional and remarked, "Well, this is just beautiful. You can really do this well writing?"

"Some people get lucky," Noah shrugged, feeling embarrassed.

"It helps if the stories are violent and dirty," Jacob chuckled. He was petting Gilder and idly listening to both David introducing him to the pets and Polly and Noah's conversation.

"Do you write nasty books, Mr. Asheborne?" Polly's eyes, lined with chunky mascara on her sparse lashes, widened with a mixture of disbelief and interest.

It was Noah's turn to chuckle, "I think if I said 'yes' I would be exaggerating."

"Could some people say 'yes'?" Jacob injected.

"*Yes,*" Noah returned to the stove and checked the three pots, adding salt to one, turning down the temperature on another, "But *a lot* of people could also assert they aren't even close."

"Well I—"

Gilder pushed past Jacob and a second later there were two knocks on the door.

"More early birds," David was grabbing for Mama Cat when the knocks came.

"Hey there," he heard his daddy say from within the small hall. He said something about coats, but the rest of the talking was lost in a jumble David resented because there was suddenly a lot of laughing over there.

Fawn wanted through the herd of adults at the door and fled to the living room where she hoped she could be ignored until the meal was served.

Noah was careful when he shook Naana's hand; it felt like cotton swabs in a latex glove full of pudding.

"It is so nice to meet you," he told her earnestly. "My son is really fascinated by you."

"Your cat is fat," she answered.

"Umm. Yeah, she's not very svelte, is she?"

Naana didn't answer, but wandered much like Polly into the zone that wasn't living room or kitchen. She was stooped and wobbly.

"Should she maybe have a place to sit?"

"Yah. Would that be okay?" Solomon agreed.

"Sure. Sure. Anywhere is fine," but Noah gestured to the recliner where he thought she would be most comfortable.

"Fawn!" David called when he saw Solomon, whose closest leg he hugged when he was passing by. "That's Gilder," his small finger touched the wet nose when he pointed her out to Mr. Crane.

Noah heard his son find Fawn and he had to keep himself from going into the living room to remind him about indoor voices. He was counting on David behaving himself once he found Fawn, but he also had a pretty good idea that Fawn was the kind of person who might remind him herself. Noah appreciated that.

*Don't let me down.*

Polly and Jacob talked over each other and asked questions about this and that while Solomon tried to get in the normal first few questions, the "how are you's" and "what have you been up to's" and "smells good in here". That might have contributed to David thinking he would have to be loud to be heard. When the Toullet's, Rachel and George, showed up with their son, Charlie, it suddenly felt like there were thirty people in the house.

Mister and missus Toullet were both about forty. George had a long wiery beard and an accent he later said was Ukrainian. He said a lot of people around there were, but he had actually moved from there to marry Rachel, the daughter of the friend of a cousin or something who was of Ukrainian descent. They seemed to be very much in love, but after meeting their son, Noah could tell they had to really stick together to not hurt him.

Noah didn't take it as an outright affront when the kid kicked off his shoes against the wall, toppling over the footwear lined up there. Some people just don't think about stuff like that. He also didn't think too much of Charlie picking through the appetizers, complaining when one he wanted had a garnish that couldn't be removed without also removing the cheese, spitting one into a paper towel, crumpling it up and leaving it on the counter, or taking the whole of a tray of the basic meat, cheese, and cracker assortment, going into the living room, putting his really dirty socked feet on the coffee table and turned on the TV. He even turned up the volume after he'd said vaguely, "Hey!" twice, but must have not been able to hear over the visiting.

Fawn and David stared at the older boy from the floor by the fireplace.

"What the f—"

"That channel is blocked," David informed the older boy punching numbers in the remote and tried to do the parental code several times.

"No shit. Well I'm not a child."

"*It* says you are," Fawn offered a couple cents of her own. She had discipline enough not to smile, David didn't.

"Get your dad to unblock it," Charlie ordered.

"I can't," David said grimly, he'd already fought that battle and lost.

"Hey Asheborne, wanna unblock this so I'm not bored to death?" Charlie asked through a mouth of crackers, greedily stacked cheese, and meat that almost looked like a multi-color striped cock before he crammed it into his mouth.

"You can join us," Noah offered instead.

"Yeah. Right. Uh-huh," was the answer to that.

"You'd think we twisted his arm to get him to come," his mother said.

"Really? You didn't?" Noah was surprised.

"No, he wanted to come," she dismissed it with a flip of her hand, the compactly charmed bracelet made a pretty sound as it danced around her wrist. "Had been bragging to his friends about it probably. Most of them have seen you on TV, you know, with interviews or whatnot. I told him I was surprised he even knew who you were—which he took as a personal attack—I was surprised because he doesn't read, even what he's assigned to read. I'm afraid he's one of those kids who likes things just because they're popular."

"I didn't really think I was, not to any significant scale," Noah shrugged at this too.

"My husband knows your work, but I'm a purist of Joyce Carol Oakes."

"My wife read her," he blurted without really thinking about what kinds of questions this could open himself up to. He saw their son picking his nose, just beyond the father's massive and densely haired arm. Someone said something to Noah so he didn't see what happened in the aftermath.

"Fawn, why is Naana so weird?" David weighed his options and found that it might be a good time to ask a rude question when someone else is being worse.

"She lost her mind when she lost herself in the muskeg," the girl answered absently, she was watching to see where the quivering booger went, but looked away when Jacob knocked over his glass and the whole table erupted with laughter.

Noah thought Jacob might be acting drunker than he was, but everyone seemed happy with it so he tried to enjoy it too.

Suddenly David was there, mooching for something to eat and Fawn was with him, but she looked like she just wanted to escape. Noah had a feeling that her arm *was* twisted. This might be a little too busy for the quiet little tomboy.

He appreciated that too.

God blesses the meek, right?

Fawn and David were allowed to eat in the living room because Noah could see they weren't happy at the big table even before everyone was seated.

Mrs. Toullet said something about a child that small and food that stains and "such a nice sofa" as if she were reading about someone that died.

Charlie was less than pleased to be cooped up with the grownups and groaned a lot about it before his father firmly and shortly told him to, "Shut-it."

Noah had a feeling these moments of firm parenting were too few and far between to have been any good on the little bastard. This late in the game it would take the worst kind of reality check to do him any good—if anything could help.

"What are your plans after school, Charlie?" Noah asked, hoping against hope that he would say he was enlisting.

The coming year's senior, with lips that looked disproportionate on his face, leaned back, chewing slow, and fully opening his mouth between the occasions when his teeth actually got to do something to the food, almost purposefully, it seemed, to show them all what was going on inside his mouth. Noah had only ever saw people chew gum like that.

"Ahh-dun-know," he slurred boredly. "I'm nah really thinkin' about that. I got time. I have a lot of things to do as a boy before I think of what I'm going to do as a man. Know what I mean?"

Noah had a feeling he did and didn't want to.

"Never too early to be planning for the future."

"Carpe Diem, man," Charlie said, obviously, by the look on his face, thinking he was pretty smart. Probably felt like he had the world by the balls, so why worry?

"How are you liking the place, Noah?" Roger asked. "Do you do any hunting or fishing?"

"Not a lot of hunting in the city is there, Asheborne?" Charlie chuckled.

Noah shook his head slowly and rolled his eyes toward the big teenager, "Not a lot, but—" he turned back to Mr. Toullet and clearing the condescendence from his face, "—I wouldn't object to giving it a try sometime. Do you have any tips on good fishing spots?"

"Randomly ask anyone and you'll get a 'yes' from that one, Noah," Polly laughed. She laughed after almost everything she said, did, or heard and he kind of liked her for it.

"Finding those secret fishing holes is the trick and people will want to charge you to tell you or show you," Jacob remarked just as the phone rang.

"I'd bet they do," Noah agreed, pushing away from the table.

"Well, I print maps that some of these fishermen sell to campers and tourists and stuff, no fooling," Polly exclaimed.

Noah took the phone into the other room, pushing talk as he walked away so it wouldn't go to voicemail or that the person would hang-up before he got away from the noise.

"Asheborne's," he said into the mouthpiece. He noticed that the air between it and his lips felt warm from the hot meal and couldn't wait to get back to it. He had been so busy getting the house and supper ready that he barely ate anything all day.

"They won't let you stay unless you play," a man with an unfamiliar accent whispered.

"Excuse me?"

"The children."

"Right. I know," Noah dismissed flatly.

"Then why the fuck did you bother unpacking?" hissed the male voice.

Noah cringed at the sudden ferocity and didn't know how to respond without being concerned about antagonizing the stranger on the other end of the line.

"Look. I got the message. Whoever you people are, you need to lay off. Every last cent is put into this move and this house. I *can't* leave without losing everything," he lied. "So all these warnings are for nothing."

"What if you didn't have the house?"

Noah's stomach flipped with fear and anger.

"Don't call me. Worry about your own fucking problems—it sounds like you have some serious ones."

Noah hung up and took a second in the deep end of the hall and tried to compose himself. Eyebrow raised slowly, turning on the lamp, Noah leaned in on the console in the hall and focused on the few items always in the bowl: keys, pens, a pad of paper, spare change, maybe a pack of gum, and other stuff emptied out of pockets. Only it wasn't inside the bowl, but crammed up around the outside of it.

They weren't like that an hour ago.

He'd have to ask David about it later.

"Was it for me?" Jacob joked when Noah returned.

"Yeah. It was—" but he couldn't say what he wanted to because it wasn't the kind of thing you say around people you don't really know—unless you don't care what they are going to think of you. He didn't want to make that kind of impression—a foul mouthed smart ass.

Instead, he smiled and returned to his seat. The smile Noah offered Jacob he hoped not only apologized for not finishing his sentence, but also told him that it would have been a good answer.

"Are they going to make a movie out of *Held Hands Severed*? I heard they were?"

Noah shrugged with one shoulder, "The idea's been picked

at, I think."

"How much dough would you make if it was?"

"I'd have no idea. Probably not as much as anyone else involved," Noah laughed with the others, but with a little less mirth.

"That's the way it goes, isn't it?" Roger said bitterly. "It's the people that make the world work that get paid the least and the people that do the least get paid the most to make the rest of us work."

"Amen," said Polly.

Then Jacob called her out for owning her own business, but she pouted that she still had to answer to her bloodthirsty clients.

"This sounds like the time when the Indian's due to say something about what the white-man takes," Charlie said, throwing his glazed eyes toward Solomon.

"Charlie Don Toullet!"

"Do you—" Solomon began.

"Charlie," Noah interrupted, "save your rhetoric and stereotypes for your own time and place—there's no time and no place for it here."

"I kinda figured that," Charlie made a snorting sound.

Noah expected his parents to say something and didn't know how long he could bear to wait. He wondered what they would do if he kicked the shit out of their son, threw him out of the house, and ran him over.

Over the stillness that settled on the table was the sound of eating, clinking of utensil and dish. Naana ate heartily through the tension.

"Good," she praised after slipping in her first bite of the cherry pie, between bites of chicken, and a Mediterranean style salad.

Charlie looked triumphant. His parents looked embarrassed, probably because they felt the same way, because they felt chastised.

Naana went for more chicken, eyes shiny and big with innocent greed and pleasure.

"I'll trade you furs for the recipe, white-man," Solomon offered.

Noah was afraid to smile at first, but when the others started laughing, Solomon too, Noah felt free to let it happen. He hoped the smile looked grateful, because it was.

So was Solomon's.

The Cranes were the last people to leave that night and Solomon shook Noah's hand goodbye twice before letting go.

"It was a good evening," the older man said as he took the few steps down to the small path across the yard to the driveway. Fawn was ahead helping Naana in the truck.

"I don't like Charlie," the little boy by his side announced.

Noah wanted to say that he didn't either, but instead tried, "No?"

"Nope."

Noah took in a breath of the clean night air.

"Well, what did you think of Naana?" David asked.

Gilder looked up like she wanted to know too.

"She was flattering," his daddy answered.

He raised a hand to usher dog and child inside and followed behind, telling himself he was just seeing things when something moved out of the corner of his eye.

# *WHISPERS*

To the people of Nibebiitam, Waverly Brindle was a yuppie. Her modular home was brought in all the way from Thunder Bay, where she'd lived for over forty years. When her daughter and son-in-law were expecting their first child she dropped everything to come stay with them. More like *near* them. She brought more than just a suitcase—she brought a house.

Waverly was a big hearted woman and loved her family almost excessively, protectively, but she was set in her ways and what was hers was *hers* and her space was *her* space and she got really nervous when those standards were compromised. That wasn't all. Her family—enormous family—sent her things from the "big cities" because more expensive items could, allegedly, serve her better than, essentially, the same things from Nibebiitam, or even Kapuskasing.

The Brindle's eight children took very good care of their long since widowed mother, and bought her many things so she wouldn't have to dip into the small principle that her deceased husband left her. The only child who couldn't take care of

Waverly was the daughter who moved to Nibebiitam to marry the "Paper Mill Man" who promised to take care of the Brindle's youngest daughter and love her forever. But he was Native and that just didn't fit into the "family standard". She was dead as far as the rest of the family was concerned.

If Mrs. Brindle, *Waverly please*, hadn't been the head of the household she'd have been zombified right along with her indiscriminate youngest daughter who had the audacity to love a man, regardless of ethnicity. Waverly loved him too, for *some reason*. Maybe because the guy loved her child and treated her well.

Locals said Mrs. Brindle's love was bought.

Yes, Waverly was living it up in Nibebiitam, throwing all that money in everyone's faces to show how good she had it.

Then her son-in-law got her *that dog*. That's how the people in town always referred to it. *That* dog. The Paper Mill Man, the "no good redskin", bought it for his mother-in-law to take care of her and keep her company.

"A waste of money," people said.

"Five thousand dollars was it?"

"At least."

Waverly reportedly also faked a disability. Desperate for more attention and probably government assistance, people thought.

No one really believed she was blind. They were pretty sure all she wanted was sympathy. So people were suspicious when no big deal was made about the old woman's frequent black and blue marks.

Mrs. Brindle might have claimed the bruises were from bumping into things, but they all *knew* it was really her son-in-law. And when the rich old woman died, he would be blamed for that too.

Waverly settled down on the plump-cushioned kitchen chair she always left near the front door, where she took in the evening breeze and a cup of mint tea that was supposed to sooth her stomach—she'd had some pains the last few months.

Her butt barely had to exit the chair to answer the scratching at the aluminum door. The dog she loved went immediately to rest his head on her knee.

"That didn't take long," she praised and treated the retriever from one of the many caches of treats in the deep pockets on her gray-blue skirt.

She rested her hand lovingly on his head while he was still smacking down the treat. And still smacking. And smacking. The dog's hot breath was penetrating the skirt's fabric and warming the knee opposite of the one its head was on. Smacking. Smacking. His long slobbering tongue was saturating the patch of cloth it touched. His breath was damp as the air in a sauna.

"Numm-num. Numm-numm-num," came through the slapping of wet jaws.

Her skin began to crawl. The feel of ants ran under her skin, a shiver raced ahead of the sensation, up her limbs and spine and made her thin, balding, white hair prickle at the same time she noticed that the dog's head seemed long. Too long. Not even long like a collie, but long like a crocodile. Maybe even longer.

Then she heard it chuckle, wetly, deeply, arrogantly.

The blind woman began to sob.

"I know what you're thinking," said a voice that matched the laugh, from somewhere between her knees. "And you're right."

# CHAPTER 7

◆

# CONJURING NORMALCY

Father and son were both wet from shower and bath respectively—they were trying to get into a routine of running again, something they used to do weekend mornings. At first just Gilder and Noah. Then Gilder, Noah and baby.

It was nice to run in the country. Only once did they have to move to the side of the narrow road for a passing vehicle.

The routine went pretty much the same as it had in New York. Noah would run ahead a little and run back. It was David's job to try and make his run back as short as possible, if he could. Then Noah was still able to get a good workout, while including David.

Gilder always came along. Mama Cat had for a little while, but after mewing pathetically for about a hundred yards, David decided to carry her. Noah ended up carrying both cat and child for a fourth of the run. He was impressed that Mama Cat tolerated the method of travel, since she acted like a lunatic in the car. In his arms she looked pompous and smug, like she shouldn't have had to wait so long.

So now, as David described it, it was time for them to "clean up and get their act together".

The six-year-old delighted in the grating sound of the razor skimming the whiskers off his father's face. Shave cream smelled of hugs and kisses. It smelled of warm morning's hands that pat faces and rumple hair. Shave cream, the fragrance of daddy. The aftershave, oh the temptation! The cool splash of intense daddy smell made his eyes roll. The routine was the epitome of manliness and dadliness. He never blinked, not once, during this part of the regime. The smooth run of the blade along a face that slowly appeared as the billowy cream was cut away. The shadow of weekend low maintenance stripped away with every skilled swipe.

The child readily handed a towel to blot away the last few fluffy white streaks. Then a splash of the "ambrosia", rub of the hands and patting of the newly smooth face.

"Need any?" David held up the square of toilet paper he'd earlier removed for this critical moment.

"Doesn't look like it," Noah scanned his face. "Looks like we did a good job."

They did mini high-fives and father helped son off the sink. The family of four were all in good spirits that morning. While shaving, Noah noticed his cheeks hurt from smiling.

"Can you towel your hair better, kiddo?"

"Gee!" David went to the towel closet.

"Well, then don't whine at me that you're not feeling well."

"I never do!"

"The hell you don't," Noah laughed.

"Daddy!" David came back into the room, assaulting his head with an angry towel. "That was soap talk."

"Sorry, just got a little vinegar in me today."

"And what does vinegar make you do?" David asked knowingly.

Noah bent over to get and gave a kiss.

"You pucker," the father answered.

"I do. I like vinegar chips," the six-year-old declared.

"Not by the faces you make."

"I do."

"I'm not so sure. I—"

The phone rang and Noah left David to go get it.

There was a "beep" when the "TALK" button was pressed and Noah raised the phone to his ear, "Hello?"

"Locking your doors won't keep them out," warned a masculine voice on the end of the line.

"Who is this? Is this about those kids?"

"They're going to kill you and your family," the voice said matter-of-factly.

Noah hung up.

Immediately the phone rang again.

"*Yes*?" he answered stiffly.

"LEAVE OR *DIE*!"

Gilder raised her head and growled at the phone.

Noah held the phone away and looked at the name and number on the Caller ID.

He hung up again.

The pen bit deep into the legal pad as he recorded the names and numbers that came up from the phone calls.

The cellophane wrapper on the phone book removed, Noah clenched and unclenched the plastic in his right hand as he got the number for the police and dialed it quickly, pretty sure that there would be another threatening call before he had a chance.

"Nibebiitam Municipal or can I transfer you to RCMP, or OPP? Do you have an emergency?"

"Municipal Police? And no. A complaint."

"Let me transfer you to an available constable. Please hold."

He got about three seconds of jazz music before the line picked up.

"This is Phil," said the constable.

"Good morning, my name is Noah Asheborne and I'd like to make a complaint."

"Go ahead."

Noah blinked at the phone. He wasn't sure what the tone meant. Was he being sarcastic? Agreeable?

"Umm, okay, well, I've been getting a lot of strange phone calls. Some of them are pretty pushy, but I've gotten a couple aggressive ones this morning and the last few nights. I can give you names and numbers, but I think I know who it is."

"Oh yah?"

"*Yes.*"

There was a brief silence before Noah felt like it was still his turn so he continued, "I just moved here—"

"Yup," the constable injected.

"—and it was barely a day before all these guys drove up and started telling me all these stories about these troubled kids and that I needed to protect my family. They more than subtly suggested that it wasn't a good idea that I live here. That's been the nature of the phone calls too and frankly, I'm sick of it."

He heard the constable breathing evenly. Noah listened for typing or the scratch of a pen or pencil working.

"I think everyone knows about you Mr. Asheborne. Don't let that alarm you. Around here everybody knows when anything happens. Not a lot of people move to Nibebiitam. Mrs. Brindle was one of the last to move here. You should almost be surprised there wasn't an article about it in the paper."

"I'll count myself lucky."

The constable chuckled. Noah heard his chair creak and it was really easy to imagine the guy leaning back and putting his feet up on the edge of his desk.

"Alright, why don't you give me their names and the numbers," Phil said, finally sounding serious.

Noah read the list and for the most part the constable didn't have to ask Noah to repeat anything. This time he heard the sound of what he was saying being written down. And he was glad.

"Can I tell you something, Noah? *Can* I call you Noah, Mr. Asheborne?"

"Sure," he paused, "to both."

"Okay, Noah. What I'm going to do is promise you that I'm going to look into this and do the best I can to discourage it from happening again. Now I'm not telling you that there is anything okay with what's happened out there, but I feel that I should let you know that this is, unfortunately, pretty typical behavior. Even tourists and campers get it."

"You're kidding?"

"I'm afraid not. Now if it isn't any of the people you mentioned, it's going to be one of their friends or neighbors doing it. They want to think they are doing people favors. Superstition is reality to some of these people. And there is this belief that any white people around here are going to be murdered by evil spirits. The fact of the matter is that we live in a pretty rough country and people go out and explore it. Accidents happen out there and it's pretty darn likely for them to be nasty. People have accidents at home too and *all of these* are blamed on evil spirits."

Noah sighed, "Okay, so what do I do?"

"I just want you to know that they don't mean you any harm. They just have a shitty, excuse me, *poor* way of sharing their superstitious concerns with people."

"So what you're really telling me is there's nothing you can do and not to worry because they have good intentions?"

Then it was Phil's turn to sigh, "I will do what I can to discourage it. I already promised that."

Noah nodded angrily and took the moment to see what David was doing. He was getting dressed.

He couldn't take the chance that David would overhear, so he didn't ask if there was any truth to there being a lot of caucasian people dying in Nibebiitam.

"And there's no doubt in your mind that these accidents aren't caused by these misdirected Good Samaritans?"

The constable hesitated and sighed harder. The chair complained again as its safety was compromised.

"I'd be a fool to exclude anything as a possibility, but I can tell you that none of the accidents we've seen have looked like the work of people."

"Okay. Well I'll appreciate anything you can do to resolve this. And sooner than later. I don't want my kid catching wind of any of this crap."

"I understand," the constable sounded genuine.

Noah hung up and passed the weight from his shoulders to the hands he clamped on his sides.

"I hope so," Noah said to no one. He crumpled the list and threw it away.

He also hoped he'd be able to do some writing. Maybe he'd start a new story. One about a town misfit who is pranked by any number of bastards in town and goes on a killing spree. The misfit, who never got anything other than nasty phone calls, would track his first victims down by the numbers left on his phone.

"If this was the 80's maybe it would have made a good movie," he muttered to himself.

"What're we gonna do for lunch?" David hollered.

"What do *you* want to do?" Noah asked. He wasn't sure if he answered loud enough to be heard.

"Burgers," David answered matter-of-factly.

Noah tapped his pen on the empty tablet, feeling there was something he wanted to write down. He looked up from the paper as the six-year-old reached him. Gilder was beside him. Both had mooching looks on their faces.

"I think we can do that," Noah decided. The pen hit both ends before it lay flat on the pad of paper. "For now, why don't you worry about what kind of cereal you're going to have?"


Despite how the day began, by lunchtime Noah was in high spirits. He got a phone call from Derrick. They had a nice talk, and while it no longer affected him, Noah didn't mind getting the latest gossip from work. He hoped to stay in touch with many of the people anyway.

After getting off the phone, he was ready for that burger too. David had been ready all day. Gilder was ready, but Gilder was always ready to eat.

Feeling up for the drive, Noah decided they'd check out a restaurant in Kapuskasing this time. David had been itching to run around after no more than a minute or two in the truck and then didn't want to leave it when they got there.

"Can I just wait out here?" David wondered boredly. He squatted to test a pebble to see if it made marks on the sidewalk.

Reflexively Noah wanted to say, "No." But this was Kapuskasing, not New York, and if it would be fine *anywhere* it would be here. He needed to make himself relax, because he needed to be able to enjoy how good life could be here.

"Stay *right here*."

"Don't forget what I want," the boy called after.

To prove he didn't forget, Noah recited what they agreed: a Happy Meal and a special dessert if they didn't have one. They *wouldn't* have a Happy Meal because this wasn't McDonald's, but David insisted there might be something like it here, but a Canadian version.

As he entered, Noah scanned the dessert counter for something David would like.

"*Everything*," he muttered.

The servings of take-out burgers and fries were half the size they served at the diner in Nibebiitam, but still plenty. He balanced the drinks, bag with the meals, and a clear plastic container with a huge slice of apple pie *a la mode*, and pushed open the door.

"Look what I found in the dumpster!" David exclaimed.

Already horrified, Noah looked just in time to see David stuff the last portion of a burger into his mouth and rifle again through the crumpled bag he clutched.

"Drop it!" Noah yelped, louder than he meant to.

David's hands jumped away and raised them level with his shoulders. The bag fell to the ground.

"David! What were you thinking?"

"I was hungry and it smelled good and someone wasted their food!" David explained in a high, pleading voice.

"You know better than that."

"Homeless people eat it and they don't die."

Noah stared dumbly at the child for at least three minutes.

"Throw that bag away, because you're already nasty. Don't touch *anything else* until I get the hand-wipes."

"Oh-Kay!"

"Okay your butt back here before I reach the truck."

"You bet!"

"You bet," Noah echoed under his breath. Then he wretched a little at the thought of the partially eaten burger. He thought of teeth clogged with bun and meat and that the fringe of every new bite being rimmed with this stranger's saliva softened dough— and it going into his baby's mouth.


They agreed, on the way to town, that they would go to the city park to eat lunch.

They loaded into the truck. Gilder and David squeezed into the small seat behind the front seats. The meal got shotgun. Noah bought a newspaper out of the machine by the restaurant and the food and drinks sat on top of it.

The park was perfect, the special way that most city parks are. Noah was hoping there would be a few kids around, but they had the park all to themselves for the moment.

While David ate and shared with Gilder, his father was completely absorbed in a newspaper that made him feel really stupid for thinking David was okay to be left alone outside the restaurant. After reading about the librarian in nearby Hearst that was killed during a robbery. Even though it happened at night by a known criminal with a drug habit, even though the guy was now dead—having tripped, apparently and landed on the same knife he'd used moments before to slay the librarian. It was unnerving.

Noah found the sound of perking coffee in the bottom of the fast food cup. He shook the 24 oz. cup, half-full of ice, and tried again for just a sip's worth to try and clear the film from his dry mouth.

The paper said they thought the mugger might have also been responsible for killing Angela Cleary, a babysitter, and the toddler she was watching, in a separate botched robbery earlier that week. On the next page were updates on another murder. It looked like they arrested the son-in-law of that old lady who was killed last week. The people, who the suspect worked with, at the paper mill near Kapuskasing said he was a gentle human being and refused to believe he could hurt anyone. According to neighbors in Nibebiitam, the guy sounded like he was no good anyway. That he was controlling and abusive—even to his elderly mother-in-law who was "allegedly blind".

That comment struck Noah as odd.

*Was she or wasn't she?*

The article made Noah wonder how many "no goods" were around here. Was it like those stories he heard about people living in Alaska all being drunks and suicidal? Was that what northern Ontario was like?

Derrick told him that a lot of these small towns couldn't afford to have their own Municipal Police Force, but not to worry because Nibebiitam did. At first Noah was comforted.

Now he was concerned. Obviously the people were willing to put up more money to have police right there. He wondered why.

Noah wasn't feeling very good about the constable's assurance that the people calling the house were good intentioned people going about things the wrong way. He'd be calling a locksmith first thing when they got home.

◆          ◆          ◆

Because it made him feel better earlier, Noah also gave Derrick a call when they got home.

Derrick wanted to talk about a quickie he'd acquired during his lunch break.

Noah was always somewhere between impressed and disgusted by what Derrick was able to accomplish sexually. Sometimes he didn't mind hearing all the raunchy details. A lot of the time he felt wrong hearing the specifics. Derrick used to always press for information about the sex between Noah and his ex, Terri. Citing how bangable she was. Then after David, how she'd become such a MILF. They actually had a pretty nasty fight about it one time when Noah got sick of saying "no".

There was something sacred about being a wife and a mother that Derrick didn't appreciate. And before she was Noah's wife and the mother of his child, she was his first love. So their relationship was always too sacrosanct to discuss like porn.

"So Derrick," Noah interrupted, "Nibebiitam is so small, why do they need their own Municipal Police? Kapuskasing is close and they have their own OPP station, or office, or whatever."

"You're at the end of the earth, buddy. A lot of people go up there to test themselves against nature. A lot of people go up there to go camping, hunting, fishing, all that outdoor crap. There are a lot of people from out of town here and there throughout the year. Accidents happen. And, even though Kap's close, you'll find out that the people of Nibebiitam like to take care of things themselves."

Noah nodded throughout his friend's explanation.

"Do you think you can get that investigative reporter friend of yours in Connecticut to look into some things for me? Umm, what was her na—Kendal. Do you think she would mind doing a little freelance work for me? I'm gonna do some footwork on my own during lunch breaks, but she was pretty damn good at her job, as I recall."

"If you mean blowjobs!" Derrick laughed, "Okay, okay. Sure thing. I'll tell her to get ahold of you and send you her digits just in case she forgets. But I don't think she forgets anything."

Noah made sure David was out of earshot before replying, "If you mean blowjobs, I'm sure she'd rather forget."

Derrick chuckled. He never seemed to take anything sexual personally. As Noah recalled, Kendal didn't really either. So perhaps in this case, no harm no foul.

"What do you know about these delinquent children that, according to my aboriginal neighbors, are intent to drive all white people out of the area?"

Derrick laughed in a way that suggested he'd heard a lot about this before.

"Wait until you hear about Nibebiitam's alternative church if you think those reds are disturbing. They just *want their land back*," he finished the last sentence in a slow drawly voice that he used whenever he was mocking something he thought was stupid.

"What happened to the last person who lived in—"

"Crap," Derrick interrupted. "I have a business call on the other line. You're lucky you don't have to do the nine to five grind like the rest of us suckers."

Noah detected a hint of irritation similar to what he'd heard when they'd talked the first day at the house.

He didn't know how to respond to it.

"Okay, so—"

"You're going to see the school soon, right?"

"We—"

"Have a good time."

Then the line went dead.

Noah sat his phone on the counter and sighed. He didn't feel any better.

The house phone rang.

"Can I answer it?" David asked loudly.

His daddy leaned in and looked at the caller ID, there had been a lot of strange phone calls. He didn't want his son hearing any of that bullshit.

"Sure kiddo."

The six-year-old lunged onto the chair by the counter and picked up the phone. Maybe it was mommy.

David recited what he was taught to say when he answered the phone. His disappointment was obvious even before he said, "It's for you, dad."

"Thanks sweetheart," Noah rumpled the head of curls as it passed and held it still long enough to embed a kiss in it.

"Hello?"

"Hi, Noah?" a woman's voice responded. "This is Rising Moon. I just wanted to see how you're liking the truck?"

Noah smiled and said how much David liked it and reaffirmed how good it would be on winter roads.

"Yeah, once you find something that works, stick with it. My dad drives this rust-bucket he calls a pick-up. He says it's been loyal to him so he's loyal to it."

"Your dad? Is your family from Kapuskasing?" he wondered because she seemed to have connections there.

"Her daddy's in charge of the police," David informed. He was laying on Gilder who was laying on her side, like a black letter "n". Mama Cat waddled past and David did nothing to protect his face from her butt as it glided past it. He noticed a piece of grass sticking out of it and snickered.

"Phil?" Noah asked David.

"You know him?" Rising Moon, thinking he was talking to her, was only half surprised.

"Only in passing."

David listened to the conversation for as long as he could stand before it was just too boring. He had more important things to do and think about. Like when he was going to see his new school for the first time.

Even as the boy busied himself with toys and things, after Gilder couldn't stand the kid laying on her anymore, he was well aware of when his dad laughed, and sometimes caught him smiling. He was aware of how long the conversation lasted. That his daddy didn't end the call even while he took care of things around the house, like starting dinner, doing dishes and tidying up things here or there.

# *WAYSIDE*

The old yellow light above the four gas station pumps offered little to combat the moonless night encroaching on the space big enough only for four vehicles. Anyone pumping gas on the side nearest the road would be mostly submerged in darkness.

Mary Lynn had been battling with her bladder for the past forty minutes. Back then, she was telling herself she wouldn't have any trouble getting home before she'd need to go. With still twenty miles left on her journey, the painful jiggling in her tight, swollen bladder was starting to feel like death more than just wet pants. To cope with it, Mary Lynn rocked, wiggled, and bucked in the seat—moves she joked to pass the agonizing minutes, she might do well to remember the next time she saw her boyfriend.

Whipping her vehicle into the first gas station she saw, and the last she knew of before the outskirts of town, Mary Lynn parked under the dimly lit walkway at the side of the station entrance because the restroom was around back—a necessary courtesy for visitors and residents living in the middle of nowhere.

Every step she took made her aching bladder jump, the fluid slosh inside.

"Oh God, oh God-oh God, oh God, oh God," she groaned the mantra almost exactly the way she had been an hour and a half ago when she was still at her boyfriend's.

A forty-watt bulb, that even moths and mosquitos weren't interested in, was perched above the blue restroom door. It was open half-way and so she burst into the closet sized room, slapping on the switch to the fluorescent light over the sink. It buzzed and flickered stubbornly before lighting as much as it was going to. Mary Lynn's eyes already locked on the toilet and wasn't afraid of having to do her work in the dark.

Her left hand reached absently behind her to pull the door shut and hooked her fingers into the rough cavity of where the knob was supposed to be.

"What?" she whined incredulously. A semi-curtsey allowed her to spy out into the nearly pitch blackness.

A printed note taped to the door explained why:

*"In honor of our visiting fecalphiliacs (shit artists) who tried in vain to protect their paintings by locking the door when they finished, it is with deepest regret that we can no longer permit the locking of facility doors, lest the thoughtful and less evolutionarily challenged patrons of this service station be denied their own time to create here.*

*If anyone knows the identities of the stinky finger painters, please inform the clerk right away—we want only to formally thank them and make sure they are rewarded for the creation of art that so easily invoked such strong feelings in visitors and patrons alike. "*

*Please use "Courtesy Cup" to plug the hole.*

Mary Lynn stared dumbly at the orange plastic cup hanging from a hook by the door.

There was poop in it.

"Oh—*whatever!*"

The thirty-nine year old woman yanked her red and white knit scarf off and threaded it through the latch hole, tying that end to the door and the other to one of the pipes below the sink. Her neck was still burning while she urgently clawed through her bag for the travel-sized pack of tissues she kept handy. The wad filled the hole well enough—not that she was really worried someone was out there at this hour—at the moment she honestly didn't care.

The restroom wasn't exactly clean, but she'd used worse when she didn't have to go as bad. Ordinarily Mary Lynn would have laid out a barrier of t.p. on the seat—at the moment she honestly didn't care about that either.

The rush of piss and contact with the seat happened simultaneously. As the pressure was dying, she read the sign again and shook her head.

"I'm sure the artists appreciate the 'courtesy'," she snorted.

*Why didn't they just buy a knob that doesn't lock?*

"Cheap bast—"

WHAM! WHAM! WHAM!

A small squeaking scream jumped into her mouth.

"It's occupied!" she yelped.

No answer.

*Duh,* she thought when about fifteen seconds passed without another knock.

Pretty much the only people out at this hour were cops—it was too late even for drunks—so she hoped constable Do-Right was embarrassed.

The tissue made a short whispering sound as it was poked out of the hole. Even though it took nothing to evacuate the opening, the finger shoved all the way through.

It was big enough to fill the hole.

Then it was yanked back into the black oblivion on the other side.

A bigger scream froze in her throat—her eyes saucers of fear rounded disbelief.

She wanted to get up, even as she hadn't wiped—at the moment she honestly didn't care, but she was afraid to expose herself by standing. Mary Lynn leaned forward so her sweater and coat fell over her knees and shimmied her tight jeans up her thighs.

Then something else started to come through the hole—it reminded the poor petrified woman of a home video of a birth, but within seconds of it crowning through the void it was clearly inhuman—except, perhaps, in its choice of skin.

Mary Lynn didn't dwell too much on the matter of what exactly the toothy, veiny thing was oozing through the impossibly small opening—at the moment she honestly didn't care.

# CHAPTER 8

◆

# VENDETTA

Mama Cat lay on the edge of the sun-warmed gravel road. Her fur was tinted with the dust of the fine dirt she'd been sporadically rolling in between naps and batting or twitching flies off her perpetually animated and permanently kinked tail.

She gazed lazily past the ditch and at the front yard where dog and boy rushed purposelessly around on grass that was still a little too cool and wet for her standards.

Upon the first vibrations of an approaching vehicle, her eyes narrowed with annoyance—she waited until the last minute before waddling into the ditch.

The man kept the grass short, but even so, she felt confidently concealed when she'd laid out at flat as possible.

The boy kept her up last night wanted to play with and pet her, but he had no interest in playing with her now. Her tail swished jerkily, like a fisherman's rod. She'd claw him if he tried to play with her now.

Not just out of spite, this time, but because she didn't have time.

*They* were there. The most horrific and annoying creatures—children who always want to play.

Mama Cat flexed her paws in a passively threatening way, the curved, pin-like nails cresting dangerously past the short brown and white fur. As predators they were nearly matched and both already knew too well that killing the other wouldn't be easy.

Because of *them* her people up and left so fast they never spared a single thought to where she was or even that she was. Because of them she—

David watched Mama Cat dart like a grey hound around the opposite side of the house—she was out of sight before the reeds in the ditch stopped wobbling. Mama Cat was hunting—she only took off like that when she was after a squirrel, bunny, or other varmint. Something was in trouble.

The child took off in the other direction, hoping if she caught a bunny it would be alive to pet and play with a little.

She was on the back steps, facing down the children, with a snarl pulled back on her teeth that sent ice through David's veins.

Suddenly her front legs were flapping, claws flying on paws that looked like little catcher's mitts, like when Gilder goes after her cat food or even Gilder's own food, if Mama Cat wants it—then the cat sped off again. It didn't look like her feet touched the ground until she reached the edge of the back yard.

David didn't notice the grass part in front of the scruffy tabby stiffly standing her ground.

He didn't see the tall line of raised fur down the middle of the black dog's back or hear the low rumble of her growl.

# CHAPTER 9

---◆---

# PREY OF THE SPIRITS

The records office was a harmless looking building. It, like the few other businesses or offices in Nibebiitam, appeared to have been a house first.

That made sense, Noah thought, raising his gloved hands to blow heat through them, there was a time when all the business was in the woods or underground. That left just a lot of houses in what would someday be the sleepy center of an isolated little town.

Why, Noah wondered, was it taking so long to make himself go in?

He found himself looking over his shoulder, up and down the sidewalk, feeling like he shouldn't be there. Feeling like everyone in town was watching or would soon know he was there and why. It seemed really likely that someone would show up and exclaim in joy that it was him, stranger or no, and invite him to the diner to talk about things that would subtly make him feel it was futile or foolish to be interested in all those stories, in all those "accidents".

The collar of his jacket scratched at his chin as it dipped behind the coupled zipper and flapping second layer with velcro closures. The gloves, with a newly frosted patch from his breath, were driven into his pockets forcefully. The morning's were getting cold. There was almost no growing season, Jacob told him. This morning it was thirty-three degrees.

"Just go," he muttered.

His brown eyes swept left and right for the last time. Someone was walking this way and anything but moving looked too suspicious, but part of him wanted to be heading back to the truck, not *there*.

A brass curl bounced when the door below brushed it. The small gold bell in its center rang like a threat delivered with a smile.

"Be right with you," a woman called from the back.

Noah pulled off his gloves and rumpled his cold stiffened hair with his empty hand. He guessed it probably wasn't totally dry from his shower.

The foyer was lined with, he thought, very old wallpaper. The kind painstakingly reproduced in classy Victorian style homes that never quite look authentic. The processes of producing them were probably a lot different, he assumed, but there was something unique to the look, feel, and even smell of old wallpaper. The yellowing effect of age, cigarettes or sunlight gave it character. There were a lot of old photographs hung along the walls and behind them, he ventured, perhaps a glimpse nearer to what the paper looked like originally.

The rug too had once been beautiful, but long abused by traffic and what the traffic brought in on their feet. The grayish, washed out path showed the favorite courses of visitors to this office and perhaps even whatever it was before that, if the rug was part of the deal.

To the right a stairway swung sharply and steeply behind a wall. To the left, the former parlor, was the office, as labeled by the handwritten sign slipped in a protective three-ringed plastic sleeve.

It pained Noah to clear his boots, of whatever dirt or grime they brought in, on that old rug. He hated to contribute to its wear.

He was putting the gloves in the left pocket of his coat when he went into the office where there was more wallpaper, some curling and with a little water damage, and more old rugs. The lighting wasn't original, but the old fittings for gas were left up, just painted over.

The reception desk in the service area looked like the counter of an old bar—

*Maybe that's what this used to be.*

—and a painted wall screamed out from behind cream colored towers of file cabinets, "I don't belong here!"

The rounded shape of a butt under a flowery dress swayed gently back and forth as the owner of both fingered through the bottom of a drawer, by the sighs, with little success in finding whatever she was looking for.

"That's not a good way to start the day," Noah tried to sound like sunshine and smiled toothily.

*Too toothily.*

His lips closed over his teeth, but without ruining the smile.

"Oh goodness gracious!" the elderly woman blustered, spinning away from the drawer. She looked horrible, in fact, and made Noah feel bad about trying to make light the apparent predicament.

"I'm sorry," he blurted.

The woman stared at him for a few moments. A look of recognition pulled up on her eyebrows and she quickly banished as much of the panic from her features, but her eyes still looked worried and perhaps fearful.

"You must have lost something important," he tried to sound concerned, but he was looking at the keys dangling from the open drawer and had a gut feeling it was not the kind of place things get misplaced from.

"Not really," she said earnestly, but with obvious frustration.

"I think Nibebiitam must have elves. I can't believe how things around my place have this way of growing feet," Noah chuckled. He watched her cool blue eyes steadily, even as he worked up what he thought was a dopey smile.

She laughed in a high forced way.

*They must not be used to having to lie about it,* Noah thought, nodding unconsciously to himself, and smile falling away without noticing.

"So what can I do for you this morning?" the woman said brightly.

"Yeah, I was looking for local periodicals..." he'd decided last night that would be the least alarming of the records he was hoping to look at on this visit.

"Sure. Sure," she agreed, in a unique bastard of accents, and came out from behind the desk. "From when, dear?"

"All of them," he tried not to sound too serious.

"Whatever for?" she wanted to know, but clearly tried not to sound too serious either.

"I love old periodicals. I was hoping to find some old photos to maybe enlarge and use for art in my house," he felt smooth and believable.

"If you like old photos you should invest some of that time on this floor. Got a whole lot of them on display," she gestured left and right as she led him down the hall with deliberate slowness.

"What's this place?" Noah pointed to a comparatively larger and somewhat over-exposed photograph of a great old Queen Anne style house backed by a curtain of tall black pines.

"That's the Melnyk house. He was a dentist," she said proudly. "Not one of our founders, but he helped make this mining settlement into a real town. Brought it sophistication."

"Why did he come all the way up here?" Noah asked absently as he admired the fine work of the architecture and character of the old dark photo.

"Invested in the mines and even though he had no need to work and was certainly old enough he might as well not have, he was a generous man and offered his professional services at little cost."

"An early health plan for the miners," Noah mused with an easy smile.

The clerk beamed.

"What was his name?"

"Doctor Oleksandr Melnyk."

"Wow, that's beautiful," he remarked again of the house and stood back from it. "Is it still standing?"

Her thinning dome of white and gray hairs wobbled as she nodded.

"*Oh* yes."

"I'll have to check it out sometime. So where can I find those periodicals," he pressed gently to see the disappointment settle on her face like a child finding out there's no Santa Claus.

"Of course," she said briskly and led him to the basement where the door was tied to a solidly fixed hook on the stairwell wall.

"It must like to close on its own," Noah remarked as he followed her down the worn spots in the brown painted steps.

"Uh…Yes. The building leans a little, I think," she answered.

He observed the fairly new hardware on the door and couldn't help but wonder if it had trouble with locking itself too.

"Here you are Mr. Asheborne," she was standing in front of the wall of bound periodicals conveniently located nearest to the stairs and within view of anyone standing at the top of them.

"Mind you we had a fire," she said apologetically, sort of.

"Of course," he said without surprise. "That's a shame. I bet a lot of other records were damaged too."

"Regretfully yes."

He looked over the bindings, his curiosity tempered by his resentment at being treated like an idiot.

"Has this always been a records office?"

"It's served as a courthouse too," she chuckled. "You'd never believe what it was before all that."

"A bar," he guessed, rolling his sparkling brown eyes in her direction.

She sounded surprised when she told him he was right.

"I heard you were a bright one," she remarked.

He had an impulse to say, "I wouldn't forget it."

"The building seems to have survived the fire pretty good," he commented absently while absorbing the complete absence of any fire damage.

"It was an isolated fire," she supplied quickly.

"It looks like even the old bindings held up," he observed, running one hand down the old, mildewy spine of the earliest collection. "Nineteen...," he squinted and tilted the heavy binding, "Nineteen thirteen. That's got to be about as old as Nibebiitam."

"It was officially founded in 1913, but it was settled in 1853. You will find fire damage inside ones where the oil lamp turned over and lit them."

"So how did the other records get burned?"

He avoided looking at her that time, wishing he hadn't had to be such a smart ass, wishing he had just let her keep lying, like he already expected her to.

"Please don't shut the light off when you come up," she sounded like a commercial. "There might be other people down here."

He wanted to ask how she couldn't know if there was, but he supposed there could be other staff working on things... like running lighters along the edges of pages they tore out.

"Is there a place where I can work down here?"

"There are tables in the study upstairs."

Noah spun on one heel slowly, taking in the rest of his surroundings for the first time. The rows of file cabinets and shelves of folders fanned out from the wall of periodicals, wasting a lot of space, if you asked him. It seemed strategically arranged that a person need only rotate to see to the end of every aisle. He didn't see how he couldn't realize if someone else was down there.

It seemed pretty inconvenient to bring the heavy articles up and down the stairs to wherever the study was, but they clearly didn't want or expect people to look—every record in this basement was there just in case someone did look. Just in case someone did say, "I'm looking for the death certificate of my great-great uncle Waldo Woodcutter." or "I'm looking for articles about our very earliest lacrosse team." They had to keep up appearances or else suffer the interest of a scrutinizing mind.

"Fantastic, thanks," he said, pretending to already be absorbed in just reading the dates on them.

"Sure thing dear, see you soon."

"Yep."

Noah knew she would look back before she left, maybe on the stairs or at the top of them, so he wouldn't let himself watch her go or look to see if she had really left. Instead he waited, struggling to open and cradle one of the massive volumes to look as if he was just giving them an unparticular look over—just for pictures—and spending some time admiring any picture he found that wasn't just a portrait. Only then did Noah raise his head, focused on looking like he wanted to ask her something, and saw the stairwell and doorway empty.

He propped the volume on the floor, against the shelves and moved into the nearest aisle. He was looking for death records, police or court records and was pretty sure they would be in a locked room on another floor, but discovered that he wouldn't even know if he was looking right at them. The files, the shelves, everything was coded. For all he knew they could have had one death record slipped into every 121.03S-T folder so that they would know where to look for it and no snoop would ever have time or go through everything. On the other hand, Noah reasoned, there really had to be a normal looking system too, so not to draw suspicion.

It was the deeply seeded locals that seemed to have the secrets to keep and all the others had the stories to tell. There were people in Kapuskasing with relatives in Nibebiitam that would have a much more legitimate reason to come looking. People don't like conspiracy and so pick up on even the possibility of shady dealings so keenly that a lot of the time the treachery is not only fake but completely implausible—that is, to anyone but those who faithfully believe in it.

Noah randomly pulled a drawer in a cabinet.

"Deeds…" he muttered and closed it silently. His sight barely cleared the top of the cabinet, but saw a portion of a door that was all but hidden, especially standing at the bottom of the stairs, because it was underneath them.

"Records," he read the chipping black letters on the door painted to match the wall around it. He didn't think it was a tongue-in-cheek, roll your eyes label, but the entrance to an older portion of the storage area. Maybe even the original place, when it was sometimes used as a courthouse.

He was hardly surprised to find it locked.

Just then he heard a creak on the hallway and returned to the periodical mere seconds before the tan hushpuppies with sagging violet socks reached the top of the stairs.

"Everything alright down there Mr. Asheborne?"

"Oh yeah," he said in a cheerful and dismissive way, "I just want to find something promising before I start however many hours' worth of step aerobics."

Her snicker carried eerily down the echo fertile stairwell.

There was no way, to know which volume, if any, would have the kind of information he was looking for. The fact was that Noah probably would have to spend the whole day making trips, trying to sound ignorant and enthusiastic about old snapshots of storefronts and smiling strangers. The first volume was where he left it and the best place to start.

"I'd love if I could see some of the old birth and death records," he said when the last of the stairs were behind him, the clerk was, of course, waiting.

"What on earth for?" she tried to sound casual and discouraging—she was really saying, "Isn't that just the silliest thing? Oh the things you crazy young people get into! You don't want to do that! You don't."

"I have some relatives from the area and I was curious if they ever lived here. I'd love to know there were more than fur traders and coopers in my family," a handsome smile spread with undetectable force across his stubbly face.

"Oh, no Asheborne's ever lived *here*," she dismissed.

"No, the MacPherson side," he thought he remembered reading they were a notable family in, at least, the Kapuskasing area. This notion was verified by the way her face went blank and she stammered for the right dissuasion.

"Well, not just anybody can view those kinds of records."

"But death records are public," he began to protest, trying to sound half-hearted.

"Not in Canada," she contradicted, eyes narrowing triumphantly.

"Really? Because where I worked before I had to request vital records from Canada all the time and no one ever said anything like that. Geez," he scratched his chin with his left hand, while the other was working on going completely numb with the weight of the book on them. "Hmm… what a bummer? My buddy in the RCMP said I should think about looking into those records since I was here. My family in the states didn't keep a lot of those records themselves. I'm surprised he would have told me I could if they weren't public."

"Well, a body doesn't think of those things unless they get stuck in the red tape themselves," she tutted and smiled stiffly. He was starting to really dislike Ms. No-Name-the-Liar.

Noah sighed helplessly, "I suppose I'll have'ta see if he wouldn't mind coming here himself to look at them for me."

Under her thin, loose skin, something hardened. Her sharp, careful eyes narrowed ever so slightly and relaxed.

"Well, if it's that important to you, I guess I can bend the rules, but I don't have the key. Lyle has it and he won't be in today."

Noah had a feeling there was no Lyle at all.

"I don't want to get you in trouble, I can just—"

"It's no trouble Mr. Asheborne," she smiled with both rows of removable teeth. Then she was moving to help an unreasonably handsome man who was waiting by the desk. The man didn't hide that he was listening to the exchange. Noah watched the clerk make eye contact with him and work herself into fairy-like cheerfulness.

"That was fast, Mr. Merchant, did you get what you needed?"

"It would actually help me a lot if I could get a photocopy of this instead of trying to do it right with pencil and paper," he held the folded sheet up to her. She said something like, "I see."

"The whole thing?" she asked loud enough that Noah could hear.

"Actually just this section," he flattened his hand across the face of what turned out to be a map.

"Oh, easy as pie. Will cost you ten cents?"

An easy chuckle carried before his answer, "I can handle that, ma'am."

"Alright then, it'll be just one second."

Then she hurried out of the room—she didn't just go quickly, she was hurrying to get back.

"I'd look in Kapuskasing," the man said as he went to retrieve his coat, long-sleeved shirt and sweater from one of the round study tables. The muscles in his strong shoulders made complicated pockets and strains as he raised his arms to pull the first layer over his t-shirt. Noah noticed an equally complicated watch and wondered if Mr. Merchant wasn't one of these survival junkies notorious for getting into trouble in the wilderness up here.

After all layers were applied he finally looked right at Noah, "Most news in Nibebiitam reaches Kapuskasing one or way or another, much to the chagrin of locals. You might look there. There's a museum and the papers themselves will probably have copies. They might not get as much information as people here, but it will be a hell of a lot more reliable."

"Why are you telling me this?" Noah wondered if he was being baited.

"Her b-s-ing you," the man shrugged.

"Do you live here?" Noah guessed not, thinking he himself looked more local than this guy—now anyway.

"Hell no," the stranger grunted, pulling together the last of his papers and stowing them in a pack. "Just thought at the last minute I better get some kind of map—a lot of people get lost up here."

"It seems that way—"

The clerk looked flushed and shone with fine perspiration as she flew into the room.

Mr. Merchant was ready, holding out the dime and with his thanks. He barely regarded her after and left the room.

"Strange man," she was shaking her head.

"Not from here?" he passed idly.

She answered, "Probably one of them hippies that isn't really from anywhere or everywhere."

"Probably," inside he was shaking his head, "You know, I think I'm just going to put this back—this is turning out to be a lot more work than I wanted to do."

"Pity," she crooned sympathetically. "I'll put that away for you then."

Noah thanked her and excused himself with a, "Have a good morning."

On the way out, he was looking at his watch and calculating how much time he could put in over at Kapuskasing. He was anxious to find out.

Noticing the empty street and remembering no other vehicles when he walked up, Noah wondered if there would be consequences for the stranger who stuck his nose in, if the clerk overheard—he worried there would be consequences for himself.

◆          ◆          ◆

There was no dread approaching the Kapuskasing Public Library. He found the deceptively over-scaled brick building, green roof and dark brown trim welcoming and home-like too. It, in fact, looked like a giant's house. He felt miniaturized approaching the entryway that was proportionate to the door that would have fit the scale of the building, but with normal sized glass doors set in the back of the entry—the *Alice in Wonderland* effect of that reached the child in him.

There were a few other visitors using the library that morning and between them and the staff he was only looked at twice before he reached the desk. There would be no "Mr. Asheborne" from strangers here, they didn't know, didn't care—it felt wonderful. It seemed like a long time since his business was *his* business.

"Excuse me, ma'a—" he read the stick-on name tag, privately resenting the clerk in Nibebiitam who was still nameless, "—Megan. I'm looking for periodicals. A lot of them. Old ones. The older the better."

The middle-aged woman smiled shyly at the attractive stranger who looked very serious.

"The publishers themselves, or maybe the museum, would be the best places to go for complete collections, records and really old pieces. I can show you what we have," she sounded apologetic and Noah cringed, "but then you're going to have to know better what you're looking for."

"Old local periodicals, ones that would cover Nibebiitam."

Megan laughed in amusement, "That narrows down your choices. You got us, Hearst, and Nibebiitam itself—not much to that one either. Most people in Nibebiitam read our paper. The writer or writers over there do short and sweet and not much meat, if you know what I mean."

"I think I do," he agreed.

"Something horrible happens over there and anyone else would write: 'Tortured Man Found Dead Hiding in his Oven'. In Nibebiitam you get 'Local Man (58) Dead'."

The librarian laughed.

Noah wanted to, but couldn't, even to be polite.

"Did that really happen?" his English accent injected its two cents.

They'd reached the archives then, she studied his face before replying somberly, "It did."

To accompany the Wonderland feel, he was once again in the land of giant books. He'd once seen a huge chair on the PBS series *Market Warriors* and he thought it an appropriate place to read books of this size if they had one.

"I don't even know where to begin," he didn't mean to say aloud.

"What sort of thing are you looking for?"

The picture excuse wasn't going to fly this time—Noah kind of enjoyed using it on the lying biddy before, but he wasn't sure about telling Megan the truth either.

"I'm pretty new to the area *and* Canada, for that matter. I'd heard a lot about those weird incidents and was curious what the papers said compared to the rumors I've been hearing."

"Have you straight up asked anyone there about them?"

"Not exactly."

"*Don't.*"

He was a little alarmed by how severe the word came out of her kind and motherly face. "People out there are superstitious as hell about any little or big thing that happens. They don't want people talking about it and yet there are others that will chew your ear off unraveling stories much bigger than what really happened. I think the middle ground is the truth and people need to realize that things happen and isolated living often carries a lot of risk—to safety and sanity."

Noah nodded and licked his lips. Even his tongue suddenly felt dry.

"So, any suggestions on where to begin?"

The librarian put her hands where her skirt choked the skin between her muffin-top and flared hips.

"*Anywhere*. It might be easiest to flip through Nibebiitam's *Gabekana Gazette* and then find the corresponding story in ours or Heart's."

*That made sense,* he thought and was nodding again.

"Okay, I'll see you sometime next year. Can I use my cell phone in here?"

"Sure thing dear, we'll page overhead when its closing time too. If you need one there are a couple pay copy machines in the main library. The one back here's broken. See us at the desk if you need change."

"Thanks Megan—oh," he extended a hand and shook hers. "It's nice to meet you. I'm Noah."

Her light brown eyes took in his face admiringly. She said it was nice meeting him too.

Facing the possibility people from Nibebiitam might use this library too, Noah was eager to find somewhere isolated to work. When Megan left, the only person in sight had her back to him, browsing the reference bookshelves. She didn't look like she was just pretending to be engrossed in her search so Noah assumed she probably wasn't Nibebiitam's version of a pod-person.

It was a good time to call Solomon and asked if he would watch David late, that he didn't know when he'd be getting home. It was okay.

*Nothing to stop me now.*

Only before opening the first volume did Noah take the time to like the way it smelled and felt—he liked the flaking glue like dead skin, that old yellowing tape with threads in it, the rough fabric binding often discolored by human oils or sunlight. Once he was looking, there was very little to enjoy in them. There was nothing to like about how he made notes so hard and fast, Noah thought he'd never be able to open his hands again—this was only after he used an obscene amount of change on photocopies and an obscene amount of trips to make them.

Noah realized he was right to be worried about who knew he was looking into these happenings, because they obviously invested a lot of energy in keeping it hidden from the rest of the world, even if they couldn't keep it hidden from Kapuskasing—no one here seemed all too excited about the frequent incidents, but Kapuskasing is a slightly older community and probably accustomed to the weirdness, dismissing a lot to coincidence, bad luck and eccentricity. The people in Kapuskasing were too sensible to believe the account of a person who says they were chased for three miles on their snowmobile by Bigfoot—any more than they believed it was anything but a lot of bored drunks who one night, coincidently, at almost the exact same time on different roads, decided to take dead runs out in front of passing cars. Ten people, eleven vehicles. Every one of them sprinting out into headlights at ten o'clock at night, give or take a minute. They were tested for drugs and alcohol—two of them were drunk. One of the drivers told the reporter that, just before the vehicle struck, the victim was looking over her shoulder and looked "…scareder than he saw a body in his life…".

There was the 1961 article about an "Unprecedented Decline in Missing Pets. What had changed, the reporter asked the constable of Nibebiitam:

"Most people aren't keeping pets anymore."

Then there was the man who was found dead in a field. About half of his bones were broken—that, the blood-spatter, and disturbance to the ground suggested he'd fallen from a great height. The last tree to ever touch that spot had been cleared almost eighty years before. There were no ladder impressions, even if there was a ladder out there somehow tall enough to inflict that kind of damage by falling from it.

They only found the body quickly because the afternoon before, right before sundown, the widow who owned the plot saw a man standing out in the field, holding partially open fists out from his sides and walking like a soldier, pulling his knees high—"…like he was taking steps…"—the widow said. Being alone, she was too afraid to confront the strange man and just prayed he would be gone by morning. Well after the sun was up, when she was satisfied he'd gone, the widow went out to see what he was up to… which literally ended up being the real mystery.

What was clear, however, was that he had been walking around in circles for hours.

The newspaper in Nibebiitam defamed the witness and said they knew the man to be a drunk and had likely been thrown by one of the logging trucks frequenting the road near the field. That he hadn't fallen anywhere, but prey to the evils of drink.

Noah didn't know why it, at first, surprised him that Nibebiitam should have its own coroner—who confirmed the death as a drunken traffic accident—any more than having their own police force—who put an APB out on the assumably damaged truck that allegedly struck him.

Unseasonable hypothermia was to blame for the six children who drown.

…a lot of heart-attacks in healthy people.

Silver in the mines kept people moving north—

…wild animals to blame for mangled hikers and campers.

Big timber, soaring economy, young people trying to have the good life—

…a person is found folded four times in and out of their wrought-iron front steps.

A huge hotel, hospital, and paper mill in reasonable driving distance—

…a mounted policeman leaves work fine and loses his mind by the time he reaches home.

Peace and quiet, the great outdoors—

…a family tacked to a dead tree's limbs like sticky-notes on a fridge.

Bear attack.

There is a point where the classifieds are twice as thick as the papers—

…lost…missing…

There was point where the ads were so few, it seemed like people stopped even bothering.

Megan tapped Noah on the shoulder—he was glad the scream went inward instead of out. He missed the page that the library was closing. He laughed it off and thanked her. It took a few minutes to put everything away and stow his things, for which he apologized then and on his way out.

"You're white as a sheet," she said, turning off the lights and locking the door behind them.

He felt cold all over, knotted inside, and probably was looking pretty shitty after that.

"Megan, how do you feel about the stories?" he was almost afraid to ask.

The librarian's narrowed eyes barely swelled open as her irises passed to the left and right. She leaned in and saying lowly, but not so that anyone who might be watching could tell a secret was about to be passed:

"When strange things happen in small towns—like alien or Bigfoot sightings, there is a collective strangeness about the communities—almost like reality denial, should their small town become despicably normal again.

"Sometimes I think when something strange happens that, even if they don't believe, they still tell everyone about it because they're afraid of that slim possibility it is true—as if talking about it now will make them more credible, should they ever actually witness it themselves. In their hearts, they probably all *know* the explanations make sense and that it isn't real, never was or will be. Holding onto the myth makes them special, like the tall-tales eccentrics conjure up for attention, even if it manifests itself negatively. The difference between being afraid it's true and *being* true is Nibebiitam."

Noah involuntarily shivered and rubbed it away quickly, hoping he just looked cold. The laugh or smile that suggested she was joking never happened. She waved goodbye solemnly with most of her left-hand fingers.

All he could do was smile and wave goodbye too.

Noah tried to dismiss how sincere Megan sounded—of course, if someone believes something they are going to sound sincere. But he didn't want to hear the bells toll "one less sensible person" in the wake of what could be a horrifying, community protected or orchestrated string of countless murders and attempted murders.

On the drive home, Noah was thinking about the death records and other relevant documents that he felt were being held just out of his reach. He didn't know what he was going to have to do if Kendal, his contact through Derrick, didn't come through for him. Calls would have to be made. Strings would have to be pulled. Favors might have to be called-in. It was evident to Noah, with the time he had, the volume of information to go through, regardless of the limited access to records, that he'd barely glimpsed the tip of the iceberg. There was a lot more going on here and he had to know it all—if that town was covering up murders…

He thought of the Sneider's and the jokes about them being devil worshippers.

"What are the chances that this small town is being influenced or intimidated by a cult?" he asked aloud as the truck door closed solidly beside him.

If the people of power in the community, the forestry and mining people, were behind all of it—that could make a lot of people tight lipped.

*A lot of people.*

# *EARLY BIRDS*

Beyond the heavy white breath of mooing cattle, an old farmer raised his head to face the forest beyond the pasture. Shimmering in dew, the still and beautiful woods shone with the soft pink and blue morning light.

The man craned his ear to the forest, the bow of his neck smoothing wrinkles on one side and gathering them on the other. He was hard of hearing, bawling cattle all around didn't help him hear any better either.

Paul thought he was so smart to get up early, get the cattle out to graze before his old lady even let her morning fart. Everything seemed to take so much longer, as they got older, that one simple joy they shared in life was competing to do things first, especially things neither one of them really wanted to do. He didn't especially want to get out of a warm bed to go stuff his feet in his crusty old boots and let out a bunch of fat cows into the cold wet pasture. Even though he was doing something he knew his biddy didn't want to do either, she would yell at him like he'd ruined something for her. It was their way of doing things for each other without being too sentimental about it.

Without being certain why, today Paul wished he'd just stayed in bed. Maybe in half an hour he'd have never heard *it*. Maybe in half an hour whatever it was would be long gone. Then he wouldn't be standing there shivering in his long underwear, thin jacket, and crusty boots wondering what the hell it was.

One gray and white eyebrow, like a scruffy furred creature, twitched as if *it* heard the sound too, but already knew what it heard, even while the seventy-eight-year-old, whose face it occupied, was still unsure.

The next time the old man heard the sound, he had to tell himself he heard wrong. He just needed to hear it again to be sure. Both eyebrows worked together to cut deeper furrows into the elderly brow. The first was twitching uncontrollably.

"You lollygagging?"

The old farmer cried out at the voice that arrived with the touch of a mittened hand. He laughed just as quickly, so it almost sounded like one sound.

His wife, whose hand held his forearm, laughed too, mostly at the sight of her poor hubby.

Standing their looking stupid, in his tattered plaid hunting jacket, with patches needing to be patched. Thin hair, that hadn't been combed in days, seemed desperate to escape from the sweat stained cap that was almost as old as the man wearing it. His skinny, turkey-like neck was stretched out like God was pulling his hair.

Paul's light gray-blue eyes pled for understanding that, over almost sixty years, he almost always found. He was about to speak, but her expression killed the words in his mouth. She saw the fear in his eyes and her love for him made her feel it too.

"Sweet Jesus, Paulie, you're white as a—"

Their faces jerked simultaneously to woods that no longer looked beautiful. In fact, it looked closer and darker and mean. It looked ferocious.

They heard it again. Closer.

A scream.

"Marta…" he croaked in the tight voice of a child.

The cattle fell silent and all at once charged back towards the barn instead of out to pasture where Paul was leading them.

"Paulie?"

His yellow work glove stabbed toward the ground ahead of them. Circling them, in grass otherwise shining with dew, were the impressions of at least a dozen sets of child-sized feet.

Neither Paul nor Marta knew if the other was first to share their scream with the morning.

About a mile down the little dirt country road, their friend and neighbor lifted his head, held his breath, and listened to hear if he'd really heard what he thought he heard.

# CHAPTER 10

◆

# LITTLE ONES

A damp basement smell surrounded David as he moved through a gray-green fog illuminated by a full moon too close and white to be real. That was when he realized it wasn't real, he was dreaming, but he didn't feel safe knowing it. He felt vulnerable. He thought about himself sleeping and was worried about his body. Something deeper than instinct told David if he got through this that everything would be okay, he just had to go. He wasn't sure where, but he also felt like he could only go forward.

The ground was deep and sticky with tar-black ooze. That was what was stinking. If earth could rot it would smell like this. The child was less afraid of what was in it than what was in the darkness around him, even though he sensed there were things in the muck.

"Where am I going?" he asked the nothing—maybe the consciousness that created the dream itself.

The consciousness answered only by making him feel like he had to move.

The fog thinned and the pervasive blackness took over the dreamscape before the little boy, as the moon had less of it to light. The ground thickened so much that David had to get on his hands and knees to crawl onto the harder surface. That was when he noticed that the blackness had a shape—and depth. It was a cave.

David woke up breathing like he'd run for miles. The hot quilts molded over him and a layer of sweat formed between himself and his pajamas, his pajamas and the quilt. His hair was damp and the small loose curls of dark brown hair were drooping. He flung the layers of bedding back and a wave of cold air replaced them. The floor was freezing, even through the feet of his jammies. If they had not been soaked with perspiration David would have dressed over them, like he'd planned. He quickly tore them off and tossed them aside like he'd pissed on them. He was glad those days were over or many times he'd have pissed himself these terrible sleepless nights.

He reached for a pair of red sweat pants, but his fingers curled into a fist before he touched it. Loose cotton was bound to snag on something. Jean was better.

The denim felt cold to the touch and cold to pull on over skin still hot from overheating. The elastic waist snapped softly around his middle. He never bothered to unbutton them. The gray and blue striped polo shirt went on quickly; the bottom, he tucked inside the waist of his jeans. His small denim jacket and shoes were by the door.

There was a chance of frost last night and he couldn't wait to know—no—he *needed* to know if what Fawn said was true. He told himself nothing would be there. At the same time he was really excited… anxious?

He couldn't wait to tell her he hadn't seen anything.

He knew a little bit about frost. He knew he had to get to it before the sun came up because it wouldn't take long after that before any evidence would be gone. It was already later than he would have liked. He *knew* it was later because of the color of the light coming through the curtains and he could hear his daddy in his bedroom—at the closet door. Then a drawer closed.

David stopped in the open doorway of his daddy's bedroom and watched him setting out his clothes.

"Up to no good?" his dad said with a knowing smile.

"No!" the small boy cried in false defiance—there was no point denying it.

"I'm gonna jump in the shower quick," Noah gave his suspiciously "already dressed" child a once over and added, "Stay in the house, okay?"

"But!"

"But what?" Noah asked absently as he slipped past David to grab a towel out of the closet.

"I need to see if there are tracks in the frost."

Why ask why some things are so important to children? Noah's smile sweetened and he hugged David with the arm not occupied with the towel.

"I'll make it quick. The frost will still be there when I get out. Okay?"

David considered this and smiled brightly, shiftily, as he agreed.

Noah closed the bathroom door and walked to the shower. As he passed the mirror he caught his own eyes and paused to look back.

"Yah, I know," he said to his reflection. He was pretty sure if he took the time to listen he'd hear the front door open in a minute or two.

He turned on the shower and undressed. The water drowned out the silence that would have told him David never made it to the door. It drowned out the sound of one desperate cry for "daddy" and the howls of a cat in pain.


Meanwhile, hot tears ran down David's cheeks. He wasn't sad. Only a little, *maybe*. He was scared or maybe just nervous. Definitely, he felt about a million things at once. He felt emotional and knew it could only be PMS.

The terrible yowls made the tears swell larger and run faster with each high pitched cry. The bloody orifice he watched yawned at him—something started to come out.

"Oh God! Oh God!" he prayed harder than he had in his whole life.

The small boy looked down the hall, panicking. Hadn't daddy said he was just going to have a quick shower? Why was it taking so long? He was too scared to leave her to go into the bathroom for his daddy. He didn't know what to do.

He didn't care about the frost—he would, in fact, forget about it for some time after this.

"Dear God!" David wept loudly.

The square of paper towel he ripped from the roll of Brawny—the most absorbent—lay like a catcher's glove in his right hand.

A small face pushed out of the gaping bloody cavern.

His stomach flipped. Despite himself he scooted closer. Something like slimy plastic wrap slipped off its tiny body as the newborn was passed with a rush of fluid and something like a relieved cry. Then it was cupped in his hands.

Snot, tears, and drool poured down David's face—he could hardly see or make sense of anything, but he wiped the baby dry—its face and ears, pear shaped body, small legs and short stiff tail. The cat was interested and licked the kitten to help clean it too.

"Oh Miss Mama Cat!" he wailed, laying it beside the first two. He felt so proud he thought he might split in two.

Another was coming—

"What's going on out here?" still dripping Noah left the bathroom, cinching the towel around his lean waist.

"Oh God," he said, before David could answer.

"She popped?" Noah asked with an easy smile and really, *really* tried not to laugh.

"Oh *God*!" David echoed, feeling this pretty much said it all.

"What do you think?" his daddy asked as he dropped to one knee beside the hastily improvised birthing room.

"Can we keep them *all*?"

Never before would Noah have considered having so many cats. But there was something kind of comforting about having more animals around. He liked the idea of it. Comforting wasn't the right word... he felt safer.

"Four kittens?"

"Five!" David's voice soared high.


When it was all said and done there were eight kittens, to what looked like eight different dads. It would be easy to remember which was which after David named them. At the moment there was only Adam, the first. It didn't matter if it was a boy or a girl. Gilder used to be Goldie, until David started talking and calling her differently.

The kittens monopolized David's attention. Noah had to threaten to "count" to make David come to the table for supper.

Noah praised every possible god when David agreed to let them put the kittens in the outbuilding around the left side of the house, close to David's bedroom window.

Mama Cat would want to hunt to feed them and it was better that she got used to bringing back little animals to the shed than bringing them in the house. Most of the time she wanted to be outside anyway. It was getting later in the year and Noah agreed to let the kittens live inside when it got really cold, but for now all of them would be happier this way.

"For now" was about as long as the happiness would last.

◆          ◆          ◆

Over the next couple days it was hard to keep David in the house, as he was always checking on the kittens and asking how long before their eyes would open. Noah didn't know. He thought it took a couple weeks. He didn't want to tell David how he kind of liked the kittens too. They were so cute and helpless and utterly perfect in their smallness, it was almost impossible not to care about them. He plucked at their stiff short tails as they fed, once when he brought a can of food out to the tired Mama.

David talked him into that, she ought to be spoiled because of everything she went through, and needed better food because she was feeding more than "just her own mouth" now.

So when the day to bring David to see the school and finish registering came, Noah was afraid he would get trouble from the kid about leaving the kittens.

Luckily, as with preschool and kindergarten, David was eager to go and socialize, for which Noah was always grateful. David regularly returned with excited stories about the culturally diverse kids he met—so here, Noah hoped, that too would be no different. David didn't care for being alone, craving the stimulation of others, so it was probably good that in not too long school would be starting and Noah was finally getting registration out of the way.

David would be getting a fix from the school environment, though devoid of children.

After filling out some paperwork, the efficient and very sweet middle-aged secretary pointed them to the principal's office.

The principal, Noah guessed was native, with high cheekbones and penetrating dark eyes. His grin brightened his whole face, lifting the cheeks impossibly higher and broader to display the biggest and whitest teeth Noah ever saw. The faux ivory bar resting on the front of the desk said Thom Redclaw.

"I've been expecting a visit from you Mr. Asheborne. I heard you had a son. I'm Thom Redclaw. Principal, Lacrosse coach, and casual bus driver—this town's too small to do anything less than multitask if you want to get things done."

"You can call me Noah. This is David. He's six."

David wanted to talk about the kittens.

"First grade, aye? And joining us all the way from New York. What in the world brings you to Nibebiitam?"

"Work," Noah answered flatly, feeling it flatly.

"A better job than in New York?"

"A more peaceful job, I hope. More time to work on my own projects and spend time with David."

"Your own projects? You're a writer, right?"

Noah nodded once. David nodded enthusiastically.

"I like Jules Verne and Isaac Asimov and don't read much else," Thom laughed. "But you must be somebody if *I've* heard of you."

"Thanks," Noah said dumbly. He never knew how to respond to people talking to him about his writing. He appreciated criticism, positive and negative, because he could do something with it. He didn't know what to do with "nice things" except pad his ego and he wasn't comfortable with that either.

"Can you tell us about David's class?"

"Sure. Mr. Han is the first grade teacher. Only person on faculty that doesn't work somewhere else during the summer."

"Most people would rather make money I guess."

The principal laughed loudly, "Are you kidding? Most people burn through every penny they make—bills evolve for it—most people can't afford not to work."

"Why's Han different?"

Mr. Redclaw sobered up with a sigh version of his last chuckles that died away as he wiped his eyes. "Han is a different kind of guy. In more ways than that. He's a good teacher, but he's murky. And he must be frugal. I wish I could answer your question. Maybe he saves up so he doesn't have to."

"Will I like him?" David piped in.

"Wouldn't you rather decide for yourself?" the principal asked.

David nodded, but inside he was thinking he wouldn't mind a little heads-up.

"This is a list of all the things David will need in his class and the calendar for the school year. They'll be mailed to you after this," Mr. Redclaw handed a folder with the Nibebiitam school logo—an arrow and leaves of some plant—on it. "You will have a little over a dozen kids in your class—"

"That's all?" David interrupted.

Thom Redclaw smiled, both father and son liked his smile—a smile that felt genuine. A smile that looked like it belonged to an honest man.

"That's all," the principal replied. "Is that okay?"

David smiled hard and looked at his dad, who was looking at him for the response.

"Dad, I'm gonna know *everyone* in my class."

"That's going to be nice," Noah said to both David and Mr. Redclaw.

It really could be nice here.


After talking a little while longer, the principal walked them to the first grade classroom. He showed David where he would hang his coat—adding, more to father than son, that a coat would be needed for most of the school year. He showed them the door in the classroom that opened to a bathroom, the large multi-stalled bathroom by the office, the lunchroom, the library, the gym, how to get back to the office, and asked David if he remembered how to get back to his class.

He did.

Once they got back in their truck, David started talking excitedly about the school, as if Noah hadn't been there. He pointed out things his dad hadn't bothered to notice. Like pictures he'd seen on the doors of other classrooms. Like what different things he saw in the playground. Like the stack of new books, that were "just like the books in New York" that were waiting for this years' students.

They stopped at the little grocery and convenience store in town because David just couldn't wait to get the things on his list. Noah might have ordinarily pressed the issue of patience, but if David was enthusiastic about school—he might as well fuel the flame.

It seemed, to Noah, that the community was either white or native, nothing else and little in between. He kind of had a feeling that this Mr. Han wouldn't fit in either category and he wondered if that might have something to do with feeling "murky".

"Colors?" David read.

Noah was already leading them to the aisle with all the pens, staples, glue, tape, and other inedible household things like light bulbs and plastic forks.

He stood back and let David grab items that were on the list and a few things David asked if he could have because he thought they could be useful. Why not, Noah figured, he could afford it and David hadn't asked for anything that actually wasn't useful. His son was happy. They were both happy.

This sense of contentment only lasted as long as it took them to reach the checkout.

While David laid out his supplies, most of what the list said he needed—they would go to Kapuskasing for the rest of it—an elderly white couple joined the line behind them. The old woman's face startled Noah because her eyes were so pale and the black specks of her irises looked so intense. Her wrinkles made her look mean and he was immediately overcome with the willies.

Like the antique teller, in the only other lane was doing to the person she was ringing up, the old couple started to ask Noah things that were none of their business. And in voices that might only be described as obnoxious:

"Why are you buying those?"

"Where do you work? Do you make good money?"

"I think I've heard of you. New fella. Haven't seen you in town. Are you a God-fearing man?"

"Are you alone? Where's this little dear's mommy?"

"Is he your son?"

"Where are you from? Where do you live now? Is it just the two of you?"

"Do you go to church? You probably wouldn't like the one here—" and the wife wrinkled her nose at the air in what, Noah assumed, was the direction of the church "—but there is a community of aware people who hold services down on Maple Street. I think that would suit you *perfectly*."

When Noah had tried to answer, or deflect, their first question, he could tell that the young woman behind the counter wanted to say something but couldn't. He understood, he couldn't say anything either. The young man could hardly concentrate on their questions, which had barely a pause between them, and had almost fused the gnawing sound of their interrogation with the similarly nosey questions from the next lane. Even if Noah wanted to respond, he wouldn't have been able to get a word in. He did want to say things, but they weren't very nice.

The teller, her tag said "Cassie", managed a, "You have a good day, now" as she finished ringing them up.

They'd try.

◆          ◆          ◆

Noah refilled his cup from the teapot and put the spent teabag into the fresh water. He laughed as Derrick carried on about some of the odd white folks he'd met when he was visiting his uncle.

"I might know the people," Noah said, still chuckling. "I don't think they've changed a bit."

David was stupefied that his daddy was meeting people he wasn't. Even though he was being watched at Solomon's, in his heart, he assumed his dad wasn't doing anything but what he'd done that first day of work.

"Jacob tells me how the Sneider's are so concerned and always trying to help out. Of course, they really just want to know what's going on in people's lives. They have their own church in a basement. Did he tell you that?" Derrick continued. Noah shook his head and sipped the tea as he listened. "She's got these bugged out blue eyes that are just a little too pale and this smile that, with a few more stains, would make a smile from Pennywise look sweet. Do you remember Pennywise?"

"Yeah."

"So she always wants to know who people are when Jacob has company and brings him stuff she thinks he can use and is always telling him these personal private things about other people in their 'congregation' and turns around and tells him that he *has to* come sometime. Uncle Jacob has the good sense not to go. Who makes up their own religion? I think there's some business law statute of limitations if you want to be considered anything but eccentric. And it's been up for a *long* time with those freaks."

"Personally I think they're a cult," Noah said seriously. "I hate when people are creepy and intense like that. I catch myself wanting to call her Minnie Castavet."

"Minnie Castavet looked like a transsexual," Derrick corrected, "The old guy looks like that Russian serial killer, Andrei Chikatilo, the Rostov Ripper—with a ponytail. The old lady is like… I dunno. Most old ladies don't give me the willies like that."

"She could be—"

"The radio lady from *Exorcist III*!" Derrick interrupted. "*That's* who she reminds me of!"

Noah felt a crawling sensation up his back.

Yeah, he remembered that movie too and Derrick was right.

# MORE THAN THEY COULD CHEW

◆

Brandon Merchant loved to be out on the lake early enough to watch the sun rise. He brought a cup of coffee to sip for the hour or two he just enjoyed being out there, before even wetting a line. The first few years after he moved out and went fishing without his dad, Brandon was afraid to be by himself on the water. It wasn't fear of drowning or anything like that. It felt dangerous in a way he couldn't put his finger on.

After twenty more years, he was desensitized and even felt a little foolish to have ever been so afraid of something so ridiculous. He stopped being afraid of the boogeyman when he was probably ten, ghosts when he was in his teens, the dark by his twenties—why it had to take so long to realize this was just another kind of monster, he had no idea.

He guessed it was just because it was a monster that, as far as he knew, was only *there*. Like the more people that know about something discredits it. And the oldsters definitely did their best to keep people from knowing about it. He supposed that helped too.

When the coffee was gone, Brandon cast his line and settled in to reading Lois L'Amour's *The Quick and the Dead*.

L'Amour or Jack London, peace and quiet, good fishing, what more could a man ask for?

This morning, he could have asked for a little better light. As autumn unignorably announced its intended arrival, it did so with a lot of fog every morning and night. It was so dense that particular morning, Brandon was having a hard time reading.

He rubbed his stubbly jaw and scanned the puffy whiteness with the intelligent eyes of a hunter—which he did for a living, either by guiding hunters, or dodging bullets when his country needed him to.

Lost in the fog, in a boat barely rocking, on a lake he could no longer see, there was a sense of floating high above the earth.

Then there was the sense of something nibbling the bait.

Brandon was sharp enough to hear the bobber jumping up and down through the surface of the water. He exchanged the book for the pole and waited for the fish to make its move.

"Whatcha doing out there?" he asked the thing on the other end of the line. "Don't waste my time."

He just about decided that his bait was probably eaten off when he felt his second favorite jerk. With a yank, the hook set and the line started running, but it was running out faster than he'd ever seen. Brandon watched in disbelief and listened to the high whirring sound of his racing line. It was like he'd hooked a torpedo. There was no way to stop it without breaking the line, he was sure of that.

Brandon tightened his grip on the rod, afraid of what would happen when the line ran out, which it shortly would. But instead of drawing until the very last, the line relaxed in the water, the momentum of the pull taking it a handful of spins before emptying the spool.

After a minute or two of staring dumbly at the line, he started to reel it in. At the very first rotation in his favor, the loose line and firmly held rod were yanked from his hands. He heard it splash nearby.

Brandon's heart was pounding and his eyes hurt from trying to pierce the wall of fog. There was a deep moaning sound, like the sound of water through the hull of an old ship, but from something living.

He flew to the motor and tried to start it without success.

Somewhere in the not so distant reach of the lake there was the sound of something swimming noisily.

It was swimming toward him.

*Fuck it*, he thought, not about to wait around, and plunged into the cold water. He was a strong swimmer and could think only of getting to shore, getting in his truck, and getting the hell out of there. He had a feeling that, even though he was good about maintaining his boat, no matter how hard he tried that the engine would not turn over. Brandon's gut told him the idea was to keep him in one spot. Sitting duck was a term he'd never let himself fit.

Ignoring the sound, which he could hear getting closer, and ignoring the dark water underneath and around him, were the hardest things he'd ever done in his life—which was sometimes a really hard life.

His fingers found bottom before his feet did and so Brandon scrambled onto shore like an animal himself, on fingers and hunched legs. His clothes hugged an athletic body that felt like all its joints were made out of jelly. Will sealed against collapsing, like his trembling body wanted it to, he shambled with what was left of his resolve to the truck waiting for him.

It had been a long time since he had been scared like this—no, he'd never been scared like this. How stupid it is that fear either helps or cripples you. He felt like a bird that was hit by a rock, at the same time knowing he'd swam farther before, ran longer, been in real danger before that hadn't affected him like this. Only there was a part of him that felt like he'd never been in danger like this.

The truck was never locked, but he was sure it would be. He spotted a rock that would be perfect for smashing the window if he had to, but the door came open easily.

Then Brandon was suspicious why.

Was it because there was something in there?

For a split second he had the urge to look over his shoulder to ensure that whatever it was wasn't coming up behind him, but if he did, whatever was inside would get him.

He got a good look in the back seat and tail of the truck before jumping in. The tires spun and spit gravel before they grabbed dirt and the vehicle lunged up the narrow lake access road.

Brandon Merchant was no stranger to the children—putting in countless hours on the lake and even more mastering the wilderness of northern Ontario—they'd always wondered what he'd be like to play with. It went about as poorly as possible.

A deep throated chortle rose out of the fog choked forest—its wordless voice told them what fun it would be to wait for someone to discover the boat and play a naughty trick on them. And what a good prank it would be to tangle the legs of children in the line.

The day was young.

# CHAPTER 11

◆

# A BRUSH with DEATH

Autumn returns a lot faster to the north, Noah acknowledged the next morning, the first morning with a hard frost. It was also the first to strike Noah with inexplicable dread, so much that he had to force himself to even leave the house—half expecting a bear waiting for him in shadows the sun had chased away just an hour before. This trepidation, he realized after immersing himself in the brisk air, was so familiar it felt like *deja vous*.

*This fear* was almost palpable and nameable—it was a presence as much as a feeling. It made him feel like a child again—because it had been that long since he felt it—when fear was Fear. When it was an entity that waited for you under beds or in basements. In the maw of fierce dogs and now in his front yard that August morning. This fear alerted the man to every subtle sound, to every detail of the distant woods, every possible shape in the shadows.

A man walked down the few steps to the yard, but it was a child's eyes scanning the lot—the heart of a small scared beast, not so much beating as rapid pitter-pattering behind a ribcage that resonated the sound like drums in his ears. The task of putting out the mail took minutes. The residual fear subsided within the hour, but the uneasiness would never quite leave Noah; not for the rest of his life, this time.

He did not see the spindly child on four equally long and spider-like limbs, panting, eyes bulging in their rotten face—uneven, clustered teeth—staring inside, brow pressed to the screen exactly where the door struck its face when it closed behind Noah.

David woke to a heavy weight pressed against his back—the source was trembling and making small pitiable sounds somewhere between a whimper and whine. For a split second David was certain, when he rolled over, he'd see Fawn's naan, her great-grandmother, lying there. But he could smell it was Gilder. Then David realized he was wet.

"Gilder!" David exclaimed sliding off the bed and into a run. Gilder lay stiff, eyes bulging, body racked with tremors as her security bolted down the hall.

The smell of coffee perking led the child directly to Noah. There he slowed down and walked—*no running in the house*—and leaned on the bent arm resting on the table edge.

"Gilder peed in my bed again."

Noah frowned and lowered the cup just as it reached his lips.

"I don't know what's come over her kiddo—sometimes animals get weird when they feel like they're competing with other animals. Gilder's had a lot of extra peeing to do here. Maybe she's a little overwhelmed."

In terms of trees alone, Gilder's favorite things to pee on, David could definitely understand how she could feel overwhelmed. What he couldn't understand was how she had any pee left? He thought about it all day and by nightfall, fell asleep still thinking about it.

David's eyes popped open. Something woke him.

What?

A sound?

His room was particularly dark thanks to the new moon's starless night and an untimely effort to be a big boy and outgrow his nightlight.

"Gilder?" David whispered into the perfect black.

He whispered the dog's name two more times before he got up.

On his nightstand he found his cow-shaped flashlight and held it to his chest. He hoped he wouldn't need it because that would probably wake up his dad.

Going first to his daddy's room, David's eyes bugged out at the dark as if that could possibly help them adjust to it any more than they already were. He heard the bed creak slightly and Gilder pant at the presence of her other master.

So it wasn't Gilder.

Then what—a horrible wail penetrated the walls and seemed to travel through the rooms and out the other side of the house.

The sound made David's skin crawl, but he wanted to know what it was. The trembling child stood at the front door and reached for the lock. He knew he shouldn't.

*I'll just peek outside*, he told himself as he opened the inner door.

"Moo!" the mouth of the plastic cow dropped open and the flashlight came to life. David's heart pinched in his chest and he practically sucked his lips into his stomach to keep from squealing. He'd forgotten it did that. Not that it mattered—it was his only flashlight.

He didn't need it to get from his bedroom and through the house, but with the night staring back through the screen door, he wouldn't go another foot without it. The old aluminum door whined as he pulled the handle with both hands. The flashlight mooed again when the mouth moved. The child froze and stared into the dark hall behind him, finding his father's room with his memory and listened. Not a sound. Chewing hard on his lips, drool gathered in the corners of his mouth, David squeezed through the partial exit.

The cold air shocked the small boy. He shivered and hugged himself to keep warm. The spot of light from the flashlight danced around the porch and finally settled on the ground like a pendulum losing momentum.

The damp ground sucked at the feet of his pajamas and they sucked back at the moisture, quickly numbing David's toes. There was the sound again—a low whining, sickly sound.

The corner of the house seemed a long ways away and the darkness beyond it, threatening and hungry. Hungry for little boys. The light pressed into the shadows below the porch, where something could be hiding, and spread a swath of darkness around the posts supporting it.

He thought he heard a woman make a sound somewhere in the darkness ahead of him—it was high and throaty like sounds he sometimes heard his mom make behind closed doors.

The next time he heard it, David was a lot closer to the source—he must have heard it wrong—just because he was so far away, because then he knew it was Mama Cat. She was yowling in the dark, in the small shed close to the house. It was her squalling, but it was different, and it was horrible and miserable and ferocious.

There were other sounds too, sounds that drove David to run away.

Though only giving off a pathetic spot of light, David missed the beam when his flashlight died. He was close enough, even in the pitch black, he remembered where the stairs were and tripped and banged everything he possibly could hurt when he fell against and down them.

Laying on the sidewalk he heard the clear sound of something running toward him on the concrete. It sounded just like Gilder, like the sound of her nails. But it *wasn't* Gilder.

David shoved himself up and ran, too scared to feel the pain. It took him a second, a wretched eternal second to find the door handle—all the while hearing things coming toward him across both the deck and yard. He closed the door behind him and locked the deadbolt first and was almost shaking too bad to lock the one on the doorknob.

He ducked into bed—eyes burning from unblinking—though there was no way he would sleep. He closed his eyes and prayed that he would. He prayed he already *was* asleep.

No sooner had the boy prayed for sleep than he was disturbed by a familiar and comforting sound entering his room. At first he was startled and then quickly relieved by Gilder's thunderous sprint to jump onto the bed, only to be gripped by terror by a landing far lighter than any dog her size could accomplish.

David closed his eyes as quickly as they opened—a sudden weight joined him on the bed. He felt something over him, pressing on either side of him, tightening the bedding on his small body. He wanted to think it was Gilder, its presence warned the contrary.

Nestled inside a bundle of quilts, head sunk deep in a feather pillow, he heard the thing's muffled breathing. Mortal terror told him not to let it known he was awake. So he pretended to be restless and turned his body on one side. He felt the moisture of its gaping mouth, panting against his turned face, and whimpered aloud when long hands caught his shoulders and rolled the child back over.

Its eyes pierced through flesh into feelings. David only meant to peek, but was met with such horror his eyes widened as though caught, bottom and top, by hooks and line.

*Something* like a dog grinned down at him with hundreds of tack sized teeth. Its impossibly long neck hung in a bow to boney shoulders on an emaciated dog body with very long, very human arms and legs, and hands on all four limbs. It wheezed and panted crazily, aroused by the boy's fear, the most afraid the child had ever been. Though David could not recognize an erection, the sight of it sparked a fear for self he'd never known. He longed to be hidden and invisible.

"What in the world is going on?"

David gasped and sat up straight and stared in disbelief.

Noah stood in the doorway. He'd no features, just silhouette. What little light there was behind him traced his outline.

The child's mouth was too dry to answer. It was filmy and felt like it was pasted closed. He scanned the room to see that it was really gone, but behind the door the thing was panting so hoarsely and loudly he couldn't believe his daddy didn't hear it.

"You okay, kiddo?" Noah worried. The hall light cast a rectangle of yellow artificial light into the little room. David looked so small, thin, and pale. Almost gaunt. "You not feeling too well?"

David and the creature behind the door locked eyes. He tried not to tremble. Not to squirm in the pee soaked bedding. He felt a hundred different screams bouncing inside his throat. Then he let himself think, *Dad can protect me.* And the thing smiled with so big a smile, in so big a mouth that David knew it could bite his daddy's head off in one chomp *and it would,* the smile promised.

Too many teeth, an impossible amount of teeth, crowded into the beast's smile. Its eyes twinkled out of the darkness behind the door. All he could see of them was the twinkle, but he knew they were black and small like marbles set deep behind eyelids that closed like they had drawstrings. If David called for help, it would kill his daddy. If he didn't, it would kill him. If his dad found it, it would kill him. And after it killed one of them, it would kill the other.

Though panting, the thing couldn't hold back a chuckle.

A fresh stream of pee warmed David's lap. He looked alarmed at his dad, who clearly hadn't heard that either.

*You're not real*, David thought at it. But seeing is believing. He couldn't make himself really believe what he was thinking.

David screamed and Noah screamed when David screamed and the thing behind the door recoiled into the dark, impossibly backing, into the tight angle near the hinges. The phone rang again and this time David didn't make a sound. Father and son looked at each other stunned.

"Oh my God," Noah exhaled shakily and went after the phone.

Somewhere through the walls David heard the muffled sound of his dad talking on the phone. After a little while he heard the sound of Gilder being goaded for hiding under the table again. His daddy asked her what was wrong. Tried to get her to come and when she wouldn't, told her she was silly.

David and darkness stared at each other.

It took a long time before David realized that was all that was there, darkness.

He squished down into his wet bedding and willed himself into that instinctive security children find under blankets. He grabbed handfuls of excess bedding and packed them around his shape so if he felt something against him maybe he could tell himself it was just his blankets.

◆         ◆         ◆

The next morning David was up well before his dad. Noah heard the TV while he was getting dressed. He woke with a splitting headache and was eager to nurse it with a cup of coffee, since he suspected it was caffeine withdrawal. He slept restlessly through bad dreams and strange sounds.

Sometime during Noah's last hour of sleep, a poor frightened dog made a courageous dash to be in the room with him. Now Gilder wasn't interested in leaving the bed when Noah was ready to leave the room, even when the words "potty" and "food" entered the sounds coming out of her human's mouth.

Coffee. Frozen waffles. Let the dog out, if she'd go. Let her in. Feed the dog.

All of that would have to wait until he made a phone call he kept forgetting to make.

Fawn answered the phone tiredly, but it was late enough in the morning Noah thought it would be safe to call.

"My grandfather isn't home. He'll be back in not too long," Fawn told him after he said who he was.

Noah frowned. He wanted to tell her she shouldn't tell anyone that, even people she knows, but he just wanted to get the call over with. He made a mental note to mention that to her the next time he picked up David.

"Listen, just wanted to ask a quick question."

"Sure," the teenage girl agreed.

"I'm sure you know all the stories about these weird kids that cause all this havoc around here—" he could almost imagine her nodding as she made the "mm-hmm" sound "—and I just wanted to ask if you would not to tell David about it. I can't image Solomon saying anything because he already knows how I feel, I just wanted to ask that you don't say anything to him about it, okay?"

He pressed his palm to the middle of his throbbing forehead with one hand and looked in the direction of the living room. Fawn didn't answer.

"You there?"

"Umm. Yeah. No problem, Mr. Asheborne."

"Thanks hun, I appreciate it."

"Okay."

"Alright. See you later. B'bye," and hung up.

Music and dialogue from a familiar DVD gnawed at his head. David watched the same DVD yesterday, more than once. He hadn't even bothered to take it out of the machine. What was the point? The six-year-old never tired of it. Noah was the same way when he was a kid. When he liked something that was all he wanted. Maybe all kids are like that.

He made coffee and sat at the table massaging his temples while he waited for it to finish perking.

"David, can't you watch something else?" Noah snapped. His head pounded. How much had he slept last night? An abbreviated hour? All those strange noises. The phone call with "no one" on the other end. So his nerves were shot and he couldn't rest. Somewhere in the early morning he must have went unconscious. Only to be subject to, what? Four straight hours of Bob the Builder?

"David!"

This was the warning bark.

Then came counting.

The DVD sang on.

This was just not his day, not David's either if the boy was cut off from TV today and maybe the next day or two after. "*One…*"

When the show wasn't stopped even then, Noah forced himself to get up and deal with it. Discipline, one of his least favorite parental duties since even before David was potty trained. He almost never had to count to two. Not on David's *worst* days…

The short span of hall beyond the front door was all that lay between the Headache Machine and the unshaven, rumpled, under slept father who was on his way to lay down the law.

He almost walked right past Mama Cat. There was nothing remarkable about her anyway. She didn't make a mess. She went in her box. He really only noticed her when she wanted his attention. But something was different this morning and he realized at the exact moment he also saw that David was *not* in front of the TV.

"Mama," he exhaled in a half groan, half yelp. His now large brown eyes fixed on the mess between Mama Cat's front feet. He followed a thin trail of blood from her to the partially ajar screen door and saw where her face slid across it, when she forced the way to her people. The blood-drenched kitten tried to raise its head from the ground where the somewhat deflated looking cat laid it. Like the kitten, Mama Cat's face was matted with blood. The striped cat nudged the pathetic mewing baby and then looked up at Noah. Her yellow-green eyes asked for help. They begged for it.

Outside, David shrieked.


Noah flew out the front door and hurdled over the porch rail at the scream, or perhaps series of screams that continued from the outbuilding.

Dusty morning light poured across the bloody scene, quickly eclipsed as the young father filled the doorway, calling out to his son who was kneeling in blood and little furry bodies.

"Dad!" he screamed, and for a second his voice distorted in reaction to the senseless horror his six-year-old mind was trying to understand.

The boy turned on his bottom and for a fraction of a second Noah thought it wasn't really David and actually screamed himself. Then his left hand clamped over his mouth, then between his teeth as David raised his small cupped hands so they almost touched Noah's stomach. Cradled in them was a kitten, its fur still lying flat and fluff-less in its newness. It's almost perfectly round head, with its tiny ears and little pink nose, and fused eyes that looked like sperm in their early stages of opening. In the perfect dome of that little head was a deep, bloody crater. Each and every one of the kittens scattered across the floor were destroyed in the same way. A single bite.

◆       ◆       ◆

"Son-of-a-bi—" Noah bit off the last words and rumpled the head of the little person who joined him to watch Solomon drive away.

"Whud he say?" David asked fearfully. He was thinking about what happened outside last night. Whatever killed the kittens was whatever chased him was whatever had been in his room.

"Badger, probably," Noah answered as he turned them both to leave. He was really hating badgers right now. "Solomon said they do stuff like that."

David felt anger fill his chest. Solomon knew more than Fawn and Fawn would say it was the children. Even though it wasn't a child in his room—somehow David knew it was a child, just the same. It was whatever it wanted to be, but it was one of the things Fawn told him about. Solomon lied.

"Why would badgers do that?" David wondered.

Noah couldn't tell him that animals do that kind of shitty stuff to each other all the time. You can't turn on *Nature* without seeing—along with all the necessary deaths that are part of the food chain—all kinds of vulnerable animals who are the victims of the creature world's version of murder. He couldn't say, 'Sometimes animals kill for fun'. He couldn't say, 'Yeah, and all that's true for people too. Because we're all animals.'

Fawn came around the side of the house then, carrying a bucket and discolored sponge. She paused a second before approaching the father and son. She slipped the sponge into the bucket where it was out of sight.

"I got inside too," she informed Noah in little more than a mutter.

"Thanks so much for staying to help out Fawn," Noah said gratefully.

"The itten-kay id-day ot-nay ake-it-may."

"I didn't think it would," the father admitted, but he was still disappointed. He extended an arm to the girl and hugged her shoulder when she moved into it.

"Do you think it was badgers too?" David asked Fawn.

Fawn looked knowingly at David. She heard the way he asked. That's called rhetoric…

"Badgers *do* do that," Fawn told him.

The kids looked at each other for what seemed like a long time to the lone adult. There seemed to be a battle of wills going on.

"Hey guys, don't dwell on it. David, Mama Cat's going to need a lot of TLC. So let's just try to focus on her right now. That's all we can do," he bent and hugged David warmly and apologetically because he'd been so cross about the DVD. David started crying. Neither father nor Fawn could console him.

Sweat beaded on the child's brow, while nightmares churned and furrowed through it. Tears squeezed through red rimmed eyes to cheeks flushed feverishly. He told himself he was just tired. He told himself that it was all a bad dream. It was his turn to lie and he lied about everything that seemed so real and everything that seemed unreal.

"It's okay to be sad, David," Noah squatted to look his son in the face, who nodded knowingly. "Do you want to talk about it?"

Then the little boy shook his head.

The father stroked the boy's teary, sweaty, and warm face, then kissed it.

Noah was 100% certain now that David was sick. Last night, by the time he got back to check on David, he was asleep so hadn't bothered him. But the six-year-old looked so small, fragile, and pale. Later, when he discovered his son peed the bed, was the last verification he needed, but David was already laid up to mend his aching heart with juice, crackers, and *Bob the Builder*.

# JOY RIDE

◆

Somewhere beyond the cloud of dirt was a black Camaro going almost forty miles over the speed limit, barely keeping all four wheels on the road. The taillights illuminated the dirt like a red nuclear cloud while the headlights ricocheted off trees. Inside were three seniors from Kapuskasing, Craig, Mike, and Charlie. There was also Katie, a girl from a freshman class.

A bottle of vodka bounced around the front seat, much like how the car passed down the road. In the rearview, the driver, Mike, caught glimpses of skin and the busy movement of discarded clothing. It was hard to watch and drive, he preferred to watch.

"Where do you want me to stop?" Mike asked the mass of limbs in the back seat, over deafening music.

"Find a side road," Charlie grunted somewhere between "Ohh-yeah!" and "Come on."

The three boys had been friends for a long time. As their last official summer vacation, since they all planned on working at the mill after graduating, they wanted to make the most of it. One of the things they'd always put off was heading up to Nibebiitam to find out if all the stories were true. They brought Katie along because even if they didn't see any proof, she was bound to get so scared they might all get lucky.

Tonight was the night. Summer was wasting. The full moon raised their confidence.

The passenger in shotgun, Craig, howled wildly as he leaned out of the window.

THWACK!

A mailbox reduced the hollering boy's head into a pulpy mess on the small rear passenger window. The force of the impact slung the car into the ditch and into a tree before anyone had a chance to scream.

Charlie and Katie were crushed together in the floor space between the front and back seats.

"Mike!" Charlie called wetly, blood was running over his face. Going into shock, he had no idea if it was his or someone else's blood. He cried again, harder and louder, when Mike didn't answer.

"Shut up!" Charlie screamed at the babbling body crumpled into him.

When she started crying, he tried to shove her off, but could only move one arm and there was no chance of moving anything else. He was sure he was broken, a lot.

Then Charlie drifted into unconsciousness.


When he came too, the car was flooded with light and he heard the sound of the driver's door being pried open. A lot of people were moving around outside of the vehicle. He hoped they would hurry up too before the bitch died on him.

"Hey! You out there! I'm alive! *Help*!" he screamed.

A large person passed through the light, mumbling wordlessly like a Gremlin.

Anger cleared Charlie's mind enough to realize that most of the light seemed to be from flashlights, as it moved all around him.

"Hey fuckers, I'm in here!"

The driver door came loose and fell off the car. All at once, the lights simultaneously jumped away from the car. There was giggling and more "talking". Somebody came back to Mike and started fighting with the seatbelt. They jerked and jerked. Two more came and together jerked the body free with enough force to leave behind any parts of the youth reluctant to move. Through the space between the seats, Charlie saw what was left of his friend after that.

Somebody got on the trunk where Charlie could clearly see them—could clearly see because the glow came from *them*, not flashlights.

Then the light in them went out too, illuminated only by the beams of full moonlight which they appeared to absorb. They were clear and bright, but no longer blinding like high beams being thrown through the glass on all sides.

He was thinking they were like vultures that prefer to eat dying, not dead, prey. They had been circling and circling. He used this as reason to hope his friends were still alive. Charlie tried to tell himself the white people were angels. He even tried to tell himself he was a good enough person to make it to heaven someday. His soul, as much as the things outside, knew what he'd never admit—Charlie hoped they'd take the others and spare him. He thought if he could stay still and quiet now they might think he died, because his gut was telling him they were not people, they were not vultures, and they sure as hell weren't angels.

The small legs and bare feet on the trunk hadn't moved, while the others stayed busy.

For a little while, that seemed like a long while, Charlie thought himself successful in his possum act, if only he could ignore the thing on the trunk, but he couldn't make himself take his eyes off it for long.

The front seat bucked and jerked as one of the things jumped out, laughing wildly. The movement jarred the entangled teenagers—Katie could only raise her head enough to conceivably slip a sheet of paper between them.

"They're real," the bloody girl mangled into him mumbled wetly.

Alarmed, Charlie looked at the back window, just in time to see the thing squat and start to lean in.

*Please don't see me! Please, please, please! Fucking bitch! Fucking stupid fucking bitch! Just fucking die! Just die!*

*If you gave me away, I'll kill you,* Charlie thought. And he would have if he'd had the chance. He wanted to strangle her skinny neck, but he needed to think of himself right now.

Charlie Toullet tried to think of any possible escape. It would be impossible if it was aware of him. He had to steal a look at it, if he was ever going to know. Did he *need* to know that bad?

It was probably better just to keep playing dead and hope for the best.

But Charlie had to know if it knew.

"They always know," Katie bubbled out before going silently into her last breaths.

It put paws instead of hands to the glass and peered in with something that should have been a child's face, but wasn't. And its smile wasn't sweet, but full of canines that seemed too large and thick for its face, like a toddler putting in their grandparent's dentures.

When Charlie looked over his head at the back window he screamed so hard he tore the hinges of his mouth.

# CHAPTER 12

---◆---

## SOJOURN into the MUSKEG

"Why did Solomon lie to my daddy?" David asked Fawn the next day.

They were exploring the woods and, according to Fawn, they'd found some kind of trail, so they'd been busy with it for a while. David guessed he could kind of see where the earth might have been packed before, but if it was used, it was a long time ago. There just weren't as many plants there, but it was still grown over.

It was late in the afternoon and his dad would be there to pick him up soon. David wanted to ask her about the lie all day. So it was time to spit it out.

"It really made you mad, didn't it?" was her answer.

"He didn't have to lie. He didn't have to have an answer," David pointed out.

Fawn held his soft upper arm to help him over a log. She nodded, but he didn't see.

"Is it safe for us to be out here?"

The forest was beautiful. The light was changing and the whitish yellow illumination was so intense that it almost looked like paint where is struck the western facing edges. In this light the spongy, moss covered ground looked lush and full of life, instead of a life-choking growth that hid pockets of mud and water.

"You're safe David. I promise." Fawn heard sincerity in her voice that she wasn't even aware she could feel. At the same time she realized just how much she liked this little white boy from New York City. She could have hugged him.

"Fawn," David swallowed hard. He felt tears returning at the thought of the creature he was both sure had been in his room and sure could not have been. "The other night—"

Fawn stopped abruptly and David mashed his face into her backbone. Before he could even push away from her, the girl was backing up. He could hear the ground sucking at her feet and realized that water was seeping into his shoes. He almost fell, but Fawn didn't stop backing up. She had to grab his arm and tug him to the side. If he hadn't strapped the Velcro extra tight, for a walk in the woods, he'd have lost both of his shoes.

Since no adult was there to hear, David growled, "What the hell?"

He scowled hard at Fawn to let her know that 'yes, he was serious'. She glanced at him and then away.

At the sight of her face, David thought, she almost looked white, *if* white was actually a little more gray than creamy. He wasn't mad at her anymore.

"Fawn…"

He wanted her to say something, start explaining, and stop scaring him. He included all these needs in her name and how he said it, somewhere between pleading and sorrowful.

David didn't see anything scary. A broad green-brown swamp spread out in front of them. The smell of algae, dead water, and rotting trees filled his nose, but nothing about this place was new. There were thirty-thousand-million of these swamps up here. This one was particularly duck-weedy. Big hairy deal.

They were facing down the expanse of a swampy forest pond. The light shifted suddenly and the contrast of illumination and shadow made visible things they couldn't see before. One thing in particular, the low mouth of a moss and vine covered cave. When the light was just so, the mouth filled with blackness.

He yearned to go to it.

David felt like he'd been there before.

"Do what I tell you and everything will be just fine," Fawn said calmly and almost frosted—like a bitter cake concealed with the sweetest icing.

The older girl's hand snapped onto David's wrist, hard, so hard he cried out. Her other hand made a cup over his mouth and shoved the sound back in. Before he could resist David saw what was wrong.

From the thick trunk of a dead tree, just across a sparkling expanse of shallow open water, the bark peeled apart and an old cracked-faced pushed out between roots. He perfectly matched the darkness, light, texture, and colors. Perfectly perhaps, all but the shining blackness of piercing eyes narrowed by heavy lids, swollen, and sunken all at once in skin that could have been made of ash and clay.

Fawn gathered David closer because she was too afraid to run. This white child in the wood could never grasp her explanation of the man, but his small trembling body told her he understood enough. No one needed schooling to tell their instincts when something in the spirit world is wrong… or among them.

"Is that—?"

Fawn's hand tightened so hard on his little face that her fingertips were starting to hurt his teeth.

The eyes, no less than slivers of watery obsidian, flicked up to the mortal children huddling on the fringe of the tiny clearing. They didn't waver, even as he oozed from the skin of the tree. The penetrating, omnisciently intelligent eyes never blinked—fixed on them.

From the wooden mouth that released him, the man seemed to pour out on the forest floor. His fingers sunk into the moss and tangled roots. The very slightest upset made the afternoon light start to dance on the greenish brown water. Both Fawn and David would later agree that they thought he was drinking. His body shook, like a wet dog, and a fountain of long silver and black hair erupted from the scalp that had been no more than cracks and knots a second before.

Then he stood.

As he did, his bark-like skin began to form clothes. He found a dead, limbless branch, and took it up like a staff. The man of the woods turned his head and surveyed the land as if it were his realm. Indeed it was.

Even as his head turned to look around, his face never left the children, even as his hair rotated rightly—the face was under there. There might have even been a face where there should be, but it was out of sight.

The forest responded to him. There was an energy that hadn't been there before and it spread like roots from this entity. It sounded like all the wildlife in Ontario surrounded them. The trees were busy with the motion of wings. Weasels and fox and other small furry things darted in and out of sight.

The man stretched his back, like it was stiff, and turned away from Fawn and David entirely, moving into the darkening forest with a nod to the changing sky and one last meaningful look in their direction.

*"Aandi ezhaayan?"* an androgynous voice from everywhere and nowhere said.

Fawn seized David's shoulders and spun him around, in the direction of her home.

Without saying so, David felt her tell him it was time to go. It was time to hurry. To run. Carefully.

"Did you see the cave?"

"Uh Uhh," Fawn shook her head. She stared in disbelief at the bizarre little boy. "Why—"

"There was a cave behind the—"

"You were seeing things."

"Was that—"

"Silver Fox Man?" Fawn interrupted.

David nodded breathlessly.

"Oh David," she grunted, helping him back over the tree they crossed before. "I think so."

"Can we tell anyone?"

Solomon's voice resounded through the woods. He was calling them.

"I don't think so."

Solomon was standing in the backyard waiting for them. He raised his eyebrows at their hectic faces and then raised his hands onto his sides.

"What have you two gotten into?" he pressed accusingly.

"The woods," David answered. His tone said he wasn't being smart. It was all he could think to say.

"Well your dad said he's going to be a little late."

"Why?" the boy worried.

"Jacob needed him to finish something and he was going to stop for a few groceries."

"Coffee," David said. His dad had added that to the list this morning and probably wasn't going to take any chance of running out.

"Actually he said it was a big shopping day; he thought you might have forgot." He had. "But he hadn't planned on working late, so not to worry. You go ahead and go in," Fawn's grandpa told him. Then Solomon watched the child until he was through the back door, thinking he looked so small for his age.

Then Solomon went to talk to Fawn.


"Oh *Naana*!" David sang as he made for the back porch, sloshing all the way.

She didn't answer. He didn't think she would, but he wanted her to hear him. He wanted her to be glad that he was coming and let her know that he was glad to be coming to her. He didn't have any grandma or great-grandma. No naan. His family was so small. Was so much smaller now. He wanted to be a part of the love that was here. Maybe, he thought, the broken parts of both their families would somehow fit together.

He was glad the wind-chimes were silent as he entered the screened in porch.

Even as the century old woman sat there silently, David felt the kinetic energy of her consciousness. She knew he was there, just as well as she heard him call. He felt her hug him back as he threw his arms around her neck, even as arthritis kept her from returning it physically.

The plasticy smile left on Naana's face was as beautiful a smile as anyone could hope to have. David could stare at it forever and ever—which was easy because it never really left her face. Not when she was left undisturbed. If you went out to the porch, where she always was, and didn't try to talk to her, that smile would never falter.

The three or four dozen, or more, wind chimes along this side of the house would sometimes ring and the smile would tremble like a mouth when someone's eating their rage or that special smile when people try not to cry. That's a heavy duty smile that says, "I'm just fine, really."

And maybe the person or persons will believe it. Maybe they'll believe it themself. The way that Naana was, was not because of the accident that orphaned Fawn. It was something *out there*.

David pried his eyes off the elder and gazed curiously and accusingly at the acres and acres of woodland surrounding the modest house. *Home*.

Something was stolen from Naana and David knew what that thing was.

He felt creepy all over as the woods changed before his eyes; it became darker and more secretive as the realization came to him. Naana's will was gone.

*God gave us free will*, his dad told him so. So maybe only the opposite entity could take it away, David considered and feared.

David left his arm across her shoulder and knew he loved her so much. He wanted to talk to her about what they saw. He wanted to talk to her about everything. He wanted to say, "Was it real?"

She would know. People that old know everything because they've lived everything. And she'd lived everything *here*. She'd got this old living here. Among all these bad things.

"You cannot show what you're doing. And they can read your mind—" David was startled by her old and gritty voice, "—the *only thing* they do not know is what's inside your soul," Naana thought aloud. "They can't know. Can't know. Can't. Little things live in the mouth of wickedness. If only something could shut its mouth."

"The children?" David felt himself tremble.

"They are *so* playful," Naana mused almost fondly.

"What can't they know?"

The old woman began to rock, even though her face gave nothing away, he felt her tension and held her tight.

"Naana," he whispered against the warmth of her head, "Is the Silver Fox Man bad?"

Clarity bloomed in her eyes. She turned to his face. Nose to nose she whispered slowly and monotonously, "He is shepherd of the seasons. He is the balance of nature and the spirit world. Balance is neither good or evil. And yet it must also be entirely good and evil."

A thin, boney hand rose to cover the hand on her shoulder.

"When *he* is there," she paused and swallowed hard, "everything in his presence is in balance. Anything out of balance in this world or the spirit world has no strength. If he is there and you do not harm nothing, then you are safe. They say if you see him he will protect you."

David kissed the side of her head and hugged her again. If that was true, then he knew that Naana never saw Silver Fox Man. She didn't seem protected by anything.

◆         ◆         ◆

It was all Noah could do to keep from screaming as the world's oldest teller rang up his groceries in line two of two in Nibebiitam's answer to a grocery store. The store itself wasn't that bad. The prices weren't great, but they had to freight so far that it was expected. Most of the staff were friendly and it was just kind of charming. This was the second time he'd been stuck with *her*. Noah thought he was safe when he saw Shirley and started unloading "Big Shopping Day's" groceries onto the worn black tread of the second oldest thing in the store. Then the first oldest thing showed up, graciously offering to take over so Shirley could get her lunch break. Not only was she incapable of scanning items without having to punch in their numbers, but it took her forever to type the numbers—mainly because she could hardly see them, but she also had to comment on *every fucking thing* he bought.

He had to watch her like an eagle too, because she wouldn't always type the numbers in right and he'd end up being charged for all kinds of obscure things if he wasn't paying attention. Then, afterwards, he had to go through his entire receipt to make sure it was right.

A "ping" on the white and grey tile caught Noah's attention and he watched a four-year-old in a sweat-suit chasing down the penny she'd dropped. When she retrieved it, she thumbed it into the half-full gumball machine and cranked the knob as hard as she could—just the way David used to. A perfect shiny yellow ball landed in the palm of her tiny hand when she carefully lifted the little door so it wouldn't get away, like her penny almost did. Her face screwed up when she looked at it.

And then the adorable cherub with a sweet-tooth reeled on aisles one through two and screamed in a teeth-grinding pitch, "I want my money back!"

And the words "want" and "back" each lasted at least ten seconds.

"Wow," said the Ancient as Eden teller.

"No kiddi—"

"I didn't know they made this juice in tangy!"

Noah's elbows fell painfully against the counter and he dropped his face into his hands. He disgusted himself a little for wondering if he could talk Fawn into grocery shopping when she was old enough to drive.

He was suddenly joined by the strong smell of someone who had recently marinated in a cigarette smoke filled car.

"Noah Asheborne!" the husky voice said cheerfully.

He looked briefly at the prematurely wrinkled face of the fifty-something-year-old woman who was standing way too close to him. She'd curled her recently colored hair to look freakishly youthful against her strikingly androgynous face.

"Mrs. Sneider?" he thought he knew.

"I know what's on your mind."

He hoped she wasn't saying what he was afraid she was suggesting by her almost "sultry" tone.

So he didn't answer.

"You have those spirit kids on your mind. Been hearing the stories. Well, I am here to tell you those stories are nothing but nonsense."

"Thanks. I'm glad someone clarified that for me."

"I knew you would be. The stories are so disturbing. Nothing but red heathen superstition."

Noah's eyebrow twitched.

"Where's that sweet little boy of yours?"

"With a *heathen*," he didn't bother hiding his irritation.

"Sweet Heavens, no! You need to bring that boy on over and me and my hubby will be glad to watch him. Get some religion into the both of you and you'll find their nasty red devil stories won't bother you anymore."

"Stories are stories. It doesn't bother me."

"We have been working on a blessing for the town to ward off the evils of godless people. It has been too long coming. Keeping people hostage by a myth. My husband knows powerful—"

"*Please*, Mrs. Sneider."

"Oh, I know, you have that Solomon Crane watching your kid—"

"Don't say another word," Noah stabbed his finger into her bitchy old face. "Either shut up until I am gone or go to another line. I don't give a damn what a vicious gossiping bigot has to say."

Andrea Sneider's lips tightened into a straight line and she left the line and left the store—having not had any items with her, except what she put in her pockets.

"You okay, hun?" the teller asked slowly as she watched him watch the woman leave.

Noah felt safe to answer anyway he wanted because he knew the teller almost certainly wouldn't hear what he'd say—his give a damn was pretty much exhausted, "You know? You make me want to gouge my eyes out with a corkscrew."

He noticed, while his face was still close to the counter, white hairs all over the rubbery black conveyor.

"No, I'm fine. Thanks," he assured the old woman. He looked at his watch and couldn't believe how long he'd been in line. He worried that David would be worrying. He was still worried about David's health. A lot more bad happened the last few days than good. He didn't want David to know this much shit. As far as Noah was concerned, the divorce alone was more hurt than he wanted David to ever know. Nature is cruel, but David didn't have to find out the way he did.

## *HOPING FOR A QUICK DEATH?*

◆

Everything about this moment made Lawrence Weinman glad he abandoned the trail. He thought getting off the beaten path in nature, as well as in life, was the only way to really experience anything worth experiencing.

Nobody was going to believe this was a real stump. Not with what Photoshop can do. It was almost as if bark had grown over carvings of forests, mountains, rivers and animals, even human faces. Seeing was believing and he didn't really care what anyone thought. This moment was *his*.

The camera lowered and Lawrence let it hang beneath his knees as he squatted to look at it again, without the lens. He couldn't stop looking at the huge knots all over the base of this enormous broken tree.

Swollen beads of sap gleamed back at the hiker like eyes. If they were real eyes, they would look amused.

Funny the way bark can resemble anything. Another tree, a snake, mountains, a toothy grin—a toothy...

The bark... was that a face in it?

A flourish of movement, beside, above, before him.
All the search party would find was one shoe.

# CHAPTER 13

◆

## STRANGER than FICTION

After David was put to bed, Noah retired to his room to work. He was bothered by the conversation he just had with his son. A conversation that ended with the child's insistence that he was fine and didn't know why Noah was asking and actually started working himself up to tears to make his daddy put it to rest. For some reason, these results didn't resolve any concerns. Noah brushed his teeth and got into his pajama pants while Gilder claimed her spot on the king-sized bed. The ladies of the house, Mama Cat and Gilder, couldn't decide which one of them was going to sleep in which bed.

The other night, Noah pretty much decided that what was happening was Mama Cat could only tolerate sleeping with David a night or two, then she would want to switch beds and *that* dictated the sleeping arrangements because Gilder wanted to sleep by her people, especially the little boy.

Mama Cat was out of luck tonight.

Hands resting on the sides of his flat stomach, Noah watched Gilder make her nest, when she was done, maybe he would get some work done.

"Forget it buddy, no toys in bed," Noah discouraged the mutt when she realized something was missing and started plowing her mug through blankets outside her nest. "You'll drool all over the bed and if you don't keep me up squeaking all night I'll roll over and find a soggy stuffed animal that smells like dead fish. I think not. Lay down."

Loving her family, the dog obeyed, but she didn't understand why he wouldn't help her look.

The young man put on his reading glasses and crawled onto the bed with a file box and his laptop sitting on top. Within minutes he'd surrounded himself with a circle of protection guaranteeing he wouldn't get a lot of shuteye that night. He needed the sleep, but more than that he needed to keep his mind busy so he wouldn't be thinking about tomorrow—David's first day of school in Nibebiitam.

Most of the notebooks and reference books were related to the manuscript he was working on, but the red notebook was for ideas and now also for all notes about the stuff that had been going on in Nibebiitam. He'd started writing down details about the calls—who, when, the numbers—when the concern became legitimate that, at some point, he might need documentation for the harassing phone calls and the weird incidents that might have been the "well meaning" harassers too. One of his friends was a lawyer who always stressed, "Document, document, document—everything."

The guy even started documenting every fight and other problem between him and his wife, just in case it ever came to divorce, especially if they had children. He also said, you start a job, you document every negative thing that happens so if it comes to legal matters you have pattern, you have habit—you have documentation. It made Noah self-conscious visiting with him, wondering if he was building a dossier about him too.

He pulled his feet up under him, like a pretzel, and balanced the laptop between his knees.

What felt like a few minutes of writing lapsed the night almost four hours.

Somewhere in the dark house, on the other side of the bedroom door, came the sound of Gilder's nails clink-clinking across the kitchen floor and then loudly lapping at her water bowl. Apparently she was really thirsty, at first making Noah feel bad for her. Then he smiled when he thought about how he'd long since learned late night drinking like that would always lead to early morning whining and walks.

Instinctively turning to tease Gilder, where she still lay at the top of the bed, Noah stared at the black egg-shaped mound of peacefully sleeping dog.

His throat felt like it folded over in his neck. Eyes reluctantly and heavily crept toward the door while his mind tried to decide if he'd really heard what he thought he had. There was no sound at all outside the room. Staring at the door, Noah somehow felt certain, if he waited, the answer would come on its own.

When the phone rang he jolted out of his trance. At the second ring, Noah realized it was his cell phone and almost relaxed. He didn't know if he could handle a doomsayer's phone call right then. It being his cell, he was sure he didn't have to worry about who was on the other end.

Noah looked away from the screen to check the caller ID. Excitement and apprehension surged through him as he saw a Connecticut number.

He pushed "talk" and put the phone to his ear, trying to sound casual, "Hey, Kendal, what'd'ya come up with?"

Her somewhat girlish voice jumped on the line with an air of impatient excitement:

"Noah, you are just not going to believe this shit."

"Try me," he said tonelessly, but he didn't mean to. Thoughts about what he might have heard in the kitchen were pushed aside and forcibly forgotten.

The sound of riffling paper sounded like static on the other line.

"Nasty ass history. Internment camp, missing people—enough to make the Appalachian Trail sound as safe as a Sunday school picnic. Mysterious deaths, fucked up death records. Fires with major casualties, including both a hotel and a hospital, a bus driver that goes crazy and drives headlong off a bridge, murders, bizarre accidents," there was the sound of sifting paper again. "Want more?"

"I want it all."

She sighed heavily, "I hope you have a few hours. I'll mail you what I've got so you'll be getting a pretty substantial box in the mail. I'll send it with all the bells and whistles. In a second here I'm going to tell you how sincerely I think the people up there would rather no one knew about what's been happening. I've got to tell you something..." then she trailed off.

"What, Kendal?"

"I'm sorry, because the last thing you need is someone making you feel like shit, but I don't feel so great about you being up there," she tentatively admitted.

Noah leaned back, his shoulders complained, his eyes were burning, and his muscles ached from being tense. The move was supposed to make their lives better. So he had to admit, "Most the time, I don't either."

"If you need to bail, you can crash at my place," she offered.

He cringed at the idea. She was a great person, always

available, always willing, always caring, brilliant and trustworthy. But she was also into *everything*, he didn't know if her compulsion for learning let her be otherwise. Maybe not the right environment for a child, even temporarily. Maybe not the right environment for an adult either.

"I appreciate that," said Noah and that was one hundred percent true. "And hey—"

"Yeah?" said the women's voice.

"Before we get too far into this, I wanted to say how much I appreciate it."

There was a sound as she smiled, breathing out of her nose.

"Okay then, hope you've recently gone to the bathroom, or you may shit yourself," Kendal warned.


Three hours later, with two hours left before the alarm would go off, Noah got off the phone and, by the armload, put his work on the dresser and lay down.

His lean muscular limbs felt old and ached as he stretched out on top of the comforter. A crackling sound leapt from his left knee as he pushed the left heel out and pulled the toes back toward his knee.

Tap. Tap. Tap.

His back flew off the bed and he leaned in toward his bedroom door to hear better.

Tap-Tap-Tap at the front door.

Gilder let out a low growl.

"Who in the world—"

BOOM! BOOM! BOOM! against his bedroom door.

The black mutt flew of the bed and ran to the farthest corner from the door, flashing white as she barked ferociously at it.

Noah spilled out on the floor on the opposite side of the bed from the door without even realizing he was fleeing. He was pushing off the ground when he heard the click of the latch giving and watched paralyzed with fear as the door slowly swung open. Behind him wafted the sound and smell of Gilder peeing.

"You okay daddy?"

*It's not David,* he thought.

"Dad?"

Gilder's paw found his ass crack through his pajama pants when she hurtled over his crumpled body.

"Yep," the father said, sheepishly picking himself off the floor. He didn't like to lie to David, but he apologetically explained, "I tripped. Everything's okay, you can go back to bed."

The boy looked at his father in a tired mixture of annoyance and doubt, both of which vanished with a shrug.

They exchanged "Goodnights" as he left the room with Gilder.

Noah kept a lamp on and, when he lay down again, pulled the blankets up so high he could barely see over them. He tucked the blankets close to his body so if he woke feeling like something was up against him he would immediately think of bedding first—just like when he was a little boy. He didn't feel any safer, which hardly mattered.

There was little chance of sleeping.

◆          ◆          ◆

A few hours later, at the kitchen table, Noah felt completely alone in his nervousness as David prattled on about this-and-that—he had a hard time paying attention. And it wasn't just being overtired. Even after the last sip of coffee, the butterflies in his stomach weren't drowned. Sometimes the gnawing feeling in his gut just told him his caffeine addiction needed a little attention. Then again, the call from Kendal, and the pounding on his bedroom door, gave him enough reasons to be sick to his stomach.

This morning his baby would be starting his first day of *real* school. From how casual David was acting Noah was concerned for a split second he might have forgotten to remind the kid today was "the day". But last night the six-year-old picked out his clothes, asked for a special lunch, and went through the school supplies in his bag one last time. And this morning father asked son if he was excited. Son said "yup" and went directly to turn on the TV.

Noah was feeling down. He saw the little boy, who was not as little as he had been this time last year, and he couldn't help thinking how he'd have to live that realization every year for probably another twelve or fourteen years and maybe a few more than that, depending if David went to college or if he ended up living at home. What made Noah feel bad about it was that he so often was struck with these profound moments, almost epiphanies, when the love he felt for his son seemed so big it was overwhelming. He felt bad about that because of things he thought and said and fought about with David's mom—something he could never take back feeling—how he didn't want this baby. He vehemently, earnestly, whole-heartedly protested having children—only to fall helplessly in love with a tiny newborn boy, with his hair and eyes, and Terri's lips and nose. Noah felt guilty about that, even though he thought he had good reason for feeling the way he did. He could hardly remember why he'd felt as strongly as he did, once he felt the pull of fatherhood.

This was only half the guilt.

While he hoped David would never know the way he once felt, it broke his heart when he considered the possibility David might know that his mother abandoned him. Did he ever wonder why his mommy never tried to see him, talk to him, never asked about him?

Did he ever wonder why she left? Does he feel unwanted? That would be enough to traumatize someone for life, but if David ever found out that, at one point, his daddy didn't want him either?

Noah got up from the table, he thought he was going to be sick, but when the sensation passed, he was still able to pretend he'd just gotten up to put his cup in the sink.

"You about ready? You don't want to be late your first day," Noah heard the strain in his voice and kept his back turned to David. Tears burned in his eyes. He wiped away one that was too heavy to hold onto his eye lashes, braced his hands on the edge of the counter, and let his weight hang on his shoulders.

David didn't answer for a couple seconds. His dad didn't hear him eating, as he often could.

"Yah," he finally responded. Noah heard the clinking of dishes and turned only enough so he could see if David got them okay.

"Thanks a lot buddy. That's very grown up of you."

The dishes were pushed over the lip of the sink and clattered against the few dishes waiting to be cleaned.

"We got to work together," David hugged the waist beside him. Noah hugged the boy's head.

David knew they were pretty much all each other had in the whole world. So it made sense to him that his daddy should be sad today. He'd seen parents be upset on TV when they sent their kids off to school. So he understood. It wasn't uncommon for him to catch his daddy looking teary and distant, at least since his mommy left. So David thought maybe his daddy was afraid that when he was away from him, that he would go away too.

"Do you have to work?" the little boy asked.

"I'm going to work at home today."

"For Jacob?"

"Nope. For me. Gonna try and write today."

David was happy. Writing was the work his daddy wanted to do most and he always seemed to be in a better mood when he was working on a book.

"What's it about?" David asked, though he knew there wouldn't be a good answer. Derrick said his daddy wrote historical thrillers. That meant David wouldn't get much more detail than, "this guy was bad and yadda yadda."

"Well...," Noah began, slipping out of David's arms and heading for the closet by the front door, "It's about a man who got in big trouble."

"What did he do?" David's eyes got wide. He and Gilder looked at each other and both looked excited. To be fair, most of the time Gilder looked excited.

"He went to jail because his son was late for school."

"You can go to jail for that here?" the boy exclaimed as his coat was passed to him.

"Oh yeah," Noah affirmed.

Boy out and headed for the steps, dog out and tail free from the doorjamb, he locked the door and followed David to the truck.

"Oh my God!" David hurried for the passenger door. "How much time do we have?"

"Five minutes."

David's face went blank. He stared in disbelief as his dad casually walked up to the truck, let Gilder in the back seat, and got in himself.

"We'll never make it to town in five minutes!"

Noah let himself smile. At the first crack, David saw he'd been tricked. His gut instinct was to punch his daddy in the arm, but the first day of school was not a good time to forget that hitting was bad. He thought about letting out a swear, a big one, just to see what his daddy would do, with him about to be gone all day. The little boy wondered if his daddy would remember it happened. He seriously doubted there was any dish soap in the truck.

David almost talked himself into it when they had to brake to let this huge, dark brown cow-horse-like creature cross the road just ahead of them.

"Is that Bullwinkle?" the child asked, awestruck.

"It sure is," Noah answered, lifting his cell phone to record with one hand and the other on the handle to be ready shift gears if they had to make a run for it.

"What are you doing that for?" David noticed.

"I've heard these fella's can be a little grumpy sometimes when people are in their space."

They watched for the next minute or so as the moose dissolved into the woods lining the road.

"Are you going to show Derrick?"

Noah nodded and put down the phone. He didn't like David to see him use it when he was driving. Most of the time he didn't, but there was no point in planting the seed that it was ever okay. There's no place to be that's more important than being safe, he often told David. Especially when they met scary drivers on the road. "Where's the fire?" was David's favorite thing to say at those moments. He was glad that's all David picked up from Derrick, considering all the other things he heard his godfather say about other drivers—not that Derrick should have said *anything* about the way other people drive. You know you're driving like an ass when a kid thinks they're on a theme park ride.

When they arrived at the school, Noah was disappointed that he hadn't been able to keep the gag up about being late, because when David saw the kids from town just arriving he would have realized he was being kidded then. The fun hadn't lasted very long.

"So I'll ride the bus most the time?" David asked.

"I didn't know how you were going to feel, so I told them I'd bring you in today. I think it's better for you to ride the bus and be around the other kids, but sometimes when I work in town you can ride in with me if you want a little change. Do you want me to walk you to class?"

David considered for a second and, after trying to remember if he could remember the way to the classroom, shook his head.

"Nope. I'm pretty big now."

"Yah," the man felt weak and foolish at the crying feeling that wanted to take over him. "I noticed."

David smiled proudly.

"You going to be able to climb down okay?"

The boy wasn't so sure about doing it alone, but he didn't want anyone to see his dad having to help him with *that*. He wouldn't feel as grownup as he had been feeling all morning. First grade— felt like he was starting graduate school.

"Yup."

"Yep? Okay."

Noah reached over and helped him push open the door.

"David," Noah began as his son started to get out. "You feeling better today?"

"Better?"

"The last couple days I thought you were getting sick," he thought about mentioning the wet bed, but decided against it.

The little boy thought about what his dad had told him—that you can have nightmares when you're awake, but what you're experiencing isn't real. He'd been thinking about that a lot and knew it was true. It was just hard to tell himself that something isn't real that's scaring you. When it's something good, it's really easy to know it isn't real. He wondered why.

"I haven't been feeling good. My heart is broken, you know?"

"Your heart is broken?" the young man echoed. He looked worriedly at his son.

"I feel so bad for Mama Cat," David answered.

"Oh… me too buddy."

David took a kiss and a hug before getting out of the truck without incident.

He ran toward the school so his dad would know he was confident, but when he heard the truck pull away from the curb he stopped to watch it go. He blinked at the fierce morning sunlight and shaded it with his hand.

He knew his daddy's heart was broken.

The herd of children from the buses now joined the other students pouring through the two sets of tall glass double doors.

The hall within was lined with cheerful posters about reading and math. Colorful cutouts of numbers and letters and basic math were hung with small rings of cloudy tape that made places in the cutouts cling just a little tighter to the porous wall of lemon-yellow painted brick.

The freshly waxed floors were already scuffed by the time David got inside, but it still smelled new and clean, maybe even more than the day he'd visited the school before.

All the classroom doors were pine and looked warm, like gold, as the morning light ricocheted down the sunny halls. David knew the other classrooms, like the classroom he was told was his, had new erasers at their clean blackboards and unworn cylinders of new chalk laying in the clean troughs below the aged black surface. There would be stacks of new books and old books and workbooks—maybe they would be able to take the plastic off themselves. He wondered what all he'd get to put his name on. It was on every possible thing in his bag, with the exception of individual colors, markers, pencils and the like.

At the first door on the right side of the hall stood a sweet faced woman with almost white blonde hair, and curves that made every section of her body look stacked inside her black dress and floral sweater. She was the only adult in the hall who wasn't leading little people around. Her lips were red and smiling and her eyes were blue, blue, blue. David wanted her to be his teacher. He heard her greeting students she knew. Her laugh was like bells and her voice was sweet and clear. She was standing in front of a classroom and it wasn't his.

"You lost, sweetheart?" she asked him over the heads of the other children.

He shook his head.

"Who is your teacher?"

"I'm in first grade," he let her know. He'd wandered close enough that he could smell her perfume.

"Then you know you need to go to Mr. Han's class, right?"

David nodded. He remembered.

"You're in Han the Yawn's class?" a little boy with flaming orange hair called out. He had a smile like an upside-down triangle.

"Mitchell Davis, be respectful," the beautiful teacher scolded.

"Yes Ms. English," said the grinning boy that was suddenly standing beside them.

"English? This is English class?" David poked his head into the room.

"Her last name's English," the boy corrected loudly.

The teacher put her hand on David's head, her perfectly oval red nails looked like jewels in his hair as she turned him toward the hall. "You *both* need to be getting to class."

"Mrs. English, what class do *you* teach?" David inquired with wide eyes.

She crouched low enough to look him in the face when she answered.

"Just 'Ms.' English, sweetheart, and I teach third grade," she pointed to the sign above the door, just in case he could read it. "You two don't want to be late the first day, so go on."

David *didn't* want to be late, so he hurried the way he remembered. He wanted to run, but he knew not to do that. At the fastest pace he felt he could go, David overtook the boy Ms. English called Mitchell.

They looked at each other curiously as David passed him.

The door to the first grade class was closed right after the warning bell rang. By that time, David hadn't been in his seat long enough for it to be warm. Mitchell Davis came in just as the final bell rang. He breezed past the only adult in the room, a slender Asian man, a little older than David's daddy, who was dressed in what his dad called "business casual", so David was sure it was Mr. Han. The man held the pointer for the chalkboard. That was another clue. His naturally narrow eyes followed Mitchell as he passed.

A number of the kids laughed when Mitchell darted into his seat, as if he'd been there the whole time. There were others with laughter filling their faces, but they thought they'd get in trouble. By lunch David found out that the difference between the children laughing and those just wanting to, were those who had older siblings or not. Older siblings warned their younger brothers and sisters that Mr. Han was no nonsense and that was true.

David was grateful for the temporary distraction Mitchell's hasty entrance had given him from the staring eyes of the small town children. In small towns, either you know everybody or you're a stranger. David was a stranger, even though a number of his classmates heard about him.

"Since this is the first day, this once, we can dismiss your tardiness. If you know you are going to be late you need to bring a note from your parents explaining why. If you don't have a note your name goes up on the board," Mr. Han pointed at the right side of the chalkboard which was separated from the rest by a line of red electric tape. At the top of this column was written "WARNINGS". "After your name goes up, you get a check behind your name for the next offense. One check, extra homework. Two checks, detention. Three checks, I call your parents. They have to leave work or come in special during lunch break and have a conference. Nobody, including me, is going to be happy about that."

Mr. Han's eyes, barely more than slits lined with short straight eyelashes, moved over the class. No one had laughter in their faces, or anywhere else, anymore.

"I expect you to be in class *before* the warning bell. Now that Mitchell has shown us what is not okay, there's no excuse for *any* of you."

Several of the other students shot glares at the red-haired boy.

"Turn around Tara," the man said as he walked over to his desk. He wrote something in a red notebook and stored it in a desk drawer. Then his middle finger read over a sheet on his desk.

"There's a new addition to your class and the town this year…"

David felt his gut flip. Instantly the stares that could find him without turning around, did. He tried to focus on the teacher and raised his hand so it was level with his shoulder. He felt stupid because Mr. Han was already looking at him before he even mentioned there being anyone new.

"David Asheborne?" the man said his name as if he were reading it.

David nodded.

"There he is, class. I'm sure you'll all make him feel welcome."

In his school in New York, when there were new kids, they had to stand up, say their name, then everyone had to say "hi" and if they wanted to say anything about themselves, they could. David couldn't decide if he was grateful or not.

The teacher picked up a binder and started taking roll. He said to raise your hand when you heard your name.

After taking attendance the first grade teacher introduced himself.

"My name is Mr. Han," he pointed to where it was written on the chalkboard.

"Okay," the man closed the binder and put that away too. "Next we need to get through some other rules."

Noah's anxiety about David starting school was tempered by his eagerness to get writing. But his eagerness was tempered by the vehicle he saw idling just past the end of his driveway. The car was full of at least five, maybe six people. He wondered if they weren't wondering if no one was home. He decided not to slow down and drive by to see what they would do when someone saw them and to see if he recognized anyone.

Only one person even looked when he passed, the others were fixated on the house. All of the people were thirty-ish and Native. He wasn't surprised and he didn't feel like having a confrontation. Once he was out of sight, he called the police.

During the second ring, the car tore past him, leaving the pickup in a cloud of dust. Noah threw the truck in reverse and started back toward the house.

The secretary went through the same spiel about forwarding calls and if there was an emergency.

"I don't know if there's an emergency, I haven't gotten in my house yet to find out if it was broken into," he explained just as he parked the truck and jumped out. The secretary told him that he was going to be transferred to an available constable. He got Phil again. Noah wondered if he wasn't the *only* constable in Nibebiitam. He wouldn't be surprised.

"Yes, hello, Phil?" he said as he unlocked the door. "I just got back from dropping my kid off at school and there was a car full of people hanging out on the road in front of my place. I don't know if anyone tried to get inside, but when I went past them a minute later they whipped past me. I couldn't tell if there were more people in the car than there had been."

"Are you back at the house?" Phil asked.

"I'm going in right now."

"Whoa, whoa, whoa!" Noah could almost picture the officer leaning forward on the desk, over donuts, in sudden full attention. "Wait until I can get someone out there to secure the premises."

"You know—never mind. I'm sure it's just more good intentions executed in a bad way." He hung up and angrily stuffed the phone in his pocket.

Noah didn't want to wait. He didn't want to hear any more excuses. A scenario played out in his mind where he did wait and there was someone inside, destroying everything they owned, and the constable patting the person on the back and letting them go. He wished he hadn't even called. He wouldn't have, if instinct hadn't kicked in.

The first thing Noah did was retrieve his baseball bat from the coat closet right by the door. Then he pet Gilder when she came to welcome him home. She was calm—definitely a good sign.

Everything looked just how he left it about forty minutes earlier. The windows were all locked and intact. The back door was still locked and didn't look like it had been tampered with from the outside. He checked the closets, under the beds, and even in the space under the sinks. He wasn't that enthusiastic about checking the attic or basement. There are some fears from childhood that are strong enough to come back to haunt you even as an adult. He was so wound up he felt really susceptible to fear.

The morning light filled most of the stairway to the attic so Noah was glad he decided to check there first.

He was about halfway up the stairs when he heard something. Even though the house was still pretty new to him, he had a bad feeling it came from the basement.

"Shit," he exhaled.

He told himself he could be wrong about that though. Sound is tricky.

"Gilder? Where'd you go girl?"

*Please come up the basement stairs. Please come up the basement stairs.*

*I might have a heart attack if she does*, he considered.

"Gilder?"

She sent out a single high note that sounded like a dog whistle. Her black face and part of her neck were visible at the base of the wall at the end of the hall.

His body jerked like every muscle hiccupped. The cry he made sounded halfhearted—he was embarrassed to spite himself.

"Wanna come check this out with daddy?"

The dog's head withdrew and he heard her cross the kitchen floor to the rug in front of the sink.

Adrenaline surged through his legs and arms. He heard the sound again before he returned to the top step. It sounded like a metal pail, or something, rocking against concrete. His heart started hammering. It felt like he had earbuds in that were pounding pure bass through his head.

After hearing the sound a third time, Noah had tracked it to the top of the basement steps.

Little light reached the basement, so from there he could only dimly see what was at the immediate bottom of the stairs. Someone was standing there.

Suddenly they broke into a run—like a greyhound out of the gate, on all fours, bounding up the stairs—just without touching them. Noah slapped on the light, jumped back and raised his bat. There was nothing there.

Everyone has had those moments when they see things out of the corner of their eyes, but this was getting ridiculous. He made a mental note to call someone out to check the house for gas or something else that might cause hallucinations.

Not since he was a little kid did he "miss-see" so many things.

"Mr. Asheborne?" the call was followed by three strong knocks on the door.

Noah tossed the baseball bat onto the couch. He was pretty sure who would be there. He just didn't know if what he pictured would be the same as the real thing.

"I must be psychic," Noah announced as he opened the door to an average heighted, middle-aged man with a pronounced belly, so pronounced he looked pregnant. He looked at the uniform and then looked at the truck that might have been the Webster's Dictionary image for the word "junker". The only thing that surprised him was that the constable didn't look as Native as his daughter. If at all.

"Hi Phil," Noah said through the screen door.

"Looks like we got off on the wrong foot. I'm sorry," the officer apologized.

The young father studied the older man's face for sincerity. It was there.

Noah stopped in mid-reach to let him in.

"You need to know something," he began, looking Phil sternly in the eyes, "I have a child here who counts on me to keep him safe. No matter how trivial or impossible something is that bothers him, I look into it for him. And no matter how certain I am that it's nothing serious, or perhaps nothing that's even real, my son would never think I was taking it any less seriously than something more momentous. I would expect the same thing from you."

Rather than getting angry, which was what Noah was sure would happen, Phil nodded somberly.

"So should I," Phil agreed.

After a second, just to make sure he wouldn't find a snicker in the constable's eyes, or a smile jerking on the corner of his mouth, Noah believed he was being listened to.

"Would you like some coffee?" Noah offered and held the screen door open.

"You bet."

◆            ◆            ◆

Awkward might not be a strong enough word to describe the feeling between the two men, but it wasn't unbearable yet. The constable's daughter was the only thing they had in common that was amiable. So Noah decided to make a go of conversation in that.

"So, no offense, but how does someone named Phil end up with a daughter named Rising Moon?"

Phil, who turned out to be a big nodder, nodded at the question.

"Her mother's name was White Moon."

"Was? God, I'm sorry," Noah frowned. "There seem to be a lot of families up here without mothers."

"Yours included," Phil noticed.

It was Noah's turn to nod, but he had nothing to say.

"Is that why you left New York?"

Noah took a breath to keep himself from saying something he might regret. The nicest thing he could think to say was that it was none of his business.

"I'm sorry. That's a little personal isn't it?" said Phil.

Noah slid back in his chair and met the constable with a blank face. He thought that was the perfect answer.

"Can I ask if his mom is still around, then?"

"Obviously, not."

It was Phil's turn to lean back.

"We just can't iron this out, can we?"

"You know what they say about first impressions," Noah said as much to himself as Phil.

"Can you give me a break because you work with my daughter?" the constable tried.

That detail *was* all but forgotten at this point.

"I think people control their own destiny. You make your own breaks. You want to fix this—*fix this*. It's as simple as that."

"I wish I could fix your problem, Noah," Phil conceded earnestly.

"You need to crack down on this shit," Noah jabbed his finger into the tabletop. "What pisses me off is that you obviously knew this was a problem, you probably know who's doing it and you're doing nothing. No more excuses. Do something," Noah raised his hand when Phil tried to cut in, "You feel like you can keep doing nothing because the world is looking the other way, but you don't want this shit posted on the couple hundred sites and blogs my friends run. You don't want me to write a nice long article about it for the tens of thousands of people who follow my author's page. You don't want the world looking this way. No one around here does. I'm not blind."

"But—"

"But *nothing*. I've been doing some digging. You tell me why there are so many accidental deaths in the area. This year alone there have been forty-four deaths ruled as accidental. This month alone there have been six. And how many people from out of town are still looking for their loved ones who were supposed to be in this area before they disappeared. And then try to tell me how, even though the population of Nibebiitam is about sixty-four percent native, that eighty-five percent of these accidents are white."

"Do you think because I'm Matis that I'd turn my back on these things?"

Noah shrugged, "You tell me what it looks like, then."

"I understand that," Phil put both hands out flat, knuckles up, the classic "calm down" position. "But you need to understand some things you're not going to find in any old newspapers or death records."

"Go ahead."

Phil opened his mouth. It hung open for several seconds before he took another sip of coffee instead of answering.

"We can't call all those deaths undetermined," Phil explained. "That would make the world look this way and all that would bring was a lot of trouble and, I'm afraid, more deaths. No matter how you feel about the things people are telling you, there's something to it. Because there are a lot of unexplainable things going on here. I'm not local either, Noah, I went through a whole lot denial and confusion before I did the only thing I could do and that was accept that this is the way things are here. This is how it's been for the past maybe two hundred years. I'm not inexperienced in police work, even if I work in a small country town. I have seen a lot of murders in my day, believe me. A person just can't explain some of the things that happen around here. People can't stomach it—that includes the Native people around here too—including the people that have upset you. They can't stomach the deaths. Getting to know neighbors and um dying so reliably they *count* on it happening. That's why they want you to move on. Because you're a white guy living in the woods with his family. There comes a point when you believe something is so dangerous that you feel responsible for the harm that happens when you did nothing. At least, they are probably thinking that they tried."

After a long silence Noah managed to look Phil in the eyes, "You're telling me you believe in all that crap?"

Phil shook his head adamantly, "I didn't say that. I just said when you can't find answers, you accept what seems to make sense to other people."

"Well then," Noah stood up and dumped out his cold coffee. "Please let people know that I got the message and thanks, but no thanks."

"I have talked to some people who are probably the ringleaders and told them to back off," Phil let him know.

"Fantastic."

"Noah," the constable rotated the chair so he could face the younger man. "You don't feel like you can go back, do you? You feel cornered."

Noah shook his head, but the truth was, he always felt that way.

After a little small talk, which was unrelated and probably purely meant to leave things on a better note, the constable took his leave. Noah hadn't missed, for the whole duration of the very long visit, that Phil hadn't received a single call. He felt pissed again. That was one thing he wasn't sure about, how busy the police were. One time isn't enough to claim a standard, but it was a start.

Noah sat down to get back to his writing project, but what he really wanted to do was start writing about this. There was a book here. He didn't usually write non-fiction, not unless text books count, but he loved history and Nibebiitam's was sordid to say the least.

Hours had passed and Noah came out of the writing purge realizing he had to pee and that he was hungry. He felt like he'd only just sat down. The whole time he was working he was thinking about the things he'd turned up, not to mention the plethora of information Derrick's friend was able to dig up. Kendal was someone who they went to college with. He thought she was interesting, but a little intense in her sense of sleuthing. Derrick thought, her being bookish, she'd be an easy lay and they often hooked up over the years. At a New Year's Eve party Derrick threw one year, Noah asked her if she saw much of Derrick, she told him she only slept with Derrick that first time to find out what sex was about. She craved information. And so, to answer his questions, they only got together when he promised to show her something new. Apparently, she didn't have any use or time for a boyfriend.

Before Noah knew it he had to pick David up from school. He was actually a little late.

Gilder wiggled like a fish on land when she caught sight of her other human running up to the truck. Noah reached across the seat and let the door open enough so David could get in.

"Hey, hey, hey! You look like you had a good first day," Noah remarked as the smiling child climbed into the seat beside him. David was breathless and beaming so hard his father couldn't tell which was making the boy's cheeks so rosy.

"Dad, I missed you!" the first day first grader threw his arms around as much of his dad as he could hold.

"Did you have fun?" Noah pressed, since David didn't immediately go into a long explanation of all the things that made the day good.

"Mr. Han hates kids. I wish I was in third grade," David pouted.

"What's in third grade?"

"Mrs. English," David said the name lovingly.

"Oh yeah? Then she must like kids," Noah guessed.

David shrugged. He didn't know. It didn't matter.

"Did you make any friends?"

"Umm, I met everyone. Mostly everyone was nice, but Mitchell is a bad boy."

"He *is*?"

The little boy nodded. He looked so serious Noah had a hard time keeping a straight face.

*What the hell did this Mitchell do?*

"Yup, he got his name on the board and *three* checks!" David explained, his voice drenched in disgust.

"What do three checks mean?"

"That means he went too far."

Father and son looked at each other to make sure all the details of the story were understood.

"So this is someone I shouldn't allow you to have visit?"

"Nope, dad. He was a red-headed stepchild."

"*David*," Noah said disapprovingly.

"Well that's what Derrick says," the six-year-old protested.

"Your uncle Derrick says a lot of things I wouldn't want you to say."

"Like the effer?"

"Yep."

"Well, he is bad. He was kinda mean to some of the kids. He made up a mean rhyme about Mr. Han and got some of the other kids to say it too."

"Don't you ever repeat it," Noah said sternly. He knew how children can get each other excited enough about things that they do stuff they know they shouldn't.

"I won't," David agreed. "It has the effer in it."

A mental note went up on the memory board in his father's head. Mitchell was officially blacklisted.


After supper, Noah put in one of David's videos and went to have a shower. Mama Cat was pissy and anxious. Noah told her twice not to bully Gilder because she was having a bad day. He didn't know what was up with her, but during supper she started getting hissy and even took a whack at Gilder's face when the poor sweet dog tried to sniff her.

"Mean little kitty," Noah scolded as he took out a towel and closed the bathroom door on her almost flat, angry looking face.

He needed to clear his thoughts. There was something about showers that took his mind to a place where he could organize the things going on in his head. In the relaxing heat of the soothing water, setting his mind free, he often came up with a lot of ideas for stories.

Noah leaned into the jets of hot water, the shampoo suds rushed softly across his lean muscular body. The water pressure for a moment felt like a hand pressing down on his head. He ignored the fleeting sensation as simply that, but it made his heart jump a little.

His left hand scrubbed out the soap while his right hand wiped off the largest collections of suds. His fingertips brushed the base of his penis as he pushed away the lather. He looked down through the glassy spirals of water running off his head. A not unpleasant ache arose in his gut and started to work through his body.

*Why not*, he thought and felt. There was no one else to do it for him.

He began to massage the already stiffening shaft when he heard the rumpling sound of the shower curtain being disturbed.

His eyes had automatically closed as he worked on a mental prop to help things along, but now they were open wide and staring at the creamy, semi-transparent sheet between him and the foggy bathroom.

*Foggy?*

Noah released himself and pulled back one side of the curtain to look out into the room. Mama Cat wasn't there. It wouldn't be the first time she put a scare on him while he was in the shower. David wasn't there. Fog shouldn't be either—at least not this bad but—he'd forgot to open the window.

"Damn," he muttered and closed the shower curtain again. There wouldn't be any point to open it now. He really needed to get an exhaust fan installed.

Obviously, he'd just brushed the curtain himself.

The curtain slowly billowed inward as if a slight but constant breeze filled it.

Noah shoved back the curtain, expecting to see David using the toilet. There would be a breeze if the door opened. But, again, he was alone.

The shower curtain suddenly flapped and bowed inward like a sail full of wind. A sound of roaring winds filled the bowl-like shape of the curtain. Noah threw himself into the corner, bruising his hip on the faucet of the tub and knocking the showerhead-wand off its stand. It landed loudly in the bottom of the tub. The pelting water felt like teeth, or beetles, or small hands feeling up his legs and testicles as the showerhead rocked in the draining water by his feet. He fled the sensation and the shower and spilled out onto the bathroom floor. The pain in his shins, from tumbling over the porcelain wall between him and security, left him believing he'd broken both his legs.

Regardless, he threw himself over on his back at the unequivocal sense that something was bearing down on him. He raised his arms and cried out at the anticipation of teeth.

It did him no good to keep thinking to himself how he didn't believe in ghosts. He found no comfort in it either. Comfort was exactly what he hoped to find.

His eyes darted around the room and fell on the flapping window curtains.

Panting and shaking like a leaf, Noah cocked his head and frowned at the sheer dancing sheets of three gold tones and a print of coppery leaves. He smelled the air outside. He felt the air trace his body, cooling as it found every inch of available skin.

"Oh my God, you're fucking stupid," Noah forced a laugh. He raised up on his elbows and watched the curtains for about a minute to be sure he was seeing what he thought he was seeing. He just hadn't been able to tell the window was open because of the curtains.

*And,* he told himself, *I didn't really look very hard anyway.*

But that was only true for his explanation of what happened. Despite being so afraid, his erection was showing how much braver it was than him. He got up on his knees and worked at finishing the job.

Sex was always so good with his wife. They didn't have a lot of problems. Even when they fought they always ended up making love. After fighting, sex almost always felt like their first time. He didn't like to ever call it "fucking" but sometimes there was no other word for the sex they had. That was what he was thinking about, as he leaned on the side of the tub for leverage against the desire and loss his body was arrested in. In the back of his mind was a little voice that said it felt a little stupid jerking off after having just being scared like that.

It was also saying that the window *had* been closed.

*It had*, the voice insisted.

# TREATED LIKE DIRT

◆

Amy Proctor moved stiffly in her unforgiving uniform. The stiff cotton material might look sharp on slim nurses or cute on pudgy little housekeepers, but most days Amy felt like a log being rocked from side to side to create motion. She was too uncomfortable to be comfortable with people and, over the past ten years, had all but alienated herself from friends and family she once was enviably close to.

She couldn't tell them that she was afraid all the time. So afraid when she was around them that they would see through her silence and uncover her darkest secret and thereby the reason why, or at least the best reason she could think of, why her life was falling apart—the one thing she didn't mention about the night she was robbed in the parking lot.

Amy was in tears, as she often was.

It was safe.

It was safe to cry, at least.

She rarely saw anyone while she was working the night shift and she wouldn't have it any other way. She didn't like to see people. She didn't like people to see her. She thought about what they were thinking. What were they thinking of her? What did they want to do to her? Did they want to hurt her?

Why?

Because she was big?

Because she wasn't doing a "respectable" job?

She was, after all, treated lower than the sprayed shit she often cleaned off the walls behind toilets.

Because she was a woman?

Because she wasn't beautiful?

Because no one would miss her? Which was only true to her...

So, Amy was in tears. She often was.

No one would see, so no one would ask what was wrong.

Her leg, that she thought looked the same size from her hip all the way down to her foot, extended to drive the gray, rubbery stop under the bathroom door. A mop was already in her hand, as she'd followed tracks from the vestibule, through the lobby, and to the small one person unisex bathroom.

*So someone bee-lined here before registering. That figures,* she thought. It would have been easier to vacuum this crap off the enormous carpets leading to the front desk. Carpets "Muddy Feet" completely bypassed.

By the time the tracks reached the bathroom, they started to dry and were less sloppy and more defined. Amy thought she'd followed boot tracks to the restroom, but it started to look like the prints were made by bare feet. She stopped mopping to get a better look at them. She reached into the room and flipped on the light switch. She cursed under her breath. Half of the mess was caused because "Muddy Feet" felt it necessary to bring a dog—a

BIG fucking dog into the clinic and track half the mud in Ontario in with them.

The tracks looked strange.

They looked like someone walked in on the front of their bare feet and went to sit on the toilet. But the tracks to the toilet and where she would *expect* to find them, at the base of the toilet, looked more like the dog's tracks.

At some point a good housekeeper could almost do "mess" forensics. But even if she hadn't been a good housekeeper she couldn't have overlooked the fact that this muddy trail went only one way.

Amy felt like she wasn't allowed to realize that until that very moment. There were a lot of other things she didn't realize until that moment either.

She didn't realize until that instant that once the "boots" or bare feet went into the bathroom, there were *only* the dog tracks. These tracks were almost the size of her hand. It was no part of a bare foot. Even though she was sure she saw boot tracks, she was sure she also saw bare footprints in the bathroom. *But they weren't there.* It was as if every spot she thought they were was smudged now or clean.

She briefly entertained the thought that "Muddy Feet" rushed the dog, that wouldn't be allowed, into the bathroom and locked it in while they went to their appointment. But Amy was a good housekeeper and she couldn't entertain that idea for long.

The clinic's bathroom doors can only be locked once they are closed, otherwise they will unlock again. So nothing would keep anyone from finding his pet.

Besides, and probably most disturbing to Amy, there was only the set of tracks leading to the toilet.

A quick glance told her there was no way this person, a guy—by the size of the tracks, had cleaned up in the sink and thereafter left no tracks. One—she'd never seen anyone, at anytime, anywhere, whose version of cleaning up was even remotely what a conscious patient care cleaner would do. For their best intentions, people always leave something, but the sink was almost perfectly clean. And two—there wasn't enough waste in the garbage or missing from the paper towel dispenser to clean up the mess this would have been.

*And why*, she wondered as she realized more and more of what she couldn't see or wasn't there before—*why are the prints in front of the toilet the dog's*?

For a split second she had an irrational, but what felt like the only logical, explanation for this: a werewolf. And while she wanted to laugh, she felt terrified instead—that's how sure she was that this was the only explanation, no matter how implausible. It was almost as if the tracks suddenly looked like "werewolf" tracks to her instead of a dog's. Like she should know what a werewolf's tracks are supposed to look like.

She had a feeling in her gut, in her consciousness, as if she was coming out of a coma.

*Are those handprints?*

Amy was staring so hard at the prints that she was afraid her vision was blurring and distorting. She told herself not to trust what she was seeing.

She was too afraid to rub her eyes, because for that brief moment she wouldn't be able to see.

She had a feeling something was still in the room—no matter how empty it looked.

The hair prickled on her neck and she backed from the bathroom door like it was the toothy maw of a gigantic beast.

Until that very moment, Amy hadn't believed in werewolves. When she saw the tracks change, she believed with all her heart. That had been enough to make the housekeeper temporarily forget something else she did believe in.

What dread she felt of werewolves was instantly erased by terror a hundred times that—when she found out the truth about a local legend she always felt had too much evidence to not believe in.

"No. No, no, no, no," Amy stammered, backing away from the room that appeared empty, but felt like it was bursting with life… or, at the very least, presence.

The shadows in the sparsely lit lobby were inadequate to conceal the creatures racing between "hiding spots".

They looked like patients.

She swore they wore hospital gowns, but she couldn't really tell. She didn't dare look, because what she *couldn't* see, in the restroom, was more threatening—or so she thought.

BOOM! BOOM! BOOM!

Someone or something heavy was running down the hall on the floor above her. It was running toward the stairs, stairs almost directly behind her.

The pounding made her eardrums vibrate. A box of disposable gloves fell off the back of her cart. Her dust mop and duster fell out of the rubbery slots that were supposed to hold them.

*It* was coming down the stairs.

The waves of sound reverberated through the air, a sound like heavy boots. Distinctly, and from all directions she heard the sound of nails on hard floors, and throaty animal panting.

Something tore in Amy's neck as she whipped her head around to look up the wide flight of steps. Teeth sunk into her arm and released and clamped and released, like a machine, more than a beast. She stared down at the thing and it stared up at her. Many others were there, staring up too.

Then she felt a rough wet tongue under her fingertips and the hot, humid cavern of a mouth seconds before its teeth severed them from her hand.

A bite took her elbow, the strong yank that followed, tugged her face and throat within range of more teeth.

She couldn't even scream.

She tried.

Amy opened her mouth in pain and filled her lungs with air enough that surely someone would have heard if the scream hadn't miscarried. Her mouth filled with the long narrow snout of something like a hairless dog and the thing, starting with her tongue, began eating its way down her throat. It chewed at the roof of her mouth and gums. Its teeth sunk into the pink flesh among the roots of her teeth and yanked stubbornly to pull them. When it couldn't, the thing's little fingers pawed at her face. Its thumbs fit into the corners of Amy's mouth, beside its bald, wrinkled mug, and shoved down on her jaw until it tore away from her skull.

Through the maddening pain they made her feel their feast. By their will alone they demanded she live and live a little longer. The housekeeper felt the things eat the meat and snap the tendons behind her knees. One nuzzled against her bottom, ripping through the fabric and resumed eating. She was conscious that it tried to push its muzzle into her anus, even as the efforts of several of the things spilled her guts out on the floor.

One of these started to fight with that who was now inside up to its ears.

They were yipping and yowling and every inch of her was bitten. If they didn't bite, their course tongues licked away her skin. They licked her hands and feet—which were calloused from hard work and fun to chew. One of them squealed when her keys fell loudly against the floor.

Between these pale fiends that toyed with her waning existence, something black with long, dark, spidery limbs moved throughout them. Supervising them. It was something like a man. In its nakedness, clearly male. Something about its posture reminded her of a hyena.

Amy was nearly dead when she felt this dark monster stand behind her. Her last thought was that there was nothing left for him to eat but her soul.

She'd never seen anyone, at anytime, anywhere, whose version of cleaning up was even remotely what a conscious patient care cleaner could do. For their best intentions, people always leave something.

There wasn't a trace of Amy.

Her cart was in its closet. No sign of "Muddy Feet" remained in the lobby or in the memory of any who were there when the clinic closed. Staff were left to wonder if she even showed up for work. Until later that week when Amy's keys were found under one of the chairs in the lobby by a housekeeper that wasn't quite as good, didn't even try to be, and didn't care.

Not until the night *she* heard something rushing down the stairs.

# CHAPTER 14

◆

# HUNTER's MOON

David put on the last of the six pairs of socks to silence his footsteps and prayed for the best. The *best* would include Fawn remembering to bring her bike around back because that was only a few steps from his bedroom. He rarely slept with his bedroom door open, thinking this would keep the monsters out, but tonight his daddy hadn't questioned the change of pace. Everything was going as planned. He was soundless and smooth, gliding across the floor like a shadow.

"Oh shit!" he exclaimed.

Noah had added a chain and deadbolt on the backdoor because they hardly use it and might be more likely to forget to lock it. Noah also didn't like the idea of a regular doorknob lock being the only thing between whatever might be outside and them snuggled warm in their beds. These locks were well out of David's reach. His daddy had been pretty pissed when they were installed so high, but rather than having more work done, he put a single step stool by the door, in case of emergencies. David wasn't confident to be able to move the stool without waking up his dad.

*Oh well*, he grumbled silently, *my shoes aren't back here anyway*.

Everything, just *everything* was going wrong.

Suddenly his feet flew out from under him and his head hit the hallway wall. One flailed arm hooked the stand with the hall lamp and it sounded like he took the whole house down with him as he landed in the position of a gingerbread man under a lamp, a drawer from the stand, some junk mail that was never moved, any number of toy cars and action figures, and other things. The light crashed and a cup of pens, a notepad and keys spilled all over the floor around the pool of David.

"Solomon already asked if you could go to the pow-wow, David," Noah called from the bedroom. He was wide awake and had been the whole time. David had thought it weird for his dad to go to bed at six.

"Come in here," his daddy called in a tone that meant the boy was going to get a talking to.

It took a moment to sort himself out of the pile. David hoped that wouldn't be held against him.

Noah was sitting with his legs folded underneath him, his laptop in his lap, notebooks, and a few library books around him like a force field. He took off his reading glasses only far enough to put the end of one arm against his lower lip so it was accessible to chew on.

"You were going to sneak out?"

"But—"

"You're lucky, mister, that one of you had the good sense to just talk to us. Just because we're living in the sticks doesn't mean that you can just take off into the world whenever you want, at any time of day. It's dangerous here. Just dangerous in a different way. You're six years old. What are you thinking?"

"Well—"

"Are you scared of me?" the lenses of the glasses touched the laptop keyboard when he asked his son this.

"No," David answered matter-of-factly and shamefully.

"So why did you feel like you couldn't ask me?"

When David started over to the bed his dad made room for his son to climb up beside him.

"I thought it was something secret that I couldn't talk about. Because I'm white I have to sneak in."

"Who told you that?"

"No one," David replied.

"Well, I can promise you that it's not true. Anyone can go to pow-wows. Solomon said that we'd be welcome there. That *anyone* would be, as long as they observe the rules and respect the traditions. And I know you're going to listen to Fawn and do whatever she says so you can both have a good time tonight, right?"

"Right!"

"So no more sneaking?"

"Nope," David agreed, but he wasn't sure he would never need to, again.

"You know you can tell me everything. *Anything*. No matter if it scares you or if you think it will scare me. And it really scares me that you were willing to sneak out. We're in this together David. We can't be a team if we don't work like a team, can we?"

"We *are* a team, dad," the little boy crammed himself into the space below Noah's right arm and his waist.

"Alright. So I'm gonna help you out kiddo. You better get ready because Solomon said he'd be here by 7."

"I knew I'd be out past my bedtime," David added guiltily.

"Every once and a while doesn't hurt," said the man who was completely aware that David staying up late only hurt himself.

"I'm going to the *partaaaay*!"

"It's not a party," Noah pointed out to the little body rocketing toward the door. David shot him a smile and disappeared. The reading glasses slipped back on and the man returned to his work.

He wondered how often he'd have ever smiled without David and The Guilt returned. The Guilt that reminded Noah he hadn't wanted to be a dad, *ever*.

◆          ◆          ◆

Solomon separated from the kids shortly after they arrived at the pow-wow, saying he would meet them in an hour or two, after being flagged down by a group of half a dozen men around his age.

Fawn took David's hand and lead him through the crowd of mostly First Nation's people. His heart was pounding and had been since they were near enough to hear the sounds of the gathering through the open truck windows. It was exciting to be out late and the fires and warm bulbs of strung lights gave the event a fair-like feeling. The drums made his pulse race. There was a sense of being in another world. It was like Mardi Gras for First Nations people, or something. Everyone was dressed up. Many people, both men and women, had their dark shiny hair pleated into very long braids. He was fascinated by the colors and the feathers. The beads and the paint.

Fawn looked like the dolls that they'd seen in a lot of the gas station/gift shops that they stopped at on the way from New York. She looked just like the Indian dolls. David never would have guessed she could actually look that much like a girl. He was proud to come here with her and Solomon. They looked so good, but he was a little embarrassed to have nothing special to wear himself, even though Fawn assured him he didn't need anything.

When Fawn told David the things he should and shouldn't do, he felt a little overwhelmed. He was concerned about offending people. If everyone looked like "normal people" he wouldn't have been so concerned, but the outfits rang the truth loud and clear, this was something *completely* new. If David wanted to get the most out of it, he needed to pay attention and observe the rules. He could learn a lot from what other people do and then the next time it would be easier.

The smell of pot wafted through the air, but Fawn insisted it was the scent of burning sage. She said drugs and booze weren't allowed at pow-wows. He grinned at the thought of NYPD hearing *that* as an excuse, even though it was true. David knew *that smell* from the older brother of one of his classmates who was "toking-up" when he was supposed to be minding David and his friend overnight. It was called "marijuana", among other things, in New York, David had explained to Fawn, but she'd bored of insisting it was sage.

Either way the odor was thick there. That and the smell of tanned leather and the dusty, earthy smell of feathers. There were other smells that interested him a lot too. The aroma of food, and he was getting hungry. Whenever he was anxious he got hungry.

People were eating and he wanted it.

"What is that?" David was careful not to point, even though that wasn't one of the rules Fawn told him about, it was one of his daddy's rules, but it made it impossible for Fawn to know what the six-year-old was talking about.

"What?"

"That," David said again. Then realizing the problem he added, "What the lady in yellow is eating."

"You don't know what wild rice is?"

He didn't, but he liked the sound of it.

"I'll get you something to eat in just a bit," Fawn promised.

Painted faces looked down on the little white boy. Hot mustard yellow streaks and dots ran along one man's rust-colored skin. A mask of glossy black wrapped across another man's face, and a point like the blade of a butcher knife shot down from his left eye. From what would be the edge of the black blade was a curtain of white paint dressed with red spots. His eyes were like black pearls and his skin looked like some kind of dark peanut butter, to David.

Either of the men's long hair was joined with feathers of large birds and something, the boy guessed, was hair. There were a lot of people with these very soft looking and dramatic flourishes that responded to every movement they made, to the very slightest disturbance in the air. Porcupine quills and black beads gathered in bands around another man's wrists and neck. A hundred-million-billion brilliantly colored beads in sharp geometric patterns temporarily gave David ADD.

Some of the people's clothes rustled in interesting ways, other people (like Fawn) wore clothes that made sounds like bells.

Fawn told him this was for a jingly dance.

That was why David couldn't have any food right now, because he needed to be good and stay there while Fawn went out in the open arena.

He was nervous about being alone so Fawn had left for just a minute to get him ice cream to sate him.

David looked numbly at the dripping ice cream cone clutched in his sticky right hand. Fawn squeezed her hand over his and patted his head.

"You'll be okay, just wait here a minute. I bet it won't even feel that long."

"Okay," he squeaked.

After she disappeared, his eyes fell resentfully upon that cone.

*Why do older people think treats will comfort kids*, he thought gloomily.

On either side of him stood Anishinabe men of Fawn's band. Very little of their bronze skin was exposed, and the beadwork painted the colorful fabric with lively patterns. They wore beautiful headdresses with lots of feathers, quills, and the stuff like hair. A child half his age wandered past in a full fringed leather dress, holding the hand of her mother.

David the Comfortable Anywhere, took over for David the Cautious and Sometimes Shy.

"Pocahontas, eat your heart out," he elbowed the man to his right. They both looked at him.

Boy, he wished he could be naked and covered in paint like the paintings of Indians in some of the history books at the library. And, in fact, many of the illustrations he'd *ever* seen of Native people. All those pretty beads and feathers, or fringed pants with moccasins. Maybe *just* moccasins and the biggest headdress in the world.

"I'm David," he said, suddenly timid again, to the man on his left. The one he elbowed.

"*Boozhoo*, David," he answered, smiling kindly.

The other man was smiling too as he looked down at the curly headed boy around his waist level.

"Boo shoo?" David repeated uncertainly.

The two smiled again. They looked an awful lot alike. He was pretty sure Fawn planted him between brothers and he felt bad. No one should separate family.

He started to fidget after they fell quiet. With the heavy pounding of the drums and the chest swelling singing and dancing he couldn't believe he'd feel so awkward and set apart—these things were the very air he breathed, but between these men...

"Don't you like ice cream?" asked the brother on his right.

David looked at him alarmed and hurriedly licked around the drips. Was he mad? Defensive? Offended? He couldn't remember any rules about food.

"I like it," David wailed. He wanted to cry. Where was Fawn?

"It's a little different here, isn't it, David?" asked the, assumed, brother on the left who smiled comfortingly.

David nodded.

"Why do you have pow-wows?" David asked whichever of them wanted to answer.

"Lots of reasons," said the man on his left, "We had an Acorn Festival and a Harvest Moon pow-wow. We're getting together now as harvesting is over and it is now the time of the hunter. This is a gathering for the Hunter's Moon."

"Hunter's Moon?" David felt a chill run up the back of his head. He wasn't sure which one of them it was, but there was a big hand on his back that rubbed away the fear. He had a feeling they knew what he was thinking and what he was feeling.

Changes were happening in the arena and suddenly a lot of women covered in bells like Fawn, including Fawn, entered the circle. More and more people filled the space behind them. The tall young men squatted at the same time, conscious that their height blocked the onlookers who came up behind them. They were now on David's level. The brother on the left pointed out Fawn. She looked like a piece of the night sky in her dark blue dress with long silver bells. Every move of her dance made the narrow silver pieces on her dress bounce and make watery tinkling sounds. There were countless women and girls with similar dresses on. The sound of their jingling defied description.

The brother with the black blade painted on his face put his hand on David's shoulder and patted it.

"You like the Jingle Dance?" asked the other brother.

"I like it all," David admitted dreamily.

That was true.

# CHAPTER 15

◆

# INDEPENDENT STUDY

Noah's sat up straight in bed; so fast and hard, he thought he might have pulled something in his stomach. While he rubbed at the soreness, the rest of his body was tense and alert to hear again the sound that woke him. Somebody—some*bodies* were whooping and crying out in the yard. It sounded like kids.

He heard at least two run across the deck. No less than three in the chorus.

"Sons of bitches," he muttered angrily as he tossed the covers aside.

David got home from the pow-wow pretty late and should be sleeping hard, but he needed to check on his son before addressing the disturbance.

After peeking on David, to make sure he was asleep, Noah went to the front door, the baseball bat from the closet clenched in one hand.

Looking over his shoulder to check the time, 4:11am, he spotted Gilder. She was crammed into the corner by the kitchen sink. She'd pulled the runner rug up against and somewhat over her. She whimpered when he reached for the doorknob.

Mama Cat stood in between the living room and kitchen, stiff like all her legs were in casts, being pissy again.

Seeing her made the hair on the back of his neck prickle.

*Maybe I should call the police*, he considered. He didn't want to be hasty. What grown man can't handle a few punks?

*Remember the French movie* Them*?*

The kids were starting to make sounds like pigs and dogs, and other indistinguishable animal-like sounds. He turned on the porch light, expecting the little bastards to run like hell, but they only became more excited.

Unable to bear the grunting, smacking, panting, hackling, cackling any longer—Noah slammed through the two closed doors. In the heavy silence that met him, the screen door's hard, tinny, bouncing effort to close made him scream. His throat and the door rattled and whined as each settled. Too wound up.

*A mosquito's fart would probably kill me.*

Shaking in the absolute quiet and empty yard, Noah felt embarrassed, though he knew he didn't have any reason to be. There was no way he imagined all of that—was there?

He reached out hesitantly and pushed the screen door closed securely—he heard the click and then looked back at the property. Noah was alarmed at how winded he sounded. A cold sweat broke out on his trembling flesh. The fingers of surplus terror trickled down his back and along the sides of his face.

*Where are you little bastards?*

In the back of his consciousness, a little voice asked if he'd ever seen anything besides animals tremble like this. He didn't have to answer "no", he felt the word behind his chattering teeth.

Animals hear things, see things, all the time that only some people experience some of the time.

The voice insisted: *What you are facing down?*

*What is facing you down is that* something *animals have always tried to warn us was there.*

*There.*

Whatever it was hadn't left—the woods?

The outbuilding?

The yard?

The front porch?

Whatever they were, were biting their lips to keep from laughing.

*They'll bite your lips off and their teeth will kiss yours.*

They were shifting their feet to satisfy the urge to chase Noah to his death. They salivated at the dumb horror they struck in the man.

When the young father's desperately probing eyes—

*You don't really want to see*

–incidentally met theirs in passing. Eyes, glinting like pinholes in a pleated fleshy blanket, fixed unblinking on Noah and drank up his sudden and unsettling awareness of mortality. Mortality, the things adored and resented. Mortality was the mother of fear, but inevitably the device to end their very favorite games.

Noah didn't want to see.

*I don't want to know.*

He knew what it felt like to be terrified at his own home. This was his second "do-over" and it pissed him off to be scared again. The anger was enough to bate his fear, a little, for a moment.

The two inch step up through the front doors almost tripped him, but the invisible force that successfully urged him back inside also kept him from falling.

*They'll get you!*

The same invisible force that drives all gut reactions.

*They will get you!*

The dead bolt slid solidly into its reassuring position. The lock on the door knob clicked pathetically in place next.

*False security.*

Within the next few hours he would interact with them a record number of times.

*No one sees them until they decide to kill.*

When Noah misplaced his coffee cup.

Did he really leave the kitchen towel there?

*Put it back.*

How did it get on the floor?

*Put it back!*

When a step ends in a—STAMP!—because your feet brake so hard when you think—

*Did I just see the shower curtain move?*

Just like later, when he was shaving in the small round mirror in that shower and he was sure—

*Certain*

that a child's?

a dog's?

a child's face was pressed against the cream colored lining.

*Not again...*

For the rest of the shower, when Noah shampooed, when he rinsed, whenever he looked away, the curtain had opened just a little bit more…

Had it?

*Just a draft.*

That's what they always say…

That night, too close to David's bedtime to sensibly start a movie, father and son settled on the couch for "Guy's Night."

*I don't care if he's cranky tomorrow*, Noah told himself, *This'll be a nice end to this crazy week.*

After a while, despite his best efforts, Noah could not tell himself the mohawk running down Gilder's back wasn't a sign that

*Something's there…*

and why Gilder would not look away from the picture window no matter what father and son said.

Something in his—

*flesh preserving soul*

—gut told Noah to stay the hell away from that fucking window.

*Just stay the fuck away from it!*

David fell asleep at his regular time—

*Dammit!*

—and slept peacefully on his father's stiff body.

Fear induced rigor mortis?

*That's when you die of fear.*

He ate an inappropriately huge laugh.

Noah barely blinked, much less slept.

So, come morning, father and son matched each other in crankiness.

David was almost cheerful when the local news talked about the cold weather. There was a good chance they would soon get snow.

◆        ◆        ◆

With every southbound migrating flock, the more desolate North felt. Leaving behind a sense of abandonment, even as the earth filled with cold. Winter is the anti-energy—like a vampire, it drains life to raise cold and quiet. Dark geese, with great pale bellies, cut through the sky while some mammals, amphibians, and reptiles bed down for the long sleep. For a short time there is an abundance of life and sounds, but little other than man seems foolish enough to stay around or stay awake to witness the dying of the year.

David was preoccupied with a lot of things, two of them involved the season. He wanted to find the cave he saw when they encountered Silver Fox Man.

David was convinced there was no coincidence meeting him there. He felt like he and Fawn must have been in danger and he was warning them. They were out in the woods pretty late. Naana said he would protect people.

David wasn't scared of him anymore, it was just scary to be near something that felt like he did. It made the boy feel helpless and breakable. Like everything in nature, including himself, could do nothing against Silver Fox Man's will.

Even so, David wasn't afraid to go back. When it was winter, there wouldn't be as much crap over the opening. Somehow he'd have to force Fawn to take him back. He knew it would come to that, because Fawn had already refused thirteen hundred times.

She said it was probably a bear den or an abandoned mine—two things too dangerous to be poking around in.

The other thing he was thinking about was Fawn's promise that he would have proof when the first snow fell. It was getting really cold. There had been flurries. It was only a matter of time, maybe days, maybe hours. He was pretty diligent about asking his daddy what the forecast was. But it's not always right.

After school he would be at Fawn's. Then David would put his plan into action to get Fawn to go to the cave with him.

◆          ◆          ◆

"Mind if I join you?" Noah asked the barrier of newspaper and the fingers holding it open.

During his lunch break Noah liked to have a cup of coffee. This was the first time he ever saw David's teacher there, having noticed him through the glass. Once inside, he would have seen only the paper. With that in mind, maybe this wasn't the first time he'd "seen" Mr. Han there, but Noah sensed a rare opportunity to pick the pedagogue's brain about Nibebiitam, since, as rumor had it, he was an "out-of-towner" too.

Mr. Han lowered the paper, folded it indifferently and half tossed it on the window sill under the "NER" of the neon sign reading "DINER." The deceptively youthful teacher's impossibly narrow eyes somehow indicated that he looked up at Noah. He nodded and said, "Sure."

He'd no sooner sat in the seat than the waitress, none of which were under forty, served him with coffee, his regular, and a menu.

"Do you mind if I share your lunch break?" Noah asked.

"Sure," said the quiet schoolteacher.

After ordering, Noah settled into the pervasive silence of Kim Han's presence.

"My son, David, is one of your students."

Han didn't react. He blinked a couple times at the obvious and shifted on his seat.

"How long have you been teaching?" Noah asked.

"Nine years," he paused and added, "Three here."

"Where are you from?"

Kim Han wasn't used to questions. He wasn't used to anyone bothering. Not even the basement church people bothered him anymore. He felt a little bombarded by *three* questions, usually being a "one question's all they have" kind of guy.

His mind went blank. For a second Han wasn't sure if he *could* remember. Then he guessed what he was probably *really* being asked.

"Do you mean '*originally*'?"

"I suppose there aren't a lot Asians up here. You must get asked that a lot?"

Han shrugged. He didn't feel like explaining how diverse Canada is. In Nibebiitam he was the only Korean, now.

"Sorry, I meant 'where' as far as cities go. Are you not Canadian?"

"I'm Canadian," Kim took a breath and tried to get ahead of the next question. "I was born in Montreal."

"But most the time people are really asking, 'Where are you *from*'?"

The reserved schoolteacher could only force himself to nod.

"Do you mind if I ask you a strange question?"

"How strange?"

Noah smiled before he realized Mr. Han wasn't joking.

"When you moved here, were you bombarded with stories about evil spirits that run-amok and kill people, well beyond their regular duties as Mr. Nobodies?"

Kim Han looked up at Noah for only a second, the closest he'd come to looking someone in the eyes in months.

His dark brown eyes flicked almost unregistered while barely panning his head to take in what the other patrons were doing. "Do *you* really want to be talking about this?" Kim wondered grimly.

"It's become pretty intrusive. I'd like to hear someone else's thoughts about it. I feel bombarded."

"No matter how it seems, there are a lot fewer people who can't stop talking about it than people that treat the mention of it like cursing," the teacher answered tonelessly. Noah wasn't sure if he was even talking to him.

"I guess it would make sense that I wouldn't notice the people that don't talk about it when there's enough people that do."

"Just so you know when to stop, if a person doesn't jump on the subject or changes it. Some people take it really personally, the idea of some scandal blackening the town," then he met Noah's eyes steadily as though making certain the meaning wasn't lost to the practical stranger.

"I see…"

Han unfolded the newspaper again suggestively.

Noah didn't miss the hint and quietly attended his coffee for the next few minutes before Kim retreated. He looked at his watch and realized the teacher probably just needed to be getting back to the school.

Anyway, he hoped that was why Han left the way he did.

"And for some people it's like cursing," Noah repeated and thought aloud, "Wonder why that is?"

The world's fastest waitress was there clearing Han's spot and answered his thought, "You ever speak of the devil?"

Noah nodded understandingly.

Inside he felt his mind roll its eyes. Then she added:

"Just between the two of us, I think there are a lot of people here in denial."

His eyes flicked up, but all he caught was the ties of her apron waving goodbye.

David was bugged out all the time. Having nightmares. Pissing the bed. Noah was afraid of their psychotically, "helpful" neighbors. Gilder was a nutcase half the night...and sometimes during the day. The city had secrets—secrets about dead people—secrets about how they ended up dead.

Han was maybe too private to have inside information.

*So who can I talk to?*

*Jacob?*

Jacob liked to talk too much.

Rising Moon seemed nice enough and, while also not from there, she seemed to know a lot more than he did. He started dialing her number, wondering what she was doing for lunch. She was at home. Maybe that was better. He asked if she'd mind company.

◆       ◆       ◆

Noah and Rising Moon looked at each other infrequently over their cups of coffee. Neither drank much before the steam subsided and not even one word passed between them. Noah was the one that asked to come over, but the only thing he said after "hi" was "please" to the offer of coffee.

Finally, after struggling and mentally rehearsing, it came down to "say something" or run like hell and pretend it was someone else.

"Please don't take this the wrong way, but I have to tell you something that's been bothering me," Noah blurted after the longest uncomfortable silence he'd felt since being convinced to go on a blind date with a personality deprived, egotistic, dimwit from college who liked to sing about everything.

"You know, in real life, there's no eccentric friend who coincidently has the answer to a person's obscure circumstance—monsters no one else has even heard of or even written about—yet ironically some incidental acquaintance has twenty books on... that's how it is in movies," Noah trailed off. "So I didn't know who to go to."

"Go ahead," said Rising Moon. She smiled reassuringly, seeing him struggling. She was flattered that he felt he could come to her.

Noah hesitated and thought about other people who he could have went to, Solomon, Jacob, even Fawn or Derrick, but he'd brought it up and now he guessed he would go ahead and say what he had to.

"When we first moved up here it seemed like everywhere I turned I was being told about this ghost or spirit crap," he resumed. "And I thought that maybe people were trying to scare us away. I don't know how much your dad has told you about our discussions."

He watched Rising Moon's face for honesty when she answered. Noah wondered if she'd lie for her dad if he was blabbing all over about the raving, shit-headed white man who just moved to town.

"Father wouldn't tell me anything about his dealings with people. It would be on a need-to-know basis. He told me that he met you. He was a little nervous about me driving a stranger all over," she giggled like it was the silliest thing to worry about.

Noah believed her, but had to build up his courage again to continue.

"Every day I pass by those other houses, big, nice houses where, you'd think, people should be living. But I see the broken windows. It looks like vandalism. I see where there were fires and I wonder if they were driven out by whatever happens when the campfire stories don't work."

Noah thought long before continuing, bracing himself in case he offended her. "I know we're in the minority here and… I'm starting to wonder if it's accidental."

Before she could answer he continued hurriedly, "All these American Indians," he chose carefully, "who *live out there* come to my place and say it's dangerous to live there, scaring my kid *and* me and…" he trailed off.

"Hey Noah," Rising Moon said as brightly as she could to show she was okay, "It does seem a little off doesn't it? And if you are wondering if whites owned those houses you mentioned? They did. And so, in a way, the reason your tribal neighbors are coming *might be* to make you leave. But I promise, it's not because they hate you, but because there are things that happen too often around here for them to think they wouldn't happen to you too."

"What do you mean?" Noah worried deep lines into his brow. *Here it comes*, he thought.

"I don't know if the things we do to protect ourselves from Manjimanidoo actually help—some people think there's only one that's evil and is leading the others to attack whites—either way, your neighbors have seen it happen and happen, again and again—"

Rising Moon paused and frowned through the possible ways to say what, now, she *had* to say. She didn't want to sound eccentric. At last she put her hands over his and continued, "Their white neighbors die. They are trying to protect you. How do you tell people these things but straightforward. By the time most people find out on their own… it's too late. Sometimes they fall down stairs and end up folded up in ways that could just never happen from a fall. Sometimes they freeze to death on their porch and their doors are unlocked—no reason they couldn't get in. Sometimes they freeze to death inside their homes. On the coldest day of the year, with their doors and windows open and they are found just sitting in an armchair, with fear written all over their faces."

"You're saying if we stay, we'll die? And it has *nothing* to do with people just wanting us out of here" he looked at her incredulously.

"Yah," she nodded firmly. "Every race up here has "accidents". But they tend to happen more to whites. Out there—and I'm not trying to scare you—but if you want to know the truth… they literally chew you up and spit you out."

"No…" Noah trailed off. Rising Moon didn't know if he was refusing the explanation or refusing to leave their home.

"Noah," she was hesitant to touch his troubled face, but she already wanted to so bad that she almost ached at the possibility to finally get to do it, "I *don't* want you to leave, but it scares me that you live *there*."

She was grateful that he didn't recoil from her touch, but she didn't know what it meant that he didn't respond right away to what she said.

"This is really unbelievable," he said at last. "I don't know what to do. If this is true—it's *not* true! This is ridiculous. I can't listen to any more of this crap. Your dad told me the same damn ghost stories."

He stood up and moved to the other side of the room, "This *isn't* true. If it was, why would *anyone* live here?"

"It *isn't*—" he cut her off when she tried to answer.

Rising Moon sighed helplessly.

*Believing is all about the will to.*

"I don't believe in ghosts," the father added.

"They're not ghosts. Not exactly I mean, these things, they're *something* like ghosts. Not how you think of them, but most people are wrong about what ghosts are," Rising Moon began tentatively. "*They* are the poltergeists. *They* are the boogeymen. *They* are Mr. Nobody. Ghosts imply spirits of all living things, in general, if they are in that state. But they aren't just anyone. Only children. Spirits in limbo—ghosts—can only be *children*.

"Children don't always know the consequences of their games. Sometimes children hurt each other or animals just to try and make sense of pain, cause and effect. Some are almost sweet—they move things, hide things, and sometimes help people find things. Some are demented—they trip people, they hide important things, they break things, they scare people because they think it's funny. Like grabbing your foot when you're swimming. They shape-shift. They can look like anything. They can sometimes convince living children to do things for them. Bad things. Things they think are funny.

"Sometimes they knock things over or make sounds in people's houses to trick people to come running. Sometimes they make you think you see something in the shadows, to feed off the pounding of your heart.

"All children can be led astray. They can be confused. No matter how brutal, they are children. Children are the only beings who inhabit a state where the veil of reality is so thin that make-believe can be reality. I don't believe there has ever been a ghost of a baby or full grown person.

"Infants don't know confusion and no adult can retaliate against death, because they *understand it*, even if they don't want it. Ghosts are angry and confused."

Noah didn't agree with what she was saying. It didn't account for adults with child-like mentality. He didn't think that everyone that dies could understand why they are dying—like if they were murdered or were in an accident. What if they weren't prepared to die? He knew if he died, he wouldn't leave this earth until he knew David was going to be alright. To him, this explanation didn't account for a lot of things.

"And you refuse to even consider the possibility that all these deaths are done by people? Because I haven't seen anything people couldn't do. I don't know that there's anything people aren't capable of. You're not from here. These aren't your people. You don't know. You can't *know*. I just wonder why you'd rather believe in a bunch of monsters than what is not only more realistic, but more obvious. There *is* a big secret in Nibebiitam, but it's not an epidemic of supernatural activities. I—"

He couldn't say, 'I have proof,' not to her or anyone else here. And definitely not someone who believes it's spirits—

"If people are killing people, don't you think something has to be done?"

"Yes. I don't know why I find that more frightening than what I know about the children," Rising Moon agreed nervously.

"Maybe because it *is* possible. Why do you think people retreat to fantasy, even if it's terrible too? Because in the back of their mind they know it isn't real. And for a little while, they get to be free."

"How can you be sure that people could have done all of these things? Have you looked at every case—every accident? These deaths *were* investigated."

He bit his tongue and held onto what he knew.

"But people up here believe so strongly in this that if they could get away with having a section on their death certificate that says 'Death by Spirit' they would probably use it," he replied. "I think these spirits are a convenient scapegoat. It scares me that people would buy into this. Whoever is responsible has got to be pleased."

"Are you going to leave?" Rising Moon asked in alarm enough that her high voice startled him.

"Here?" Noah returned, gesturing to the room.

"Nibebiitam?" she elaborated.

"I don't know—" even though he knew there was no way in hell he was going to stay "—I don't see how it's worth putting my kid through this."

Rising Moon didn't want him to leave Nibebiitam or her home, for that matter. She couldn't bear the empty space. She wanted Noah in it. She needed Noah in it. She didn't know how to keep him there.

She thought about seducing him, undressing, putting her hand between his legs, between his jeans and his underwear, touching him, blowing him, whatever it took to give him something worth staying there. If she knew how to do those things, she might have tried.

She wanted him, but she didn't even know if he was attracted to her. She didn't even know if they were friends. He might laugh if she tried. Without knowing what to do, he might. She looked him over and thought someone that sexy would have to know a lot about sex. She ended the thought with thinking that she didn't like her boobs. That took the wind out of her sails.

For the moment.

"I need to get going if I'm going to get home before my son," Noah caught the time out of the corner of his eye. He checked his watch to make sure it was right.

"I'm sorry," she said.

"It's okay. And *I'm* sorry, but I just don't understand why people around here think if they serve up shit that people will eat it."

"It would be shit, somewhere else," she argued. "It's different here. I had a hard time accepting it too."

"Were ghosts just anybody before, or just kids?" he threw back.

"Anybody," she said sheepishly, "but I know differently now."

"How long did it take for you to believe that racist ghosts were going around killing people? What did you think, at first?"

"I thought it was just a dangerous place. Mostly I just worried about my dad being in the thick of it," she explained.

"They never leave any witnesses?"

She sighed.

"They say, if you see the spirits real form they won't let you live."

"Is their real form children?"

Rising Moon shrugged. It was hard to explain and tiring too. No one survived to say what they saw. Noah didn't believe anything she said.

◆        ◆        ◆

David got off the bus with Fawn. He would have been disappointed to learn that she suspected something was up, but it didn't help her prevent it.

Once they got in the back yard, he took off in the direction of the path they found. He was pretty sure he remembered where it was.

He didn't count on Fawn being faster than him. He would have, if she was a grown up, but he felt like he was on an equal playing field with another kid.

She called his name and asked him to stop. He wouldn't.

Fawn's slender fingers locked around his upper arm and both children spilled out on the crunchy, leafy ground—only then did they stop moving.

"What the hell are you thinking?" the girl demanded.

"I'm going to the cave!"

"NO-YOU'RE-NOT!"

"I'll go no matter what! I'll sneak out when you're in the bathroom. I'll get you in trouble with your grandpa and when he's yelling at you I'll go! I'll tie you up!"

"I'll tie *you* up," Fawn threatened.

"Get off of me!"

Fawn sat back on her heels and brushed the leaves off her jacket.

"We can't."

"I just want to peek," David pressed.

"You won't. You'll want to go inside."

"No, I won't. I'll just peek. I have a flashlight," David opened up his bag and took out the big-headed plastic cow with a "moo" and a light in its mouth. "See?"

"If we do this, you'll leave it alone?"

"I will. I just need to see."

"David, you don't go poking around in places like that. Old mines collapse all the time with no warning."

Fawn *hadn't* seen the cave. All she saw was something she still had a hard time accepting that she saw. She had a bad feeling there was no cave at all, that in the fading light there had been a black bear and David thought it was a cave.

She also had a bad feeling that there *was* a cave.

They moved fast and deliberately along the path they had taken when they were just exploring the woods. At the time, Fawn thought it was cute, because the closest to nature David ever explored was Central Park. She felt good that she had an answer for most of the times he asked, "What's that?"

It made her wish she had a little brother.

She thought she'd have liked that.

While neither said it, they both were anxious to get there and back to the house before the sun got too low—which was earlier and earlier every day.

They crossed the large log, Fawn had to help David again, and soon the ground was squishy. It was close.

Much to Fawn's disappointment she was able to spot the cave when they reached the pond. Its black yawn reminded her of the mouth of a deep sea monster. But the little light beckoning victims inside was David's flashlight, which looked like a cartoon cow. And she was the dummy who had to go to it.

"It looks like it should eat," Fawn commented absently.

David nodded in agreement.

Happily, they swung wide to avoid the pond and the tree. Fawn wondered if Silver Fox Man travelled through trees or if he just resided in them sometimes. She was afraid to think that it wasn't just any tree, but *this tree* in particular.

Was he in there right now?

In a matter of minutes they were moving into the No Man's Land between the tree and the cave and it didn't feel safe. It didn't feel good at all.

"Here, let's—"

David tripped hard, his little body crashed against a hard path under the leaf covered forest floor. With Fawn's help, he was pulled off the ground like a piece of chewed gum, lip busted wide and cherry red fluid already dripping on his shirt and racing down his skinny neck.

They were stunned for a moment, David surprised, Fawn horrified.

"It's all fun until it hurts," the little boy chastised himself.

Fawn took off her coat and took off her blouse and undershirt. She balled up the undershirt and pressed it into his face, obscuring it. Then she redressed and went to kick at the leaves where David fell.

"Ow!" she cried and jumped back.

"What's wrong?" the little boy worried.

"I stubbed my toe."

Fawn crouched to move the leaves away more carefully, but her sacrificed foot had done enough to the foliage to expose the metal track. She swiped at the leaves and saw the rotted boards between it and another row of tracks.

"It's a mine," she said breathlessly.

After she cleared enough moss and vines away she was able to see a short distance inside. Therein the track was clear, running like a tongue down the blackened throat of the serpentine mine.

David had rearranged the shirt and was standing beside Fawn now. They looked at each other, a cocktail of fear and wonder in their stricken faces.

The cow's inevitable "moo!" echoed down the mine.

"Cool!"

"Not cool! I told you these mines are dangerous."

David passed through the entrance and stood on the sparsely leafed gums of the mine's mouth.

Fawn's head barely cleared the opening.

"How old do you think it is?"

Fawn shrugged. All she knew was that it was before her grandpa's time. Otherwise she would have known there was a mine out here. She could see, from the dead vegetation at the opening, how the small entrance could be easily overlooked, but she couldn't believe her grandpa wouldn't notice it. He didn't seem capable of missing anything... except people. She was looking around, busy with her thoughts when she realized she was alone.

"David!" the teenager called through clenched teeth.

He'd wandered so deeply into the shadows that all she could see was the pathetic light given off by the flashlight. She was afraid to call out any louder, for fear the mine would collapse. "This whole place could come down any second!"

It felt like nothing but the air inside held the shaft up and disturbing even that could bring it down.

"What's this?" David called to her without the same consciousness.

"What?" she asked, catching up just as the little boy was opening a bag partially covered with embroidered flowers, their color either washed out or too filthy to recognize.

He didn't have to answer. The light was fixed on several bundles of dynamite stuffed into the tattered bag.

"Oh my God, David," she whispered. "We have to go now!"

She didn't have to explain after using that tone.

David grabbed for her hand and ran. What he really wanted to know was if they were what he thought. And they obviously were.

Fawn was ordering David to do things:

"Look out for that!"

"Climb over this!"

"Watch out for that"

"Hurry!"

And any number of demands.

To David, it seemed like she never stopped yelling.

When they burst out into the backyard, the six-year-old lost his footing, but Fawn didn't lose the grip on his wrist and ended up dragging him almost fifteen feet before he got his feet back under him and was able to keep up the pace, somewhat.

The front door slammed behind him, from the weight of Fawn's body thrown against it. She reached over her shoulder, slumping there, and locked the deadbolt.

"Was something after us?" David worried. His breath hitched like he meant to cry.

"I felt like there was," she distinguished that sense among the many reasons for her pounding heartbeat.

The little boy panted. Then, feeling like a chump to be using his legs when he didn't have to, he collapsed on the floor.

"You okay?"

"Yah," David exhaled.

"I don't think Solomon is home."

"I hope not. Will you get in trouble, Fawn?"

Fawn slid down the door.

"I don't like keeping secrets from him, but I think it's better if he doesn't know we did this."

"Will Naana tell?"

"Tell what?" Fawn wondered.

"Tell that we weren't in the house and that we slammed the door."

Fawn nodded, "I don't think she knows what's going on."

The idea made David sad, even though he didn't believe it. Naana knew a lot. She knew when he was there. Sometimes he thought she knew what he was feeling. She just didn't talk a lot. Sometimes she'd surrender a thought or two.

"Oh my God," realization washed over David. He sat up while making sure what he was thinking made sense.

"You said the cave looked like a mouth?" he double-checked.

"Sure. It did. You thought so too."

"Naana," he called as he leapt up and raced to the back porch with Fawn on his heels.

"Naana!" he said excitedly.

She didn't respond, not with words, but David felt her waiting for a reason why he was being like this.

"Naana," he held her knees and looked up into her face, "Is the mouth of wickedness a cave?"

Her semi-glossy eyes moved to meet his.

"Is it a *mine*?"

A tremor moved through Naana's delicate old frame. Her lips pressed together solidly by the few teeth clamping them together. She folded in on the space over her knees—literally vibrating.

"Naana!" both children exclaimed.

"What are you talking about David?" Fawn asked bewildered.

"Something she told me," he exclaimed.

A wind raised music through the wind-chimes. The old woman's shudders became violent. So severely and rapidly she quaked that she appeared slightly blurred.

"Did you see it?" the little boy wanted to know.

Naana stopped moving, like someone pressed a pause button on her.

"*Gitchie Manito*, Little *Waabi-ma`iinganag Weshkiniigidjig, aaniish eshnikaazyin*? It is pain, pain, pain. *Mukaday*, Black *Wabizhashi*, is so naughty, naughty, naughty. Hear *bapeewug*; feel *winanimiziwin*, know *Niboowin*. Keep what you know 'til your last breath," she babbled happily. It was as if nothing ever happened.

"What is she saying?" he asked Fawn.

"It's about the Children, but it doesn't make sense. I guess I don't know all the words," she regretfully admitted.

David nodded thoughtfully.

"Sorry for upsetting you before," he said at last. David hugged Fawn's waist, "Sorry for upsetting her."

"Why were you bothering her with that? Do you want to give us away?" she whispered into his face.

David shook his head.

He wondered if it was an accident that Naana's room almost directly faced the path, that only this side of the house was so densely covered in chimes, that she kept vigil about sixteen hours a day.

He decided to take the elder's advice and keep his thoughts to himself. And he was thinking, that Naana tried to stop them. Probably, he guessed, after Fawn's parents and sister died.

Then Fawn was leading him away from the porch and into the bathroom.

"How are you going to explain your mouth?" it was Fawn's turn to worry.

"I fell. We were playing. That's all true," David suggested.

"We *weren't* playing," Fawn corrected. "Speaking of which, so much for keeping your promise."

"My promise?"

"About going so far in!"

"I'm sorry! I didn't realize. I didn't mean it. I didn't mean to lie," David wailed. "I don't mean to be bad. I just get carried away. I meant to keep my promise. I really did."

"Shh. Shh. Calm down. It's over," Fawn comforted. She held his little body and was surprised by its smallness in her own tiny arms.

"We need ice for it," David offered, "That's what my daddy would do."

"That's what Solomon would do too," Fawn agreed.

"I don't think we're that different, being white and being native," David told her shoulder.

"There are differences," Fawn disagreed.

"But that just gives us something to talk about, doesn't it?" David agreed. "We all start out just as people and need the same things. The rest are the stuff that make us pretty."

"This doesn't make you pretty," she teased his bruising face.
"It makes me look tough?"

Fawn laughed. "I don't think so."

He consciously clenched a fist in each hand and, with the assistance of a determined face, flexed his baby soft arms.

"You don't think I look tough?"

Fawn laughed hard. "I'm seriously going to piss myself if you don't stop."

"Get pull-ups. They help," David suggested in absolute seriousness.

"I'm well beyond that," she wiped tears from her eyes as her laughter subsided. "Where are your ancestors from?"

"Ancestors?" David cocked his head to one side. Fawn was replacing the bloody undershirt with a face cloth soaked with cold water.

"Where your grandparents or whoever came from before America."

David considered this for some time because he thought he should know something, but he didn't.

"I don't know where my family comes from," David confessed. Because he felt like he should know, but didn't, he assumed his daddy didn't want him to know.

"We must have been the first Americans," he guessed.

Fawn's eyes widened along with her mouth, which she quickly covered with her hand when she began to laugh.

"You are insane, kid," she sighed out the last of her laughter for the night, since later Solomon didn't believe he was getting the full story and she was grounded until he had.

◆          ◆          ◆

That evening father and son asked each other what they did with their days. David was happy to hear an almost perfectly concealed tone of frustration when his daddy briefly mentioned Rising Moon. When Solomon dropped David off he'd repeated the story Fawn told him about David taking a spill somewhere when they were playing. He also told Noah that he was going to look into it.

"Is there something else I need to know about your face?" the father asked.

"I tripped over something in the leaves when we were outside," David explained. "Then I fell on something else under the leaves. Fawn took care of me."

His father smiled easily, "That's why I trust you with her, because she's a responsible young lady."

"And the only sitter you know," David pointed out.

"That too, but sometimes people just get lucky."

They both felt lucky to know Solomon and his family.

"Hey, guess what?" Noah said in a voice like he just woke up in a good mood.

"Huh?"

"Forecast's calling for snow by morning."

"Oh?" David exclaimed. "Oh…"

◆         ◆         ◆

By the next afternoon, the gray sky was spitting flakes.

David nervously watched the winter's first snow falling. He had no doubt that he would find the tracks Fawn told him he would find. He was prepared to believe that the girl might have come over last night and did it herself. Expectation wrapped the child in a blanket of fear and would not let him slumber.

They would leave impressions in the snow. They would leave proof, Fawn told him.

Fear of truth kept his eyes wide and unblinking.

What if there *were* tracks to his window? After everything that happened, he had no reason to doubt, but even so he told himself Fawn was full of crap and that was finally enough to ebb his fears.

He closed his eyes.


Way back when Fawn told him that he would have his proof, David imagined how this day would go. He would spring awake and rush outside, much like the rush to presents on Christmas morning.

David already believed in white wolf children. He didn't really feel like he had to know, but he *had* to.

He hadn't bothered getting dressed. He rarely did before leaving his room *any* morning.

Gilder had left wet tracks all over the floor in front of his bedroom door. Sometimes it was hard to stop her from running around after she did her business. A few ballet-like moves took the small boy across the puddles and to breakfast.

David was about to sound the alarm that there was a mess, but his dad was already cleaning up. Gilder wriggled and wagged her tail from her bed in the living room.

"Mess maker," David teased her, temporarily distracted from his mission.

"The snow was so wet it just stuck to her and became water right away," Noah explained.

"So the snow isn't staying on the ground?"

"It wasn't, but it looks like things are going to get a little white. Take a look."

David leapt over to the dining area and the sliding doors that went out onto the porch. There was a set of tracks in the snow, pressed clearly through the inch of white to the dark wet green of the grass below it.

The only thing that kept David from throwing open the door and rushing out to check was that his daddy didn't want those doors used. There was even a brace in the track to keep it from opening. So he ran to the front door instead.

He heard his dad call after him, something about a coat. Maybe boots? But David felt warm in his pajamas *and* they had feet.

David spilled out on the wet grass, he was down for a few seconds, jumped up and went after the tracks.

They went right under his bedroom window.

His knees slammed together over the pee that almost happened. One hand went to help, the other covered his mouth.

No tracks went away.

He didn't think there would be.

They don't do things that make sense. They only mean to scare. They wouldn't leave tracks if they didn't want to. Would they?

David was taking one last look around when he saw two half-moons melt the frost on the bottom half of his bedroom window. The prints looked something like small lumpy gourds or pickles. He would leave identical marks if he put his hands beside his eyes, trying to look through glass.

Maybe they do leave tracks when they leave.

The ground felt particularly hard when he slipped running back to the front door. He landed face first in the slush. He wasn't sure if he was pushed or not. So he tossed the idea out of his mind. Up on his elbows, David was face to face with the tracks he'd followed. He hadn't bothered to look. They weren't dog prints or footprints—they were handprints. Only hands.

Little hands.

"Do you have a good reason for this?"

His daddy was standing at the corner of the porch, leaning forward on his elbows, so he could see around the side of the house. He had a cup of coffee in his hands and had a sip while he was waiting for David to reach him.

"The tracks," David explained.

"Following the trail of Gilder's duty?"

"It wasn't Gilder," he protested.

"There are *lots* of critters around. Remember when we'd go for walks in the winter and you would see all the bird, squirrel, cat, mice, and dog tracks in the park or on the sidewalks? You don't realize how much stuff's around when you don't see them. Which is why you don't take off without telling me where you're going. I'm going to have to start punishing you. You know the rules. You need to abide by them for your own good.

"What if something had happened and I hadn't noticed you come out here? What if I'd locked the door and went into the attic to get sorting through that stuff and didn't hear you needing to get back in."

The boy opened his mouth to answer, but the man was quicker.

"No coat. No boots. It's a degree above freezing, maybe?"

"What kind of punishment?" David wanted to know.

"One you wouldn't like."

"How much?"

"Enough that you'd never do it again."

David raised his eyebrows. He doubted that. He so often forgot the rules when he was too into the moment, he didn't know what would keep him from never doing something again. Probably something his daddy would never do.

"You doubt me, buddy. I see that face," Noah accused as his son came around and up the front steps. "I think I'm coming down with something. This might not be a good time to test your limits."

"Sometimes I forget."

Noah made a sound, something like "uh huh". He did sound like he was getting sick. David knew he'd have to be extra good. Daddy always told him that people needed to rest to feel better. It was just so hard when daddies were sick, because then there was no one to play with him when he needed it to be his daddy and not someone furry.

David made a face when he got back to his cereal that was now mushy.

The rest of the morning was uneventful. The kid didn't think too much about what he saw. That wouldn't surprise him. Much worse already happened and he *expected* this to happen.

He didn't need proof.

If there was a white wolf child there, why didn't it hurt him? How couldn't it have known he was there? Did it not care? Are they not all bad?

They are ghosts, he decided. Ghosts get stopped all the time. What stops ghosts?

David was beginning to think he knew.

# EMULATION

———————◆———————

Mrs. Ashley Jenkins left the backyard light on just in case the kids couldn't last the whole night, camping out—rather, when the kids scared each other so bad that they had to come inside. She already moved the coffee table out of the way so there was plenty of room to spread out their sleeping bags.

She was standing at the kitchen sink, where she had a clear view of the tent. For the moment, she could see most of the yard, because the sun hadn't completely set, and watched the three eight-year-olds and her husband, Wesley, who was acting at least that age himself. They were sitting around the little Weber grill making s'mores while Wes was priming the pump for late night fleeing.

He already planned on scaring the hell out of them, after they fled inside, just when they'd almost be feeling safe again and sleeping downstairs.

She scolded him, but she felt attracted to Wes' youthful energy. It reminded her of how they were fifteen years ago.

When the marshmallows and daylight were almost

completely gone, her husband extinguished the coals and told the kids goodnight. They shot into the tent and zipped it up tight.

Wesley Jenkins smiled wolfishly as he came in the back door.

"What did you do?" she asked accusingly.

He ignored her, smiling bigger, and hung up his jacket.

"Zombies?" she guessed.

He shook his head.

"Aliens?"

"Uh-uh," Wes denied, coming up behind her to hug her shoulders. "*Better*."

"No, you didn't!" Ashley wailed. "I never went into the woods again after you told me those horrible stories."

"It's historical, cultural," Wes advocated. "If you're going to live around here, you have to know about wendigos."

"You made me hate Ontario."

"Liar," he said, kissing the back of her neck. "I made you love Ontario."

"I can't believe you told them that. You'll traumatize them," his wife shrugged him off. She did wonder if they would be able to handle it, since stories about wendigos had scared her so bad.

"The one with the guide and the tent?" she pressed.

"And the disembodied voice crying out about his burning feet."

"And how he followed the guide's tracks until they stopped, as if something had plucked him off the earth," Ashley added. "I hate you."

"Not as much as they're going to when I unzip their tent, quiet as a mouse, and start dragging out their sleeping bags."

Mrs. Jenkins spun around and dug her hands into her full hips. "Don't you dare!"

"You're only young once," her husband defended. "I'd rather make memories they can laugh about later than worry about traumatizing them today."

Wesley left to have a shower before calling it a night, to get the smell of grill off him so his wife would let him in their bed.

Ashley looked once more at the tent, now illuminated with several circles of light and went to bed herself.

Whenever he woke up, out of habit, the first thing Wesley Jenkins did was check the time. It was exactly three in the morning when husband and wife woke simultaneously.

"What was that?" Ashley whispered, inexplicably too afraid to lift her head off the pillow. Wesley was already getting out of bed. She heard the whisper of his boxers rising up his legs.

"It sounds like the boys finally gave up," he said cheerlessly.

She heard him leave the room and start down the stairs. About four steps down they heard the sound they couldn't remember as what had woke them—boys screaming.

Ashley soared past Wesley, almost knocking him down the stairs—but he held the rail so tight nothing could have removed his hands.

"Well, come on! Help!" she screamed at her husband as she reached the bottom of the stairs.

He sunk to the stairs until he was sitting.

"*HELP!*" her shriek could have shredded a block of steel.

Then a third and final scream, which at first sounded like it was right at the back door, at last was barely a whisper as it arched over the house and into the night.

Wesley chased the cry, breaking his toes on the last step and spilling onto the landing. It was a cry he knew by heart, one that had changed a lot in the past eight years, but one he would know anywhere. Their son's.

"Jeremy!" he called, leaping up and clawing down the attic stairs in one jump.

"It's not him," Ashley whispered to Wes, two stories away, without strength to do anything more. She grabbed the knob and let the door open slowly.

Her son's name rang out again and again, until Wes must have reached the attic window, because then all he said was, "NO!"

His wife padded out into the dewy night and stared into a clear and starry sky. Two sleeping bags were strewn across the yard—she spotted the third in a tree.

Their shoes and socks would later be recovered almost a hundred miles away, lined up side by side on the end of a dock.

Their disappearance would be categorized as a kidnapping, of course.

# CHAPTER 16

◆

## SAGE in his SHOES

*Am I drunk? I'm not drunk. I feel like I'm hung-over*, Noah thought, delirious with fever. He lay on his stomach, face to the corner of the couch, arms wrapped around his head. He didn't even remember how he got home from work or how he ended up on the couch. How long had it been? What day is it?

The last thing Noah remembered must have been a fever induced delusion or maybe he hadn't even been awake—he had been laying in the dark, in his room. There was a clink in the hall, like something bumped the lamp.

When he turned on the bedroom light there was huge clattering, crashing, and pounding—like someone running down stairs.

The feeling of an ice cold spider scurried up his back and made goosebumps rise on his arms.

His scalp prickled.

*Oh God, I could puke.*

Head pounding, bones aching, his every nerve tense. He felt murderous at the slightest sound.

"Sweet po-ta-to pie!"

"Please shut up," Noah moaned against the upholstery.

"Go!" the boy screamed against his neck, "Go with your wind! Nobody gonna go again!"

"Goddamn it, David!" Noah growled and turned his face to see the boy that most of the time he really loved. The child's head was an uncombed bush of brown curls, the Christmas tablecloth tied firmly around his neck, a tenderizing hammer and spatula in either hand—the flushed boy looked slapped.

"It's the song of the south," David explained, puzzled by the anger it roused.

*Its sounds like a spanking*, Noah's ears urged.

"We…" David whispered, "ALL live…"

Noah's eyes pinched shut.

"In uhhhhh… yella! Oh! Uh, yella' tambourine! WE-ALL-LIVE—"

The Nyquil knocked him on his ass. The flu left him helpless. The sound made him want to crush hot light bulbs in his ears.

*If I yell I'm gonna throw up…*

"Don't drink and drive, do the whopper meadow drawl!"

"DAVID!"

The six-year-old's perceived size decreased by 25%.

"Daddy?"

"What time is it? Did I bring us home?"

The room was a blur. David became a part of that blur as he ran off to look at a clock and ran back. The room was tipping. If he puked, he would never make it to the bathroom.

"It's night out."

Noah started to nod and he felt the couch rock like the Pirate Ship rides at theme parks. He suddenly had the most inappropriate thought, that of one of the first times he and his ex-wife had sex. It was kinda like that ride, he was thinking.

"Night out? What's the first number?"

"Eleven," David answered.

"Oh God…" his daddy groaned. David backed away from the wet sound of imminent barfing. "You haven't been to bed?"

"Nope."

David sounded proud.

Then he started to hum. Noah couldn't tell what it was, but he knew he didn't like it. The humming gained volume and energy. It was going to become words soon.

"Do you want me to call Solomon?" the little boy asked.

"Did you eat?"

"I had cereal."

"Go to bed," Noah felt like his whole face was pushing to one side of his head. He tried to think about what was around the couch. What could he puke in?

"Aww!" David wailed.

Noah bristled. His sweat soaked t-shirt allowed David to see every muscle tightened on his daddy's back at the sound of his voice.

"Sorry," David pet him.

"Let Gilder in. Lock the door. Brush your teeth. Shut off the TV. The lights. *Go to bed*."

In a matter of seconds Noah was practically unconscious.

David padded away silently. He suddenly felt really vulnerable. He kind of enjoyed that his dad was there, but not interfering at all with his fun. It was nighttime and David wanted his dad to be alert and available. He felt like he was all alone.

"Guh?" the child gasped as he opened the heavy door, about to call for Gilder through the screen door.

Someone was standing on the stairs.

A *stranger*.

She was standing like a gunslinger before a duel. Her ratty shawl obscured her face and torso. There was a quality to the fabric that made everything it touched out-of-focus. Her arms and legs were visible. The girl's arms were skeletal. Her legs were horrifically thin, but they were a dog's.

David squealed and slammed the door shut. He pinched the lock into its "locked" position on the knob. He panted on the other side of the heavy inner door for a minute or two.

Then he sprinted to his bedroom, slung the door toward its frame, and landed on the bed at the same time his bedroom door closed.

He felt safe to sleep with his dad being right out there on the couch.

◆　　　　　◆　　　　　◆

David stood frozen in the hall. The morning light filled the house, lighting the inner gold of the pine walls. The sun's kiss was given to every inch of every surface. It was so beautiful. It wasn't tranquil: it was full of life. But David's chest felt cold, sick, and scared. His father called again for him to let Gilder in, but he couldn't, there was someone out there. A child. He saw their greyish silhouette through the screen door, coming and going as it paced the front porch. All the boy wanted was to run over there and close the heavy inside door, but he couldn't.

Gilder was out there with whoever it was.

She was in danger.

When the wolf child outside disappeared from sight, David sucked in a breath and, though his flesh and soul protested, he ran for the door. He heard the footsteps returning, but he couldn't stop. He couldn't stop now. He cried for Gilder, but no sound came out. He knew it would reach the door before him. It would let itself in. His feet made loud thudding sounds on the floor—far too few—he thought, for how many steps he'd taken.

Then all at once he was there, the screen door inches away from his nose. A naked Indian girl, his height, stood with her back to him. Though too young to possibly be, David felt it was Fawn. He called her name too, mutely. When she turned to face him, it was Gilder. On her hind legs, furless—her front legs hanging like arms that could reach the deck if they were not bent to reach the knob.

A squeak escaped as the six-year-old woke. He'd wet the bed again.

Embarrassed, David slithered away from the wet spot. He worried what his daddy would think. He was too big for wetting the bed. So he started crying.

He ground the tears out of his eyes with small fists. The room was a blur of twinkling and wavering light. His sleeve worked better to dry his eyes and clear the gleaming of the brilliant morning sunshine. Sunshine that made the gold of the pine walls glow as if they had a light of their own.

David's chest tightened.

The bedroom door swung open smoothly and the brightest of autumn mornings poured into the room.

He was afraid to leave.

Out there, he heard his daddy making sick sounds. And he was muttering "no" over and over again, as if he were using "no" as the sound of a choo-choo train.

Peeking down the hall, David saw his daddy in his "cozy sweater" all rumpled and crouched near the front door. The heavy interior door stood open. The bottom half of the screen door was mangled. A hole the size of a medium pizza was punched through the shredded screen.

A soundless mass of what looked like only black fur and blood lay at his daddy's feet.

*Not Gilder too!*

David stared down the hall. Guilt kept him from moving, from making a sound.

Would Gilder look at him accusingly?

Would daddy yell at him?

Would he be punished?

Would Gilder hate him forever?

For *all* four worries, David thought he deserved the answer to be "yes".

The one time when father and son looked at each other, Noah said nothing to him, just gave him a look. *The* look. The parental look that says *whatever* the parent wants it to say.

To David, the look said "disappointment".

What else should it say?

It *could* say, "You disobedient little brat! See what happens when you don't do what you're told. How many times do I have to tell you? How many times *did* I tell you? Make *sure* you let Gilder back in. Make *sure* you let her *in*. You saw what happened to the kittens. You could have put *them* in the garage and not the shed, to keep them safe. If you loved them, you would have thought of that. If you had thought of that, then you might have thought about *what* did that to the kittens. A badger, Solomon said. But *you know better.* Even if there was a badger. There *could* be a badger. You left Gilder out with a badger because you didn't love her. Because you didn't *listen.* Because you're an *ungrateful* little *brat.* Maybe that's why your mother left. Maybe she was suffering the way you're making Gilder suffer now…"

David let out a bawl that made tears shower from his eyes.

"Gilder!" he wailed.

"Bring me the keys to the truck," Noah directed as he removed his sweater and swaddled the big black dog as firmly and gently as possible. A duality that any good parent masters pretty damn quick.

In a flash, the sobbing, shaking, nose-draining child returned with the keys and Noah's wallet—so he could drive. Noah was pale and sweaty with fever, his eyes were busy with the internal struggle to be clear enough to deal with this.

"Okay, you hold the keys, and I need you to open the door for me."

David did.

Once outside, Noah told David how to lock the locks, while using a porch chair, and the three of them quickly loaded into the truck. Gilder remained half-cradled in Noah's arms. Her head was both slumped and supported on his right elbow.

David cried harder as the truck shook and shuddered down the dirt road. He felt so bad for Gilder. He didn't want her to hurt any worse.

After some time and about three miles left on the dirt road, David realized his dad was talking to him.

"Hey—kiddo—"

"Huh?" David choked, gagging now from crying so hard.

"You okay?"

They looked at each other as long as Noah dare take his eyes from the road.

"Dad!" David wailed. "Gilder's gonna die! And it's all my fault!"

Tears jumped into Noah's eyes.

"It's not your fault and that's not going to happen."

David considered this a second and took the moment to transfer snot from his nose onto his arm.

"Promise?"

Noah swallowed hard and looked down at his other baby. A breath that was supposed to be an answer hitched in his throat. He had to swallow several times to do it without his feelings getting in the way. He felt too sick to control his emotions at all.

"I want to."

They drove in silence, besides David crying, until they reached the vet.

By the time they got there Noah couldn't keep from puking. He had to bend in a funny position to do it without getting anything on Gilder.

Noah couldn't tell if she was breathing.

◆　　　　　◆　　　　　◆

It felt both good and bad to pass her off to the able arms of the staff at the veterinary clinic. They would let the Asheborne's know as soon as they knew anything.

Within seconds father and son were crying inconsolably.

"I'm so *sorry*!" David wailed against his father's shoulder.

"Shh," Noah comforted.

He was sure he would be sick again if he tried to form words.

What would he say when they asked what happened? He thought he heard someone ask that when they first arrived, but it was such a jumble. He wasn't thinking clear. Not that he was thinking so clear, even now. But what could he say?

But they *hadn't* asked. And they wouldn't.

All they said was that she was lucky.

◆       ◆       ◆

Noah stood in his bedroom doorway, looking at dog and boy laying in almost the same position, facing each other. He hadn't been able to sleep. It didn't make him feel better to think that an animal could have done this. No good would come of thinking it was demented youths.

In spring, he thought, they would leave. There was something wrong about this place and whatever it was only seemed to be getting worse. He didn't want to mess with moving during the winter, but he would leave everything they had to protect his family—the dog was family. She might as well have been his daughter, but he hadn't been treating her like that. Gilder wasn't getting the attention he knew she deserved—beyond that, he felt like he'd let her down. She was scared all the time. Stressed.

Seeing her wrapped up and bandaged, Noah didn't feel like being sick was a good excuse for letting down someone you love. That was the reason, but not a good one.

He was the only adult here—it was time to focus on what mattered.

It was almost Halloween, he'd almost completely forgotten. That would be a good time to start raising morale around the

Asheborne house. David could have a Halloween party. It would be a good opportunity to meet other parents in the community. It would be good to see if they were happy.

Tonight he would order a costume for David—his son liked to be surprised about "what he was". Tomorrow, he decided, he would go to Kapuskasing and buy shitloads of Halloween junk for gift bags, invitations and decorations to surprise David. It would be a good way to get him enthusiastic. An enthusiastic child is a happy child. He wanted David to be happy. David deserved to be happy. What child doesn't?


A lot of effort was required to convince David to go to school the next day—he wanted to stay home with Gilder. Solomon had been called and was going to take good care of Gilder while Noah "went to work" and David felt good about that.

"Will Naana be okay home alone?" the little boy worried.

"Sometimes when you are there with Fawn, isn't it just her and Naana? Doesn't that mean Naana was alone before Fawn gets home from school?"

"Yah," David answered absently.

"Solomon will take good care of Gilder," Noah assured him. "I promise."

David wasn't worried about that. Not ever.

Solomon might have lied, but that was the only time David knew of. And that probably wasn't as big of a lie as he thought it was, at the time. His daddy didn't want to hear anything about the white wolf children. He heard him tell Derrick. Constable Phil pissed his daddy off talking about it. Solomon was more subtle than that and more sensitive. David figured he knew the truth was more than his dad could handle. Ghosts, fairies, boogeymen, monsters, and stuff are things you have to *stop* believing in. Children are born believing.

"He puts sage in his shoes," the little boy commented offhandedly.

Noah smiled.

"Isn't it uncomfortable?"

"Fawn says it keeps him safe," David explained nonchalantly. Almost too casually.

Noah caught his son's glance and followed it to the row of shoes and boots by the door. No doubt of what he would find when he put on a pair.

"Well I'm sure it doesn't hurt anything to be careful."

David almost told him that it smells like pot when you burn it, but then his daddy would want to know how he knew that. He'd smelled it on people before, but he didn't *know* what the smell was until he spent the night at his friend's. He didn't want to tell his daddy that.

In a few minutes Noah was bundling his son for school and helping him keep an eye out for the bus.

In no time David was pointing and saying, "There!" and throwing open the door. The broken screen door was propped against the outside of the house—he planned to replace that today—so after the inner door there was nothing to slow the boy down.

Noah grabbed David's backpack to stop him and pulled him back into a hug.

"I love you," he said against the top of his son's head.

"Love you too dad!" David declared loudly as he was released.

"Stay back until the bus stops!" his daddy yelled after him.

David hollered something inaudibly, but Noah was sure it was something like "yeah" or "I will".

After closing and locking the front door, he went to give Gilder medicine. She'd made a mess. Noah didn't care. She was still a little dopey from the visit to the vet and he didn't know when she'd be able to go outside again.

Her dog bed was lined with one of the potty training liners they kept from when she was a puppy. He changed that and washed her soiled fur.

Solomon came at about 9 o'clock, like he promised.

"So you have a sad baby!" Solomon cooed when Noah led him into the bedroom. Gilder wagged her tail and raised her head a little.

"Yep. She hasn't tried to get up or anything, but I think that's the pain killers. It looked like something took a machete—" his voice strained and he threw away the rest of the thought.

"Did they have to do surgery?"

Noah shook his head. "Thank God."

"How is David?"

"Morose."

Solomon smiled brilliantly, "It's always something more tragic than 'sad' when you're little. Speaking of which, you look like shit."

"Sorry. I hope I don't get you sick. I was so out of it that I forgot to let Gilder in the other night. I guess I told David to do it, so he's blaming himself."

"I see…" Solomon nodded. "So morose probably isn't an exaggeration?"

"I wish it was," said Noah. "He puts on these shows that he's okay. Sometimes I feel like that's worse."

"It's worse," Solomon began, "when they can't pretend anymore."

"Hey, I gotta get going, but I really appreciate this," Noah hurried, looking at his watch.

"You bet."

"The coffee is pretty fresh. Cups are in the cupboard just above it. Help yourself to anything you want to eat or whatever. I'll get back as soon as I can."

Solomon nodded through the explanation of benefits.

"Hey!" Noah turned on his heal, pointing at the silver-haired man. "Do you think you could stay a while after and help me hang the new door?"

Solomon smiled in a way that looked like he should be about to laugh, "What if I don't know how?"

Noah looked at him soberly. "I have a feeling there's not a whole lot you *can't* do."

"And hey," the young father added.

"Yeah?"

"I'm going to pick up a bunch of stuff for a Halloween party. Do you think you and Fawn would like to come?"

The cheer drained from Solomon's face.

"We don't celebrate Halloween here."

Noah squatted in the doorframe and leaned on it, his legs felt weak and watery yet from being sick. He laced and unlaced his fingers, until finally raising his eyes to his neighbor.

"Okay," Noah's abandoned accent rising strongly as he spoke this one word and remembered to put it away with all other hidden things as he continued. "Tell me why."

# CHAPTER 17

◆

# FREAK STORM

"October 31, 1977 we were hit by a freak snowstorm..."

More than a foot of snow fell in twenty-four hours and, at the Nibebiitam nursing home, the residents somberly watched the blowing snow and ice and knew there was no chance the elementary school children would come in their costumes as they had for the past thirty years.

Jared Christianson shuffled into the room, holding a green plastic bowl full of Mary Janes, Sky Bars, and Zagnuts. He wore his red robe and slippers, one of the nurses added felt horns to a headband for him. The Devil sighed and felt he really was evil when he had to let the others know he'd just heard school was cancelled.

Agnus, who had three great-grandchildren in the elementary school broke into tears.

Only four of the nurses showed up so far, and the costumed quartet joined two of the three overnight nurses to get breakfast going and try to raise the shut-ins' spirits. The third overnight nurse, Patty, was attending the phone at the main desk.

Claude Baptiste, who was notoriously cranky and complained all week about the children coming, making noise, and messing up his routine, was the first to the sitting area that morning and had a bag full of Sugar Daddies and Wax Lips.

"What the hell am I supposed to do with these?" he grumbled disgustedly. "My lips are already in my mouth most the time and I don't have any goddamn teeth!"

The youngest nurse, Cindy, laughed louder than she thought was polite—she was on a caffeine high after the nightshift and already had two cups of coffee this morning to deal with the overtime.

"Wonder if I can get extra rations by trading Candy Cigarettes," the fourth oldest "and-don't-forget-it'" resident, Gregory Perdeaux solicited one of the other nurses as she passed.

Collette was about to answer when a blast of wind rattled the shutters and made the whole building cower. Lights flickered, but stayed on.

"I'll get some candles," she said instead.

Cindy went with her.

"They would have been here in an hour," Agnus said absently.

Mr. Christianson hugged her small shoulders and kissed the top of her head.

"We'll make up bags for the kiddies and the teachers will walk them down the next good day. It will just be a little late this year," he comforted.

"I suppose," said the old woman who only saw her great-grandchildren when they came on school visits, family was always too busy.

"I'm peeing," Claude said idly, "and I don't care."

"Thanks a lot," said the nurse who just put his oatmeal in front of him. "You know, these are just kids. What the hell do you people do when Santa doesn't come?"

"Why the hell would Saint Nick visit us old bastards? We ain't worth salt to nobody no how—the devil's standing right there—" he jabbed a knotted finger towards Jared "—and between him and us we'd *use* any coal he gave us, so it wouldn't mean a damn thing."

Then the room went black.

The whirring of equipment, vents, motors and lights ceased.

Patty whipped open her lighter and pushed out from her desk. The yellow dancing light raised a face from the darkness by her knees—unlike any Halloween mask she'd ever seen. A sudden flourish of movement on the other side of the desk made her drop the lighter. She thought, *Of course*, when it closed and put out the little flame.

She was trying to be calm. She was trying to think when someone could have went under there and who had brought their kid to work. It must have been Cindy, since she was raising her child alone after the logging accident.

Patty ignored her instincts and told herself there was an explanation and it was stupid to be afraid of a child.

"Can you get that?" she asked the tiny person in the dark.

The sitting room resounded with the sound of her scream.

Someone else had a lighter and one of the nurses had a flashlight. Witches, ghosts, goblins, imps, monsters—the room whirled with racing bodies. The double doors leading out to the garden flew open so hard the glass shattered, pelting and nicking residents and staff.

"People said that the storm did it all, cut the power, and broke the windows that made so many freeze to death, but Jared Christianson—one of only seven survivors of twenty-five patients and seven nurses there that day—insisted there were children there in Halloween costumes. Jared asked local authorities about the horrendous things he claimed he saw done to his fellow residents and the staff. The coroner, who was also a logger and preacher, said there was no evidence of any such things and none of the other survivors, including the desk nurse Patty, would ever be well enough to tell their side of what happened. Some people felt like what wasn't said, said enough, especially after some of the bodies were 'accidently' cremated," Solomon concluded. "The next year, most folks in Nibebiitam and even some in Kapuskasing could barely stand to answer the doors. One child was killed with a shotgun when he rushed for spilled candy, the nervous hand of the homeowner's wife had dropped. Then later, the wife died from internal damage, because of the shotgun going off just behind her waist."

"So they just stopped doing it," Noah nodded as Solomon finished. "I guess I can understand why."

Solomon didn't push it, because he knew it was hard for Noah, but he wondered if Noah understood because he was sympathetic to the tragedy or because he believed that what happened wasn't as simple as a winter weather disaster.

"What will you do now?" the older man asked the younger sitting beside him.

"Want to play dominoes?" said the man from New York City, who could not say "dominoes" without sounding like this was not the first time he'd pulled up roots between countries.

"Don't you have to work?"

Noah shrugged, an embarrassed smile tugging at one corner

of his mouth.

"I lied," the man confessed. "I just didn't want you to resent coming over here to babysit for a dog while I went shopping for party supplies."

# LET NO GOOD DEED GO UNPUNISHED

———————————◆———————————

By the light of a barely announced morning sun, the constable's brown truck plowed down the minimally kept and now slushy, wintery road.

A family was reported missing, after they didn't show up to view a property they were looking at, a hunting cabin down this road. Phil didn't expect to find anything good. Since he started working in Nibebiitam, his well of optimism sat dry as far as missing people went.

When he was twelve and on a trip with his grandparents north of Wendigo Lake, a similar situation occurred. Some people, camping near them, were frantic when their friends were supposed to meet them at their campsite for supper and didn't show. His grandparents, with him in tow, went with the campers to check, assuring them that people get caught up in what they're doing and lose track of time.

What happened was the friends had went fishing and left their catch in a cooler by the tent.

Bear live in the woods. Beat eat fish. Sometimes animals have bad moods. Sometimes animals get a taste for blood.

It was atrocious.

Phil remembered the bodies looked a lot like butchered deer—with little meat left on them. Only the heads made it wrong.

He shuddered at the memory.

Now *this* family wasn't fishing—the pike and perch weren't even running on the Kapuskasing and this was no weather for camping, but it *felt* the same.

It always felt like this, like that one event would forever spoil the ending of all tales of missing people.

Maybe this time would be different, he always told himself.

This was no way to start the day, he told himself that too often, too.

Just around a corner in the road Phil saw the pale blue minivan pulled off the worn tracks, almost leaning on the trees. The road was so narrow, much more than a couple feet off the road and you don't have much choice but to lose some paint to a tree trunk or two. He'd probably lose a mirror trying to go around it, if he didn't get stuck himself. The "ditch" was basically a furrow to keep the road moderately dry. The corduroy underneath was supposed to do the rest.

"Got themselves stuck," he laughed in relief. "Okay, we'll fix that."

As the truck straightened, the engine sputtered. Then it quit.

Phil sat there several seconds staring dumbly at the dashboard.

"Okay… Then they can help *me* out."

*Damn junker. No budget*, he thought.

He tried to turn the engine over again and again, they might need it to get the van unstuck, but with the second try something inside him started running. An unjustified urgency filled his veins and crawled through the fine hairs all over his body. His scalp prickled.

Unconsciously, the constable pressed down the lock button on the door.

There's no way to know what percentage of the times when people think they're going to die that they actually do. Only survivors can say, "I was *sure* it was my time."

The constable was thinking it. And he was right.

Almost in slow motion, the side door of the van slid open and a pair of small bare legs and feet slid out and began swinging and kicking the air from the back seat. They were horrifically thin and chalky.

His own door handle rattled.

Phil lurched away from the door, restricted by the seatbelt. His head knocked the rearview mirror down sharply. Like being punched repeatedly in the chest, his heart slammed against his ribcage. Unprecedented fear swelled in him. He felt he was dying, like he couldn't breathe, and the horror made him wish it all would end.

It stopped.

His flesh ached like he'd been beaten as his muscles started to loosen. Cramps started to ease out of his legs, ass and arms.

"Jesus Christ!" he exclaimed as the terror diminished almost completely. He couldn't understand why it did. It was as if something decided for him.

He straightened the rearview mirror.

Reflected in the small space behind the front seats were the small pair of swinging legs.

# CHAPTER 18

———◆———

# GAMES of TAG and HIDE-AND-SEEK

"Hello?" Noah answered his phone.

"Hey, are you on your way into town?" Rising Moon's voice came over the line.

David made a face.

Noah confirmed that they were. Or they would be, if he hadn't had to pull over to answer the phone.

David had been dawdling a lot and ended up missing the bus. The only consolation was that Noah had to work in town that day and David probably wasn't going to be late for school.

"Can you do me a favor? Dad went to answer a call this morning and I'm afraid he's broke down. He didn't answer his phone. Dispatch was able to raise him on the radio, but couldn't make out a word he said. Are you past Nigig Road?"

Noah looked over his shoulder.

"About four hundred feet. I can go back. Did you want me to check on him?"

"Could you?"

"Sure," Noah agreed.

If Phil had been able to hear him say it, Noah wanted to remark that he was sure the truck didn't break down, it was just going about helping him the wrong way.

"Dad," David whined, "I have to go to school!"

Noah considered.

"What's the road like?"

"Probably pretty shitty, this time of the year… to be honest, pretty much all year," Rising Moon told him.

His daddy looked at him, the right corner of his mouth tucked thoughtfully.

"I'll call the office and let Mr. Han know you're going to be late. Then you won't get your name on the board," Noah was sensitive to the anguish David felt over the thought of getting his name on the board, but the boy didn't seem fazed.

"I can stop there," Rising Moon offered. "I'm walking to work right now."

David scowled.

"Not my mommy," he muttered almost inaudibly.

"Thanks, but I think they need to hear it from me," Noah thought.

"In Nibebiitam?" Rising Moon sounded like she was going to laugh.

"I hope they do," Noah said tensely. "I wouldn't want anyone to be able to—cover your ears David," Noah watched until the ears were securely covered, "—I wouldn't want anyone to be able to snatch my kid, tell them he was going to be late or be sick, and have until school was out before anyone would know something was wrong."

"I guess I wouldn't either," she agreed.

The man reached over and rubbed David's elbow so he knew he could bring down his hands.

"I'll give you a call in about fifteen minutes. Better yet, I'll have your dad give you a call."

"Thanks!"

After they hung up, Noah called the school and explained why David would be late. He took the opportunity to ask about their policy about who can make those calls. The secretary answered very seriously that they'd actually prefer face to face excuses, when possible, from parents and guardians *only*.

"Up for a little adventure?" he asked, putting the truck in reverse.

*Why didn't she do it herself*, David was thinking. He shrugged. His daddy didn't even like the constable.

Not that long ago a truck turned off on Nigig. Masked only by a thin blanket of snow was one other set of tracks, too small to be Phil's. These would have been from someone who took it the afternoon or night before. Even though the new truck hadn't had any problems handling bad road conditions, Noah lost a little confidence when he first saw the narrow, ugly little partition through the wilderness. But if the vehicle with the little tires made it, the truck would be okay, he told himself.

They'd never taken Nigig Road. He assumed it was one of those old logging roads that were all ruts and mud. Trees grew up near enough to the road that branches occasionally slapped the sides of the truck.

"It sounds like big wings!" David cheered.

"If there were enough, it would kinda be like a carwash, wouldn't it?"

David giggled. He imagined a log cabin carwash where everything inside was taken from nature. There'd be spinning pine trees and mini-geysers. He belly laughed when he started imagining how skunks and porcupines might contribute.

"Shit!" Noah exclaimed as they rounded a corner. He knew he shouldn't brake hard, but he did, and slid a few feet on the unmanaged road. He didn't even want to know how close his bumper was to eating the rear license plate of the truck blocking the road.

"You asshole!" he said to Phil's truck.

"Oh, ho ho!" David laughed. "You said swears!"

"Sorry kiddo. Don't repeat dirt words," Noah said to the little boy grinning beside him.

He'd have to apologize to David again when he repeated the dirt words to the dumb bastard who almost got them into an accident.

Noah got out.

A second later the passenger side door closed.

"Hey Phil!" Noah called ahead.

He caught his son's outstretched hand to help him walk along the rutted tire tracks. The constable's dirty brown rust-bucket sat far enough from his front bumper that David could just fit between them. Noah barely noticed the pale blue van on the side of the road ahead.

"Phil," Noah repeated uncomfortably when they reached the open driver's side door. He imagined the round-bellied constable "running to the rescue" of the stranded travelers, killing the battery on the old pile of junk by leaving the door open and then he and the family all having to wade out of the woods together.

He was feeling a laugh coming on when cold fear struck him so hard in the gut he was winded.

Crimson streaked the dash and wheel where bloody hands clenched and pawed. Impossibly, Phil's body was crammed into the space below the passenger seat, mouth gaping with terror and pain. His throat was opened into a black cave down to the spine. Noah's hand clamped over David's face and crushed it against his jacket, but the boy had already seen. While his daddy trembled and tried not to retch, David saw the scene in his mind and almost shook his head. A numbness traveled through his limbs and finally to his heart, replacing fear with a dull throbbing disgust and familiarity. After the kittens, after Gilder, he started to know their work and hated the wolf children.

David's small body was nearly crushed in his father's arms as Noah yanked the boy off the ground and ran back to their truck. He opened the door and pushed his son onto the seat. Once there, David hauled ass into shotgun so his dad wouldn't have to wait to get in.

Hurry, hurry, *HURRY*! David's mind screamed. He made little fists and bounced anxiously in his seat, even after his dad was also seated. Even after the doors were locked and they were backing up down Nigig Road.

"Are you okay David?" Noah turned the small face toward him. He thought the urgency in his voice made him sound angry. He was sorry for it, but it couldn't be helped.

David nodded.

"Did you see?" the alarm was high in his daddy's voice.

"See?" the little boy echoed.

Noah took his eyes off the road just long enough to scan the fearful expression on his son's face.

"Phil," Noah's eyes were stinging at the thought of that poison in his baby's mind, at the thought of the clearly horrible death, the horrible pain, the nightmarish scene.

"I saw a lot of blood," David answered.

"You didn't see Phil?"

"No," David lied. "Was Phil there?"

Noah opened his mouth twice to answer and couldn't say. All he could do was hold his son's face for the second he could spare and thank God repeatedly while he moved the hand away to take out his phone. He hated to use it while he was driving, especially driving backwards, but there was no way in hell he was going to stop.

He had to redial twice before he got the number right.

"Nibebiitam Municipal do you need a transfer to RCMP, or OPP? Do you have an emergency?"

"*Yes!*"

◆　　　　◆　　　　◆

Noah kept David out of school for the week.

Kim Han left a manila envelope with Jacob, bearing David's homework, only if he wanted something to do.

The funeral was in Thunder Bay, since most of Phil's friends and extended family were there. He couldn't get himself to call Rising Moon, but he sent her a card and flowers in condolence for her loss. What do you say to someone after they lose the only real family they have left? It's not like he and Phil were friends either and his friendship with Rising Moon felt strained since he'd talked to her about the stuff going on.

More importantly, he didn't even know what to do for his son.

Noah sat at the kitchen table, having tea. It was Saturday, four days after the incident happened. He watched his son staring blankly at the TV screen. It didn't tell him anything about what David was feeling. If David wasn't laughing or energized by what was on, blank staring was the kid's only other TV watching look.

That week David busied himself with clipping pictures from magazines, mostly National Geographic, and "writing books" on construction paper. He worked so hard at it he almost seemed obsessed. He stopped three times only when he was working on them, and that was to show them to Gilder and, once, Mama Cat and explain them. They were guidebooks or reference books, or something.

Solomon and Fawn stopped by to check on them on Thursday. David wanted to show them to Fawn. From the porch the men heard bickering that ended upon the girl's loud insistence that, "They *aren't* wolves!" Of course, when the father and grandfather came to check on the flustered looking children, they said nothing was going on.

For the past hour, since having breakfast, David was apparently hypnotized by cartoons. Noah leaned out to see what was on. Something new. No, it was *Sesame Street*. Definitely not the way he remembered it.

"How are you doing kiddo?" Noah wanted to know more than anything. He asked David no less than three times a day, but David not only didn't seem to know why, but was confused, though not ungrateful for the time off from school. So Noah hoped this was a phase and actually had nothing to do with Phil's death.

He hoped so. What father wouldn't?

David smiled at Noah so blatantly that it reminded him of a Troll Doll's smile.

"How are *you* doing?" the boy returned.

"I'm fine. I just thought maybe you might want to finally talk about what happened to Phil. I know that was really scary. Blood is a scary thing. For some people, even a tiny, tiny, tiny, bead of blood makes them so sick they pass out—" David snickered and said something like 'silly gooses' under his breath "—and I know it was really scary for you. It was scary for daddy too. Sometimes when things are scary it can be hard to stop thinking about them. Have you been thinking about it a lot?"

David shrugged. "I didn't really understand it."

Noah studied his son's face from across the room, the similar brown eyes looked back at him, doing the same thing.

"Have any requests for supper?" his daddy asked.

"Can we have sundaes for dessert?" David countered with a cherubic smile. Noah had to smile too.

"We'll have to be imaginative with toppings, because we aren't really prepared."

By the gleam in David's eyes, his father wasn't sure if he should have said it that way, but at least it seemed like the old David.

"I can be that," David promised.

Noah had no doubt.

"Dad?"

"Yah buddy?"

"When can I send my list to Santa?"

Noah smiled gratefully. He took his coffee into the living room and sat beside his son.

"I think we can wait a little longer this year, being that we're so much closer to where he lives, it won't take as long to get there," his daddy told him.

"I want to beat the rush," Noah was informed.

"It won't hurt for you to send it any time. I just like you to wait until the last minute because you always change your mind or want to add more things."

David smiled like this was a compliment.

"Up here there aren't as many new things to see all the time," his son explained.

That was true enough, Noah agreed.

It had been a while since he felt anything good about the move, but for the moment he was thinking the simplicity might be really good for a child. He wasn't being bombarded by ads, malls, and thousands of other kids everywhere who all had different toys for him to covet.

Noah would do anything to fulfill every one of his son's needs. Now there might actually be a possibility of giving David everything he wanted and without spoiling him.

"I love you," father said to son.

"I love you too," David returned so serious and earnestly it raised tears to Noah's eyes.

Whatever was wrong between him and his ex, he'd probably never know why she left. It was what it was. Lovers throw each other away all the time, but what Noah would never understand was how a parent could abandon their child. How could anyone give up something that is fused with an absolute and innate sense of responsibility to it? It is instinctive, isn't it?

Noah certainly didn't feel like he had any choice in loving their baby, all his will flittered away the very moment of his son's first bawl.

He had to.

He always assumed Terri felt the same way.

*It's just so fucking cruel*, Noah thought sadly, then remembered. He remembered animals often eat their young. And people hurt their children in ungodly ways all the time, every day, practically every second. That, he must have been completely fucking blind about her. He knew, to her, David started out as a means to an end, but he never doubted she loved their child.

Had he forgotten everything about his own childhood? Of course Noah knew there was nothing inherent about love.

◆　　　　◆　　　　◆

Noah was nervous about what David would hear when he went back to school. He wasn't sure what was going around about how Phil died. The blood was bad enough, but he didn't trust that kids wouldn't talk about how gruesome it was, if they heard.

What the Asheborne's did hear was that Phil had been in a wreck with the abandoned parked van. The newspaper said that the van ran out of gas and the family, assumedly as a shortcut, decided to cut through the woods and succumbed to the elements. Phil, the paper said, had lost control on the slushy road and crashed into the van. They knew it wasn't true, but what could they say. There were quotes in the paper from what emergency people had described of the scene.

What could he say or do?

He told Jacob that wasn't how it happened and Noah was told that he must have been so horrified by seeing the body that he must not have been able to process what he was really seeing.

Noah wished he had taken pictures of the vehicles.

During his lunch break, Noah told Jacob he was going down to the diner for coffee, as usual, but instead headed out to the junkyard just north of Nibebiitam.

The truck bounced and rattled down the ruts the tow trucks had taken the week before—there was very little other activity.

Never in his life had Noah seen such a fence as surrounded the dump. He hadn't expected to see a building there to watch the gate either.

One of the men in the small gatehouse trudged out to Noah's truck with a cheerful look on his round, eczema reddened face. The man waved as he came close and Noah unrolled his window, even as a little voice insisted that, no matter how jolly the man looked, it wasn't how he was feeling, and that both men were likely armed and dangerous.

"Hulloo there," the man called loudly.

"Hey," Noah greeted him and offered a hand to the guy when he was close enough. They shook hands through the open window.

"You guys even have heat in there?" Noah asked with a nonchalant and friendly tone.

"Nah, but we bundle up good. Later we use the little wood furnace in there, but it's not too bad now to go through da trouble."

"I hope you're paid enough to make up for the trouble."

"We do. We do," the guy waved off the concern with a mitted hand. "What we lose in comfort, we make up for in lack of responsibility. My wages seem fair enough."

"Fella can't ask for more than that these days can he?" Noah smiled broadly.

"No sir, nope," the 'fella' agreed. "So what can we do for ya today?"

"Was wondering if I can bring my household garbage here. Have had it piling up in bags in the basement trying to figure out what to do about it. All my neighbors are no help because they just burn all theirs."

The men laughed together.

Noah was glad to hear the man's laugh sounded a lot more sincere than he thought his own did.

"Sure, sure. Just toss any of your trash in over there—" and pointed to a typical large waste management bin near the gate, "—we dump it when it gets full, but it takes forever. Most people use the bins at the east side of town and they go to the big waste place outta town," the man said through all the appropriately timed "oh's" from Noah, who already used the eastside bins.

"East side of town?"

"Practically in town," the guy said.

"Well you've made my day. That will save me a little mileage and a lot of time. Thanks."

"You betcha."

Noah turned around by where the guard's truck was parked and headed back out to the road. He followed the road past the dump farther north, until he saw what looked like a road, or what maybe once was a road, cutting into the woods. He took it until he was sure to be as close as he could get, without passing the dump entirely, and got out.

"Sorry Jacob, gonna be a little late getting back from lunch," Noah mumbled as he locked up the truck and slogged through the shallow ditch and into the woods. He just hoped Jacob wouldn't ask him about the delay or anyone else about it, for that matter.

He had to hike about a mile through the woods before he found the dump and the fence. For some reason, Noah hadn't thought to bring wire cutters, but wished he had. He wasn't actually sure if he owned any, but he was wanting them now a lot more than he was wanting to climb chain-link ten feet and deal with barb-wire.

*No. That's fucking razor-wire up there.*

"You psycho-sons-of-bitches," Noah breathed, shrugging off his coat. Before starting up, he looked over the grounds for activity, but couldn't even see the front gate from there. Coat wrapped around his elbow, Noah reached just above shoulder level. His fingers curled around the cold metal, through diamonds of air, and accepted the hold. It had been a long time, but—like riding a bike—he quickly felt comfortable with the climb.

When Noah reached the top, he fumbled, and almost dropped the jacket trying to double it up enough to feel safe using it to cross the coil of wire and blades.

The razors bit at his jeans as he flung his legs out of harm's way, followed by his torso and hands. Once on the other side Noah only climbed down a couple feet before dropping to the ground. He was afraid the jacket would fall and, if it did, to the wrong side of the fence. It held so securely that, Noah knew, there wasn't going to be a lot left of the jacket when this was over. He guiltily felt like he was going to need to burn, bury, or hide the jacket—like it was evidence.

Trying to keep the entrance at a distance, Noah stealthily slipped between the masses of junk. There was little sign of anything but animals in this area of the junkyard, but by the age of the forsaken items and vehicles, he was about sixty years from what he was looking for.

Noah was about to comment to himself about an old ringer washer when he glanced into the backseat of a sea-green classic car. The cream colored interior was bleached white where the sun had returned to it day after day over the past, maybe forty or fifty years. The sun could not wash out the bloodstains. It looked like no less than buckets full of blood were tossed throughout the vehicle. There were slits in the seats like someone had hacked angrily at them with a butcher knife. Only the cuts, too close together, told him the real culprit was an animal. Maybe a large cat?

*Are there lions in Ontario,* Noah thought, reaching through the open window to touch the clean edge of one of the gashes.

"There'd have to be," he quietly answered himself.

Touching something softer than the padding under the old vinyl, Noah pinched out a small clump of dense white hair.

*Or that goddamn killer bunny from that Monty Python movie. Guess they didn't have a Holy Hand-grenade.*

Once he was looking, it was clear that this car wasn't alone in hoarding DNA. Even the washing machine ringers were stained with blood where the weather hadn't washed it out. The wooden pins were discolored, having once eaten a tremendous amount of blood.

Noah thought he was only there to take pictures of the truck and van. He was starting to worry if he had enough shots left on his camera. There wasn't time to think about that. He needed it all.

Everywhere he looked there was more and more to shoot. There was a tent, what remained of a tent, that he was sorry was so weather beaten that there was barely more than a few stained ribbons of the fabric left. It didn't make much sense to even lower the camera anymore.

Through the lens, Noah saw the earth freshly dug by tires and knew that just beyond the heap of trash in front of him was the "X" in this treasure hunt.

His gut was ready to retreat, it even threatened him with purging and made him so sick Noah felt nauseous down to his numbing fingertips. What would they have done to the vehicles to hide the truth?

What would they do to him?

When he saw the truck and van, they were just as they were that Tuesday morning around eight o'clock. The fact of the matter was the truth was already hidden. Looking around at the masses of vehicles and scattered junk, it was painfully clear how many truths were buried with it.

Dread washed over Noah and he snapped through the last shots on his camera, eight. Four of which would be too blurry to make out, because the hands holding the camera were shaking so badly.

He ran like hell for the fence and cut his inner thigh and calf in his haste to get out. He almost forgot his coat and had to climb halfway back up to yank it off the wire. So desperate was the invader that he didn't notice the set of small barefooted tracks that led up the fence and continued beyond it, without interruption.

A low branch on an evergreen slapped the man's face cruelly, ripping away the first couple layers of skin.

He didn't care about explaining the injury.

Maybe he tripped on the sidewalk. Maybe he grazed his face on the side of a building when he wasn't paying attention.

The silent and undriven span of broken woods didn't feel empty. It didn't feel like it was as far away from the dump as it was. A mile should have felt safe.

Noah leapt behind the wheel and roughly turned the key—the truck roared to life and retraced its path back to the main road. He expected sirens. He expected his camera to be confiscated— the dump to mysteriously empty and close. He would be told by men in dark uniforms that none of what he thought had happened, happened. None of what he saw had he actually seen.

That evening David told him he was a "weirdo" so many times that Noah started to feel really silly about being paranoid.

When Noah sat on his bed, with the camera in his hands, he forced out a chuckle and tried to convince himself that he meant it.

"It is silly, isn't it?" he asked himself or tried to persuade himself.

The camera rolled over in his hands, seeing a few more cuts he hadn't noticed the first, second, or third time he had administered first-aid.

"Where the hell am I going to go to develop this?" he leaned into his palms and wondered how long it would take to get them back from the developer he used in New York.

As the month drug on, Noah spent less and less time looking over his shoulder and looking forward instead to Halloween, no matter how forbidden. In a way it was almost exciting to celebrate the holiday in secret—it helped the atmosphere of the day.

David had no idea about all the plotting going on behind his back—at the very least he could usually *sense* a secret a mile away.

Nothing at school reminded David when it was Halloween morning, but he came home to a decorated house and last year's treat bag full of new candy. Noah helped David decorate three brown paper bags with bats and pumpkins from construction paper. They'd have to hurry to be done before Solomon and his family arrived.

David's costume arrived on time. He was a Flying Monkey— which in some ways was true. That was the trick to making David happy with surprise costumes, somehow being able to explain how it brought out a secret part of himself. Last year he was Sherlock Holmes.

If the problem with Halloween was people being afraid who was coming to their door, then they would have expected guests and their own party. Solomon agreed that there wasn't really anything to stop them from having a private party—it was worth it, for David's sake.

They were living on the edge.

In a little while they'd be bobbing for apples, beating the pumpkin piñata, and pinning the nose on the witch—contraband was all around them. Even the pets were outlaws. Gilder had a cowboy hat on and for the occasion was moved out of Noah's room to her corner of the couch. Mama Cat was a bumblebee. They both thought how great it would have looked when she was preggers.

By the time the witch, the scarecrow, and the grumpy looking Raggedy Ann arrived with homemade treats and a couple "scary" videos, David was in high spirits, never once asking why Halloween wasn't the same here as in New York.

Nothing was.

## *ALL HALLOWS GETTING EVEN*

◆

The Fredrick's only lived next door to the Sneider's for four months before they decided to raise a privacy fence between the properties. From the study on the second floor, William Frederick often saw the comings and goings of his rude, self-righteous, and invasive neighbors. He couldn't see into their basement, but at night, when they were holding service, William saw that the light cast from the basement windows flickered wildly with candlelight. He was always afraid and somewhat certain of the day when he would see members of the congregation bringing children.

It was October 31st and it felt like everyplace in the whole world, but this small community in northern Canada, acknowledged it was also Halloween. The Fredericks, like everyone in the area, accepted that it was better to leave that one day alone—to not tempt fate.

Apparently, William saw from the study's window, his neighbors did everything contrary to what the rest of society accepted, while tonight, also doing the one thing he and his wife feared most—involving children.

Mr. Frederick didn't see any parents and, in the dark, could barely see the children, but their white clothes ate the moonlight and made their little bodies glow like fog in headlights. Clearly playing together, they ran and rolled rambunctiously around the yard on the other side of the eight foot privacy fence.

William was writing an email to his son, who was away in college, while also thinking about what to do about those freaks. He didn't think it was a good environment for children. No one, but the people who attended, really knew what happened in that basement, but no one else's ideas about what happened at the services were very flattering.

Every few seconds he would look up, to keep an eye on the kids. Only a few minutes after he noticed they were there, William had to leave his desk to get a better look, which was almost impossible with both the overhead light and desk lamp glaring. Tentatively he turned off both and crouched by the window, staring horrified.

The children, whose hair was paler than blonde, carried on like puppies. They might have even been pretending to be animals, but most people who pretend to be animals don't nip each other. Their arms and legs sure as hell don't change their length so they can run on all fours. Some of them had very long arms or very short legs and moved very, very fast on their new limbs.

These things were interested in what was going on in the Sneider's basement. They ducked in and out of the window wells, watching someone in the candlelit room. Mr. Frederick wouldn't be able to tell from the second story window and, he thought with a little wicked pleasure, maybe even in person he wouldn't know which Sneider he was looking at, when they passed near the basement window.

William hit the light on his watch. It was 9:45. Services began at 10:00 and they were surely down there setting up their "church".

Scattered and busy now, the children no longer played. They dodged looks from inside. They climbed the wall to peek into windows on the main floor. All but the lights in the neighbor's basement went out.

*Maybe they always shut the lights off.*

They were running through the first floor.

They looked out windows to spy on the ones spying into the basement.

The candlelight flickered.

For the first time since they were installed, the Sneider's basement windows opened, and little bodies slid in like otters on their bellies.

A lot of people thought the Sneider's were purposely gender neutral—Mr. Sneider wore his hair long and years of hard drinking and smoking and scowling made Mrs. Sneider look and sound just as masculine as her husband. Once they were robed, it was even harder to tell them apart, but Mr. Brian Sneider was the one busy setting things up this last night of October.

It was suddenly very cold in the basement, Brian thought, as he was pulling his robe over his head, when he heard a heavy wet sound, as if someone just dropped an armful of drenched clothes. When his eyes passed through the neck hole, the first thing Mr. Sneider saw was a pile of steaming guts.

Instantly in shock, he thought dumbly, *So that's what it was.*

Then he followed one stubborn line of gut, still attached, and saw the cavern of his wife Andrea's empty torso, empty save the dangling ornaments of her lungs and heart.

Rather than finish pulling down the robe, Brian's fists clenched the fabric to his mouth to manage the scream growing deep inside him.

"Don't cry," said a high childlike voice in a very soft way. It seemed to come from under his feet. Against his better judgment, his will, his sense of reality, Brian felt a strange, forced, oppressive calmness wrap around him like the rings of a barrel, like he was drugged.

As the emotional anesthetic broke apart and a voice boomed around him that was almost too deep to understand:

"I THOUGHT YOU LIKED TO PLAY WITH CHILDREN!"

A heavy set of footsteps landed at the top of the basement stairs. He felt like a child, in perfect disbelief and terror—as if the boogeyman had begun to crawl out from under the bed.

Long hairless black doglegs emerged as it descended. Each step thundered with weight that did not match the length and build of this spidery limbed being.

The world spun, every vein felt like it was bursting from the pressure on his chest—he saw its face. Its eyes that sparked like flint inside wrinkles that cinched around them. Those wrinkles loosened as Sneider's heart began to fail.

He was *cheating*.

The wolf children ran on the walls, the ceiling—rushing, yipping, screeching—outraged that his body would try to get away with it—to get away with such a cheap trick.

The pain that followed surpassed mere moments—they could make thirty seconds feel like thirty hours.

When Mr. Sneider was through, the spindly black monstrosity crawled like a bat over the old man's body, following the line of entrails, he reached the woman. It held onto the denuded ribs and drew itself off the floor and up to Andrea's face. It wanted to know she was still looking. Of course she was—one of the little ones tore off her eyelids.

Long nails like sickles slashed away her cheeks and pried open her mouth until her head was open like a set trap. Then it chewed her teeth off her gums like corn on the cob. They popped and crumbled in the sable black darkness of its salivating mouth. The little ones pawed greedily for their turn. There wasn't much time left with her, but it was given to them.

How does one describe the sound of a scream when it comes from a mouth set like this? It is surely clear and unhindered—perhaps the purest scream there ever was.

William listened hard as he watched the candles go out and the house next door eclipse in night. He thought against opening his window. He thought against looking anymore, but he was afraid not to. He was afraid to tear his eyes away—like a pile of junk in your room that looks like something dreadful in the dark. Like taking your eyes off gives it the opportunity to become real and taking your eyes off will surely give it a chance to sneak up on you.

Headlights turned onto their road. There were two more cars behind that. Mr. Fredericks wasn't surprised to see them stop outside the Sneider's house. It was ten o'clock.

Then, Mrs. Frederick's wind-chimes played pretty tinkling music in the flowerbed in his own yard—below his window.

In the deepest reaches of his consciousness, William felt a sigh move through his soul, along with the sense of being spared.

# CHAPTER 19

———————◆———————

# PRETEND TIME

November 1<sup>st</sup> rang in with a phone call.

Jacob, Noah's boss, had to call him right away to let him know what happened to the Sneider's. Noah wasn't broken up by the news, but it rubbed him the wrong way that Jacob sounded so happy or excited by it.

"You're kidding," said Noah when Jacob said "unofficially" that they accidentally killed each other performing bizarre rituals in their basement—even though the other members of their church said their services had nothing to do with violence, bloodletting, sacrifices or anything—and that they were hurt by the suggestion. *They* thought it was a hate crime against the church. They were afraid of it happening to them too.

*Isn't everyone?* Noah thought. *These little monsters have the whole town hostage.*

After he finished going through what Kendal sent him and his own research, Noah was going to send a copy of his findings to the RCMP.

That day couldn't come fast enough, as far as Noah was concerned. For how protective and secretive most people were about the matter, he thought they better be more than packed and ready to leave when that day came. Nobody was going to like it. But if shit didn't stop happening long enough for him to catch up, that day might never come.

Officially, the Sneider's deaths were being investigated as a murder suicide or accidental death via their religious practice. Jacob said Donald, one of Nibebiitam's remaining two constables, told him they found traces of blood and fluids all over the basement. Some of it was old and remained only as stains. Brian Sneider grew up in that house. There was bound to be something sordid to it, but on the evening of the first day of November the house burned to the ground.

The town of Nibebiitam was more tore up about the house than any of the deaths Noah knew of since they moved there.

The house was historically significant, that dentist having lived there. An important man.

The Fredericks started packing so they could move first thing next spring. William would never tell anyone what he saw the night of the fire or the night before.

One look in William's eyes told his wife and anyone else, there was no talking him out of it.

But a lot of people talked about it—as much about the Frederick's leaving as what happened next door. Someone started the rumor that the Frederick's son was having emotional problems and the family had to go to him.

Pretty much the whole community accepted or promoted the idea that everything that happened at the Sneider's house was an accident. Soon enough, even members of the congregation did too.

While people in town talked about William Fredericks' plan to leave, phone calls resumed bombarding the Asheborne home, urging him to do the same thing. They were starting to leave notes in the mailbox too.

Noah changed their home phone number for the third time, still getting at least one call from a weirdo every day—after that, he didn't bother to try and get it changed again. So on November 16th, he almost didn't answer the unknown number that came up on the caller ID display of the home phone.

"Yes," he gritted his teeth against the expected rant and warning.

"This is Mr. Han," said the calm, flat voice on the other end.

"Hi?" Noah said to the silence. No TV, no talking, nothing cooking, no radio. It was almost impossible to find silence in his own home. It made him wonder where the school teacher was.

"Do you have a minute to talk? It's about David," said the voice he barely knew.

Noah pulled his butt onto a stool by the island in the kitchen. "Of course."

"How is he today?" David's teacher asked.

"Well, he's acting six. He's destroying magazines and using up glue-sticks while the TV rots his brain."

"What is he making?"

Noah frowned and leaned out to look at the little boy—half expecting to see something completely different happening, by the way Kim asked.

"Books."

"Yeah."

Noah waited for him to continue. He wanted to ask what difference it made, but he didn't have to.

"He's been making a lot of books during free-time. I know he works on them at home too. I have a feeling you probably haven't looked at them."

"No. He says he's not done."

"I did, when I had a chance. There's a lot of gibberish in it. Not scribbles, but made up words. I think they are some kind of journals or reference books. There are maps and drawings of people."

"Such as…"

"You can understand, being his father, that it might be hard to tell what things are sometimes—but I think David is creative enough to get the point across. I think he's having a hard time with what happened to Phil. It looked to me like he drew a lot of pictures of his truck—that was where he died, I understand."

"It was," Noah's throat was tight.

"He has also been acting funny in class. Distracted and silly—more so than before or what I think is typical for someone his age. At his worst, before, it never took more than saying his name once or twice to bring David back from LaLa Land. Now, sometimes I can't, at all. I sent him to the nurse. I thought she'd call. When I didn't hear from you I decided to call you myself."

"No, I haven't got a call about it. If something weird happens in Nibebiitam, isn't that when you don't hear about it? Sorry for the sarcasm. I don't know. Well, David's mind can wander," he looked at the deeply engrossed magazine snipping child, "But I don't think he's been sleeping very well. Between the move, some different things that have happened, the stuff I talked to you about at the diner too, and what happened to Phil—I know he's affected. But it's also nothing, even before, for him to get so lost in these fantasies that I practically have to scream at him to wake him up."

"How long has that been going on?" Mr. Han wondered.

"Maybe once every few months…" Noah didn't think that was weird, not for a six-year-old. He took the phone into the other room, unaware that David stopped to watch him.

"When the divorce happened, I felt like his need for pretend time went through the roof. I thought that was getting better, he seems to have so many 'real' interests here. He's all over the place."

"It might be his real interests distracting him," Han suggested.

Noah nodded because he didn't think he could talk. His left hand closed on his face and his heart ached. It felt like it was wilting and bleeding out.

"Mr. Asheborne?"

Swallowing hard, Noah managed, "I'm here."

"It might not be anything to worry about," Kim offered. "I wanted you to be aware. Between the two of us we can start comparing notes and see if there's anything to worry about or not. You've named a lot of good reasons for him to be distracted."

"His schoolwork is normal," Noah knew because he always looked through David's papers. David always wanted to show them.

"You'd hear about that slipping before the gradebook, Mr. Asheborne," Kim assured him in an almost grave way, "Problems in kids show their faces pretty fast in their work."

"I appreciate that."

"I just wanted to let you know that he's been disruptive and that he might be using these journals to cope with some of those issues."

"I appreciate that too."

Noah went back out where he could see David, who was still busy working on his books.

"Will let you know if anything changes for better or worse, okay?"

"Okay," the young father agreed, said goodbye and left the space between the kitchen and living room to join his son at the couch. Sitting between it and the coffee table, David laid over the open pages and raised his eyebrows at the prying face.

"What have you been working on so hard?" his daddy asked. "Is it a journal?"

"It's an encyclopedia set," said David.

Noah raised his eyebrows too and said, "Oh? Can I see?"

David groaned reluctantly.

His daddy's eyes told him it wasn't really an option and he peeled himself up from the covered pages.

Noah carefully flipped through the sheets which were, just as Han said, completely full of bibble-babble. He saw a page full of drawings of what, to him, were clearly Phil's rust-bucket.

"Do you know what I think?" Noah said without pausing on this page.

"Huh?" David wanted to know.

"I think somebody maybe looked at his daddy's binder. The one with his red notebook inside?"

"Huh?" David repeated, screwing his face up.

"Are you making a file like daddy's? You need to tell me."

"File?"

Noah stared at the boy exasperated.

Maybe he didn't know.

Maybe he hadn't seen.

"You know you are never supposed to snoop in my things David—sometimes there are good things I don't want you to see, sometimes there are things that are for older people to see—but either way they are only David's Business when I say so? Right?"

"Yah, but I never looked," David claimed. "These are Encyclopedia Ashtannicas."

*I feel like you're lying to me*, Noah thought at the little face staring up at him.

In not too long, Noah wouldn't be able to tell.

◆        ◆        ◆

David was still busy with the books that evening, so Noah thought it was a good time to work on his own. Ordinarily, he liked to work in his bedroom. During college he did so much typing in bed, that it was habit now. He thought he could think better, even though it was harder and harder on his back all the time. He didn't like David being exposed to his writing, even though he couldn't read very well yet—he did a lot of research for his novels, sometimes involving history and pictures just too scary for him to consciously have in a "David Okay" zone.

He'd make an exception tonight to be near his son and moved his work to the kitchen table.

He had that feeling again, to not let David out of his sight, only to be lost quickly, deeply into his work.

The faintest hint of movement flashed through Noah's peripheral vision. He lowered the screen of his laptop, listened and looked—seeing nothing, he went back to his work.

A minute later it happened again. This time two shapes zipped past.

Noah closed the laptop and sat his glasses on top of it. He rubbed his aching eyes and sat still for a moment before he decided he had to get up to check. The living room was probably where it headed, so he went there first, but when he passed the short division in the hall there was something there.

"Son of a bitch!" he cried out in surprise at Gilder lying there. She wagged her tail as much as she could and was thrilled to see him too.

Noah looked at the small dirty stocking feet poking out of the open closet door. Something that looked like a striped fur candy cane passed back and forth against the butt and back the man couldn't see. Then Mama Cat's face ground up against the edge of the door, incidentally pulling her stubby mug back so her teeth rubbed the wood. She didn't seem to mind. No more than she minded falling asleep on the sharp edges of wood stacked by the fireplace, or with her head and half her arched torso hanging off the couch, or being upside down, or with her face stuffed into spaces where he was sure she couldn't breathe.

There were clinking and rummaging sounds near ground level. Little mutterings and grunting, Noah imagined David's little pink tongue held in the corner of his mouth while he concentrated on whatever he was doing.

"What's up, kiddo?" Noah asked as he stepped into the hall and sat on the floor beside Gilder in her dog bed, who he pet generously and gently. Then Mama Cat got jealous and wanted some love too.

The boy in the elastic waisted jeans and long sleeved t-shirt wasn't as concerned with getting his share. He wasn't even sure if he really heard anything.

"David?"

Then he was sure.

"Yeah dad?" his son asked, sitting back on his heels so he could turn enough to see his daddy's face. His daddy's heart ached when he saw how peaked David looked—and it wasn't just overhead lighting. There were dark circles under the puffs of the boy's eyes.

"What are you doing?" Noah wanted to know.

"Making stuff."

"What kind of stuff?"

David considered his answer a minute.

"Making chimes and stuff," he finally replied.

"Need any help?" Noah offered.

"Aren't you working?"

Noah shook his head and reached out for his baby, who gladly climbed into the arms open for him. The child felt so small and light, like hugging an arm full of feathers.

"It can wait."

His son looked doubtful.

"Sure?"

"Of course," his dad asserted.

Mama Cat raised up on her back legs so she could rub her face on one of the arms wrapped around David.

"You cat!" David snickered, reaching for her tail.

"How are you feeling, kiddo?" Noah felt for fever under the guise of brushing hair out of the little face.

"Okee," a little hand tried to help slap the mess away.

"You need a trim, I think," his daddy smiled warm and handsomely.

"You too, daddy," he touched the stubble on his daddy's

face. Stubble enough it was almost interning for a beard.

"Jacob told me everybody grows beards up here in the winter."

"It makes you look old."

"I am old."

"You *are*?"

Noah's smile spread, "Mm-hmm."

"How old is old?" David wondered.

"You are as old as you feel. Some people who are very young have lived a lot—it shows."

"Have you lived a lot?" the child wasn't sure if he could ask—his daddy never talked about his past. He didn't know if this counted as asking about it or not.

"Sometimes I feel like I have," Noah put his face against David's forehead. Then he asked, "How old do you feel, David?"

"Six."

"Six?"

"Yup."

Noah looked at David's face and could tell his son didn't want to talk about anything serious. He kept looking back at the closet and the playing he was missing out on.

"Okee," said Noah, releasing him to the cardboard box and the paperclips and yarn laying out in the open.

The man with worried eyes watched the child for almost an hour before he rumpled the head of boy, cat, and dog—in that order—and went back to the kitchen table where his laptop looked flat and disgruntled. He rubbed his jaw thoughtfully, surprised that he'd let the hair grow so long—no matter what Jacob told him or he told his son—Noah hadn't even noticed. David would like helping get rid of it in the morning.

He logged back into his computer account and stared at the

words that seemed too dark on a screen too light.

Dates. Places. People. Tragedies. Tragedies. Tragedies.

Flukes. Freak accidents. More people. More places. More dates.

It was more than just the muskeg, Noah recognized, that kept internment prisoners in Kapuskasing from running away—it was legends. It was blaming legends for accidents. Anger, violence, murder on ghost stories. Even blaming folklore for incidents of gravity.

Hundreds of pages. Hundreds of victims. Maybe one, two, ten, fifty, a hundred murderers who were overlooked because of legends and fears. Superstition and scapegoating.

A big chunk of time was missing from when a Nibebiitam official took it upon himself to destroy records to hide what was going on. That was when they must have realized it drew less attention to make excuses than to have no records at all.

People asked.

Of course they would ask.

The official was fired and there was a town meeting, the first real records since the official was hired, but there was no record of what the meeting was about, who went, no minutes. But the documents since then, 1967, had the look and feel of a "standard". Almost like all the records were made ahead of time, but with enough information to just about reach to the truth and then say, "Conclusion of the investigation showed death/injury was undoubtedly accidental."

On a second word document was a manuscript that had made little progress.

It was really hard to focus like he needed to. No. He didn't need to. He *wanted* to write this book.

There was something about the weirdness of Nibebiitam that

he thought he could conquer. In doing so, that he might salvage their life there. He wanted to disprove the myth.

No.

He *needed* to.

# CHAPTER 20

◆

# The VOID

Solomon called the Asheborne's the evening before December 22, the last day of school before Christmas break, to ask Noah if he could get out of work the next day because a bad storm was coming. Noah didn't think so; there was a lot of work to wrap up after all the business that came in prior to the holiday. Work he didn't think he could do at home. But that was just as well, the men agreed, because the school would call his job first if it let out early—since they knew there might not be anyone at home to take David, even though he was always welcome to just get off the bus with Fawn when it was arranged.

The next day was bitterly cold and a dangerous energy hung in the heavy gray clouds that blocked out every inch of sky.

All the kids in Nibebiitam schools starting counting down the day from the instant they woke up that morning. School wasn't cancelled. In an hour? Two hours? When would Christmas vacation begin?

David had a hard time paying attention to class. The wreaths they'd cut out, snowmen and reindeer they made, garland they'd glued, just reminded him that it was *that close* to Christmas. He squirmed with impatience.

With the collective will of almost every child within fifty miles, they wished the weather to get bad enough that they'd get out by lunch.

The cars in the parking lot looked like they were huddled together to keep warm against the cold. Not a damn lot of good it would do the little pale blue Oldsmobile nor the yellow VW bug, almost twenty years old, whose owners forgot to start them during the day. Unlike the other cars coated in a cruel dense frost—like bread in gravy, these two poor cars looked saturated in the cold that, with wind chill, felt like forty-five below.

Somewhere the school buses were coughing and coming to life to cart the children home early before the sudden heavy snows gained ground. All the teachers were getting their kids bundled and ready to go—anxious themselves to get the hell out of there. All teachers but Mr. Han, who knew the children's excitement to leave early could get them ready in a quarter of the time it took at the end of a regular day. In fact, he was in no hurry to empty his classroom because a colder, emptier home waited for him.

To the children this reinforced the idea Han was a mean, cranky he-spinster who loved to make everyone miserable.

Mr. Hanburger, to last years' first graders, to this years', Hanbenezer Scrooge. Unlike Dickens' Scrooge, more than three spirits would visit Hanbenezer.

When at last the first graders were set loose on the halls of Nibebiitam Elementary, Noah was just coming through the front doors. The pouring of little booted feet down the stairs and hall reminded him of the infected in *28 Days Later*. It made him smile.

He looked over the hordes of short people waiting at the large glass doors for their buses to arrive. A few either brave or over eager were waiting on the steps when he walked up. In this height range, there was no risk David wouldn't spot him.

"Waiting for someone?" asked a pretty blonde leaning in a doorframe surrounded by strange looking reindeer.

Noah smiled involuntarily at the voluptuous teacher who dressed older than she could possibly be. Sometimes he was horrified when teachers looked like they were going clubbing instead of teaching colors and numbers to five-year-olds, but her sweater alone was at least as old as Naana. Her dress might have been from the seventies. In a way, it struck him as classy, so he still had to smile. She was lovely.

"I'm picking up my son, David."

"Oh sure, Mr. Asheborne. Nice to meet you. Ms. English— Lillian," she took a couple steps to shorten the distance so they might shake hands.

In a second or two David was there, glad that his daddy got to see Mrs.—Ms. English. Glad that they were getting out of school early. Glad that it was almost Christmas. Glad that his daddy was there to pick him up.

Noah was reluctant to return to the outdoors. The drifting and blowing snow obscured the dark shape of huddled children on the steps and made it impossible to see when the buses pulled up to the curb until the wind paused to draw a breath.

"It was nice to meet you Lillian," David's father told her and shook her hand goodbye. "Drive safe," he said lastly, while holding the door open for his son and a dozen other children.

David ran around the door and cupped his hands on the frosty glass until Noah was able to get past the surging children.

"Are we going home?" David had to yell.

"In just a little bit. Daddy has just a little work left before his day's done."

The tissue paper wreath pinched in David's mitted hand was almost ripped away in the wind, had Noah not been ready for that to happen. David's pack crinkled and clinked with other holiday crafts Noah earnestly couldn't wait to see.

While delayed buses dumped off their last children into ever deepening drifts, Han's blood was already ceasing to drip. His body settling to room temperature, which in his small lonely house was a chilly fifty degrees. The clean spaces on the walls where pictures once hung, were the only witnesses to his death, which would not be discovered until the middle of January—after roughly three weeks. Then, his death would hardly raise an eyebrow when to everyone it seemed apparent he killed himself. Clearly he'd never gotten over the divorce. His isolation was apparent even when his family was still in Nibebiitam. No one could really relate to the Korean-Canadian teacher, except perhaps the divorced New Yorker who came up that summer with his boy.

It was a downward spiral, they all told themselves they expected to happen one day.

Slitting ones' wrists is common enough, no one knew what to think of him biting them out—or the wild look of fear that would remain on his face as long as the flesh remained. They may have been able to ignore that, but the lack of any blood on his mouth was not as easy. Of course, dozens of explanations were offered; explanations were the only forensics that let them maintain all they denied. Anything else and they'd have to question the ideality of this small country town.

Blissfully unaware that this would come to pass, David thumbed through last month's *Highlights* magazine while he waited for Noah to finish working. Inside, David's heart pounded with excitement and fear, reinforced with every brief and frequent glance through the great picture windows.

There is something between children and snow that exists for only a handful of years—there is some sort of magic that is secretly acknowledged that might translate to adults as the power and danger winter wields.

The heavy snowflakes, no one falling without being entangled in at least ten others, clouded the streets and clung to all things like glitter on glue. David thought he would never see another snow like they had in New York City.


The winter storm only grew in strength over the next twenty-four hours—it grew into a screaming, staggering wind, and raised moans and wails from the beaten houses and ravaged forest. The driving snow packed solidly into any space where the wind could no longer push it. Throughout the day the snow and wind molded smooth banks and almost unperceptively rolling waves in the yard.

The elemental power was fascinating during the day, but as night quickly settled over the unrelenting blizzard, it became an abominable monster to be feared. This was a night of wendigoes, of banshees, and wraiths. Sometime before the storm hit, his daddy assured him that all the little animals that stayed awake in the winter had settled into their downy nests to ride it out in their warm little dens. They were safe.

Somewhere, David imagined, Silver Fox Man, now an old, withered, and starving man, was meandering the limitless wilds on this very awful night. He would not be bothered by the cold and was afraid of nothing.

During an earlier storm, while waiting for Noah to pick him up from the Cranes, Solomon consoled David that for hundreds of years hunters and other travelers lost in storms like this were rescued by the same old man.

David couldn't help but hear the storm, but he wanted to hear through it, listening for the sound again. It sounded like something in boots pacing on the deck. David had been staring out the window—straining to see through the dark. Gilder, looking out in the dark beside him, didn't see anything either. She didn't like the storm and had been tense and vocal about it all day. Had she sensed anything out there, she would have done something more than huff and puff.

The distinct sound of heavy footsteps passed by the window again.

Maybe it was Silver Fox Man.

He better haul ass if he didn't want to miss him.

David closed the bedroom door to keep Gilder inside. Maybe Silver Fox Man wouldn't protect people whose dogs bark at him.

It took some effort to stuff the feet of his pajamas into his winter boots. After his coat, he didn't think he needed anything more because he was just going to look outside. If Silver Fox Man was there, he wanted to try and talk to him.

The automatic light came on as David crossed half the deck, it illuminated every single speck in the wall of snow coursing past and through the porch. Santa Claus could have been standing three feet into it and the child wouldn't have seen him. That possibility was only half of what frightened the little boy—

if he couldn't see Santa Claus, he couldn't see anything else either.

Out there, beyond the wind, there was little more than the snapping of cold branches and a scuttling sound on the roof.

Suddenly there was a "thump" on the steps directly in front of him, like something dropped off the eaves.

For some reason, David was sure the front door would be locked when he ran back to it. But the outer door flung open easily, too easily in this wind, and with some effort he managed to get it closed. Enough time, he was certain, for whatever-it-was to catch up. The window of the screen door was up and so frosted the little boy saw nothing but the porch light in it.

David went for the heavy inner door, unaware of the silhouette that joined the light filled frost of the outer door's window.

Above the storm, hung a full white moon. It threw strange shadows from the outside in, when the clouds and snow allowed. The wind groaned against the curves of the log house as the child secured the dead bolt and his safety, for at least a while.

*There* was a child that liked to play. Tag was a game he seemed to favor, though he never finished the games they thought he started.

Something, again, paced the snow breeched porch. Something, again, scampered on the roof. Something—*someone*, somewhere, would take David's turn while he and Gilder crowded in beside his father and Mama Cat for the rest of the horrible night.

◆　　　　◆　　　　◆

The next night, Noah rose restlessly from bed. Over the past few weeks his sleep was running down to only two or three hours over the whole evening. Thinking was his worst enemy—his mind didn't want to let him rest, not without solving all its problems. He wasn't sure how big the problem was.

Noah knew David wasn't sleeping well either. He hoped the kids at school weren't filling the boy's head with the same mumbo-jumbo he was getting from people, but he couldn't ask without going there, himself. The father supposed it was unlikely his son knew nothing, as there is nothing people like to do more than talk. And people like to upset each other. It makes them feel powerful, like they have control of someone else—if they can control how someone else feels and reacts—a lot of people think that's a good thing.

The young man never felt he had control of anything, not in the whole of his twenty-nine years on earth. He never felt like he was missing anything by dominating nothing. He just didn't want to be lost in the current. He didn't want to be used or hurt. Not anymore.

Structure and security were all Noah needed for himself and his family. He had the rug pulled out from underneath him when his wife, Terri, announced she was pregnant. Everything, including his personal convictions had to be reorganized to make room for the expense to their finances and his feelings—which were both disregarded. When things started going well for them, it happened pretty fast, but before that they had to manage their money carefully and save for nice things.

Then the morning came when he woke up and she was gone. Their four-year-old son was crying in his bed—the father rose automatically, since she never did.

When dreams of that morning recurred—often they tried to

explain the unexplainable—that being why she left and what became of her.

Sometimes, in the nightmares, she'd have killed herself—after coming to the horrible realization Terri might have left abruptly had she been raped. Then, there could have been a lot of things she couldn't stand. Not everyone can talk about those things, even with people they love, but he couldn't imagine not knowing something like that had happened to her. It was unbearable to think of her going through something like that alone.

Noah thought he would have seen the signs.

Other times when the nightmare returned, she'd have taken David and then the police come and tell him that his son is dead.

Other times it just plays out the way it really happened. And it plays out again and again and again, until the man wakes up crying and exhausted, or clay-cold and stiff like a hundred-and-five-year-old man lying under the watch of the angel of death. Those days it was hard to function.

People get divorced. Things happen, but most the time people know why. Don't they?

Sometimes Noah felt like he was lying on the ground with his face smashed in by the force of the fall. Reality could play no part in helping the abandoned deal with it—he had to guess about everything, because he had never even heard her voice again. It still bothered him that he couldn't remember the last thing she ever said to him. Probably "goodnight".

The divorce papers came.

She didn't want anything.

She didn't want David.

He talked to her lawyer, a longtime friend of his wife's, about selling the house. It was the most valuable property they shared and he wanted to know if she wanted any of the profit from the sale—she said automatically, "Nope. She's made up her mind. You're a free man, Mr. Asheborne."

But what he heard was, "She wants a new life. A completely new life. No strings attached."

Noah didn't know how to make excuses for the birthday and Christmas cards that never came, because other kids David knew still heard from their parents after divorces—that's why David said it was "okay" when Noah explained how mommy wasn't coming home. That's how his son made it okay within himself. Noah was sure David would hear from her too. So when those things never happened, he didn't know where to begin.

"Can David leave her a Mother's Day card at your office?" Noah asked her lawyer that first year.

"She doesn't want anything from him. She didn't want him— why would she want a birthday card from the person responsible for her stretch marks?"

"Huh?" he said in disbelief.

"Just between the two of us, I told her it was stupid for her not to take her half. I think that should tell you how over it is."

"I understood that since the moment she left," Noah told her. "All I've ever wanted to know is what happened? If I did something wrong. If something happened to her. If she was okay."

"You know how it goes, Asheborne, it's not you, it's her? Right? Try to think of it that way. Get a little pissed or something, you'll feel better."

"It *doesn't* make me feel better."

Noah hung up the phone. The worst thing about modern phones is that most of them can't be slammed to hang up. That's what he felt like doing. It felt stupid to push a button angrily.

Then he'd looked down at the envelope laden with unintentional paint fingerprints.

Getting pissed wouldn't do anything for them. There was no room in their lives for something so useless. Not that people can't get mad and will get mad. Noah had been mad, a lot. He had been mad at the whole world. He knew an age when he hated everything and everyone. So he knew it didn't help. As far as Noah was concerned, David never even had to know his daddy could get angry.

In a perfect world, but how realistic is that?

Now, two years later, standing in the doorway, watching his son sleeping against the back of their dog Gilder, the man worried. He worried about David all the time. Worse still, it wasn't being overprotective. There were a lot of things going on that could scar his son for life. He needed to figure out where his son was hurt and take care of it. If it started to look like more bleeding than he could stop on his own, he'd bring David to a doctor, as anyone would do for someone they loved.

Isn't that the best way to prevent scars?

All he knew was that he *knew* David was being hurt and had been hurt. No matter what the boy claimed, there was a little broken heart in that small helpless body.

Worst of all, there wasn't a goddamn thing he could have done to protect him. When a child needs and you can't sate, that is the worst kind of helplessness Noah had ever known.

He felt he was right about the world being the wrong place for children, but he also believed he was wrong to think there was nothing a parent can do to make it right.

In a few hours Noah would be awakened by the pattering of ten feet passing in the hall. David, Gilder, and Mama Cat would go out to the Christmas tree and start poking around. Then he would have to get up, catch his son in the act, pretend he was mad, ask him to wait—at least until he put on some water for hot chocolate. David would be thrilled that the cookies and milk were gone—and "the way it used to be" would own the day— even if "the way it used to be" only meant the last two years.

At about noon, after shoveling out the driveway, the whole family, including disgruntled pets in sweaters, piled into the truck with a few dishes of food and presents for the Cranes.

Solomon shot a turkey that fall and they were all excited to have wild harvested turkey—the older man said it kicked fat-farm turkeys in the ass. A few weeks earlier, Fawn told David that Naana's slow-cooker reindeer and wild rice was the creamiest, yummiest food in the whole world. When David started crying she was sorry she hadn't called it caribou instead.

David cradled his presents to the family in his lap. He painted a coffee cup for Solomon and insisted on giving Fawn his favorite baby toy, but he wouldn't tell his daddy why. Naana's present made pretty sounds as its pieces shifted in the box.

With the laughing and bustling of being surrounded by people he loved, David completely forgot what kind of meat was in the rice.

After filling himself on Rudolph, among any number of other dishes, he and Fawn sat by the tree and exchanged gifts.

"What is this?" Fawn whispered to David and held up the limp and matted Pound Puppy she'd unwrapped a few minutes earlier.

"A toy?" David guessed sassily.

Fawn looked at it uncertainly.

"It was mine," he added. "Sorry, Gilder chews on it if I don't hide it."

The girl looked over at the little boy sitting so close their knees touched.

"My mommy and daddy were together then," he pressed further, looking down so he could explain more. "It's the only toy I have that I remember having when I had them both. I have other toys from then, but I remember memories with it before mommy left."

He met her eyes and understood what each other was feeling.

"I want you to have it. I knew this one would be okay. It will get along with yours," then, suddenly doubtful, he added, "I think."

"Close enough," said the girl. She dropped her eyes to the battered but dearly loved plush dog. She thought she had a good idea what it might mean to him.

"I love you Fawn," David blurted.

Solomon and Noah stopped teasing Naana long enough to listen for Fawn's answer. When she stuck out her jaw and hardened it against the embarrassment of his outburst, Solomon helped by making kissy sounds. Noah smiled—he was smiling so hard his face hurt. And his stomach hurt from eating well. For the moment his heart didn't hurt. None of theirs did.

"What do you say, *noozhis*?" Naana scolded.

Fawn leaned in and whispered what she had not ever been able to say before, "You are my *niijii*, David."

"What is that?" he leaned away, staring at her with wide eyes.

"It means you're my friend," she said too low for anyone but David to hear.

"Thank you, Fawn," said the little boy.

At first she was horrified that he might be blushing, but the flush preceded tearing eyes.

"You okay, David?" Noah asked. He could recognize the most subtle announcement of tears.

David nodded, while grinding out the wetness gathered on the rim of his eyes with soft knuckles. Gilder licked at the hands and forehead.

Ever since David was a baby, she got anxious when he cried. The six-year-old laughed and shoved at her. The big dog went after his hands again, overzealous because she was feeling happy and safe for the first time, in a long time. Her little human giggled wildly and cried for Fawn's help. She tried, but choked exaggeratedly—or maybe not too exaggeratedly—at Gilder's breath when she became interested in licking Fawn's face too.

The father clearly felt, as much as saw, a wonderful truth. Everything seemed to be okay when they were all together. They were happy.

Solomon, for a moment, felt the presence of his son-in-law and daughter—he almost heard their laughter.

The grandfather clearly felt, as much as he saw, the voids in their broken families filling.

# CHAPTER 21

◆

# BELIEF is the FATHER of REALITY

Noah wanted to be surprised that Kim had killed himself, but from everything he heard about how distant and unhappy the schoolteacher was, anything was possible. He would have liked to have known the guy better. When Noah first heard what happened, all he could say was, "Damn."

With all the "accidents" and "natural" deaths in just the short time they'd been there—Phil's death, what happened with the kittens and Gilder—Noah was more than a little concerned about how a teacher's suicide was going to affect David—who wasn't doing that well anyway.

On the first day back to school after Christmas break, David was excited that Mr. Han never showed up for class. Mr. Redclaw was their substitute. David said that *all* the kids thought it would be so funny for them to put Mr. Han's name on the board.

The next day, when Kim didn't show up again, one of the

kids cleverly suggested that their teacher must not have known Christmas break was over. All the kids laughed.

Then Mr. Han didn't come in the next day or the next. Then, after missing a week of work, and not answering any phone calls, Thom Redclaw called the police.

When Noah told David that Mr. Han wasn't going to be his teacher anymore, the little boy asked what happened. His father didn't know how to tell him. So he decided to tell his son that angels came and took him away.

Then his six-year-old casually corrected him, "Those weren't *angels*."

Noah swallowed hard. This was a perfect time to find out what David knew—or what he was told about those goddamn children, spirits, demons, delinquents—it was hard to know what people were really talking about. Solomon was so general about the issue compared to others, maybe it was time to have another talk with the old guy about this shit. Right now he needed to ask his son.

"What were they then?" Noah tried to sound like he had no idea what else he could mean.

"Was it immigration?" David wondered wide-eyed.

Noah laughed.

"Your teacher was a citizen of this country—*we're* the immigrants," he explained.

David looked confused, shrugged, and smiled brightly. "Okay," the little boy said.

"Okay," said Noah.

Part of Noah wanted to take this easy out, but he knew that David would hear "the truth" at school.

"It *was* angels, David," Noah knelt on the floor beside the couch where David was working.

The six-year-old cast a look at his father that seemed very old and very knowledgeable—like when someone knows you are wrong and, even though it makes them mad, they won't bother trying to correct you. He dreaded the feeling David might ask, "Well, what was it then?"

"Okay," repeated his son, in exactly the same way.

"Do you know what I'm telling you, David?" said the father through the most uncomfortable wave of *deja vous.* He'd asked David that exact same question two years before. It made Noah feel like throwing up.

"He died?" David guessed in an almost absent way.

"I'm afraid so buddy," Noah drew him into his arms and hugged the little body he loved more than anything, that he felt he wasn't protecting.

"Are you okay?" Noah whispered against the top of the head that now leaned against his chest.

"Uh huh," the boy answered idly.

"Do you want to talk about it?" this was all too familiar too.

"Why?" the child asked loudly.

"Because sometimes it's really confusing when people go away."

*Oh God, oh God, too familiar...too fucking familiar!*

"When people go away? You mean *why* they go away?"

"Uh huh," Noah's accent played through his breath. His heart was starting to pound. It felt like they were back in New York, could almost smell traces of Terri's perfume, just like the first time he had to talk to David about people going away. He could remember the way the couch felt under his hand. He remembered it was sweaty, but that he felt cold.

"Sometimes people go away," David looked up at the underside of his dad's jaw.

"That's true, but David," he moved the little body back so they could look into each other's faces, "sometimes when people go away and we don't want them to it makes us feel a lot of questions. I am here to help you if you ever feel questions."

"Daddy," David said in the "you're silly" voice. "I know *that*."

"I'm glad."

"Even if you go away, I know you'd still be there."

"But I'm not going to go away David, ever."

David nodded, the nod weakened until he was facing into his lap where he fidgeted with his safety scissors.

"Do children ever go away?" his son asked in a small voice.

Noah's gut told him David knew all about those evil kids.

He didn't want to lie. He never wanted to lie to his son.

He wasn't a big fan of lying to anybody.

"I think they do, sometimes."

◆        ◆        ◆

Almost a month later, Noah finally made the call to meet Solomon somewhere, sometime—he needed to talk to him.

Somewhere ended up being Solomon's house.

Noah was afraid to have the conversation again, after how it went trying to get to the bottom of things with Phil and then Rising Moon.

Noah wasn't going to work as often as he should, saying that his writing project needed his time, but it was partly to avoid Rising Moon. He didn't feel good about it, but he didn't want to pretend that everything was good just because Phil was dead. He felt sorry for that. It was something else they couldn't talk about.

Jacob knew it had more to do with her than with any manuscript, call it gut instinct. He once asked Noah if they had shacked up—if it was a problem to be around her. So there was no point to lie about why he took so much time off, but Noah still answered "no", that it had to do with getting his book done. And, for the record, there was nothing like that going on between them.

Since talking to Rising Moon, Noah had been pretty successful in avoiding the topic of wolf children with anyone— even though he invested a lot of hours looking into all the strange deaths—and even not so strange deaths.

He just hoped it wouldn't hurt his friendship with Mr. Crane too.

"When I first met you Solomon, you let the others do the talking. The second time I saw you, you tried to talk to me about some things that were pretty hard to believe. I appreciated that you hadn't brought it up again, but now I think I'd like to ask you about it." Noah looked into the jet black eyes of his elder as he spoke. "Can I?"

"You can ask me anything," Solomon said sincerely.

"Since we moved here we've been harassed about staying in our home. People on the phones screaming that we're going to die, to people hanging out on the road by my place. Are these the same people who you came with that first day we met?"

"It could be," Solomon shrugged. "Has it been bad?"

"Bad enough to think there's no way I could stand to raise my child here. Bad enough to be afraid for our safety," Noah answered.

"I'll see what I can do about that," Solomon said in a way that said it would never happen again.

"When we first met, you told me that the woods were

dangerous and that a lot of strange things happen. You said that some people say that the woods are haunted. You said some things about children in the woods that sometimes cause people to have accidents... that sometimes these accidents leave people dead. To clarify here, are the ghosts and the children you were talking about the same thing?"

"I thought it would be easier if you didn't think of them that way."

"But everyone else told me they were."

"Okay. Yes. They are the same thing."

Noah nodded.

"Okay," the young man continued, "Do you believe it?"

"I do."

"How?"

Solomon leaned forward, eyebrows reaching for his hairline, "How *can't* you?"

Noah leaned back, tapping his lips with the middle and forefinger of his right hand. He cocked one eye-brow thoughtfully. Solomon leaned back and shrugged.

"Well?" asked the old Indian.

"Well, come *on*..."

"No, Noah. Tell me. How can't you believe it?"

"I think people are responsible for this. A lot of deranged people. Also, I don't believe in ghosts, Solomon," Noah explained.

"Do you believe in anything you can't see?" the older man pressed.

Noah was thoughtful a moment, though the answer came swiftly:

"I do."

"Okay."

"Okay? That's it?" Noah laughed.

"Well, what do you want? Are you trying to tell me nothing weird has happened since you've been here?"

"A *lot* of weird stuff has happened, Solomon," the younger man agreed, "but I don't know that anything has happened that can't be explained."

"Oh good God," it was Solomon's turn to laugh. "You see all those implausible storylines on TV. People can come up with some explanation for *everything*. Doesn't mean that everyone will buy it. That's the boat you're in now. In a nutshell, this is something that people believe in here. Almost everyone believes it. Maybe everyone—I wouldn't be surprised. Some people think that if they deny it they will be safe—like claiming you don't believe it will make it go away. But they all believe eventually. Once you believe then you can learn the rules and protect yourself, but until then you just have to hope nothing weird happens."

"Why do you have to believe to know the rules?"

"Because the rules won't work if you don't believe they can. That is one thing I do know. That is how we've been okay. Sometimes people get over enthusiastic in trying to either save lives by driving people out or by trying to make them believe."

"People like the people who have been calling me," Noah asked, feeling more than a little disturbed.

"I'm afraid so," Solomon admitted. "There were these fellas who were set to try and imitate the wolf childrens' work to make people believe faster and ended up killing some folks up the road. Then there were others that thought that threatening people was a good idea too, tried to take matters into their own hands to drive the family out. At least the people got out alive. It's that burnt up building just up the road there."

"You're kidding me?" Noah exhaled.

"I wish I was."

"Phil didn't tell me that."

"Phil hadn't been here that long," Solomon sounded regretful.

"So he didn't necessarily have the whole story?"

"Not everyone can accept the whole story."

The men sat silently until the younger sighed, leaned back, and asked, "So what do you want me to accept?"

"It would help a lot if you would just believe in ghosts and believe that some things help protect people from the supernatural. Once you know that I can enlighten you to the nature of the beast."

"I don't want to," Noah said honestly. "I don't believe ghosts are killing people."

"Can you really explain everything that's happened to you at that house?"

"Yes," Noah said. "And a lot of it has to do with losing sleep and being scared all the time because of the shit people are telling me and the things I've been finding out. Has anyone ever lived out here without incident who didn't buy into this ghost stuff?"

"I wish I could tell you yes, but most people believe it. And I think the majority who say they don't are in denial. Since the first white people settled here, they knew something was off. Nibebiitam means 'Watched in the Night'. It's a warning. Everyone knew back then and so they settled what is now Kapuskasing. Nibebiitam is here because some people wanted the land more than they were bothered by being scared. Things weren't as bad back then, they say."

"So if you want to live out here, you had better believe in

ghosts? The realtor never said anything about that to me."

"Are you surprised?"

"Not really. Who would be?"

"You really can't believe, can you? What do you think happens when people die?" Solomon wanted to know.

Noah swallowed hard and chewed his lip.

"I don't think about it."

"How?"

"By not thinking about it," Noah said matter-of-factly.

"You must watch movies with ghosts. What do you feel watching them?" Solomon wondered.

"Entertained, if I'm lucky."

The men studied each other's faces. After a long while Solomon gave up trying to read what was going on in the wounded brown eyes looking back.

"What in the world have you been through, Noah?" worried the elder.

Noah felt ashamed when he realized there were tears in his eyes.

"Right now I'm worried about what my son is going through. He's not sleeping. He looks sick. Mr. Han—" Noah's chest started to hurt. "—David's teacher was worried about him too. I thought the winter break would help, but it didn't. Another tragic death and—I made an appointment for him to see a doctor in Kapuskasing, but the waiting list is astronomical. I should have established care when we got here. A six-year-old shouldn't look like hell unless they've just raised it."

"Does David know about the children?"

Noah was relieved Solomon needed to ask.

"I think he does, but I would think it unlikely he wouldn't get exposed to it somewhere."

"Me too," Solomon agreed.

"What is he like when he's over here?" asked the young father who was regretting not talking to Solomon in the first place.

"Weird," laughed his neighbor. "I would expect weird, but to be honest I think he's been a little strange too. Maybe distant. Preoccupied."

"I wish I knew what was going on inside him," Noah answered.

"I wish that almost every moment I look at *noozhis*, my granddaughter."

Noah nodded, he didn't have to know to understand. With how much he deflected discussing his own history and anything about his wife abandoning them—he was loathed to ask for details, no matter how badly he wanted to know Solomon Crane.

"Do you ever wonder what those two get up to when we're not around?" Noah decided to change the subject.

Solomon nodded.

"Your son is giving Fawn back her childhood."

◆          ◆          ◆

"I'm going with or without you," David threatened.

Fawn stared hard at the pressing dark behind the window.

She felt sick with fear, her watery knees knocked.

The boy was thin and sleepless—eyes bulging with fear and sickly pale flesh. She didn't even know if he was in his right mind. The last few days, the traps he designed, the jabbering, carrying on, and scheming. Writing guides and texts and arguing points *he'd* made up in them.

"David…"

He unrolled a sheet of construction paper and pressed his finger to the map he'd made.

"We found the den. All wolves have dens."

"These aren't wolves," they'd had this argument before.

He went for one of his "reference books". In a section pasted thickly with photos of wolves, he ran his pointer along rows of scribbles.

"Yup, like I said," he stammered and closed the staple bound text.

He suddenly perked up and started scribbling on a "list" he was making.

"And cookies for the kiddies," he sang.

"David, stop, you're scaring me."

The little boy looked at her somberly.

"Oh, don't be that!" he demanded.

"Well, stop being so weird."

"We-are-duh," David stared at her as the words dropped slowly from his mouth. Then he started to talk to himself, in a way on the verge of song:

"Great mystery, Little White Wolf Children, what is your name? It is pain, pain, pain. Black, Black Martin, is so naughty, naughty, naughty. Hear laughter, feel terror, know Death. Keep what you know 'til your last breath."

"David!"

"I need to go back!" David argued. "There should be pictures on the walls. Red Riding Hood, three little piggies—wolves like piggies."

Fawn grabbed his shoulders and shook him hard, even as she felt her own body shaking harder.

"Stop! You can't. *Why* are you being like this?"

"Why are *you* being like this? I need you."

"For what?"

David's face went blank, like he had been slapped. He started to "write" furiously in one of the books.

Fawn started crying and dropped her face into her arms. David paused and then scrawled faster and began to hum.

After a few minutes she was able to make herself stop. She looked up from her arms and over his work.

"Promise me you won't go back."

"Why should I go back?"

"You said to draw pictures," she reminded.

"They're really nice, Fawn," the little boy insisted.

"Did they tell you that?" her voice trembled.

"Naana told me."

"Listen to me," Fawn forced him to look at her face. His cheeks smooshed around his mouth. "Naana is crazy. She went out into the muskeg years and years ago after my parents died. By the time she was found she wasn't the same anymore. She had barely a thread on her body. She babbled about losing her fire. And she left her mind out there in the winter. She said Old Man Owl chased her until she was close enough to town that anyone could find her. She's gone. When her heart broke she didn't lose blood, she lost her mind. They aren't wolves. There's no den. They aren't friendly. They aren't playful. She just can't deal with the truth."

The little boy's gaunt face somehow paled more. "She lost her fire?"

"She was freezing."

David wanted to know the truth, but he couldn't ask. It would ruin everything. Everything. And Fawn didn't seem to understand what he did.

Maybe, he thought, she couldn't deal with the truth either.

"Let's talk cookies," he demanded.

"No, David."

"If we talk cookies I won't go there, promise."

Fawn let go of his face and sat back against the front of the couch, unfolding her legs and stuffing them into the space under the coffee table where David was working.

"Why do you want to talk about cookies?"

David answered incredulously:

"Who wouldn't want to talk about cookies?"

# JAWS of WINTER

◆

February entered the year cold and still as rigor mortis. Along the bank of the Mattagami River, the limbless bodies of birch trees cut the deep, blue-gray night like lamp posts with peeling white paint. To see the light of each post you must meander the woods and catch the moon when the highest branches embraced the celestial bulb.

At the head of a line of racquet shaped tracks was a snow-shoed tracker, Gerald "Grim" Grimlande. His successes pressed through the wire basket strapped to his back.

He hadn't been able to sleep and decided to take advantage of the nearly full moon. Up until then he was glad to be out, but when he came across the tracks, all he wanted was to get back home. The tracks he'd come across belonged to wolves. A lot of them, more than he'd ever seen in a pack before. They were fresh. Grim thought even an idiot could tell that.

Thoughts of children crossed his mind. He pushed them out. You don't do that.

*Don't acknowledge them.*

He was afraid to turn his back on the tracks. Their path would soon take them out of his peripheral vision too.

*There's not any other sign of them*, he told himself. Nowhere in sight. Not a sound.

Gerald told himself he should be confident the beasts were long gone. But he wasn't called "Grim" because of his last name. It was a hunter's moon. He was alone and his pack was loaded with dead animals. He wasn't feeling confident at all.

The snowshoes crunched over the three feet of crusty snow as he turned to steal a glance toward their heading.

Then something flew past.

Things.

Not things—wolves!

Wolves soared over him and dissolved in the night. Then a second wave passed over and they stopped fading out. They stayed. They stopped flying and ran. They ran around him while, at top speed, he could only trudge along. Snowshoes were not made for running.

*Don't stop!*

*I won't,* another part of his mind guaranteed. They agreed, if he stopped, he'd die.

The trapper didn't dare look at them—*them,* moving too fast to stay with him. Them moving too slow to possibly keep up. They kept up. They stayed beside and all around him. They ran on two, on four, on more legs.

He tore his eyes away.

*Don't look!*

*Their faces—oh God their faces!*

*It's not faces. Not faces.*

*THEY DO HAVE FACES!*

Grim closed his eyes. Only opening them to ensure he was

still going the right way.

*They're not real.*

*THEY* ARE *REAL.*

He closed his eyes. He couldn't remember the last time he cried. He couldn't help thinking this might be the last time.

"*Nindayekoz,*" said a voice in his ear.

His eyes snapped up like cummerbunds in old comedies.

A withered old man stared into Grim's face.

He felt a scream that refused to come.

The circle of wolves was farther off, more like a mist that you cannot see when you are close to it. They were flying again and fading in and out of sight. It was like being inside a fog tornado filled with pale demons.

The old man noticed him notice them and nodded at the wolves:

"Vi v byezpyetzi."

The last time Gerald heard Ukrainian he was just a little boy, but it was all his grandfather spoke. He thought he knew what it meant. He didn't care enough to try to make sense of it—he felt a call to run and answered.

He ran like the Devil was chasing him.

He remembered being chased by a bull the size of a sofa once when he was working on a farm in Montana. He didn't think it was possible to run faster than he did that day, even without snowshoes.

The woods—the night blurred past him.

Grim thought he broke his shin when he spilled out on the steps in front of his modest cabin. The pack felt heavy on his back, like *something.* He slapped at it and struggled to throw his body enough to loosen the burden from him, enough that the straps eventually broke and the pack crashed and spilled out its contents on the deck. The trapper recoiled until the only way to back further against the house would be to dissolve into it.

Even looking at the harmless pack didn't feel safe and so he left it out on the deck. It and the thing staring out of the mass of dead animals.

# CHAPTER 22

◆

# DESPERATION

David waited until Naana needed to use the bathroom before sneaking outside. There wasn't much time, but a lot more time than if it was someone else needing to go to the bathroom.

Fawn was tired by the time she got Naana back in her rocking chair. The old woman sat in the living room during winter months, the porch was too cold for anyone to sit in—one of these days Fawn planned to take her for a walk, just to get her some fresh air.

In the almost silent living room, the babysitter noticed two things, one—the absence of David and two, the air felt cool—like the door had been open a little while ago.

It took about forty-five minutes to take care of Naana, who was constipated, but insisted she could finish. Now, it almost seemed like the old woman had conspired with the six-year-old.

It was too cold for David to be outside for forty-five minutes—so where was the kid and what was he up to?

"I'll be right back, Naana," Fawn kissed her great-grandmother's head and handed her the TV remote so she could watch *Murder, She Wrote.* It had already been on five minutes so the old woman was starting to get upset.

The teen was hardly surprised to discover the boy's coat and boots missing.

"You little shit," Fawn mumbled as she bundled up against the cold to go after him.

She stepped through a knee high drift and then fell on her face. Her feet were in a mess of coat hangers, soup cans, and yarn. Some of the knots weren't tight until she pulled on them to get them off and they cinched tighter around the mess. The cold didn't help. The mittens didn't either. After they came off she managed to free one foot so she could stand up. She saw then the little handprints in the "drift".

Fawn moved to go down the steps and almost fell again when pulling against the weight of Solomon's chair and the bench on the opposite sides of the door. The mess was tied to both.

"David!" she called and fought the snare off her other foot. She was only frustrated when she first fell. By the time she was totally free she was mad.

"What?" the little boy hollered as he came around the side of the house. His face was red and he was breathless.

"Why did you trap the front door?"

"I trapped the back door too," he informed her, almost sounding disappointed that she didn't mention it or didn't know.

"Why?!?"

"For the wolves."

"You are trapping wolves at our doors?"

"No, just seeing if it works before I use them."

"Well, where the hell have you been?"

"It took you so long with Naana that I decided to set up my traps. Then I made snow angels."

"Snow angels?"

"Yep. Wanna see?"

"No," Fawn said flatly. "You need to clean these up before someone gets hurt. It's all fun and games, right?"

"Righto," he trotted up the stairs and gathered the mess out of the snow.

"I'll start on the stuff in the back," Fawn stepped over him to get inside. "Unbelievable."

She watched the little boy who was beyond winded—he almost seemed frantic. Frantic, she suspected, to get back and look like this was all he was doing.

"What are you up to David?"

"I wanted to try out my traps," he looked guiltily at the snow by her feet.

"You wanted to try out your traps on me?"

David shrugged.

While Fawn worked to dismantle the work he did in the backyard, she watched him tearing around the yard, like he was trying to cover every inch of ground with his footprints. The only way the behavior made sense was when she reminded herself that he was not only six, but also a boy.

He was hoping she wouldn't be able to tell where he'd been, in the yard or out of it. It took a lot more time than he expected to make it through the woods when its winter.

After they got inside, it didn't take long to feel confident that his secret was safe.

As for Fawn, Noah would be there to pick the kid up in two hours. Maybe by then she would be able to get rid of the inclination to rat on the little fiend.

◆ ◆ ◆

Noah almost didn't answer the door, but when he peeked through the kitchen blinds and saw Rising Moon's car he decided he may as well answer. He suspected she might check to see if the truck was in the garage. If she knew he was home and didn't answer she might wonder why. He didn't want that to happen. It was about time they talked.

"Hi," he said as he opened the door. "Come on in, it's freezing."

"This winter has been really mean. I expect snow storms in March. We've had more snow so far this month than we had in all of last year," she said.

She looked him in the eyes.

She didn't want to talk about the weather.

He didn't either, but their reasons why couldn't have been farther apart.

"Where's David?" she didn't see him anywhere.

"In his room," Noah answered, moving into the kitchen that she might follow him.

"I heard he hasn't been well," Rising Moon said in a way that almost sounded more like, "I told you so."

"He's not sick. At least I don't think so. But he isn't sleeping very well. I'm hoping it's just a phase," he pulled out a chair for her and sat down in one on the other side. "I thought the gossips were dead."

"Gossip will never be dead in Nibebiitam," she contradicted.

"Maybe it can be if people who know better don't contribute to it," his hand cradled his forehead. "I'm sorry. I guess I haven't been sleeping so well either. Sorry. Please, go ahead and sit down."

"I'm moving to Thunder Bay," Rising Moon announced, standing by the pulled out chair. "I wanted to make things right with you before I go. I'm sorry for expecting you to accept all this hook, line, and sinker. If you only have faith in what's real, that's okay."

Noah didn't want to talk about that either, so he said nothing.

"Do you want to know what's real?" she asked.

"Sure," Noah said with a shrug.

"That this stuff doesn't happen in Thunder Bay—at least no more than you would have experienced before. You and David could move there. You could still help Jacob out. I'm still going to do work for him from there."

"That's a reality of *everywhere*, but here, Rising Moon, not just Thunder Bay. Why move there?"

"Thunder Bay has a lot to offer," she countered, dropping her coat on the back of the pulled out chair. She came around the side of the table and half sat on the edge so her resting hand was inches from his.

He almost asked, "Like what?" But he thought she was baiting him to ask. He didn't want to hear the answer.

"We got along before," she reminded him and edged along the edge until he had to lean back and push the chair away from the table a little, to not touch her. That was when she put her legs outside his thighs and straddled him.

As her bottom came down, her hand moved down his torso. When her fingertips met the top of his belt they were undecided, then chose to go behind the belt.

"Don't," his hand snapped on her wrist and shoved it away. "Get off of me, *now*."

"David's sleeping," she slurred before grinding her mouth against his. Her tongue tasted of some kind of fruit schnapps as it quickly and urgently probed for the deeper reaches of his mouth. He clamped down in an effort to drive it out. He felt sick at the feel of it and her.

Noah stood up sharply, almost knocking her over. He pushed blindly for her shoulders as he ripped himself away from the kiss. Her nails dug painfully into his hand, trying to move it to her breast—her other hand moved between his legs and squeezed hard.

She yelped when he smacked her hand away from his crotch and threw his body away from her.

"I said he's *in* his room!"

"Noah," she whimpered.

"Get out!"

"Noah, *please*. I don't want to leave without knowing if there was something there."

He barely heard her as he pressed down on his throbbing privates with his wrist.

"Get out."

"What are you saving yourself for? She's not coming back!" she pled.

He put one hand over his eyes, over the rising headache, over the rising anger. No matter how much he hated a person, he'd never felt like hurting someone like he did the version of Rising Moon he was meeting now.

"Keep your voice down," Noah's hand went out before him to tell her to stop. "My son can hear all of this. My wife is none of your business. My life is none of your business. I thought we needed to talk, but what I need you to do is leave. What's wrong with you?"

"I'm lonely and hurting and I'm fucking tired," she wailed.

Noah's eyes darted to the hall. David would be alerted to a

curse word. Cursing means trouble. Trouble means worry. A worried child is an alert child.

"You know what, I'm sorry about your dad, but you need help. Right now you also need to get out of my house and stay away from me."

"I don't need you to be sorry! You're lonely. I'm lonely!" she cried.

"You don't want to do something like that because you're lonely. Regrets will feel worse," he offered gently, though, at the moment, he really couldn't give a shit about her. His skin was crawling and he was starting to really worry about what she would do. All he could think was to try a different approach.

"Should you be giving romantic advice?" she snapped.

Noah shrugged.

"I don't need this," she clawed up her coat and started down the short hall to the door.

Neither do I, he wanted to say.

*Don't let this escalate,* an inner voice warned. *What if she was somehow even more disturbed than she seemed? What will I do if she's armed? What would happen to David if she kills me? Was she that far gone?*

"Maybe we can talk when you're not drunk," Noah didn't know if he said it loud enough for her to hear, but he sure as hell wasn't going to yell after her. Probably David was already listening and in a minute he would have to go back there and check on his son, but he needed to catch his breath. He needed to stop shaking.

"Drunk?" Rising Moon appeared at the opening to the kitchen. "Do you think I have to be drunk?"

"Aren't you?"

Rising Moon stared at him, face struck with disbelief.

"I've never met anyone like you," she said in a small, frail voice. It didn't sound sweet, to him. It didn't spark sympathy. It gave him the willies.

"Your wife was so stupid to leave you."

Noah's brow furrowed angrily.

"It's none of your fu—" he glanced at the hall to the bedrooms "—*none* of your business," his voice was stern, his eyes smoldered with the rage, "She had her reasons—I don't judge her. You sure as hell don't have any right to."

Noah knew, all too well, what reasons a person might have to just take off without saying anything to anyone, having done so himself roughly a decade earlier.

"Well, if that's how you feel," she shrugged "I can't believe you defend her."

"I'm not," he said the word like he was slamming a door. "I just don't know."

"If she—"

"Just stop. This is none of your business. How many times do I have to ask you to leave?"

"When was the last time you had sex?" she ignored.

"Don't be a creep, Rising Moon. I'll never just lay down with someone if I'm desperate. Maybe you should consider that."

"More advice, hmmm."

"Well, why would you think I'd want to have sex with you? Do you think because I have a cock that you can just fiddle with me a little and I'll be game? Like you found some secret to override the fact that there's nothing between us?"

"What about you coming over?" she protested.

"What about it?" Noah's hands went limp with disbelief.

"You trusted me."

"I didn't know who else to go to," he argued.

"Neither do I," she pointed.

They looked at each other silently.

Finally, Noah moved away from the kitchen counter and gestured for her to move toward the door.

"We'll talk later, okay?" he said, trying not to sound as angry as he was feeling by trying to tell himself he should feel bad for her. All he wanted was for her to get the fuck away from them, stay the fuck away from them and stay out of his fucking life.

"Okay," she seemed consoled and no longer gave off an aura that made him want to guard his privates.

With a closed and locked door between him and her, Noah felt okay to breathe again. If he would feel okay after he talked to David was another story.

After a gentle interrogation of the weak looking bookbinder, Noah was convinced that David had been too distracted to notice.

That didn't necessarily make him feel okay.

Noah wondered what the police would do if he called about what the late constable's daughter had done. He was afraid of what she would do if they did something about it. He was afraid of what might happen if they did nothing. He was afraid of what they might tell her.

# CHAPTER 23

◆

## The PLAY's the THING

The next morning Fawn wasn't mad at David anymore, she was mad that tomorrow was school. She couldn't remember the last time she woke up happy on a Sunday—unless she forgot it was a Sunday.

Her stomach was in knots.

It wasn't that she was picked on. People didn't really treat her like anything. Some of the boys paid attention to her because she wasn't afraid to get dirty or skin her knees. That was okay. But most of the time she felt like an alien.

Even if people accepted her or she accepted them—she was different. She had a weight in her that made her feel like her classmates were soaring above her. Like she was a sturgeon looking up at people in their boats or even soaring through the sky. There was no one down there with her.

Maybe that wasn't true.

Sometimes Fawn didn't feel alone down in that feeling. Every time the papers read or people said someone else was lost—she sensed another person or people had joined her down there. And, of course, there were creatures there. And she was terrified all the time.

The practical way to protect something weak is to add support, harden it, or lock it up somewhere safe.

Fawn wouldn't let anyone support her, so she locked herself away.

Being around people was a threat to her security.

Someone might want in. Someone might get in.

David messed around with the lock and tried to glimpse inside. He was very perceptive and aware of feelings. Which was probably why he was so good with Naana—hanging on every word.

She sat up hard, slinging her long black hair behind her ears. *Naana's poem.*

There was a knock at her bedroom door.

"I'm up," she called to her grandpa. She could tell his steps in the hall.

"You decent?"

"Yeah," she answered like she was offended by the suggestion that she possibly couldn't be.

Solomon opened the door. He was rosy from being outside and still had on his heavy gray socks with the bright orange bands around the tops.

"Look what I found," he said when he entered and held the thing out as he sat down on the bed. Fawn dropped down beside him, eyes fixed on the dusty, dirty, empty tattered pack in his hands.

"This was your mother's," he said tearily. "All this time it was out in the shed," he chuckled and felt the fabric in his hands, "After the accident, Naana kept it with her night and day. It meant so much to her. Remember when Naana first started having problems and she wandered off? I always assumed she lost it in the muskeg."

Her grandfather lovingly ran his huge knotted hands across the delicately embroidered blossoms. He looked up at the girl, checking her face for a sign of recognition. It was there, but not in a way he understood.

Fawn's eyes were wide and owly. Her mouth dropped open as if her fat lower lip was too heavy. The color drained from her face and then came back up, very red, especially around her eyes.

"Mom's?" she asked in disbelief, staring at the familiar battered pack.

"She used to tote everything in this. I think she had it threadbare in about a month," the old man reflected in a mixture of sadness and amusement. "You don't remember?"

"Not from her…" she strained to think of where. Where had she seen that filthy old sack?

It was bad—she knew it was bad. Seeing it made her feel like her skin was covered in locusts with piranha jaws.

"They won't play with you if you don't understand what's happening to you or if they don't scare you—*if they think they don't scare you*," Fawn mumbled thoughts aloud while understanding rose like vomit up her throat.

Her head spun and hair prickled.

*He was faking—he's been tricking us all this time!*

He was acting just like Naana.

"Oh God!" she screamed and sailed out of the room. Solomon followed, face knit with concern.

"What? Fawn!" he called, jogging down the hall after her. By the time he got to the front door the coats were still swaying and the screen door just rattled shut.

The old man looked at his ancient mother, who was nodding to herself to the rocking of her chair. Goosebumps rose over every inch of his flesh. Every hair short enough to hold itself up stood straight on his skin.

He had a bad feeling that Fawn would return to him in the state his mother had, after wandering out into the muskeg and being lost for all those weeks—well longer than anyone thought she could have survived.

"Stay in your chair, Naana," Solomon said, grabbing his keys and jacket as he stuffed his feet into his boots, the wrong feet in the wrong boots. He almost said 'fuck it' to swapping them, but couldn't stand to even *stand* that way.

Outside, he didn't know where to go. The yard was eaten up by tracks and Fawn seemed to have been eaten by thin air.

# CHAPTER 24

◆

# NEEJAWNISUG

"Hello?" Noah said into the receiver.

He was stretched out on his stomach, like a cat, making as much effort as possible to reach the phone without upsetting the fact that he was laying down on the couch and didn't want to get up. He was thinking about where they would move.

He was considering Washington State, maybe Montana. No prospects, no security, no job, nothing packed. None of that bothered him as much as staying in Nibebiitam any longer than they had to. When school was out for summer. Then they'd be out of Canada forever.

"Noah?" he heard Rising Moon's voice and his gut flipped. "Yeah?"

"I need to ask you something?" she suddenly hushed her voice.

"Sure," he said idly, rolling over on his back and staring at the ceiling. He tried to have happy thoughts so he wouldn't scream at her. His thoughts immediately shifted to moving and he smiled.

"Are you friend's with Jacob's great-nephew, Derrick?"

"Yeah. Why?" he was suspicious, but tried not to sound it. It was hard not to sound defensive. He didn't like the idea of this psycho even knowing Derrick's name. He thought it was weird that they should even be talking about him. He wondered if Rising Moon hadn't ended up answering the phone once when his friend called Jacob and ended up being hit on. Even Derrick couldn't handle that level of freak.

"That's so weird," she mumbled.

"Why?"

"I'm not sure," she whispered.

Noah no longer felt idle. He felt impatient.

"What's this about?" he wanted to know.

"I was going through Jacob's address book for the contact info for one of our clients. I paid attention to Derrick's card because Jacob is always talking about him—" Noah's scalp prickled at the idea of her having access to all of his own contact information. *Sure* she was looking for something with a client. He wondered how many of the psycho phone calls she was responsible for. Was she trying to make herself obsolete? She obviously was feeling pretty useful at the moment. "—Then I had to look back to see if I saw right, because I'd already seen yours, with your new address, and the old one crossed out—I assume from when you were first talking about the job—did Derrick buy your house?"

"No."

"Oh."

"Oh? Oh, what?"

"Because it was the same address."

"You're saying Derrick's address is my old address?"

"He has another address scribbled out too."

"The 1408 address?"

"Yeah."

"I sold my house to Megan Hanson."

"Really?"

"*Yes.*"

"Oh…huh," she mumbled, not without an air of enjoyment she probably didn't want Noah to hear.

"What?" he demanded.

"Megan Hanson is Jacob's sister."

There was about a fraction of a second where he had the freedom of thought enough to wonder if Rising Moon wasn't just trying to upset him to get him back.

"I have to go," Noah said and hung up.

He went to the bathroom and threw up.

He felt numb and stupid. Why would Derrick want the house? Why? If it was even true.

Noah realized he was still holding the phone. Since the move, he was never able to reach Derrick on his home phone anymore. He punched in the numbers to Derrick's cell phone.

"Why would you buy my house?" he demanded as soon as Derrick came on the line.

He felt like he was sinking down into a dark watery abyss. He felt the presence of monsters, but it was too dark to see down there. He was pretty sure they would make their presence known. But he never would have guessed how soon.

In the pause after Noah's question, the clear sound of heels on wooden floor, a woman entered the room with a question of her own:

"Babe, who are you talking to?"

Noah's chest rose and fell as he began to breathe hard, not feeling like he was breathing at all.

Terri.

*Terri.*

He could tell the difference between her sneeze or hiccup among a million. He knew the sound of her walk—to say nothing of obviously knowing her voice. It was Terri.

Derrick understood the silence—as even the most severe glare wasn't warning enough to shut her up—Noah knew—

"Hey man, don't let this hurt our friendship."

This was why Derrick wanted him out of New York.

This was why he talked up this place.

This was the reason why she left.

Noah started to wonder if he was having a stroke.

Derrick laughed. Noah felt murderous at the sound of it.

"Maybe if you'd told me what she was like I wouldn't have had to find out for myself."

"Rot in hell you worthless, two-faced, backstabbing, piece of—" he couldn't breathe. His mind felt like it was tipping. He felt he was about to black out. "You worthless waste of life—you steal from the world each time you take a breath."

Then Noah hung up, staring at the hand that fell limply onto his thigh after letting go of the receiver. He didn't move for almost an hour and a half. Then he clawed his hair and screamed so hard that when he tried to catch his breath after, he tasted the coppery flavor of blood in his mouth.

◆　　　　◆　　　　◆

David watched Noah silently for as long as he could stand to. It was strange to see a man look so small, so breakable. It was scary to see the color drained from his daddy's face and watch stinging eyes rimmed red by the brackish wet drained to the last drop. Then Noah sniffled because his nose started to run and his hands began to shake as they strangled each other. A full system scan was taking place behind eyes that stared forward without seeing. It had searched through every inadequacy, every fear and worry to sort out an explanation. The young man's eyes traveled slowly to his right where the phone lay, seeing it no differently than a crumpled sheet of paper that delivered devastating news.

"I like Rising Moon," David blurted in a small trembling voice. "She can take care of you. And it's okay with me," he assured Noah.

"I don't—" Noah bit down on his lips, his eyes pinched and color rushed to his cheeks and neck. He hadn't, at first, even heard what David said. When it registered, Noah thought, *Liar,* but his mind was otherwise consumed with unscrambling the entanglements in his thoughts, emotions, and even reality— because he had to get his shit together.

He would have to explain to David.

They had to breech the one taboo and talk about mommy.

How to even start talking about Terri? Why did he have to? The child had a right to know she wouldn't be coming back.

She wouldn't be back.

She's not coming back. And it's worse.

So much worse.

*Do I have to tell him?*

*You need to tell him what he needs to know when he needs to have an explanation. Someday he will ask. He might ask tomorrow. He might ask when he's forty.*

How do you explain to a six-year-old—how do you make them understand that it didn't seem real until now? It *didn't* feel real until now. He felt like a fool, like he'd needed a death certificate to prove a death even if he saw the mangled and decapitated body. That's exactly what his marriage was.

He'd always thought Terri might have been going through something she couldn't tell him about and only needed some time away.

Maybe something unspeakable happened and she couldn't stand to be a mother or a wife for a while.

He *never* felt that she didn't love them. He never saw it coming. They fought sometimes. Sometimes he couldn't do anything right. Every relationship has fights. Every relationship has little problems or even big problems and you still know everything's going to be alright. But it wasn't alright.

Now he was left to wonder how long *it* had been going on. If his friend had really come to Nibebiitam as often as he said, then he would have to know how messed up the people were. Had the same frightening things happened to Derrick? Was it purposeful? Had he hoped Noah would go crazy or be killed? What about what it was doing to David? Had they thought about that?

Noah appreciated customs and traditions; he appreciated a culture that could hold onto their past, but at what cost to an impressionable child? A child trying to believe in anything.

David sucked it all up and was drowning. Noah looked at the peeked little angel in the grey running suit. The clothes hung on his small frame. His tiny fingers fidgeted together and his washed out face looked fearful and ill. Making sense of the ruined marriage was easier than trying to understand what was happening to his child.

"David, I—"

"You're going to be okay dad," David interrupted. He touched Noah's shoulder and gave it a squeeze and rub.

The father looked at the little hand and marveled at its smallness, much like he had just after David was born.

Noah opened his arms to hug him, but David was running to the front door and grabbed his jacket.

"Where are you going?" his father asked surprised. He prayed he disguised the sadness from his voice enough that David hadn't noticed just how upset he was. It looked like he had.

"Gonna check the mail."

Noah waited for him to go, but the boy stood there staring back at him as if expecting something more. Moments passed.

"David?"

The boy flew across the room and hugged Noah *so* hard— just as hard as his little arms could squeeze. He kissed Noah square on the ear, pressing his face flat against the side of his father's head.

"I love you *so much*, Daddy. You're going to be okay."

"You bet," Noah smiled into David's shoulder. Then his eyes shut, squeezing out tears and David almost cried too.

"Bye Macaroni!" David called, pulling away and charging to the front door.

"Why macaroni?" asked Noah.

"Because I love macaroni!"

Noah put the phone back in its stand and slid back into the arm of the couch.

"Hey kiddo, take Gilder with you," Noah called when he heard the front door creak.

"You betcha!" David returned.

The couch felt warmer and softer, but his head felt stuffed and his eyes felt salty and raw. He just needed to rest. A little rest and he would forget about her. Just a couple winks and his system would be updated to include the fact that it was over. He just had to accept it. Basically all that really happened was those suspicions were confirmed and that wasn't so bad, he told himself. Now he should be able to start over. *Really*. With David he could get through anything. David wasn't going to be broken—he was resilient—in that quiet way that children often are.

He didn't know where his son got the courage from, but Noah was grateful for it. A strong child, with a big heart. Maybe there's a part of all children, like a back-up battery, that helps them get through tough times because they *should* still have a lot of years to get through. Because sometimes Noah couldn't believe the things people survive, overcome, or get through when they are so little.

He didn't feel like he'd come out of his own childhood very well. Must not have been one of the kids with the back-up "hope" battery.

People like David, Noah mused, are the people who get things done, even when they're down—or maybe, especially then. He liked the thought of David being in the Peace Corps or something. He could really see that for David. A job requiring fearlessness and compassion. A smile broke on his face and he almost laughed. A job requiring fearlessness, compassion, and a uniform.

"Oof!" he grunted at Gilder's sudden weight. She'd jumped on top of him and now stood on his stomach looking down at her bigger person.

"Why didn't David take you—" he noticed a scattered pile of letters on the coffee table. David had come back in. Beyond the mail, Noah noticed something else—the truck keys were missing from the coffee table.

The scamp must have grabbed them when he came back to hug him, but why would he take the keys—there was something else wrong too.

*What?*

Then his face went blank with recollection, he'd been too preoccupied to process before, but David had his schoolbag with him and it was bulging.

"David!" he called, flying off the couch to the open door. Through the screen he saw the driveway clearly and, not unexpectedly, he saw nothing of the boy, but the truck was still there.

"David!"

The screen door slammed hard behind him, Gilder on his sock covered heels.

The sun was setting and the wind was picking up. It was eerie outside and, all the more, thinking of his son out in it. The father's mind whirled, was his son running away? Was it something to do with those children?

Frantic, Noah ran to the pole barn in the back yard.

"David" he yelled hoarsely.

His eyes fixed on the snow, about to scour it for a trail to follow, but found a yard scrambled with little footprints.

In the distance a wolf howled and in the tall dead grasses along the woods a child giggled. To say only a shiver went up his spine would be like comparing a Monopoly hotel to the Waldorf Astoria. Something with claws, weight, and cold wet flesh scampered up his spine, leaving behind the impression of every touch.

"David!" he heard Fawn call from the front yard.

The screen door slammed and she called for the boy repeatedly inside. Noah met her at the door.

"Do you know where he went?"

"He's *GONE*?" Fawn shrieked. Her face flushed, hair askew from the frenzied and freezing bike ride.

"You know what's going on," accused Noah, his chest pounded with fear and anger.

The teenage girl looked at the wretched looking shadow of the handsome man-god she knew before. He'd been crying—he looked hysterical and completely exhausted, unshaved, and pallid with panic and horror. Bloodshot eyes bore into her for answers—like an addict who suspects you have their fix.

Noah *needed* answers.

The question was, "Where is my son?"

*Please. PLEASE. Where is my son?!?*

"It's not what I thought," Fawn replied. "I can't explain right now."

"Tell me!"

"There's no time! He's got these weird ideas about the children—"

"You told David about them? Why? What's the matter with you?"

"I only tried to warn him!"

"Is he safe now? What good did your warning do?"

He closed his fists against his forehead and growled in frustration, "Son of a bitch! This explains *everything*. Merciful fucking heaven you should have told me! *He's my son!* I *need* to know what he knows so I can take care of him. Then even though he lied about it, I would still know that he knew. None of this would be happening if you hadn't told him those stories!"

"You don't really believe that," she said firmly.

"I don't know. I don't know. But I know what's real. You're talking about *ghosts*."

"We're not that lucky," Fawn blurted.

He hesitated and was stupid with shock, unable to gather thoughts he was still incapable of accepting.

"Suppose it is real. When does it stop? How do we stop it? Is that what he's doing? What he's been working on, planning?"

"I think he thinks he can, but this isn't a full moon, curse, Friday the 13th, Halloween thing," the girl protested, "There is no *event*—THEY JUST *ARE*! They can't be stopped, but I think Naana's crazy stories made him think he can. You can't stop a force of nature. They're like the chaos element in the order of life's routines. How many people think they see something and turn on the lights to find it was nothing to be afraid of? Just because the monsters aren't there when you turn on the light doesn't mean they weren't there before. They are everywhere… they just always return here. These woods, they are just the home. I just don't know why they are so bad here. Unless—"

"They just want us to leave."

Fawn paused, with a look of disbelief on her face.

"Noah, they *like* people coming here."

Noah froze, her words hanging inside his thoughts and put a strangle hold on his throat. The girl stood half trembling with exhaustion, half frustration. She rubbed at the sweat and dirt on her face, her large black eyes shining with energy. Not that it would change anything, but she wished she had a watch on.

*No time. No time.*

"You know I don't believe in this."

Fawn grabbed Noah's shoes, shoved them into his chest and muttered, "When has that mattered?"

The sound of an engine alerted the father and he threw himself into the door frame, just as Rising Moon was getting out of her car. She was wearing an overcoat—which struck him as odd in the cold, until a gust lifted and opened it enough for him to know that was all she was wearing.

"Jesus Christ," Noah muttered.

"Let's not waste time on foot," Fawn's voice was high and anxious, eyes fixed on the running vehicle.

Noah looked down at her desperate dark eyes, his own were helpless and lost.

It really didn't matter what he believed as long as David believed it, the boy would be doing what a believer would do. So Noah needed a believer to tell him what that would be.

"Where do I need to go?" he pressed.

"You'll never f—"

"Are you okay?" Rising Moon called ahead, her voice strained with controlled annoyance. "I was worried about you when you hung up on me. I didn't want you to think I made up those things just to upset you."

"I need a ride," he ignored, putting on his shoes. No time to deal with that. No time. No time at all.

"I thought I would just—"

"No!" Noah screamed hoarsely. "David's gone!"

"Why not take the truck?" Rising Moon pointed.

"He took the keys."

"I'm sure he's fine," Rising Moon argued, almost reaching the steps. Her eyes were murky with booze and anger.

"Are you going to give us a ride or not?" Fawn came to Noah's side, throwing a coat over his shoulders. He stuffed his arms in mechanically. His ears were ringing so loud. The world looked gray, colorless.

The wild-eyed father threw his gaze on the teenage girl.

"You're *not* coming. You've done enough damage," Noah hurried down the steps. "I'll find him myself."

Eagerly, Rising Moon ran back and jumped behind the wheel. Noah reached the passenger side door. He looked at the demented woman behind the wheel and briefly wondered if she didn't have David in the trunk, but whatever Fawn thought was going on didn't have anything to do with kidnapping, but there was no way he was going to let Rising Moon leave without searching her vehicle. That was also the only reason he didn't just yank her out of the vehicle and leave with it. What would she do to the child if he came back while she was standing there, probably thinking about torching the house? He would rather keep her in eyesight. There was nothing he would put past her.

"You don't know where you're going!" Fawn screamed.

She was right. He just couldn't think straight.

Noah looked helplessly at the wilderness that might as well have been a universe in itself.

Fawn ran up beside him, panting out his name. He looked down at her, barely keeping his shit together, but he heard her loud and clear when she told him:

"You don't know where you're going, but I do."

◆　　　　◆　　　　◆

The weight of the backpack grew with every forced step, small soft arms clutched it to David's chest, sharing what little energy he had left with legs about to give out.

It hadn't seemed that heavy at first. It had been while since the first time he carried the weight altogether, but that was just to Fawn's house. After that, he smuggled the load home bundle by eight inch bundle.

It was time to return what he borrowed.

He only thought of it that way when he thought about it and he tried *not* to think about it.

There was only room for foolishness and silliness or they would know.

*Don't let it show. Can't let them know.*

The mouth of the mine was long past and the throat of darkness enveloped him, dissolving them.

His labored breathing sounded louder in the dark than even their ravenous howling and yipping. Their hooked claws snagged on his jacket and arms, but he could not see them or anything in the pure black. He squeezed the button on his cow flashlight.

"No!" he gasped involuntarily at the current of deformed children galloping around him.

They turned in unison toward the light, delighted that he saw them and that they finally sensed a bit of fear in him. The boy's stubby thumb relaxed and the monsters winked out of sight. He could feel their moist bodies, resonating more like breath than warmth of flesh. David imagined thousands of little mouths on their skin instead of pores. He couldn't keep running in the dark, but he was afraid to see them. It felt worse knowing they were there and not knowing what they were doing.

Turning back on the flashlight was one of the hardest things he'd ever made himself do.

The flashlight danced across their surging bodies. They were like a self-powered tidal wave of ethereal white nightmare. They bent and flowed unnaturally and in countless numbers.

How does one count the uncountable? When one and one make two, only if the second is partially absorbed by a third or even ten other beings with no beginning and no end.

They wanted to play, but the flicker of acknowledgement was only that, and then there were only thoughts of cookies, and fun little wolves, wind-chimes, and the jingle dance. The white wolf children were not in there. There was confusion or madness there—they could not yet make him play. The boy was not "with them". The boy was with weird rambling thoughts and preoccupied thinking about the bag hurting his arms.

And he was thinking:

*I'm close. I know I'm close.*

His heart raced as the light bounced off an abandoned pick and rotted skein of rope.

*Soon enough,* the six-year-old's mind whirled, *there will be an end to the tunnel. If this is a mouth, the throat must be the hole they made in Hell. The throat is close.*

He could almost smell the air coming from its stomach.

There was no turning back, there never was.

His heart slammed against his ribcage to outrun this fear. There was no escape and no time to acknowledge it.

The spirits smelled smoke, where there had been a spark of fear before.

*What big ears you have!*

Naana left her mind out there in the winter.

*Wind-chimes.*

They snapped and hissed as they took their impatience out on each other. They were hungry. They wanted to play. Their rage was mounting, while the boy only felt—

Dizzy.

*I'm so dizzy.*

He felt like he was falling through zero gravity. Like Alice down the rabbit hole.

*You don't dare slow*, he told himself.

*They'll kill you. They'll kill you. They'll kill you.*

Tears began to stream down David's face. They felt hot on skin cold with exhaustion. He whimpered and trembled. His knees slammed into each other, almost tripping him. Supporting the bag with his left arm, the child shoved his right hand in his hoodie pocket and closed on the one most precious thing he dare not let them know.

One foot grabbed the ground and didn't want to move. Suddenly faced with a corner, he wouldn't have known was there if not for the something glowing right around it. Someone? Something...

Everything hinged on Fawn being right about what the miners had done, what they had let out, where they had reached.

Both body and soul longed to see, longed to know what was behind the corner. And he had to see because he had to go. This had to be the throat.

It would all be for nothing if he was wrong.

Then his daddy would go through all the worry and hurt for sake of foolishness alone and the white wolf children would still be just as evil because the miners' hole would still be poisoning them.

*What would a fissure to hell look like?*

The only way to find out was to see where the light was coming from.

Like moving a slab of stone he stiffly sidestepped until the glowing thing was fully exposed to him. The thing was like the others. The same and different. It *felt* different.

It was a guard.

It was a trap.

It was *their* guard dog.

It never left its vigil and so was spiteful and unhinged, even among them.

It never got to play because it was guarding something more precious than its own wants. Its untapped ferocity was like a nuclear landmine with a century of demented dreaming seething to be realized.

David felt the waves of malevolent energy coursing from its small carnivorous frame.

Small and crouched, long ratted white hair spilled down the guardian's small white dress. It was drawing in the dirt and humming. It was a little girl.

She reeled on him, human face stretched across canine skull, smiling through jagged teeth. She half sighed and then her mouth threw open like a trap and she roared with the animosity of any enraged great beast, but unlike anything anyone lived to write into history.

He squealed past her and immediately into a greater light, illuminating a haggard wall where the mining was abandoned. A boy, like a walking stick, straddled the glow of a campfire, but there was no smoke, only pulsing light and heat ripples in the air. There was no wood and no ground for wood to sit on anyway— only a platter-sized gap in the floor where the miners chipped a hole in the roof of hell.

A boy if not for being so tall and spidery that its back grazed the ceiling, if not for the stench of death permeating from the gaping maw of the beast. A boy, aside from the skull of a wolf straining beneath the child face, like it were only a rubber mask. A boy aside from arms so long its fingers brushing its calves, aside from its emaciation, a child stood before him with something like a smile mimicked on the skin around its clustered teeth. It pawed at David with arms as long as legs, with fingers as long as feet. Its skin shone like it was rubbed with blackening grease or ink.

*What big eyes you have!*

He'd met this thing before, this panting, drooling thing—this thing that straddled his bed much like it did the darkest energy in the universe. This thing that then, like now, was greatly and clearly aroused.

Facing the dark monstrosity with pinhole eyes, despite himself, David turned and ran away from exactly what he came there for. He wasn't expecting *him*. He thought he only had to get past the wolf children.

Coming from the opposite direction the child saw a started mineshaft he couldn't see coming the other way. It was big enough, or even a man to enter hunched. The children were coming for him from all directions but this. There wasn't any other choice than to enter the smaller tunnel and hope there was a way out on the other side.

In the dark and narrow passage, David's flashlight did little against the dark, but being alone in it felt better than being in their light. *If* he was alone. He wasn't about to stop, even if it was the only way to tell the difference between his panting and theirs. They would kill him if he stopped. He didn't want to know that badly.

"Ahh!" David squeaked, trying to make his feet stop the way they had when he reached the corner, but instead he lost his footing and almost fell down the sudden hole anyway.

The old dusty dirt puffed up around his mouth as he picked his face off the floor of the mine. After a brief struggle with gravity he managed to get his entire self back on solid ground.

The cow "mooed" when David inadvertently squeezed it as he crawled close to the edge and shone the light down into the mouth of pitch blackness.

The hole was actually the beginnings of a shaft that was about ten feet deep, but it might have been one thousand miles for how ravenously it ate the dark and, like marrow from the bone, even sucked away the impression of light. So it was brilliant and unignorable when the weak flashlight beam struck a flash of gold in the abysmal black.

The light tried to catch it again and instead found something with wide black eyes smiling up at him. David's hand slapped over his mouth as he fixed his shaking light on the little face. A skeleton's face. And something more.

The small beam of light lowered as slow as a falling feather, to find what first caught the light. The spark of yellow blinded him angrily, demandingly. Light radiated across him, filling each crack, encapsulating every single grain of dirt. And paled. And paled. The pale paling and filling the chamber until white was too dark to describe its brilliance. Through the lids of his eyes were crimson, then brown, then orange, then pale blue. He tried to block it with the arm wielding the flashlight. Then the little boy saw things. Heard things.

Fawn was wrong. There *were* ghosts and they were not only children. There were men. Men with secrets. Even with covered eyes, David saw them. They cleared away boards lined up beside each other over the opening of the nearly hidden passage. Their lanterns passed a sign—this passage was unstable. Condemned.

Said one of the phantom men:

*Too hard to dig.*

*We won't have to,* the other ghoulish man replied.

There was a shape like a colossal maggot being drug behind the optimistic second man. Their lantern light came and went uncaringly from the limp form.

The men were dressed so nice. Too nice to be so dirty.

Dirty with what?

What indeed?

*What?*

David's heart pounded. There was something thoughtful inside that shape. Not living, but still thinking.

*Planning?* David wondered.

*Wouldn't you like to know?*

*no.*

*You already do.*

There was something thriving in the stinking white sheets. Not living, but thriving. Thriving and thinking. Unbreathing, unbleeding. But bloody. Want-less.

*No.*

*Full of want.*

"What does it want?" David heard himself ask aloud.

Said the voice of a ghost:

*Don't leave the sheets.*

*Oh please.*

*I mean it. They were expensive.*

Something tumbled out as the sheets were yanked away, but was lost in the dark. Only the most important edges of things were rewarded with lantern light. The darkness was getting heavy. David felt it start to press on him too.

Holding the sheets up against the light.

*We'll never get the stains out.*

Then seeing the limp mass as if they forgot it was there.

A voice shrieked between the now strobing images:

*Can't you get it off?*
*No!*
*Goddamn it! That's solid gold!*
*I didn't make you use it!!*
*Breathing. Breathing. Breathing.*
*I can cut it out.*
*Just forget it.*

*NEVER!*—boomed like thunder. The skinned maggot hit the bottom of the earthen pit. The startling bang resounded as much with impact as with the word.

David's arm felt like it was yanked away from his face, but it was the force of his own body revolting. Anything could be happening outside of that arm and it didn't really like what was happening inside of it. He moved back.

*No more, please!* David begged.

The radiance was gone when he dropped his arm. Down in the aborted shaft, the thing's shine was not so bright, but just as yellow as it drank the weak illumination of his cow faced flashlight, which lit every link in the gold chain around the skeleton's neck.

"Black Martin," David breathed, half awed, half petrified— and started sobbing.

Again and again, he heard the little body hit the partially dug pit. Again and again, heard the ghost men discuss the secret and how to hide it.

The tiny, cloudy spot of light walked up the wall of the hole and at its precipice saw the darkness fill up to the untidy rim. He followed the lip of it, across jagged points that looked like canines.

"It looks like a mouth," the six-year-old said absently. Then with more clarity, "More than the front of the mine."

"Oh God!"

He leapt up and ran, and ran out. Where was he? Where? Did he go the right way? He went left. He was supposed to go left to go back. Past the ones that look like beasts. Past the ones that look like children. Past, and past, and past their claws and leering snarling grins. Past them to where he wanted to be least, but needed to be most.

Maybe there was a hole in the roof of hell, but it belonged to Black Martin. A crack in hell wasn't what made the trickster spirits do evil things. That was all him. That cruel, loathing, relentless, restless, insatiable, and ravenous thing. The vengeful and mistreated thing.

*There he is!*

"Black Martin!" David screamed.

*Don't let it show. Can't let them know. Run boy run, better go, go, go!*

"Come play with me, Black Martin! You're it!"

As much as David hated to, he reached down and threw a rock at the disfigured—

*abused*

—spirit.

And ran.

The whole pack would be after him now. Albeit they already were, but not this way. They did not feel like playing with David anymore. They did feel like killing.

Something was unravelling in the boy's mind. The wind-chimes were falling. The jingle-dancers were tired. The cookies were eaten. The fun wolves were not fun anymore. They had a feeling there might be fear behind the madness after all. When the little breathing thing could no longer deny it, or hide it, they would take him. By the time they were done with David, he would feel he had never been afraid before.

*What a big mouth you have!*

His fist crawled up the side of his pack, so slow, while running, so fast he wheezed and choked on his sobs, edging toward the embodiment of all these fears. The tunnel tipped back and forth before eyes that could no longer focus. Every step threatened to be the prelude of collapse.

He almost missed the condemned tunnel, twisting something in his foot as he veered into the narrow fissure.

His strength spent, he dare run no farther, nor should he. The shallow shaft was right ahead.

The mouth.

*If only someone could shut it.*

His thumb depressed the starter on the small lighter finally inside his fist—

*I'll huff and I'll puff*

—the truck keys jingled against his knuckles.

*Don't let it show.*

*Little White Wolf Children, what is your name?*

*It is pain, pain, pain.*

*Black Martin, is so naughty, naughty, naughty.*

*Hear laughter?*

*Feel terror?*

*Then you will meet Death.*

"Keep what you know 'til your last breath."

A tiny flame danced on the end of the small blue shaft and kissed the carefully extruded fuse. The wolf children rose on two feet, loose jaws hanging on open hinges. Small glittering, coal black eyes fixed on the boy. Claws pierced him.

A shuttering, guttural scream shook out David's small body. A ball of hot white light exploded in his arms as they dragged him down into them and into Black Martin's once untimely grave.

The explosion echoed through the otherwise silent woods. Noah saw the cloud of smoke and dirt rise out of the treetops. Tripping to his hands and knees among the brush, he saw the little tennis shoe prints they'd been following, framed between his hands. His heart went still, underwater sounds filled his ears while his lungs refused to fill, shriveled like raisins in his clay cold torso.

He stared at the footprints dreamily for what seemed like a long time before he let himself see anything else.

Then he saw the ground matted with hundreds of small handprints. He nodded to himself as if he understood everything then, but it was really because David did. Somehow Noah made himself get up and eventually made his way to the mine.

The mouth of the tunnel was no more than an archway to the collapsed passage beyond it like a mouth full of food. Swirling wisps of dust rose like smoke from the crumbled earth, more alive than even he.

Suddenly arms wrapped around his waist.

A scream slammed into his lips—in the half second it took to react—it registered that these were a real person's arms. But they were not David's.

"Don't!" his yell was a bestial roar.

He twisted away from Rising Moon and scrambled to the edge overseeing the collapsed mineshaft. It was inconceivable to walk on the rubble where his son might be buried. He could still be alive. People survived worse. He cursed himself for wasted time. He should have already been here.

Every second counts.

He remembered the way the newborn baby felt in his arms. The first goofy smile. First steps. Teething. Bad dreams. Bed time stories…

*Every second counts,* he told himself again and again.

Skinned knees. Birthday parties. Running in the park…

Work harder, move faster!

He cursed himself for avoiding the truth and then denying it when he could no longer avoid it. For not listening to David. For not keeping him safe.

It didn't really matter what he believed because David did and David was living that belief—he should have kept a better eye on him. He should have never brought them here. He should have never trusted Fawn. He should have never trusted any of *them*, only David, whose fears he dismissed as just a child's.

*You never wanted a baby.*

*I NEED HIM!*

He shrugged away the wretched arms again.

"He's gone, Noah," Rising Moon said.

"No!" he snarled, hunting more deliberately, urgently. He listened for sobbing, whimpering.

"David!" Noah squalled across the ruins.

Rising Moon squatted, hid her mouth in her hands and tried not to cry. Her eyes fell to the earth and she refused to watch. No matter what she did, no matter how sweet she tried to be, all she ever got was jilted. What would it take to make him understand she was all he needed?

Just ahead of Noah, Fawn worked over the rubble.

"He's here," Fawn called. "I can feel it."

Noah went to her fearfully and nauseously. She was heavily dusted, save the tracks where tears cleaned her face. She stood trembling, wringing hands with bloody fingers that left marks on the heavy stones they'd moved and flesh on the ones they couldn't.

"I'm sorry, Noah," Fawn said in a wavering voice. "I never wanted to hurt him. I never thought he'd do this. I didn't get it. I didn't understand what Naana tried to tell us or how David would take it."

Noah's eyes followed the collapsed mine and tried to imagine how a six-year-old could do so much damage, but it was David after all.

He stared dumbly as the rubble shifted suddenly and sunk deeper into the earth. Fawn jumped back and threw her arms around his unmoving, unblinking, unthinking, and almost unliving body.

"Why?" he finally croaked out.

Fawn blurrily scanned the destruction and cried aloud into his side. Her answer came out as a muffled wail:

"He must've thought he could stop them!"

# The NATURE of the BEAST

◆

The body was never recovered. The mine looked like a crater from above and even partially swallowed some trees as one deep shaft ate the earth around it before being sated. There was no telling how deep it was. Nothing they could do, authorities said after what seemed like very little time to a grieving father. Didn't seem like much time at all.

Solomon and Fawn pretty much lived at the house for the first week before they gave him the space he needed—when they felt it was safe to leave him alone. There was no way to know how he'd take it. Or if he wouldn't.

Rising Moon came by more than once, she was looking poorly. He guessed she was falling apart—still. He had a feeling something broke in her when Phil died. But after everything that happened, he wouldn't open the door for her again.

As the days and weeks drug on Noah considered his plans to leave that spring. He couldn't. He would never leave David. That's what it felt like.

The hardest part of leaving England was the dog he buried at the corner of their lot after—after his dad got mad at him for not making his bed neatly before leaving for school, but he wasn't home to be punished.

Noah knew that if he left this place he would never be able to visit the grave again. He wouldn't be there to take care of it. Protect it from vandalism. Never be able to be close to that energy that doesn't leave. The energy that crawls on your skin when you enter a cemetery. The energy some people feel that tells them their loved one is still looking after them.

For a long time he ached to be in that energy.

Like the energy Terri took out of their home when she left— you feel when it's gone.

Sometimes when you lose a part of yourself, you can fill or smooth the chips or pits with someone else's energy. The Cranes did well in mending a lot of the fractured places in his sense of family, but it hurt to be with them now. It was like a play and the star is missing. What it takes out of the play ruins the whole act.

And Noah felt his heart become a prisoner of a new kind of pain and saw himself being cut off of even more things he dare not enjoy.

How could he?

*You're not supposed to outlive your child!*

Sitting on the kitchen floor against the dishwasher, his shoulders jerked roughly as sobs returned.

*You're so selfish. So selfish.*

*If you weren't being selfish you would have paid attention to what he was doing and he wouldn't have been able to get that far.*

*You were so busy bawling over* her!

*You let him down.*

Noah threw his head back to let out the ungodly cry that rose up his throat and clamped his hands over his ears.

*You abandoned him.*

He almost never left the house, the closest he came was walking out to sit on the steps. There were ghosts everywhere. Ghosts of *him* running around. Running with Gilder. Running after frogs and grasshoppers. Ghosts of a child sprawled out on the sun warmed wood of the deck. Sitting on the steps looking at picture books or loving on Mama Cat or Gilder.

In the house the ghosts were everywhere. Ghosts of smells and sounds. Ghosts of being touched, when trying to sleep, and he felt the little body snuggle up beside him. Felt the little hands reach up to grab his feet and wake him. A little body that didn't feel so little when it would jump on him. He was haunted.

Beyond the ghosts Noah experienced, anyone within earshot could tell the place was haunted. A mirthless spirit paced the rooms, searching for a place without memories. Sobbing, wailing, even screaming resonated through the walls of the Asheborne house.

Early on, with intent to call on the solitary resident, Solomon made it only as far as halfway up the walkway before he heard the sounds and cried too. He dropped to his knees, buried his face into his winter gloves and wept.

After a couple months the house and man within were silent except to speak to the beasts living with him, who he loved too.

Gilder, every day, seemed like she was waiting for something—sniffing the air and running to the door at the slightest rattle or sound on the deck—or sound in the night. Most of the time she lay in front of the front door.

Mama Cat often perched on the windowsills to draw the warmth, but Noah noticed she was preoccupied with looking out windows, gazing blinklessly at the world, as if expecting something.

Almost all at once the strange deaths stopped—poltergeist like mischief ran amok for a month or two before dying down to the occasional weirdness the average person experiences.

Only once in a great while did anyone get hurt—Black Martin was no longer there to encourage "games" of suffering and fear to sate his tormented spirit—but there *was* someone there telling them when they went too far. Someone who liked to say, "It's all fun and games until someone gets hurt." Someone who often asked the Man, that in the spring appeared as a tall and handsome brave, "Is it okay for me to see my daddy yet?"

And the Silver Fox Man, who held the little spirit's hand as they walked through the everlasting muskeg said, as he always said, "On the day you came into this world you may enter into it again."

"But it's already been my birthday!" the spirit protested.

The immortal looked down at the young being in wonder and corrected him, "That is not the day you came into the world."

*It was for his father to someday tell him when that happened.*

The small spirit hummed a made-up song and jumped over a patch of unmelted snow.

"I miss my daddy," the spirit often said.

"Yes," the Man always answered.

"Will things be the same when I go back?" he sometimes asked.

"People will ask questions. After, it will be mostly the same. You will tell them you were lost and afraid. They will not believe you if you try to explain more."

"Naana would," said the spirit. It spit out something he shouldn't have tasted and looked guiltily at the ageless face that seemed both puzzled and curious about him.

"Have you saved many people?" the grinning spirit asked for the first time.

A shadow passed over the eyes of the Man, that was not at all man, and troubled thoughts hardened the chiseled features of his seasonal face. Somewhere in the depths of his omniscient eyes was a world where it just began to rain and storm. The Silver Fox Man could only nod in response.

"Have you ever had macaroni and cheese?" wondered the little spirit who struggled to climb a large flat rock jutting out of the slope in the forest floor in front of them.

The Man helped him, gladly, and lovingly.

"No."

The little spirit's face was radiant as it turned on its hands and knees on the shelf of rock and gave his small hand to help the able warrior climb up too.

The Man let him try, but did all the work with his other hand.

"Fawn said you get hungry in the winter. I will bring some to you or leave some out," then he added meekly, "Will you let me see you again?"

"I cannot say, little one," and the Man touched the round softness of the boy's cheek. "Sometimes I close my eyes and lose weeks or months—but when they are open I look for what I know. I will always look for you. You will have to keep your eyes open too—then there is a chance."

"I will," the spirit promised. "Will you come for the macaroni? It's the best thing in the world."

Silver Fox Man swallowed hard and looked off—hundreds of miles into somewhere.

"The best thing is chance," the Man said sincerely and reflectively, "That is the greatest gift man was given."

The white child in the wood squeezed the strong hand holding his, "Thank you for a second helping."

# ABOUT THE AUTHOR

I have a Bachelor of Arts Degree in Writing, do freelance art, and work for a nearby hospital.

I got into writing and art as an escapist and I've always been a daydreamer. There is no better way to find a story to tell than giving your imagination a free hand. I hope I'll get to share everything I've conjured when willing myself, my soul, my consciousness—whichever—into a world or a life more interesting than my own.

Tamberlin's Account, a dystopian journal, is my first novel.

Thanks for reading about me.

# OTHER BOOKS by JAIME MUNT

◆

## *TAMBERLIN's ACCOUNT*

After witnessing the only other person in the world die, Tamberlin sees that there is no one left to remember or record what has happened to the world or to her. There's no one to remember that she even existed. Details of Tamberlin's past blend into her record of horror, reflection, confession, and day to day life in a world with billions of people, but only one still breathing.

## *DARK DREAMS and the WIZARDRY of BLANK STARES*

A complete collection of more than three hundred poems written primarily between 2000-2004 while Munt was in college. The work is an unfiltered collection of every poem she could find written during that time—the good, the bad, and everything in between.

## *CAROM: BOOK I - The Wheels of Fate*

On the world of Masfield, there is a prophecy about the birth of a second sun. Should that day come, a child would be born who, in their life, would affect the life of every living thing. The prophecy did not say if this was good or bad.

In Book I of the CAROM series, we meet a small boy who, growing up in an isolated village, has no idea that a masterful assassin has just been contracted to stop the prophecy before it begins.

LOOK FOR CHILDREN's BOOKS BY MUNT ON AMAZON.COM

www.ingramcontent.com/pod-product-compliance
Lightning Source LLC
Chambersburg PA
CBHW051534250626
47157CB00001B/45